Penguin Books
No Place Like

Nadine Gordimer was born and l[illegible]
She has published seven colle[illegible]
which *Friday's Footprint* [illegible]
Literary Award in 196[illegible]
Guest of Honour (1971) [illegible]
Memorial Prize, and *The* [illegible]
Booker Prize jointly in 1974. [illegible]
international literary prize, th[illegible], in
1975. *A Guest of Honour*, *Living* [illegible]*anions*, a
collection of stories, and *The Con*[illegible]*ast* have
been published in Penguins.

Nadine Gordimer

No Place Like

Selected Stories

Penguin Books

Penguin Books Ltd, Harmondsworth,
Middlesex, England
Penguin Books, 625 Madison Avenue,
New York, New York 10022, U.S.A.
Penguin Books Australia Ltd, Ringwood,
Victoria, Australia
Penguin Books Canada Ltd, 2801 John Street,
Markham, Ontario, Canada L3R 1B4
Penguin Books (N.Z.) Ltd, 182–190 Wairau Road,
Auckland 10, New Zealand

This selection first published by Jonathan Cape 1975
Published in Penguin Books 1978

The volumes of short stories from which this selection has been made were first published as follows:
The Soft Voice of the Serpent, Victor Gollancz Ltd, 1953; *Six Feet of the Country*, Victor Gollancz Ltd, 1956; *Friday's Footprint*, Victor Gollancz Ltd, 1960; *Not For Publication*, Victor Gollancz Ltd, 1965; *Livingstone's Companions*, Jonathan Cape Ltd, 1972.

The William Plomer quotation on p. 9 comes from his preface to *Four Countries*, a collection of sixteen stories published by Jonathan Cape Ltd in 1949.

Made and printed in Great Britain by
Richard Clay (The Chaucer Press) Ltd, Bungay, Suffolk
Set in Linotype Times

Contents

from *Livingstone's Companions*

For Pascale
3 July 1975

Introduction

'After I had selected and arranged these stories, the present publisher asked me to provide some kind of introduction to them. If they were now making their first appearance I might have recoiled from this invitation, but they have all been printed and some reprinted, and have therefore been through a period of probation. Whatever I may say about them now cannot alter what has been said by others, and can hardly increase or lessen the likelihood of their being read – that must depend on the stories themselves.'

The words are William Plomer's, but the attitude comes so close to my own that I do not hesitate to fly his declaration at the masthead of this book. William Plomer not only wrote some stories that have become classic, he also had a special interest in and fascination with the short story as a form used in widely diverse ways by others. His code holds good for me; for all of us. I take it further; if the story itself does not succeed in conveying all the writer meant it should, no matter when he wrote it, neither explication nor afterthought can change this. Conversely, if the story has been *achieved*, the patronizing backward glance its writer might cast upon it, as something he could now do with one hand tied behind his back but no longer would care to do at all, will not detract from it.

I wrote these stories over thirty years. I have attempted now to influence any reader's judgment of or pleasure in them only to the extent implied by the fact that I have chosen some and excluded others. In this sense, I suppose, I have 're-written': imposed a certain form, shaped by retrospect, upon the collection as an entity. For everything one writes is part of the whole story, so far as any individual writer attempts to build the pattern of his own perception out of chaos. To make sense of life: that story, in which everything, novels, stories, the false starts, the half-completed, the abandoned, has its meaningful place, will be complete with the last sentence written before one dies or imagination atrophies. As for retrospect as a valid critique, I realize it has no fixed existence but represents my own constantly changing effort to teach myself how to make out of words a total form for whatever content I seize upon. This I understood only too clearly when I was obliged to read through my five existing collections of stories and saw how there are some stories I have gone on writing, again and again, all my life, not so much because the themes are obsessional but because I found other ways to take hold of them; because I hoped to make the revelation of new perceptions through the different techniques these demanded. I felt for the touch that would release the spring that shuts off appearance from reality. If I were to make a choice of my stories in five years' time, I might choose a different selection, in the light of what I might have learnt about these things by then. My 'retrospect' would be based upon which stories approached most nearly what I happened to have most recently taught myself. That is inevitable.

Why write short stories?

The question implies the larger one: what makes one write? Both have brought answers from experts who study writers as a psychological and social phenomenon. It is easier and more comforting to be explained than to try and explain oneself. Both have also brought answers of a kind from many writers; devious answers; as mine may be. (If one found out exactly how one walks the tightrope, one would fall immediately?) Some have lived – or died – to contradict their own theories; Ernest Hemingway said we write out our sicknesses in books, and shot himself. Of course I find I agree with those writers whose theories coincide at least in part with mine. What is experienced as solitude (and too quickly dubbed alienation) is pretty generally agreed to be a common condition conducive to becoming a writer. Octavio Paz speaks of the 'double solitude', as an intellectual and a woman, of the famous early Spanish-

American writer, Sor Juana Inès de la Cruz. Growing up in a gold-mining town in South Africa as a member of a white minority, to begin with, my particular solitude as an intellectual-by-inclination was so complete I did not even know I was one: the concept 'intellectual', gathered from reading, belonged as categorically to the Northern Hemisphere as a snowy Christmas. Certainly there must have been other people who were intellectuals, but they no doubt accepted their isolation too philosophically to give a signal they scarcely hoped would be answered, let alone attract an acolyte. As for the specific solitude of the woman-as-intellectual, I must say truthfully that my femininity has never constituted any special kind of solitude, for me. Indeed, in that small town, walled up among the mine dumps, born exiled from the European world of ideas, ignorant that such a world existed among Africans, my only genuine and innocent connection with the social life of the town (in the sense that I was not pretending to be what I was not, for ever hiding the activities of mind and imagination which must be suspect, must be concealed) was through my femaleness. As an adolescent, at least I felt and followed sexual attraction in common with others; that was a form of communion I could share. Rapunzel's hair is the right metaphor for this femininity: by means of it, I was able to let myself out and live in the body, with others, as well as – alone – in the mind. To be young and in the sun; my experience of this was similar to that of Camus, although I did not enter into it as fully as he did, I did not play football . . .

In any case, I question the existence of the specific solitude of woman-as-intellectual when that woman is a writer, because when it comes to their essential faculty as writers, all writers are androgynous beings.

The difference between alienation and solitude should be clear enough. Writers' needs in this respect are less clear, and certainly less well and honestly understood, even by themselves. Some form of solitude (there are writers who are said to find it in a crowded cafe, or less romantically among the cockroaches in a night-time family kitchen, others who must have a cabin in the woods) is the condition of creation. The less serious – shall we say professional? – form of alienation follows inevitably. It is very different from the kind of serious psychic rupture between the writer and his society that has occurred in the Soviet Union and in South Africa, for example, and that I shall not discuss here, since it requires a study in itself.

I believe – I *know* (there are not many things I should care to dogmatize about, on the subject of writing) that writers need solitude, and seek alienation of a kind every day of their working lives. (And remember, they are not even aware when and when not they are working...) Powers of observation heightened beyond the normal imply extraordinary disinvolvement; or rather the double process, excessive preoccupation and identification with the lives of others, and at the same time a monstrous detachment. For identification brings the superficial loyalties (that is, to the self) of concealment and privacy, while detachment brings the harsher fidelities (to the truth about the self) of revealment and exposure. The tension between standing apart and being fully involved; that is what makes a writer. That is where we begin. The validity of this dialectic is the synthesis of revelation; our achievement of, or even attempt at this is the moral, the human justification for what we do.

Here I am referring to an accusation that every writer meets, that we 'use' people, or rather other people's lives. Of course we do. As unconscious eternal eavesdroppers and observers, snoopers, nothing that is human is alien to the imagination and the particular intuition to which it is a trance-like state of entry. I have written *from the starting-point* of other people's 'real' lives; what I have written represents alternatives to the development of a life as it was formed before I encountered it and as it will continue, out of my sight. A writer sees in your life what you do not. That is why people who think they recognize themselves as 'models' for this character or that in a story will protest triumphantly, 'it wasn't that way at all'. They think they know better; but perhaps it is the novelist or short story writer who does? Fiction is a way of exploring possibilities present but undreamt of in the living of a single life.

There is also the assumption, sometimes prurient or deliciously scandalized, that writers write only about themselves. I know that I have used my own life much the same way as I have that of others: events (emotions are events, too, of the spirit) mark exits and entrances in a warren where many burrows lead off into the same darkness but this one might debouch far distant from that. What emerges most often is an alternative fate, the predisposition to which exists in what 'actually' happened.

How can the eavesdropper, observer, snooper ever be the prototype? The stories in this book were written between the ages of twenty and fifty. Where am I, in them? I search for myself. At most, reading them over for the first time in many years, I see my own shadow dancing on a wall behind and over certain stories. I can make a guess at remembering what significatory event it was that casts it there. The story's 'truth' or lack of it is not attached to or dependent upon that lost event.

But part of these stories' 'truth' does depend upon faithfulness to another series of lost events – the shifts in social attitudes as evidenced in the characters and situations. I had wanted to arrange the selection in sequence from the earliest story collection to the latest simply because when reading story collections I myself enjoy following the development of a writer. Then I found that this order had another logic to which my first was complementary. The chronological order turns out to be an historical one. The change in social attitudes unconsciously reflected in the stories represents both that of the people in my society – that is to say, history – and my apprehension of it; in the writing, I am acting upon my society, and in the manner of my apprehension, all the time history is acting upon me.

The white girl in 'Is There Nowhere Else Where We Can Meet?', whose first *conscious* encounter with a black is that between victim and attacker – primary relationship indeed – is several years and a book away from the girl in 'The Smell of Death and Flowers', experiencing her generation's equivalent of religious ecstasy in the comradeship of passive resistance action in the company of blacks. Both white girls are twenty-five years and several books away from the whites in 'Open House' and 'Africa Emergent', experiencing the collapse of white liberalism. The humble black servant bemoaning fatalistically in 'Ah, Woe Is Me' (a very early story) could never have occurred in my writing by the time, again several books later, the young black political refugee is awaiting military training in exile and the 'Some Monday For Sure' when he will return to a South Africa ruled by a black majority. Even the language changes from book to book: 'native' becomes first 'African' then 'Black', because these usages* have been adopted, over three decades, by South Africans of various opinions, often at different stages. For example, the old Afrikaner in 'Abroad' (a recent story) still speaks quite naturally of 'natives', whereas for English-speaking whites the use of the term 'African' is now general, no longer even indicating, as it would have ten years ago, that the speaker was showing his political colours as liberal if not leftist. The use of the blunt term 'Black' is now the reverse of pejorative or insulting: indeed it is the only one, of all generic words used to denote them, that has not been imposed upon but has been chosen by blacks themselves. (Though not all, in particular older and more conservative people, feel happy with it.) Its adoption by whites has a somewhat left-of-liberal tone, but much more significant is the fact that here whites are following black, not white usage.

What I am saying is that I see that many of these stories *could not have been written* later or earlier than they were. If I could have juggled them around in the contents list of this collection without that being evident, they would have been false in some way important to me as a writer.

What I am also saying, then, is that in a certain sense a

*There is a fourth, roughly concurrent with 'African', but I don't think it occurs in any of these stories: 'Bantu'. The word means 'people', and so, used in conjunction with the English word, as it often is – 'Bantu people' – produces the idiotic term 'People people'. The use of 'Bantu' is official government *politesse*, adopted to replace the more offensive appellations with a term almost as negative – and revealing, so far as the user is concerned – as 'non-white'.

writer is 'selected' by his subject – his subject being *the consciousness* of his own era. How he deals with this is, to me, the fundament of commitment, although 'commitment' is usually understood as the reverse process: a writer's selection of a subject in conformity with the rationalization of his own ideological and/or political beliefs.

My time and place have been twentieth-century Africa. Emerging from it, immersed in it, the first form in which I wrote was the short story. I write fewer and fewer stories, now, and more novels, but I don't think I shall ever stop writing stories. What makes a writer turn from one to the other? How do they differ?

Nobody has ever succeeded in defining a short story in a manner to satisfy all who write or read them, and I shall not, here. I sometimes wonder if one shouldn't simply state flatly: a short story is a piece of fiction short enough to be read at one sitting? No, that will satisfy no one, least myself. But for me certainly there is a clue, there, to the choice of the short story by writers, as a form: whether or not it has a narrative in the external or internal sense, whether it sprawls or neatly bites its own tail, a short story is a concept that the writer can 'hold', fully realized, in his imagination, at one time. A novel is, by comparison, staked out, and must be taken possession of stage by stage; it is impossible to contain, all at once, the proliferation of concepts it ultimately may use. For this reason I cannot understand how people can suppose one makes a conscious choice, *after* knowing what one wants to write about, between writing a novel or a short story. A short story *occurs*, in the imaginative sense. To write one is to express from a situation in the exterior or interior world the life-giving drop – sweat, tear, semen, saliva – that will spread an intensity on the page; burn a hole in it.

April 1975

Is There Nowhere Else Where We Can Meet?

It was a cool grey morning and the air was like smoke. In that reversal of the elements that sometimes takes place, the grey, soft, muffled sky moved like the sea on a silent day.

The coat collar pressed rough against her neck and her cheeks were softly cold as if they had been washed in ice-water. She breathed gently with the air; on the left a strip of veld fire curled silently, flameless. Overhead a dove purred. She went on over the flat straw grass, following the trees, now on, now off the path. Away ahead, over the scribble of twigs, the sloping lines of black and platinum grass – all merging, tones but no colour, like an etching – was the horizon, the shore at which cloud lapped.

Damp burnt grass puffed black, faint dust from beneath her feet. She could hear herself swallow.

A long way off she saw a figure with something red on its head, and she drew from it the sense of balance she had felt at the particular placing of the dot of a figure in a picture. She was here; someone was over there . . . Then the red dot was gone, lost in the curve of the trees. She changed her bag and parcel from one arm to the other and felt the morning, palpable, deeply cold and clinging against her eyes.

She came to the end of a direct stretch of path and turned with it round a dark-fringed pine and a shrub, now delicately boned, that she remembered hung with bunches of white flowers like crystals in the summer. There was a native in a red woollen cap standing at the next clump of trees, where the path crossed a ditch and was bordered by white-splashed stones. She had pulled a little sheath of pine needles, three in a twist of thin brown tissue, and as she walked she ran them against her thumb. Down; smooth and stiff. Up; catching in gentle resistance as the minute serrations snagged at the skin. He was standing with his back towards her, looking along the way he had come; she pricked the ball of her thumb with the needle-ends. His one trouser leg was torn off above the knee, and the back of the naked leg and half-turned heel showed the peculiarly dead, powdery black of cold. She was nearer to him now, but she knew he did not hear her coming over the damp dust of the path. She was level with him, passing him; and he turned slowly and looked beyond her, without a flicker of interest as a cow sees you go.

The eyes were red, as if he had not slept for a long time, and the strong smell of old sweat burned at her nostrils. Once past, she wanted to cough, but a pang of guilt at the red weary eyes stopped her. And he had only a filthy rag – part of an old shirt? – without sleeves and frayed away into a great gap from underarm to waist. It lifted in the currents of cold as she passed. She had dropped the neat trio of pine needles somewhere, she did not know at what moment, so now, remembering something from childhood, she lifted her hand to her face and sniffed: yes, it was as she remembered, not as chemists pretend it in the bath salts, but a dusty green scent, vegetable rather than flower. It was clean, unhuman. Slightly sticky too; tacky on her fingers. She must wash them as soon as she got there. Unless her hands were quite clean, she could not lose consciousness of them, they obtruded upon her.

She felt a thudding through the ground like the sound of a hare running in fear and she was going to turn around and then he was there in front of her, so startling, so utterly unexpected, panting right into her face. He stood dead still and she stood dead still. Every vestige of control, of sense, of thought, went out of her as a room plunges into dark at the failure of power and she found herself whimpering like an idiot or a child. Animal sounds came out of her throat. She gibbered. For a moment it was Fear itself that had her by the arms, the legs, the throat; not fear of the man, of any single menace he might present, but Fear, absolute, abstract. If the earth had opened up in fire at her feet, if a wild beast had opened its terrible mouth to receive her, she could not have been reduced to less than she was now.

There was a chest heaving through the tear in front of her; a face panting; beneath the red hairy woollen cap the yellowish-red eyes holding her in distrust. One foot, cracked from exposure until it looked like broken wood, moved, only to restore balance in the dizziness that follows running, but any move seemed towards her and she tried to scream and the awfulness of dreams came true and nothing would come out. She wanted to throw the handbag and the parcel at him, and as she fumbled crazily for them she heard him draw a deep, hoarse breath and he grabbed out at her and – ah! It came. His hand clutched her shoulder.

Now she fought with him and she trembled with strength as they struggled. The dust puffed round her shoes and his scuffling toes. The smell of him choked her – It was an old pyjama jacket, not a shirt – His face was sullen and there was a pink place where the skin had been grazed off. He sniffed desperately, out of breath. Her teeth chattered, wildly she battered him with her head, broke away, but he snatched at the skirt of her coat and jerked her back. Her face swung up and she saw the waves of a grey sky and a crane breasting them, beautiful as the figurehead of a ship. She staggered for balance and the handbag and parcel fell. At once he was upon them, and she wheeled about; but as she was about to fall on her knees to get there first, a sudden relief, like a rush of tears, came to her and, instead, she ran. She ran and ran, stumbling wildly off through the stalks of dead grass, turning over her heels against hard winter tussocks, blundering through trees and bushes. The young mimosas closed in, lowering a thicket of twigs right to the ground, but she tore herself through, feeling the dust in her eyes and the scaly twigs hooking at her hair. There was a ditch, knee-high in blackjacks; like pins responding to a magnet they fastened along her legs, but on the other side there was a fence and then the road ... She clawed at the fence – her hands were capable of nothing – and tried to drag herself between the wires, but her coat got caught on a barb, and she was imprisoned there, bent in half, while waves of terror swept over her in heat and trembling. At last the wire tore through its hold on the cloth; wobbling, frantic, she climbed over the fence.

And she was out. She was out on the road. A little way on there were houses, with gardens, postboxes, a child's swing. A small dog sat at a gate. She could hear a faint hum, as of life, of talk somewhere, or perhaps telephone wires.

She was trembling so that she could not stand. She had to keep on walking, quickly, down the road. It was quiet and grey, like the morning. And cool. Now she could feel the cold air round her mouth and between her brows, where the skin stood out in sweat. And in the cold wetness that soaked down beneath her armpits and between her buttocks. Her heart thumped slowly and stiffly. Yes, the wind was cold; she was suddenly cold, damp-cold, all through. She raised her hand, still fluttering uncontrollably, and smoothed her hair; it was wet at the hairline. She guided her hand into her pocket and found a handkerchief to blow her nose.

There was the gate of the first house, before her.

She thought of the woman coming to the door, of the explanations, of the woman's face, and the police. Why did I fight, she thought suddenly. What did I fight for? Why didn't I give him the money and let him go? His red eyes, and the smell and those cracks in his feet, fissures, erosion. She shuddered. The cold of the morning flowed into her.

She turned away from the gate and went down the road slowly, like an invalid, beginning to pick the blackjacks from her stockings.

The Soft Voice of the Serpent

He was only twenty-six and very healthy and he was soon strong enough to be wheeled out into the garden. Like everyone else, he had great and curious faith in the garden: 'Well, soon you'll be up and able to sit out in the garden,' they said, looking at him fervently, with little understanding tilts of the head. Yes, he would be out ... in the garden. It was a big garden enclosed in old dark, sleek, pungent firs, and he could sit deep beneath their tiered fringes, down in the shade, far away. There was the feeling that there, in the garden, he would come to an understanding; that it would come easier, there. Perhaps there was something in this of the old Eden idea; the tender human adjusting himself to himself in the soothing impersonal presence of trees and grass and earth, before going out into the stare of the world.

The very first time it was so strange; his wife was wheeling him along the gravel path in the sun and the shade, and he felt exactly as he did when he was a little boy and he used to bend and hang, looking at the world upside down, through his ankles. Everything was vast and open, the sky, the wind blowing along through the swaying, trembling greens, the flowers shaking in vehement denial. Movement...

A first slight wind lifted again in the slack, furled sail of himself; he felt it belly gently, so gently he could just feel it, lifting inside him.

So she wheeled him along, pushing hard and not particularly well with her thin pretty arms – but he would not for anything complain of the way she did it or suggest that the nurse might do better, for he knew that would hurt her – and when they came to a spot that he liked, she put the brake on the chair and settled him there for the morning. That was the first time and now he sat there every day. He read a lot, but his attention was arrested sometimes, quite suddenly and compellingly, by the sunken place under the rug where his leg used to be. There was his one leg, and next to it, the rug flapped loose. Then looking, he felt his leg not there; he felt it go, slowly, from the toe to the thigh. He felt that he had no leg. After a few minutes he went back to his book. He never let the realization quite reach him; he let himself realize it physically, but he never quite let it get at *him*. He felt it pressing up, coming, coming, dark, crushing, ready to burst – but he always turned away, just in time, back to his book. That was his system; that was the way he was going to do it. He would let it come near, irresistibly near, again and again, ready to catch him alone in the garden. And again and again he would turn it back, just in time. Slowly it would become a habit, with the reassuring strength of a habit. It would become such a habit never to get to the point of realizing it, *that he never would realize it*. And one day he would find that he had achieved what he wanted: *he would feel as if he had always been like that.*

Then the danger would be over, for ever.

In a week or two he did not have to read all the time; he could let himself put down the book and look about him, watching the firs part silkily as a child's fine straight hair in the wind, watching the small birds tightroping the telephone wire, watching the fat old dove trotting after his refined patrician grey women, purring with lust. His wife came and sat beside him, doing her sewing, and sometimes they spoke, but often they sat for hours, a whole morning, her movements at work small and unobtrusive as the birds', he resting his head back and looking at a blur of sky through half closed eyes. Now and then her eye, habitually looking inwards, would catch the signal of some little happening, some point of colour in the garden, and her laugh or exclamation drawing his attention to it would suddenly clear away the silence. At eleven o'clock she would get up and put down her sewing and go into the house to fetch their tea; crunching slowly away into the sun up the path, going easily, empowered by the sun rather than her own muscles. He watched her go, easily ... He was healing. In the static quality of his gaze, in the relaxed feeling of his mouth, in the upward-lying palm of his hand, there was annealment . . .

One day a big locust whirred dryly past her head, and she jumped up with a cry, scattering her sewing things. He laughed at her as she bent about picking them up, shuddering. She went into the house to fetch the tea, and he began to read. But presently he put down the book and, yawning, noticed a reel of pink cotton that she had missed, lying in a rose bed.

He smiled, remembering her. And then he became conscious of a curious old mannish little face, fixed upon him in a kind of hypnotic dread. There, absolutely stilled with fear beneath his glance, crouched a very big locust. What an amusing face the thing had! A lugubrious long face, that somehow suggested a bald head, and such a glum mouth. It looked like some little person out of a Disney cartoon. It moved slightly, still looking up fearfully at him. Strange body, encased in a sort of old-fashioned creaky armour. He had never realized before what ridiculous-looking insects locusts were! Well, naturally not; they occur to one collectively, as a pest – one doesn't go around looking at their faces.

The face was certainly curiously human and even expressive, but looking at the body, he decided that the body couldn't really be called a body at all. With the face, the creature's kinship with humans ended. The body was flimsy paper stretched over a frame of matchstick, like a small boy's homemade aeroplane. And those could not be thought of as legs – the great saw-toothed back ones were like the parts of an old crane, and the front ones like – like one of her hairpins, bent in two. At that moment the creature slowly lifted up one of the front legs, and passed it tremblingly over its head, stroking the left antenna down. Just as a man might take out a handkerchief and pass it over his brow.

He began to feel enormously interested in the creature, and leaned over in his chair to see it more closely. It sensed him and beneath its stiff, plated sides, he was surprised to see the pulsations of a heart. How fast it was breathing . . . He leaned away a little, to frighten it less.

Watching it carefully, and trying to keep himself effaced from its consciousness by not moving, he became aware of some struggle going on in the thing. It seemed to gather itself together in muscular concentration: this co-ordinated force then passed along its body in a kind of petering tremor, and ended in a stirring along the upward shaft of the great back legs. But the locust remained where it was. Several times this wave of effort currented through it and was spent, but the next time it ended surprisingly in a few hobbling, uneven steps, undercarriage – aeroplanelike again – trailing along the earth.

Then the creature lay, fallen on its side, antennae turned stretched out towards him. It groped with its feet, feeling for a hold on the soft ground, bending its joints and straining. With a heave, it righted itself, and as it did so, he saw – leaning forward again – what was the trouble. It was the same trouble. His own trouble. The creature had lost one leg. Only the long upward shaft of its left leg remained, with a neat round aperture where, no doubt, the other half of the leg had been attached.

Now as he watched the locust gather itself again and again in that concentration of muscle, spend itself again and again in a message that was so puzzlingly never obeyed, he knew exactly what the creature felt. Of course he knew that feeling! That absolute certainty that the leg was there: one had only to lift it ... The upward shaft of the locust's leg quivered, lifted; why then couldn't he walk? He tried again. The message came; it was going through, the leg was lifting, now it was ready – now! ... The shaft sagged in the air, with nothing, nothing to hold it up.

He laughed and shook his head: He *knew* ... Good Lord, *exactly* like – He called out to the house – 'Come quickly! Come and see! You've got another patient!'

'What?' she shouted. 'I'm getting tea.'

'Come and look!' he called. 'Now!'

'... What is it?' she said, approaching the locust distastefully.

'Your locust!' he said. She jumped away with a little shriek.

'Don't worry – it can't move. It's as harmless as I am. You

must have knocked its leg off when you hit out at it!' He was laughing at her.

'Oh, I didn't!' she said reproachfully. She loathed it but she loathed to hurt, even more. 'I never even touched it! All I hit was air ... I couldn't possibly have hit it. Not its leg off.'

'All right then. It's another locust. But it's lost its leg, anyway. You should just see it ... It doesn't know the leg isn't there. God, I know exactly how that feels ... I've been watching it, and honestly, it's uncanny. I can see it feels just like I do!'

She smiled at him, sideways; she seemed suddenly pleased at something. Then, recalling herself, she came forward, bent double, hands upon her hips.

'Well, if it can't move ...' she said, hanging over it.

'Don't be frightened,' he laughed. 'Touch it.'

'Ah, the poor thing,' she said, catching her breath in compassion. 'It can't walk.'

'Don't encourage it to self-pity,' he teased her.

She looked up and laughed. 'Oh you –' she parried, assuming a frown. The locust kept its solemn silly face turned to her. 'Shame, isn't he a funny old man,' she said. 'But what will happen to him?'

'I don't know,' he said, for being in the same boat absolved him from responsibility or pity. 'Maybe he'll grow another one. Lizards grow new tails, if they lose them.'

'Oh, *lizards*,' she said. '– But not these. I'm afraid the cat'll get him.'

'Get another little chair made for him and you can wheel him out here with me.'

'Yes,' she laughed. 'Only for him it would have to be a kind of little cart, with wheels.'

'Or maybe he could be taught to use crutches. I'm sure the farmers would like to know that he was being kept active.'

'The poor old thing,' she said, bending over the locust again. And reaching back somewhere into an inquisitive childhood she picked up a thin wand of twig and prodded the locust, very gently. 'Funny thing is, it's even the same leg, the left one.' She looked round at him and smiled.

'I know,' he nodded, laughing. 'The two of us . . .' And then he shook his head and, smiling, said it again: 'The two of us.'

She was laughing and just then she flicked the twig more sharply than she meant to and at the touch of it there was a sudden flurried papery whirr, and the locust flew away.

She stood there with the stick in her hand, half afraid of the creature again, and appealed, unnerved as a child, 'What happened. What happened.'

There was a moment of silence.

'Don't be a fool,' he said irritably.

They had forgotten that locusts can fly.

Ah, Woe Is Me

Sarah worked for us before her legs got too bad. She was very fat, and her skin was light yellow-brown, as if, like a balloon that lightens in colour as it is blown up, the fat swelling beneath the thin layer of pigment caused it to stretch and spread more and more sparsely. She wore delicate little gilt-rimmed spectacles and she was a good cook, though extravagant with butter.

Those were the things we noticed about her.

But in addition, she had only one husband, married to her by law in church, and three children, Robert, Janet and Felicia, whose upbringing was her constant preoccupation. She sighed often as she bent about her cleaning, as heavy people do, but she was thinking about the children. Ah! woe is me, she would say, when the butcher didn't send the liver, or it started to rain in the middle of the weekly wash, as if, judging from the troubles in her own life, she couldn't expect everyday matters to go any better. At first we laughed at the Biblical ostentation of the exclamation, apparently so out of proportion; but later we understood. Ah, woe is me, she said; and that was her comment on life.

She worried about her three children because she wanted them to know their place; she wanted to educate them, she wanted the boy to have a decent job, she wanted the girls to grow up virgin and marry in church. That was all. Her own Mission School education, with its tactful emphasis on the next world rather than this, had not made her dangerous enough or brave enough or free enough or even educated enough to think that any place was the place for her children; but it had emerged her just sufficiently to make her believe that there *was* a place for them; not a share in the White Man's place, but not no place at all, either; a place of their own. She wanted them to have it and she wanted them to stay there. She was enough of an uncomplaining realist to know that this was not easy. She was also conservative enough not to ask why it was so difficult. You got to live in this world the way it is, she said.

The things she wanted for her children sound commonplace; but they weren't. Not where she had to look for them.

At first she rented a room for the children in a relative's house in the Location. She paid for their food and went to visit them every Sunday, and the cousin was supposed to see that they went to school regularly and did not wander about the Location after dark during the week; Sarah believed as fervently in education as she feared the corruption of the dark. But soon it became clear that Robert spent most of his schooldays caddying at the golf course (Why, why, why! moaned Sarah under the disgrace of it – and Robert opened his hand, pink inside like the unexpected little paw of a knowing monkey, and showed the sixpence and tickey* lying there, misted with the warmth of his palm) and Felicia ran screaming about the dark, smoky streets at night, as other children did. It was all right for the others, who were going to be errand boys and nursegirls; but it was not for Sarah's children.

She sent them to boarding school.

Along came the list of things they must have, and the endless low, urgent discussions over the back gate with her husband and the slow passing of folded pink notes and the counting of half-crowns out of a cotton tobacco bag. She spent, not merely a fortune on them – fortunes are things made and lost – but everything she had, her nine pounds in the Post Office, and all her wages, every month. Even then it was not enough, for the school was in Natal, and she could only afford train fare for them once a year, so that they spent all holidays other than the Christmas one at school, three hundred miles from home. But they were being educated. She showed me their letters; like all children's letters, noncommittal, emotionless,

*A South African colloquialism for a threepenny coin now out of currency.

usually asking for something. Occasionally I gave her some sweets to send them, and I received a letter of thanks from the younger girl, Janet, in reply; polite, but without the slightest hint of any pleasure that the gift might have brought. Sarah always asked to read the letter, to see, I knew, if it was respectful: that was the important thing. A look of quiet relief would come over her face as she folded it up again. Yes, she would say, there I know they're being looked after.

When Christmas came I felt ashamed to let her rent a room in the Location for the children for the duration of their yearly holiday, and I told her she could have them with her in the yard, if she liked. She put on her black dress and fringed shawl – she clung to a few old Victorian dignities – and went to meet them at the station, starting off very early, because her legs were bad again, and she could not hurry. She was away all day, and I was rather angry, but when I saw her coming home with her three children I was conscious of a sense of ceremony in her, and said nothing.

They were remarkably good children. I have never seen such good children, so muted, so unobtrusive in their movements, so subdued in their play. Too good: the girls coming to sit silently in the sun against the wall of Sarah's room, the boy sitting with his bits of stick and stone among the weeds along the fence. The girls did their washing and crocheted caps of red wool; their laughter was secret, never come upon in the open, like a stream heard gently gurgling away hidden somewhere in the undergrowth. Their smiles were solemn and beautiful, but ritual, not joyousness. The boy didn't smile at all. When I gave him a water-pistol some visiting child had forgotten at the house, he took it as if it were a penance. He's put it away in his box, Mam, Sarah smiled proudly. Oh, yes, it's a big thing for him to have that gun, Mam. He feels he's a big man now.

They were not allowed out of the yard, unless accompanied by their mother or sent on an errand on her behalf. They used to stand at the gate, looking out. Once Robert disappeared for the morning, and came back at lunch time with dust-blurred feet and grass speckling his clothes. Sarah had been complaining all morning, I know where it is he's gone. It's the golf course, I know. It's at the golf course. Her legs were worrying her, or she'd have gone up there after him. In weary martyrdom she gave him a long, hard hiding, but without anger. He cried and cried, as if in a depression rather than from hurt.

Sarah talked about the child's escapade for days; it was in the three pairs of eyes, turned up, white, to look at her as she came out of the kitchen door into the yard; it rested upon the neck of the small boy with the sun that lay upon his bent head while he played.

Sarah was sadly stern with the children, and she was constantly giving them advice and admonition. The smallest transgression set off the steady, penetrating small rain of her sorrow and disapproval, seeping down all over and about the bright spark of the child. Under the steadiness, the gentle soaking persistence of her logic, the spark damped out. I told her that I thought she was perhaps too hard on the children – that was not quite it, but then I could not be clear in my own mind about what I thought might be happening to them – and she thought a moment, and then appealed, with the simplicity of fact: But they got to come against it some time, Mam. If they learn now they can't do what they like, it won't make them angry later on. They must learn, she said – hard now – they must *learn*.

I think she bored them very much.

They went back to school, away on the train for another year. Who knows what they felt? It was impossible to tell. Only Janet, the middle one, cried a little. She's the clever one, smiled Sarah, she's going to be a teacher. She's in Standard Five already. Though two years older, and physically a well-developed young woman, Felicia was only in the same class. Plans for her were vague; but for Janet – Sarah could never help smiling in the strength of her surety for Janet – there was a place.

They never came back to our yard. During the year, Sarah's legs got progressively worse, and she had to give up her job. She went to live in the Location, and managed to get a little washing to do at home. But, of course, it was the end of boarding school; on her husband's earnings alone, with the food and rent in the Location to be paid for as well, it just couldn't be done. So the children came home, and lived with their mother, and went to school in the Location. She came to see me, troubled, I could see, by the strong feeling that they had lost a foothold; but seeing a check to their slipping feet and seeking a comfort in the consolation that although their education would not be as good, she herself would be able to train them the way they should go. She sat on the kitchen chair as she told me, slowly settling her legs, swathed like great pillars in crêpe bandage.

She did not come again herself. Her legs were too bad. She sent the children – often Janet alone – to see me. They never asked for anything; they came and stood patiently in the back yard until I noticed them, and then they answered my enquiries very softly, with their large eyes looking anywhere but at me. Yes, their mother's legs were bad. No, just the same like they were before. No, she couldn't take washing any more. Yes, they were still at school. I always had the curious feeling that they were embarrassed, not *by* me, but *for* me, as if their faces knew that I could not help asking these same questions, because the real state of their lives was unknown and unimagined by me, and therefore beyond my questioning. Usually there was an orange each for them, and an old dress or pullover that had imperceptibly slipped below the undefined but arbitrary standard of the household. Each time they came, they were – not a little shabbier, exactly, but a little slacker, a big safety-pin in Felicia's jersey, a small unmended tear fraying on Robert's pants. Even Janet, in a raggy short skirt that was a raggy short skirt, not the ironed, mended, stiffly respectable, neat rag that she had always worn before. Well, food and clothes were getting more expensive; I suppose they were getting poorer.

A long time passed without a visit from them. I used to ask the other native women: How is Sarah? Have you seen Sarah? They didn't like her very much. I don't know, they'd say, offhand. I hear she's sick, her legs are bad.

Sarah's husband isn't working, my servant remarked one

day, scrubbing the kitchen table. What, not working? I said. Then how are they managing? *Her* legs are bad, she can't work, said Caroline, shrugging. I know, I said, but they have to eat. The little boy's working, remarked Caroline. He's working in the dairy at the back. She meant he was cleaning up, washing the floor in the handling room.

I asked her to go and see Sarah next time she was in the Location, and find out what I could do to help. She came back and said: Sarah's husband got another job; he was too old for that job he had. Now he's got a smaller job. And is there anything I can do to help Sarah? I asked – Did you tell her? Caroline looked up at me. Her husband's got another job, she said patiently, as if I were incapable of understanding anything told me once.

One Tuesday morning Caroline came in from her ironing on the back porch and said: Sarah's girl's in the yard – and went back to her iron at once.

Janet was standing under the pepper-tree slowly twisting her bare foot on the stones, and from her stance I thought she must have been waiting there quite a long time. Until Caroline noticed her. Now she said Good Morning, Mam, and came reluctantly to the steps, watching her feet. She wasn't a little girl any longer. The childish round belly had flattened to the curve of hips and the very short, stretched jersey lifted with the quivering new breasts. The jersey was dirty, out-at-elbows. In her very small ears, there were brass ear-rings with a round pink, shiny bit of glass in them. She stood looking at me, her head on one side. I hear you've had trouble, Janet, I said, thinking I didn't have to talk to a child, now.

Yes, Mam, she said, very low, and the voice was still a child's voice.

Your father lost his job? I said.

Yes, Mam, she said, shaking her head slowly, like Sarah. There's been trouble.

And Robert's working? I asked.

In the dairy, she said. And looked at her feet.

And couldn't Felicia get a job somewhere? I urged, remembering Sarah's dread of her child acting nursemaid.

She's gone, Mam, said the girl, faintly.

She's what? I frowned to hear better. She's gone to Bloemfontein, Mam, she said, so faintly I could scarcely catch it. She's married, Mam.

Well, that's nice! That's very nice, isn't it? I smiled. Your mother must be very pleased.

She said nothing.

So there's only you at home now, Janet? And you're still at school? Still going to be a teacher, eh? – I was sure that she would smile now, lift up the voice that seemed to be dying away, effacing her, escaping me.

I'm at home, Mam, she said, shyly.

At home?

Yes, I'm home with my mother – The voice was escaping, struggling to get away into silence.

You mean at home all the time, Janet? I said, in a high tone.

I'm at home with my mother. Her legs are very bad now. She can't walk any more.

You mean you don't go to school at all? You just look after your mother?

Yes, Mam, she said, looking hard at her foot with her eyes wide open. Then she lifted her head and looked at me, without interest, without guile, as if she looked into the face of the sun, blinded.

I said, still in that high tone: Wait a minute, Janet. I've got something for you. I think I've – and escaped into the house. I rushed to the wardrobe, pulled out a dress and an old corduroy skirt and rolled them into a bundle. Halfway down the hall I went back to the bedroom and got five shillings from my purse.

Out in the yard she was still standing in the same position. She hardly seemed to know where she was. I gave her the bundle, saying, Here, I think these will fit you, Janet – and then I held out the money as if it were hot, and said, Give this to your mother.

Thank you, Mam, she said gravely, and it seemed that she had no voice at all. She tied the money away in a piece of cloth and folded the clothes all over again.

I lingered about the yard, not knowing quite what to do. Caroline was looking at me through the porch windows. Caroline, I called suddenly, Caroline, give Janet some tea, will you?

Caroline never breakfasts until eleven o'clock; it was just time. When I went into the kitchen a few minutes later, Janet was sitting at the table, her face in a big mug of tea, three slabs of bread and jam beside her. I said, All right, Janet? And she took her face out of the mug, and smiled, very faintly, very shyly, with her eyes.

I could hear Caroline talking to her, and presently Caroline came and said: She's going now.

She was standing in the yard again, her bundle in her hand. I came out smiling; I felt better for her. Good-bye, Janet, I said. And tell your mother I hope she'll be better. And you must come and tell me how she is, eh?

There was no answer, and all at once I saw that she was making a tremendous effort to control herself, that she wanted most desperately to cry. Her whole body seemed to surge up with the tears that pushed at her eyes. Her eyes got bigger and bigger, more and more glassy; and then she began to cry, her eyes and nose streamed and she cried great sobbing, hiccuping tears.

What's the matter, Janet, I said. What's the matter?

But she only cried, trying to catch the wetness on her tear-smeared forearm, looking round in an agony of embarrass-ment for somewhere to wipe her tears. She snorted deeply and gulped and could not find anything. There was the bundle, but how could she use that? How could she cry into that? – in front of me.

But what's the matter, my girl, I said. What's wrong? You mustn't cry. What's wrong? Tell me?

She tried to speak but her breath was caught by the long quavering sigh of tears. My mother – she's very sick ... she said at last.

And she began to cry again, her face crumpling up, sobbing and gasping. Desperately, she rubbed at her nose with her wet arm.

What could I do for her? What could I do?

Here ... I said. Here – take this, and gave her my handkerchief.

The Catch

His thin strong bony legs passed by at eye level every morning as they lay, stranded on the hard smooth sand. Washed up thankfully out of the swirl and buffet of the city, they were happy to lie there, but because they were accustomed to telling the time by their nerves' response to the different tensions of the city – children crying in flats, lorries going heavily and bicycles jangling for early morning, skid of tyres, sound of frying and the human insect noise of thousands talking and walking and eating at midday – the tensionless shore keyed only to the tide gave them a sense of timelessness that, however much they rejoiced mentally, troubled their habit-impressed bodies with a lack of pressure. So the sound of his feet, thudding nearer over the sand, passing their heads with the deep sound of a man breathing in the heat above the rolled-up, faded trousers, passing away up the beach and shrinking into the figure of an Indian fisherman, began to be something to be waited for. His coming and going divided the morning into three; the short early time before he passed, the time when he was actually passing, and the largish chunk of warm mid-day that followed when he had gone.

After a few days, he began to say good morning, and looking up they found his face, a long head with a shining dark dome surrounded with curly hair given a stronger liveliness by the sharp coarse strokes of grey hairs, the beautiful curved nose handed out so impartially to Indians, dark eyes slightly blood-shot from the sun, a wide muscular mouth smiling on strong uneven teeth that projected slightly like the good useful teeth of an animal. But it was by his legs they would have known him; the dark, dull-skinned feet with the few black hairs on the big toe, the long hard shaft of the shin tightly covered with smooth shining skin, the pull of the tendons at his ankle like the taut ropes that control the sails of a ship.

They idly watched him go, envious of his fisherman's life not because they could ever really have lived it themselves, but because it had about it the frame of their holiday freedom. They looked at him with the curious respect people feel for one who has put a little space between himself and the rest of the world. 'It's a good life,' said the young man, the words not quite hitting the nail of this respect. 'I can just see *you* ...' said the girl, smiling. She saw him in his blue creased suit, carrying a bottle of gin wrapped in brown paper, a packet of bananas and the evening paper.

'He's got a nice open face,' said the young man. 'He wouldn't have a face like that if he worked as a waiter at the hotel.'

But when they spoke to him one morning when he was fishing along the surf for chad right in front of them, they found that he like themselves was only on holiday from a more complicated pattern of life. He worked five or six miles away at the sugar refinery, and this was his annual two weeks. He spent it fishing, he told them, because that was what he liked to do with his Sundays. He grinned his strong smile, lifting his chin out to sea as he swung his spoon glittering into the coming wave. They stood by like children, tugging one another back when he cast his line, closing in to peer with their hands behind their backs when he pulled in the flat silver fish and pushed the heads into the sand. They asked him questions, and he answered with a kind of open pleasure, as if discounting his position as a man of skill, a performer before an audience, out of friendliness. And they questioned animatedly, feeling the knowledge that he too was on holiday was a sudden intimacy between them, like the discovery between strangers that they share a friend. The fact that he was an Indian troubled them hardly at all. They almost forgot he *was* an Indian. And this too, though they did not know it, produced a lightening of the heart, a desire to do conversational frolics with a free tongue the way one stretches and kicks up one's legs in the sun after confinement in a close dark room.

'Why not get the camera?' said the girl, beginning to help with the fish as they were brought in. And the young man went away over the sand and came back adjusting the complications of his gadget with the seriousness of the amateur. He knelt in the wet sand that gave beneath his weight with a wet grinding, trying to catch the moment of skill in the fisherman's face. The girl watched quietly, biting her lip for the still second when the camera blinked. Aware but not in the least self-conscious of the fact that he was the subject, the Indian went on with his fishing, now and then parenthetically smiling his long-toothed smile.

The tendrils of their friendship were drawn in sharply for a moment when, putting his catch into a sack, he inquired naturally, 'Would you like to buy one for lunch, sir?' Down on his haunches with a springy strand of hair blowing back and forth over his ear, he could not know what a swift recoil closed back through the air over his head. He wanted to sell something. Disappointment as much as a satisfied dig in the ribs from opportunist prejudice stiffened them momentarily. Of course, he was not in quite the same position as themselves, after all. They shifted their attitude slightly.

'Well, we live at the hotel, you see,' said the girl.

He tied the mouth of the sack and looked up with a laugh. 'Of course!' he smiled, shaking his head. 'You couldn't cook it.' His lack of embarrassment immediately made things easy.

'Do you ever sell fish to the hotel?' asked the young man. 'We must keep a look out for it.'

'No – no, not really,' said the Indian. 'I don't sell much of my fish – mostly we eat it up there,' he lifted his eyebrows to the hills, brilliant with cane. 'It's only sometimes I sell it.'

The girl felt the dismay of having mistaken a privilege for an imposition. 'Oh well,' she smiled at him charmingly, 'that's a pity. Anyway, I suppose the hotel has to be sure of a regular supply.'

'That's right,' he said. 'I only fish in my spare time.'

He was gone, firmly up the beach, his strong feet making clefts in the sand like the muscular claws of a big strong-legged bird.

'You'll see the pictures in a few days,' shouted the girl. He stopped and turned with a grin. 'That's nothing,' he said. 'Wait till I catch something big. Perhaps soon I'll get something worth taking.'

He was 'their Indian'. When they went home they might remember the holiday by him as you might remember a particular holiday as the one when you used to play with a spaniel on the beach every day. It would be, of course, a nameless spaniel, an ownerless spaniel, an entertaining creature existing nowhere in your life outside that holiday, yet bound with absolute intimacy within that holiday itself. And, as an animal becomes more human every day, so every day the quality of their talk with the Indian had to change; the simple question-and-answer relation that goes with the celluloid pop of a ping-pong ball and does so well for all inferiors, foreigners and children became suddenly a toy (the Indian was grown-up and might smile at it). They did not know his name, and now, although they might have asked the first day and got away with it, it was suddenly impossible, because he didn't ask them theirs. So their you's and he's and I's took on the positiveness of names, and yet seemed to deepen their sense of communication by the fact that they introduced none of the objectivity that names must always bring. He spoke to them quite a lot about Johannesburg, to which he assumed they must belong, as that was his generalization of city life, and he knew, sympathetically, that they were city people. And although they didn't live there, but somewhere near on a smaller pattern, they answered as if they did. They also talked a little of his life; or rather of the processes of the sugar refinery from which his life depended. They found it fascinating.

'If I were working, I'd try and arrange for you to come and see it,' he said, pausing, with his familiar taking his own time, and then looking directly smiling at them, his head tilted a little, the proud, almost rueful way one looks at two attractive children. They responded to his mature pleasure in them with a diffusion of warm youth that exuded from their skin as sweat is released at the touch of fear. 'What a fascinating person he is!' they would say to one another, curious.

But mostly they talked about fishing, the sea, and the

particular stretch of coast on which they were living. The Indian knew the sea – at home the couple would have said he 'loved' it – and from the look of it he could say whether the water would be hot or cold, safe or nursing an evil grievance of currents, evenly rolling or sucking at the land in a fierce backwash. He knew, as magically to them as a diviner feeling the pull of water beneath the ground, where the fish would be when the wind blew from the east, when it didn't blow at all, and when clouds covered in from the hills to the horizon. He stood on the slippery rocks with them and saw as they did, a great plain of heaving water, empty and unreadable as infinity; but *he* saw a hard greedy life going on down in there, shining plump bodies gaping swiftly close together through the blind green, tentacles like dark hands feeling over the deep rocks. And he would say, coming past them in his salt-stiff old trousers that seemed to put to shame clothes meekly washed in soap and tap-water, 'Over there at the far rocks this morning.'

They saw him most days; but always only in the morning. By afternoon they had had enough of the beach, and wanted to play golf on the closely green course that mapped inland through the man-high cane as though a barber had run a pair of clippers through a fine head of hair, or to sit reading old hotel magazines on the porch whose windows were so bleared with salt air that looking through them was like seeing with the opaque eyes of an old man. The beach was hot and far away; one day after lunch when a man came up from the sand and said as he passed their chairs, 'There's someone looking for you down there. An Indian's caught a huge salmon and he says you've promised to photograph it for him,' – they sat back and looked at one another with a kind of lazy exasperation. They felt weak and unwilling, defeating interest.

'Go on,' she said. 'You must go.'

'It had to be right after lunch,' he grumbled, smiling.

'Oh go on,' she insisted, head tilted. She herself did not move, but remained sitting back with her chin dropped to her chest, while he fetched the camera and went jogging off down the steep path through the bush. She pictured the salmon. She had never seen a salmon: it would be pink and powerfully agile; how big? She could not imagine.

A child came racing up from the beach, all gasps. 'Your husband says,' saying it word for word, 'he says you must come down right away and you must bring the film with you. It's in the little dressing-table drawer under his handkerchiefs.' She swung out of her chair as if she had been ready to go. The small boy ran before her all the way down to the beach, skidding on the stony path. Her husband was waving incoherently from the sand, urgent and excited as a waving flag. Not understanding, she began to hurry too.

'Like this!' he was shouting. 'Like this! Never seen anything like it! It must weigh eighty pounds –' his hands sized out a great hunk of air.

'But where?' she cried impatiently, not wanting to be told, but to see.

'It's right up the beach. He's gone to fetch it. I'd forgotten the film was finished, so when I got there, it was no use. I had to come back, and he said he'd lug it along here.' Yet he hadn't been able to leave the beach to get the film himself; he wanted to be there to show the fish to anyone who came along; he couldn't have borne to have someone see it without him, who had seen it first.

At last the Indian came round the paw of the bay, a tiny black stick detected moving alive along the beached waterline of black drift-sticks, and as he drew nearer he took on a shape, and then, more distinctly, the shape divided, another shape detached itself from the first, and there he was – a man hurrying heavily with a huge fish slung from his shoulder to his heels. 'O-o-h!' cried the girl, knuckle of her first finger caught between her teeth. The Indian's path wavered, as if he staggered under the weight, and his forearms and hands, gripping the mouth of the fish, were bent stiff as knives against his chest. Long strands of grey curly hair blew over from the back of his head along his bright high forehead, that held the sun in a concentric blur of light on its domed prominence.

'Go and help him,' the girl said to her husband, shaming him. He was standing laughing proudly, like a spectator watching the winner come in at a race. He was startled he hadn't gone himself: 'Shall I?' he said, already going.

They staggered up with the fish between them, panting

heavily, and dropped the dead weight of the great creature with a scramble and thud upon the sand. It was as if they had rescued someone from the sea. They stood back that they might feel the relief of their burden, and the land might receive the body. But what a beautiful creature lay there! Through the powdering of sand, mother-of-pearl shone up. A great round glass eye looked out.

'Oh, get the sand off it!' laughed the girl. 'Let's see it properly.'

Exhausted as he was, he belonged to the fish, and so immediately the Indian dragged it by the tail down to the rill of the water's edge, and they cupped water over it with their hands. Water cleared it like a cloth wiping a film from a diamond; out shone the magnificent fish, stiff and handsome in its mail of scales, glittering a thousand opals of colour, set with two brilliant deep eyes all hard clear beauty and not marred by the capability of expression which might have made a reproach of the creature's death; a king from another world, big enough to shoulder a man out of the way, dead, captured, astonishing.

The child came up and put his forefinger on its eye. He wrinkled his nose, smiling and pulling a face, shoulders rising. 'It can't see!' he said joyously. The girl tried it; smooth, firm, resilient eye; like a butterfly wing bright under glass.

They all stood, looking down at the fish, that moved very slightly in the eddy of sand as the thin water spread out softly round its body and then drew gently back. People made for them across the sand. Some came down from the hotel; the piccanin caddies left the golf course. Interest spread like a net, drawing in the few, scattered queer fish of the tiny resort, who avoided one another in a gesture of jealous privacy. They came to stand and stare, prodding a tentative toe at the real fish, scooped out of his sea. The men tried to lift it, making terse suggestions about its weight. A hundred, seventy, sixty-five they said with assurance. Nobody really knew. It was a wonderful fish. The Indian, wishing to take his praise modestly, busied himself with practical details, explaining with serious charm, as if he were quoting a book or someone else's experience, how such a fish was landed, and how rarely it was to be caught on that part of the coast. He kept his face averted, down over the fish, like a man fighting tears before strangers.

'Will it bite? Will it bite?' cried the children, putting their hands inside its rigid white-lipped mouth and shrieking. 'Now that's enough,' said a mother.

'Sometimes there's a lovely stone, here,' the Indian shuffled nearer on his haunches, not touching but indicating with his brown finger a place just above the snout. He twisted his head to the girl. 'If I find it in this one, I'll bring it for you. It makes a lovely ring.' He was smiling to her.

'I want a picture taken with the fish,' she said determinedly, feeling the sun very hot on her head.

Someone had to stand behind her, holding it up. It was exactly as tall as she was; the others pointed with admiration. She smiled prettily, not looking at the fish. Then the important pictures were to be taken: the Indian and his fish.

'Just a minute,' he said, surprisingly, and taking a comb out of his pocket, carefully smoothed back his hair under his guiding hand. He lifted the fish by the gills with a squelch out of the wet sand, and some pictures were taken. 'Like this?' he kept saying anxiously, as he was directed by the young man to stand this way or that.

He stood tense, as if he felt oppressed by the invisible presence of some long-forgotten backdrop and palmstand. 'Smile!' demanded the man and the girl together, anxiously. And the sight of them, so concerned for his picture, released him to smile what was inside him, a strong, wide smile of pure achievement, that gathered up the unequal components of his face – his slim fine nose, his big ugly horse-teeth, his black crinkled-up eyes, and scribbled boldly a brave moment of whole man.

After the pictures had been taken, the peak of interest had been touched; the spectators' attention, quick to rise to a phenomenon, tended to sink back to its level of ordinary, more dependable interests. Wonderment at the fish could not be sustained in its purely specific projection; the remarks became more general and led to hearsay stories of other catches, other unusual experiences. As for the Indian, he had neglected his fish for his audience long enough. No matter how it might differ as an experience, as a fish it did not differ from other fish. He worried about it being in the full hot sun, and dragged it a little deeper into the sea so that the wavelets might flow over it. The mothers began to think that the sun was too hot for their children, and straggled away with them. Others followed, talking about the fish, shading the backs of their necks with their hands. 'Half past two,' said someone. The sea glittered with broken mirrors of hurtful light. 'What do you think you'd get for it?' asked the young man, slowly fitting his camera into its case.

'I'll get about two-pound-ten.' The Indian was standing with his hands on hips, looking down at the fish as if sizing it up.

So he *was* going to sell it! 'As much as that?' said the girl in surprise. With a slow, deliberate movement that showed that the sizing up had been a matter of weight rather than possible profit, he tried carrying the fish under his arm. But his whole body bent in an arc to its weight. He let it slither to the sand.

'Are you going to try the hotel?' she asked; she expected something from the taste of this fish, a flavour of sentiment.

He smiled, understanding her. 'No,' he said indulgently, 'I might. But I don't think they'd take it. I'll try somewhere else. *They* might want it.' His words took in vaguely the deserted beach, the one or two tiny holiday cottages. 'But where else?' she insisted. It irritated her although she smiled, this habit of other races of slipping out of one's questioning, giving vague but adamant assurances of sureties which were supposed to be hidden but that one knew perfectly well did not exist at all. 'Well, there's the boarding-house at Bailey's River – the lady there knows me. She often likes to take my fish.'

Bailey's River was the next tiny place, about a mile away over the sands. 'Well, I envy them their eating!' said the girl, giving him her praise again. She had taken a few steps back over the sand, ready to go; she held out her hand to draw her husband away. 'When will I see the picture?' the Indian stayed them eagerly. 'Soon, soon, soon!' they laughed. And they left him, kneeling beside his fish and laughing with them.

'I don't know how he's going to manage to carry that great thing all the way to Bailey's,' said the young man. He was steering his wife along with his hand on her little nape. 'It's only a mile!' she said. 'Ye-es! But–?' 'Oh, they're strong. They're used to it,' she said, shaking her feet free of the sand as they reached the path.

When they got back to the hotel, there was a surprise for them. As though the dam of their quiet withdrawal had been fuller than they thought, fuller than they could withstand, they found themselves toppling over into their old stream again, that might run on pointlessly and busy as the brook for ever and ever. Three friends from home up-country were there, come on an unexpected holiday to a farm a mile or two inland. They had come to look them up, as they would no doubt every day of the remainder of the holiday; and there would be tennis, and picnic parties, and evenings when they would laugh on the veranda round a table spiked with bottles and glasses. And so they were swept off from something too quiet and sure to beckon them back, looking behind them for the beckon, but already twitching to the old familiar tune. The visitors were shown the hotel bedroom, and walked down the broken stone steps to the first tee of the little golf course. They were voracious with the need to make use of everything they saw; bouncing on the beds, hanging out of the window, stamping on the tee and assuring that they'd be there with their clubs in the morning.

After a few rounds of drinks at the close of the afternoon, the young man and his wife suddenly felt certain that they had had a very dead time indeed up till now, and the unquiet gnaw of the need to 'make the best' – of time, life, holidays, anything – was gleefully hatched to feed on them again. When someone suggested that they all go into Durban for dinner and a cinema, they were excited. 'All in our car!' the girl cried. 'Let's all go together.'

The women had to fly off to the bedroom to prepare themselves to meet the city, and while the men waited for them, talking quieter and closer on the veranda, the sun went down behind the cane, the pale calm sea thinned into the horizon and turned long straight shoals of light foam to glass on the sand, pocked, farther up, by shadow. When they drove off up the dusty road between the trees they were steeped in the first dark. White stones stood out; as they came to the dip in the road where the stream ran beneath, they saw someone sitting on the boulder that marked the place, and as they slowed and bumped through, the figure moved slightly with a start checked before it could arrest their attention. They were talking. 'What was that?' said one of the women, without much interest. 'What?' said the young man, braking in reflex. 'It's just an old Indian with a sack or something,' someone else broke off to say. The wife, in the front seat, turned:

'Les!' she cried. 'It's him, with the fish!'

The husband had pulled up the car, skidded a little sideways on the road, its two shafts of light staring up among the trees. He sat looking at his wife in consternation. 'But I wonder what's the matter?' he said. 'I don't know!' she shrugged, in a rising tone. 'Who is it?' cried someone from the back.

'An Indian fisherman. We've spoken to him on the beach. He caught a huge salmon today.'

'We know him well,' said the husband; and then to her: 'I'd better back and see what's wrong.' She looked down at her handbag. 'It's going to make us awfully late, if you hang about,' she said. 'I won't hang about!' He reversed in a long jerk, annoyed with her or the Indian, he did not know. He got out, banging the door behind him. They all twisted, trying to see through the rear window. A silence had fallen in the car; a woman started to hum a little tune, faded out. The wife said with a clear little laugh: 'Don't think we're crazy. This Indian is really quite a personality. We forgot to tell you about the fish – it happened only just before you came. Everyone was there looking at it – the most colossal thing I've ever seen. And Les took some pictures of him with it; I had one taken too!'

'So why the devil's the silly fool sitting there with the thing?'

She shrugged. 'God knows,' she said, staring at the clock.

The young husband appeared at the window; he leaned

conspiratorially into the waiting faces, with an unsure gesture of the hand. 'He's stuck,' he explained with a nervous giggle. 'Can't carry the thing any farther.' A little way behind him the figure of the Indian stood uncertainly, supporting the long dark shape of the fish. 'But why didn't he sell it?' said the wife, exasperated. 'What can *we* do about it.'

'Taking it home as a souvenir, of course,' said a man, pleased with his joke. But the wife was staring, accusing, at the husband. 'Didn't he try to sell it?' He gestured impatiently. 'Of course. But what does it matter? Fact is, he couldn't sell the damn thing, and now he can't carry it home.' 'So what do you want to do about it?' her voice rose indignantly. 'Sit here all night?' 'Shh,' he frowned. He said nothing. The others kept the studiedly considerate silence of strangers pretending not to be present at a family argument. Her husband's silence seemed to be forcing her to speak. 'Where does he live?' she said in resigned exasperation. 'Just off the main road,' said the husband, pat.

She turned with a charmingly exaggerated sense of asking a favour. 'Would you mind awfully if we gave the poor old thing a lift down the road?' 'No. No ... Good Lord, no,' they said in a rush. 'There'll be no time to have dinner,' someone whispered.

'Come on and get in,' the young man called over his shoulder, but the Indian still hung back, hesitant. '*Not* the fish!' whispered the wife urgently after her husband. 'Put the fish in the boot!'

They heard the wrench of the boot being opened, the thud of the lid coming down again. Then the Indian stood with the young husband at the door of the car. When he saw her, he smiled at her quickly.

'So your big catch is more trouble than it's worth,' she said brightly. The words seemed to fall hard upon him; his shoulders dropped as if he suddenly realized his stiff tiredness; he smiled and shrugged.

'Jump in,' said the husband heartily, opening the door of the driver's seat and getting in himself. The Indian hesitated, his hand on the back door. The three in the back made no move.

'No, there's no room there,' said the girl clearly, splintering the pause. 'Come round the other side and get in the front.' Obediently the fisherman walked through the headlights – a moment of his incisive face against the light – and opened the door at her side.

She shifted up. 'That's right,' she said, as he got in.

His presence in the car was as immediate as if he had been drawn upon the air. The sea-starched folds of his trousers made a slight harsh rubbing noise against the leather of the seat, his damp old tweed jacket smelled of warm wool, showed fuzzy against the edge of light. He breathed deeply and slowly beside her. In her clear voice she continued to talk to him, to ask him about his failure to sell the fish.

'That catch was more trouble than it was worth,' he said once, shaking his head, and she did not know whether he had just happened to say what she herself had said, or whether he was consciously repeating her words to himself.

She felt a stab of cold uncertainty, as if she herself did not know what she had said, did not know what she had meant, or might have meant. Nobody else talked to the Indian. Her husband drove the car. She was furious with them for leaving it all to her: the listening of the back of the car was as rude and blatant as staring.

'What will you do with the salmon now?' she asked brightly, and 'I'll probably give it away to my relations,' he answered obediently.

When they got to a turn-off a short distance along the main road, the Indian lifted his hand and said quickly, 'Here's the place, thank you.' His hand sent a little whiff of fish into the air. The car scudded into the dust at the side of the road, and as it did so, the door swung open and he was out.

He stood there as if his body still held the position he had carefully disciplined himself to in the car, head hunched a bit, hands curled as if he had had a cap he might perhaps have held it before him, pinned there by the blurs of faces looking out at him from the car. He seemed oddly helpless, standing while the young husband opened the boot and heaved the fish out.

'I must thank you very much,' he kept saying seriously. 'I must thank you.'

'That's all right,' the husband smiled, starting the car with a roar. The Indian was saying something else, but the revving of the engine drowned it. The girl smiled down to him through the window, but did not turn her head as they drove off.

'The things we get ourselves into!' she said, spreading her skirt on the seat. She shook her head and laughed a high laugh. 'Shame! The poor thing! What on earth can he do with the great smelly fish now?'

And as if her words had touched some chord of hysteria in them all, they began to laugh, and she laughed with them, laughed till she cried, gasping all the while, 'But what have I said? Why are you laughing at me? What have I said?'

The Train from Rhodesia

The train came out of the red horizon and bore down towards them over the single straight track.

The stationmaster came out of his little brick station with its pointed chalet roof, feeling the creases in his serge uniform in his legs as well. A stir of preparedness rippled through the squatting native venders waiting in the dust; the face of a carved wooden animal, eternally surprised, stuck out of a sack. The stationmaster's barefoot children wandered over. From the grey mud huts with the untidy heads that stood within a decorated mud wall, chickens, and dogs with their skin stretched like parchment over their bones, followed the piccanins down to the track. The flushed and perspiring west cast a reflection, faint, without heat, upon the station, upon the tin shed marked 'Goods', upon the walled kraal, upon the grey tin house of the stationmaster and upon the sand, that lapped all around from sky to sky, cast little rhythmical cups of shadow, so that the sand became the sea, and closed over the children's black feet softly and without imprint.

The stationmaster's wife sat behind the mesh of her veranda. Above her head the hunk of a sheep's carcass moved slightly, dangling in a current of air.

They waited.

The train called out, along the sky; but there was no answer; and the cry hung on: I'm coming ... I'm coming ...

The engine flared out now, big, whisking a dwindling body behind it; the track flared out to let it in.

Creaking, jerking, jostling, gasping, the train filled the station.

Here, let me see that one – the young woman curved her body

farther out of the corridor window. Missus? smiled the old man, looking at the creatures he held in his hand. From a piece of string on his grey finger hung a tiny woven basket; he lifted it, questioning. No, no, she urged, leaning down towards him, across the height of the train towards the man in the piece of old rug; that one, that one, her hand commanded. It was a lion, carved out of soft dry wood that looked like spongecake; heraldic, black and white, with impressionistic detail burnt in. The old man held it up to her still smiling, not from the heart, but at the customer. Between its vandyke teeth, in the mouth opened in an endless roar too terrible to be heard, it had a black tongue. Look, said the young husband, if you don't mind! And round the neck of the thing, a piece of fur (rat? rabbit? meerkat?); a real mane, majestic, telling you somehow that the artist had delight in the lion.

All up and down the length of the train in the dust the artists sprang, walking bent, like performing animals, the better to exhibit the fantasy held towards the faces on the train. Buck, startled and stiff, staring with round black and white eyes. More lions, standing erect, grappling with strange, thin, elongated warriors who clutched spears and showed no fear in their slits of eyes. How much, they asked from the train, how much?

Give me penny, said the little ones with nothing to sell. The dogs went and sat, quite still, under the dining car, where the train breathed out the smell of meat cooking with onion.

A man passed beneath the arch of reaching arms meeting grey-black and white in the exchange of money for the staring wooden eyes, the stiff wooden legs sticking up in the air; went along under the voices and the bargaining, interrogating the wheels. Past the dogs; glancing up at the dining car where he could stare at the faces, behind glass, drinking beer, two by two, on either side of a uniform railway vase with its pale dead flower. Right to the end, to the guard's van, where the stationmaster's children had just collected their mother's two loaves of bread; to the engine itself, where the stationmaster and the driver stood talking against the steaming complaint of the resting beast.

The man called out to them, something loud and joking. They turned to laugh, in a twirl of steam. The two children careered over the sand, clutching the bread, and burst through the iron gate and up the path through the garden in which nothing grew.

Passengers drew themselves in at the corridor windows and turned into compartments to fetch money, to call someone to look. Those sitting inside looked up: suddenly different, caged faces, boxed in, cut off after the contact of outside. There was an orange a piccanin would like... What about that chocolate? It wasn't very nice...

A girl had collected a handful of the hard kind, that no one liked, out of the chocolate box, and was throwing them to the dogs, over at the dining car. But the hens darted in and swallowed the chocolates, incredibly quick and accurate, before they had even dropped in the dust, and the dogs, a little bewildered, looked up with their brown eyes, not expecting anything.

– No, leave it, said the young woman, don't take it...

Too expensive, too much, she shook her head and raised her voice to the old man, giving up the lion. He held it high where she had handed it to him. No, she said, shaking her head. Three-and-six? insisted her husband, loudly. Yes baas! laughed the old man. *Three and-six?* – the young man was incredulous. Oh leave it – she said. The young man stopped. Don't you want it? he said, keeping his face closed to the old man. No, never mind, she said, leave it. The old native kept his head on one side, looking at them sideways, holding the lion. Three-and-six, he murmured, as old people repeat things to themselves.

The young woman drew her head in. She went into the coupé and sat down. Out of the window, on the other side, there was nothing; sand and bush; a thorn tree. Back through the open doorway, past the figure of her husband in the corridor, there was the station, the voices, wooden animals waving, running feet. Her eye followed the funny little valance of scrolled wood that outlined the chalet roof of the station; she thought of the lion and smiled. That bit of fur round the neck. But the wooden buck, the hippos, the elephants, the baskets that already bulked out of their brown paper under the seat and on the luggage rack! How will they look at home? Where will you put them? What will they mean away from the places you found them? Away from the unreality of the last few weeks? The young man outside. But he is not part of the unreality; he is for good now. Odd ... somewhere there was an idea that he, that living with him, was part of the holiday, the strange places.

Outside, a bell rang. The stationmaster was leaning against the end of the train, green flag rolled in readiness. A few men who had got down to stretch their legs sprang onto the train, clinging to the observation platforms, or perhaps merely standing on the iron step, holding the rail; but on the train, safe from the one dusty platform, the one tin house, the empty sand.

There was a grunt. The train jerked. Through the glass the beer drinkers looked out, as if they could not see beyond it. Behind the fly-screen, the stationmaster's wife sat facing back at them beneath the darkening hunk of meat.

There was a shout. The flag drooped out. Joints not yet coordinated, the segmented body of the train heaved and bumped back against itself. It began to move; slowly the scrolled chalet moved past it, the yells of the natives, running alongside, jetted up into the air, fell back at different levels. Staring wooden faces waved drunkenly, there, then gone, questioning for the last time at the windows. Here, one-and-six baas! – As one automatically opens a hand to catch a thrown ball, a man fumbled wildly down his pocket, brought up the shilling and sixpence and threw them out; the old native, gasping, his skinny toes splaying the sand, flung the lion.

The piccanins were waving, the dogs stood, tails uncertain, watching the train go: past the mud huts, where a woman turned to look up from the smoke of the fire, her hand pausing on her hip.

The stationmaster went slowly in under the chalet.

The old native stood, breath blowing out the skin between his ribs, feet tense, balanced in the sand, smiling and shaking his head. In his opened palm, held in the attitude of receiving, was the retrieved shilling and sixpence.

The blind end of the train was being pulled helplessly out of the station.

The young man swung in from the corridor, breathless. He was shaking his head with laughter and triumph. Here! he said. And waggled the lion at her. One-and-six!

What? she said.

He laughed. I was arguing with him for fun, bargaining – when the train had pulled out already, he came tearing after ... One-and-six Baas! So there's your lion.

She was holding it away from her, the head with the open jaws, the pointed teeth, the black tongue, the wonderful ruff of fur facing her. She was looking at it with an expression of not seeing, of seeing something different. Her face was drawn up, wryly, like the face of a discomforted child. Her mouth lifted nervously at the corner. Very slowly, cautious, she lifted her finger and touched the mane, where it was joined to the wood.

But how could you, she said. He was shocked by the dismay of her face.

Good Lord, he said, what's the matter?

If you wanted the thing, she said, her voice rising and breaking with the shrill impotence of anger, why didn't you buy it in the first place? If you wanted it, why didn't you pay for it? Why didn't you take it decently, when he offered it? Why did you have to wait for him to run after the train with it, and give him one-and-six? One-and-six!

She was pushing it at him, trying to force him to take the lion. He stood astonished, his hands hanging at his sides.

But you wanted it! You liked it so much?

– It's a beautiful piece of work, she said fiercely, as if to protect it from him.

You liked it so much! You said yourself it was too expensive –

Oh *you* – she said, hopeless and furious. *You* ... She threw the lion on to the seat.

He stood looking at her.

She sat down again in the corner and, her face slumped in her hands, stared out of the window. Everything was turning round inside her. One-and-six. One-and-six. One-and-six for the wood and the carving and the sinews of the legs and the switch of the tail. The mouth open like that and the teeth. The black tongue, rolling, like a wave. The mane round the neck. To give one-and-six for that. The heat of shame mounted through her legs and body and sounded in her ears like the sound of sand pouring. Pouring, pouring. She sat there, sick. A weariness, a tastelessness, the discovery of a void made her hands slacken their grip, atrophy emptily, as if the hour was not worth their grasp. She was feeling like this again. She had thought it was something to do with singleness, with being alone and belonging too much to oneself.

She sat there not wanting to move or speak, or to look at anything, even; so that the mood should be associated with nothing, no object, word or sight that might recur and so recall the feeling again ... Smuts blew in grittily, settled on her hands. Her back remained at exactly the same angle, turned against the young man sitting with his hands drooping between his sprawled legs, and the lion, fallen on its side in the corner.

The train had cast the station like a skin. It called out to the sky, I'm coming, I'm coming; and again, there was no answer.

A Bit of Young Life

It was not yet half past nine and the cat from the bar still lay in the cane chair on the hotel veranda where she had spent the night, licking the short white fur that covered the kittens kicking in her belly.

On this Saturday, as on every other morning, the old ladies sat looking out into the bright haze that struck off the water along the Durban beach front. Soon the young men began to gather on the steps, smoking, and poking one another in the ribs as they roared with laughter, and scratching their chests through clinging polo shirts. The old ladies smiled indulgently, liking to see a bit of young life. 'The boys', as the men called themselves, no matter what age they were, noticed the first girls passing on their way to town or to the beach: a beautiful pale blonde stepping along on her high heels like a well-bred poodle, and the arm-in-arm group from the even more expensive hotel next door, their bright faces disguised like dominoes at a masked ball by the geometrical shapes of sunglasses. An Indian waiter came quickly the length of the veranda, flicking at the ashtrays. The big doors leading to the dining room were bolted by the fat maître d'hôtel from Italy (how strange his Mediterranean voice sounded above the soft 'prt-prt' – a quick, excited purr rather than speech – of the Hindi dialects his waiters spoke) and the last stragglers from breakfast came out onto the veranda, a little feeble and wan from the gaiety of last night's club.

The cat ran in through the service door, shaking her bundle of kittens from side to side in her thin flanks.

It was going to be another hot day. By now, Indian venders with the haggard heads of prophets had started to pester along the balustrade, holding up trays of brass ornaments on which the sun leaped fiercely. Then the lily sellers ('Bundle of t'ree for two shilling – take them home, lady!'), and the whole life of the lily – whiskery roots, pearly bulb, tender stem, and gleaming petals thin and brilliant as the wings of dragonflies – hung in the air for the moment of offering, still dripping from the river; they would never grow again anywhere.

Then came the double baskets of roses – peach and yellow and red – and nobody bought them, either. It seemed that nobody ever did, unless the honeymoon couple happened to be down, when, with bird noises of pleasure, the bride, her nose peeling and her hands burned to claws, would take away a bunch to put in a tooth glass.

It was at about this time every morning that the young mother and her baby boy came through the revolving doors and out onto the veranda. Every morning since Monday, when she had arrived, they had all watched her, holding the baby's hand – he in his little swimming trunks and mannish towelling gown and little boy's flop-brimmed hat like a daisy upside-down on his head – and carrying under her other arm a trailing towel and a book and a beach-bag with a red fish on it. She was slight and small; the baby was brown and fat. Her fragile, serious profile, beneath a wide hat which sagged with the moistness of sea air, would be turned gently down to the child. 'She looks like a child herself,' one of the old ladies would say admiringly. 'So young!' And then she would stir her fat columns of legs as if she were fancying herself as once, years back, just such a slip of a thing.

The boys would stop talking a moment as the young mother passed, and then fade in again, talking in a lower key. She was attractive but withdrawn. 'Why don't you speak to her, Ed?' one of them kidded that Saturday morning. (He enjoyed suggesting to others pleasures he would not dare attempt for himself.) 'Go on. Speak to her in the lounge. Why don't you, Ed?' But Ed, the traveller in ladies' underwear who was taking a few days off midway on his usual southerly route, bit the end of his cigar and rearranged his navy silk scarf. 'I got my own plans, thank you very much.' And certainly his was the room number most frequently called to the telephone. Here was the page now, a small Indian boy with a head of stiff black hair like porcupine quills and the voice of a ventriloquist's doll, shouting Ed's number along the veranda: 'Tweu-oh-eight? ... Tweu-oh-eight?'

The traveller turned indoors to take his call, but the rest of the boys, wondering if they should go down to the club for snooker, could still just see her at the corner, looking this way and that before she crossed in front of the stand of Zulu rickshaw men who rustled their peanut-shell anklets and agitated their horned and feathered heads as if a wind had suddenly taken them up. Evidently the baby was frightened, for she hurried him past, like a puppy dragged on a lead. And then she was gone. The beach was splattered with people like bright rags – so many children shouting, so many women lying face-down that no one knew where she had got to or what magazine hid her.

But they all knew that at lunch time she would appear again, sifting outlines of sand printing the passing of the baby's feet up the steps and over the red carpet and into the lift; she would hold him on her hip in the lift and he would look around with large, unblinking eyes, and sometimes she would wipe the sand from his moist little brow while he continued to stare, unmoved. A smell of sea and fresh flesh came from them both. Half an hour later, she would be sitting at her small table at the back of the dining room, her wet hair caught up at the back like a horse's tail, her pale hands resting on the table in front of a glass of water.

To dinner she came rather late – she was never seen in the palm court, where the rest of the hotel silted in from five o'clock to drink beer or whisky, their sunburn shiny from the bath, their assorted shapes hidden in dark suits and rustling dresses – and she would walk the length of the dining room before them all with lightness, grace and haste, as if, although she did not know them and sat alone, she did them the little courtesy of apologizing. Every night, she sipped one pale whisky, bending her slim neck to drink, her long ear-rings tipping, and after dinner she took coffee in the lounge, sitting back against the banked flowers near the magazine stands, so that the family parties, the old ladies and the boys could have the larger and more prominent tables. There she would drink her coffee and then open her book, looking up frequently as the plump daughters came in to lean over their mothers' chairs a moment before leaving with their young student escorts. The older men – the boys – standing about touching cuffs and satin ties, looking at their watches and hustling one another, would go off arguing over who was to pick up whom and in whose car, and the lounge, still floating with cigarette smoke, would empty slowly of all except the old ladies in black lace dresses, drumming their fingers absently between talk.

It was one of these old ladies who was the first to speak to the young woman. The lounge was full one evening and there was a vacant chair at her table. The old lady came to rest near it. 'You're waiting for somebody, perhaps?' she asked tentatively.

The pretty, narrow, self-possessed face, which might have been rather frightening and haughty towards an old lady, dropped its look of aloof reserve, as if the girl had been unconscious of it, and opened into a smile of such warm pleasure and charm that the old lady was quite bewildered. Not only was she tolerated, she was welcomed, and spoken to with attention and interest. Her talk of the hotel food, the blood pressure that had brought her to stay on doctor's orders for three months, the hint or two about the qualities of her poor dead husband – she could tell all without the harassing awareness of the listener's impatience to which she was accustomed when talking to other young people. And what sense of the present have old ladies to live on unless they collect living evidence of it in curiosity about young people's lives? 'Tell me,' said the old lady, 'your husband's not here? You're all on your own, shame?'

She smiled. 'All alone,' she admitted. 'But, of course, my baby.'

'What a lovely little thing!' The old lady spoke as if she had never seen a baby before. 'What a darling he is! I always watch you, you know, going out with him, and he's so fat! I hear him talking.'

'Oh, he's learned to say everything since we've been here!' The young mother was excited; you could imagine her proudly writing it home; that would be the joy of it, really.

'What might your name be, if you'll excuse me?' The old lady hoped for an unrecognized daughter or niece of one of her cronies from up-country. And she was not to be disappointed entirely. 'Then your husband must be William Maisel's son,' she said triumphantly when she heard the name. Well, no; old William was the husband's uncle, the young mother said.

'A very nice family, my dear, a very nice family.' The old lady sat back and smiled satisfaction on the young woman's behalf. The young woman's smile deepened in frank acknowledgement of and apology for William Maisel's wealth and solidity. There followed a lot of questions about the ramifications of the house of Maisel – the older members, who had made the money out of hides; the middle-aged ones, who had trebled it on the stock exchange, and the young ones, who spent it becoming doctors and lawyers and even, in one instance, a painter. The young woman laughed, confused, and though she answered to the best of her knowledge, explained that really she saw them all only at weddings and other family gatherings. The old lady understood; a young wife feels strange in the first few years of her apprenticeship to her husband's family. But still, a Maisel, even if he was only old William's nephew instead of his son, would not marry *anybody*, that was certain.

'Well, of course, my dear girl –' The old lady gave her permission to the young woman to be excused; she must slip upstairs to see if the baby was asleep. And the old lady's eyes followed the small, slender figure in the swaying frock, making its way over the carpets. At the door of the lift, the young woman unexpectedly turned and smiled.

After that, everyone spoke to her. The honeymoon couple admired the baby in the lift. The mother shook her head in pleasurable denial of his obvious charm (sometimes, as now, she wore two pigtails when she went to the beach) and apologized for the noise he made in the early mornings; the honeymoon couple had the adjoining room. 'Oh, but we never hear him, really!' the bride exclaimed, 'We don't know how you do it, keeping him so quiet – we think it's wonderful!'

'It's a full-time job, I assure you,' she said, and laughed with mock grimness.

'Wonderful! Not much of a holiday for you,' said the bride, womanly and confidential. 'I'd jolly well make sure my husband came along and did his share!' And they all laughed, including the husband, who by the same time the following year would be folding baby carriages and balancing napkin bags, as harassed as he was now tenderly amused.

'Where's the little chap?' people would call out at the most unlikely hours. 'Dead to the world,' the young woman would say, with a smile, going on her way with a new book in her hand.

Even the boys got to know her. It was the evening she wore her black dress – and she looked particularly young in black, as if her childlike boning, her gentle haughtiness, her tender air, showed up in direct ratio to the sophistication of her clothes. When she wore black, she wore all black; this dress sloped down around her shoulders, flowed out around her waist, was of a heavy material. She sat in it with her hands, small and boneless as the hands in a Renaissance portrait, in her lap. She had finished both her after-dinner coffee and her book, and was simply looking around her at the lounge filled with people – without boldness, invitation or embarrassment.

The traveller in ladies' underwear was sitting near by, ordering a liqueur for himself and another of the boys. (He liked to think of himself as a bit of a connoisseur in most things.) While he was discussing the choice with the waiter, he sat facing the young woman, in the full line of her vision, and this made him feel that there was something rude about ordering refreshment under her very nose; he felt the guilty shyness that paralyses a child dipping into a bag of sweets under the eyes of grownups, to whom he has been taught it should be offered first, and this emboldened him to do what he had wanted to do for a number of nights. 'Excuse me,' he said, getting up and pulling in his bottom stiffly, 'but would you care to join us in a friendly liqueur? My friend and I here are just about to have one.'

And again, rather astonishingly, she smiled – gave the full charm of her face to him like a gift. It was the pleasantest of shocks for Ed, since, for him, as it had been for the old lady, there was that about her that made one fear a rebuff; one did not know how to begin to talk to her, any more than one would know how to open a conversation with a nun or a member of a royal family. 'Why, thank you,' she said, and her chair was brought over, her drink was ordered and there she sat, with the boys.

Two days of rain washed away any remaining stiffness. Shut in by such impenetrable sheets of grey water that it seemed the sea had come up silently over the promenade and the street and was looking in at the windows, they all huddled together in the cosiness of electric light turned on at ten o'clock in the morning: old ladies, matrons and daughters, the boys, and, of course, the young mother, now wearing a downy sweater like a newly-hatched chick. She sat with the old ladies and she sat with the boys, and this impartiality touched the old ladies and maddened and delighted the boys. 'What's the matter with us?' they would chaff. 'Would you rather talk knitting patterns than have us around you?' And she would get that teasing darkening of her eyes that was like a blush and go back to sit with them. They were admiring, they were lightly familiar, but always, as she counted up their scores when they played cards, or turned the stem of her whisky glass, the little hand, unobtrusive, dangling, one finger ringed with a narrow wedding-band, lay before them.

She was sitting with a group of the boys when one of them asked her, 'How's your husband getting on without you? I'll bet he's lonely as hell.'

'Is he a good-looking guy?'

'You bet. Trust her.'

She said, 'He's a big, fair man.'

'What'd I tell you! See?'

'Better-looking than us?' They laughed.

'You not worried about leaving him at home?' said Ed watching her face. 'Not afraid he'll run around?'

She did not answer but, looking straight at him and smiling deeply, shook her head very hard, so that her hair swung.

That decided him. 'Crazy about the chap, huh?' he said wonderingly, sympathetic as well as curious.

'Oh, Ed, leave it alone, man. The girl's married. You can't ask things like that,' one of the others said.

And all the boys laughed, turning away from something that was not for them to look at.

'Well, he's certainly got nothing to worry about with *you*,' said Ed, thinking of the futile invitations to the club, to dinner, to the cinema he had given her in the past few days.

'But I've told you, honestly,' she insisted, smiling and lifting her eyebrows with earnest concern. 'It's not that. I wouldn't be silly about that. It's just that I can't go out at nights and leave the baby.'

'All right. I know,' he said, with a laugh. 'I don't blame you. You're just missing the guy badly. But it's silly, you know – there's no harm in a show, or a bit of dancing. I'm sure he wouldn't want you to mope around, going to bed in the evenings the way you do.'

They all tried to get her to go out with them, but without success. She was charming, she was regretful, she was wistful – a young and pretty girl shut up in the hotel with a baby – but she gently refused. Her unavailability made the availability of others of greater and more obvious attraction, pall. For the traveller, particularly, who 'knew how to take a girl out', if you followed his meaning (flowers, fine dinners – the lot), and had a large and miscellaneous collection of terrific women (women with style, you know) in this as in every other town. Somehow he went reluctantly every night to call for the receptionists and models, with their big, dazzling bodies and their enthusiasm for being shown off in the best places. He wanted to go out with *her*, just once – this young woman whose only amorous tussle was rolling her baby over and over on the beach, nibbling his little neck while he laughed, who read so many books Ed had never heard of, who, despite her friendliness and courtesy and lack of affectation, unwittingly left an impress on him like the pressure of a seal: he saw it, it was the mark of someone too good for him. So, nightly, he sighed, straightened the carnation in his button-hole and went out into the town.

The old ladies, and even the matrons, who were a little suspicious of her since they had daughters to arrange for, noticed with approval that she never went out with men.

'Well, they're very fine people, the Maisels,' the old lady said, with the air of authority about the young woman that was growing upon her day by day. 'You can't expect her to behave like a bit of rubbish, like those other young women. She's not the type, that's all there is to it. And he's a charming boy, the husband' – she was really beginning to believe that she knew him – 'oh, charming! Nothing like it here.' And she waved a fastidious hand at the boys – thickset, good-natured creatures, quite unaware of the scorn in which they were held.

It was true, other young women could take an example from her, the old ladies agreed. Still, it was a shame. Young couples should go away together. After all, she also wanted a bit of young life.

The young woman was the darling of the hotel. Yet she did not seem entirely happy. In fact, the more attention was centred on her, the more the baby was played with and presented with toys and the two of them were taken for drives and trips across the bay, and she was welcomed and invited to join groups at tea or drinks, the more frequently moods of pensiveness came upon her. Often, she would rest her chin on the head of the baby and look out to the sea; her mouth pulled a little at one corner, as if something tugged at her. If Ed was there, he would say at once, under the talk of others, 'Feeling a bit blue?' Or 'Never mind, you'll appreciate him more when you get back to him.' Then she would come to the surface with a little start, which he found delightful, and begin talking again.

In the early evening, sometimes, the mood lasted longer, and it seemed to the boys as if a kind of space cleared in the air around her. The talk of racing and the road and the stock exchange precluded any romantic nonsense, but, even when she was wearing her bare sundress, the slope of her shoulders and the unconscious droop of her head, oval and smooth behind the curly fuzz of the baby's, suggested to them not the early Florentine madonnas of which they had never heard, but something further back even than that – the inspiration that gave rise to the paintings themselves.

Sometimes, too, there would show in her face a streak of strain, which, if the talk flagged for a moment, became the blankness of concealed distress. It was as if she had suddenly heard something that the talk usually managed to drown.

On the morning of the sixteenth day of the young woman's stay, Ed found her at the reception desk with a pile of notes under her hand. 'Settling your debts?' he asked, smiling. He knew he looked good in his blond Palm Beach trousers and that darkish shirt; a model had said to him the day before, 'Ed, anyone can see you don't buy your clothes in *this* town.' The young woman was pale, shadows showed under her eyes when she smiled, her hair was not as carefully done as usual; she had never looked more fascinating to him. 'I've decided to go home,' she said. 'I'm paying up.'

Home? It was a real pang that he felt, with his surprise. 'But how long were you supposed to be here? You've got another two weeks!' he protested.

'I know,' she said. 'I'm – I'm suddenly fed up. So I've managed to get a plane reservation and I'm going.' She was obviously embarrassed; he had never heard her speak so jerkily and lamely before. She even tried a funny little laugh, which had to turn into a cough.

'Well, I'm damned!' he said.

But she simply stood there at the counter in embarrassment, offering no explanation.

'You're a silly girl,' he went on. 'Really, you're a silly girl. You'll get over it in a day or two and you'll enjoy the rest of your holiday. It's a shame for the kid, too. He's having a good time. And you can do with a bit of weight. What'll your husband say?'

She shook her head, catching her lower lip in a smile, like a guilty child.

'When you going?' he asked.

'I'm on the three-o'clock plane,' she said.

'Go on,' he said, urging her bluffly. 'You phone them and cancel it.'

But she just stood there looking at him. 'No.' She smiled shyly, shakily. 'I'm going.'

'Look here,' he said, taking her by the arm and looking around to see if anyone could overhear. He was entirely fatherly now. 'I know how it is. It's just that we're not your sort, are we? You miss him, and you just haven't found any company your *own* sort.'

She protested. 'No, you've all been terribly nice. Everyone's been so nice.' He looked into her face and she looked into his, smiling.

But suddenly he saw that the smile was merely something done with her face, and that, really, she was about to cry. It was incredible – not a thing she would ever do or he would ever be allowed to witness in *her*. He was so frightened that he drew back as if he had opened a door by mistake, and he suddenly gave in. 'Look,' he said. 'Don't you worry about the airport. I'll get the car round and take you and the kid. Now, what's happening with the luggage? Will you get that ready, so that we can send it on ahead?'

He arranged everything – saw that the keys of her cases were in her handbag and her forwarding address left at the hotel, even promised to send on to her some snapshots of the baby that had been taken by the beach photographer a day or two back and were not yet ready. The news of her imminent departure flew around the hotel by lunch time. When she came down, all ready to leave, in her black suit and an elegant hat that bent back from her brow, there was somehow the unexpressed idea that she had been *recalled*, and the drama of the idea, the sense of emotion out of sight, made the other hotel guests feel a heightened touch of regret. 'We're going to lose you! What a *shame*, my dear' came to her from all parts of the dining room. And the dear little chap – Ah, there he was, adorable with his reddish-blond fluff and the wide mouth that was not his mother's; he must look like his daddy. ('Is it going to see its daddy again, then!') Even the Indian waiters collected in the foyer around the hand luggage. 'Good-bye, good-bye, Big Man,' they said to the baby. Then Ed's Chrysler drew up twinkling at the door; the sun plunged a thousand knives that glanced off its well-polished pate and chromium flanks. She came down the steps with the child by the hand, in her city clothes already a stranger to the humid, sea-blown air, the rickshaw men dozing in their shafts, and the yells of paddling children. The baby boy turned around unprompted and waved a fist. Then they were gone.

'Well,' Ed said to her as they reached the airport, 'in two hours you'll be back home.' Watching from the visitors' barrier, he saw them cross the field and climb the steps into the plane together. At the top, she turned, unconsciously duplicating the child's gesture, and gave him a last little wave of her hand, unmistakable even in its black glove.

Among all the other people trooping away, he went slowly back to the car trying to decide whether he should spend the rest of the afternoon going for a swim or playing snooker. He settled on snooker. There was not even the scent of her left in the car, the way other women shed their perfume like bitches leaving a trail for the male.

•

By Tuesday morning, it was all out. The Johannesburg papers are flown to the coast within an hour or two of issue, and everyone buys one as hungrily as if he were an exile instead of a willing holidaymaker. There it was, not even halfway down the matrimonial section of the court-judgments column along which everyone runs a half-hopeful eye: 'Maisel versus Maisel. Hugh Watcham Maisel against Patricia Edwina Maisel (born van Helm).' And that very afternoon someone arrived at the hotel who knew the whole story – a most scandalous story. (The lives people live nowadays!) The wife had been carrying on with this other man ever since the baby was born, right in the house, under the husband's nose. (Oh, the child was the husband's, all right; apparently it was the image of him.) People said she lived with both of them at once for months on end – never turned a hair. Others blamed the husband; he should have thrown her out. Evidently the lover originally had been interested in her younger sister, which made it worse; she snatched him from under her sister's nose.

Then when the Sunday papers reported the divorce proceedings in detail, the whole business was confirmed. The plaintiff this. The defendant that. Dirty business, said the boys wonderingly, crowding round the paper. The whole hotel, as if it had been stung, talked of nothing else. A kind of pyre of recollections and discussion piled up on her vanished presence, and went on smoking for days.

At home, five hundred miles away, the young woman sat and read about herself in the paper. The resort labels were peeling off her luggage in the steam of the bathroom, where it was stored on top of a cupboard. Sometimes she spent half-hours gently rubbing the flaking brown skin that flew like powder from her arms.

In a day or two, an envelope came for her, postmarked 'Durban' and addressed in an unfamiliar masculine handwriting. Inside were two postcard photographs of the baby.

Anonymous, dumb, it was a last protective touch on the elbow from Ed, the traveller in ladies' underwear. She took an odd comfort from it, and at the same moment became conscious of a guilt sharper, a burden of duplicity heavier than she had felt for all the lies, the faithlessness, the cunning of her passion. A tear, which seemed to have the tickling feet of a centipede, ran down the side of her nose.

Now no one had been spared – no one at all.

Six Feet of the Country

My wife and I are not real farmers – not even Lerice, really. We bought our place, ten miles out of Johannesburg on one of the main roads, to change something in ourselves, I suppose; you seem to rattle about so much within a marriage like ours. You long to hear nothing but a deep satisfying silence when you sound a marriage. The farm hasn't managed that for us, of course, but it has done other things, unexpected, illogical. Lerice, who I thought would retire there in Chekhovian sadness for a month or two, and then leave the place to the servants while she tried yet again to get a part she wanted and become the actress she would like to be, has sunk into the business of running the farm with all the serious intensity with which she once imbued the shadows in a playwright's mind. I should have given it up long ago if it had not been for her. Her hands, once small and plain and well-kept – she was not the sort of actress who wears red paint and diamond rings – are hard as a dog's pads.

I, of course, am there only in the evenings and at weekends. I am a partner in a travel agency which is flourishing – needs to be, as I tell Lerice, in order to carry the farm. Still, though I know we can't afford it, and though the sweetish smell of the fowls Lerice breeds sickens me, so that I avoid going past their runs, the farm is beautiful in a way I had almost forgotten – especially on a Sunday morning when I get up and go out into the paddock and see not the palm trees and fishpond and imitation-stone bird bath of the suburbs but white ducks on the dam, the lucerne field brilliant as window-dresser's grass, and the little, stocky, mean-eyed bull, lustful but bored, having his face tenderly licked by one of his ladies. Lerice comes out with her hair uncombed, in her hand a stick dripping with cattle dip. She will stand and look dreamily for a moment, the way she would pretend to look sometimes in those plays. 'They'll mate tomorrow,' she will say. 'This is their second day. Look how she loves him, my little Napoleon.' So that when people come to see us on Sunday afternoon, I am likely to hear myself saying as I pour out the drinks, 'When I drive back home from the city every day past those rows of suburban houses, I wonder how the devil we ever did stand it ... Would you care to look around?' And there I am, taking some pretty girl and her young husband stumbling down to our riverbank, the girl catching her stockings on the mealie-stooks and stepping over cow turds humming with jewel-green flies while she says, '... the *tensions* of the damned city. And you're near enough to get into town to a show, too! I think it's wonderful. Why, you've got it both ways!'

And for a moment I accept the triumph as if I *had* managed it – the impossibility that I've been trying for all my life: just as if the truth was that you could get it 'both ways', instead of finding yourself with not even one way or the other but a third, one you had not provided for at all.

But even in our saner moments, when I find Lerice's earthy enthusiasms just as irritating as I once found her histrionical ones, and she finds what she calls my 'jealousy' of her capacity for enthusiasm as big a proof of my inadequacy for her as a mate as ever it was, we do believe that we have at least honestly escaped those tensions peculiar to the city about which our visitors speak. When Johannesburg people speak of 'tension', they don't mean hurrying people in crowded streets, the struggle for money, or the general competitive character of city life. They mean the guns under the white men's pillows and the burglar bars on the white men's windows. They mean those strange moments on city pavements when a black man won't stand aside for a white man.

Out in the country, even ten miles out, life is better than that. In the country, there is a lingering remnant of the pre-transitional stage; our relationship with the blacks is almost feudal. Wrong, I suppose, obsolete, but more comfortable all around. We have no burglar bars, no gun. Lerice's farm boys have their wives and their piccanins living with them on the land. They brew their sour beer without the fear of police raids. In fact, we've always rather prided ourselves that the poor devils have nothing much to fear, being with us; Lerice even keeps an eye on their children, with all the competence of a woman who has never had a child of her own, and she certainly doctors them all – children and adults – like babies whenever they happen to be sick.

It was because of this that we were not particularly startled one night last winter when the boy Albert came knocking at our window long after we had gone to bed. I wasn't in our bed but sleeping in the little dressing-room-cum-linen-room next door, because Lerice had annoyed me and I didn't want to find myself softening towards her simply because of the sweet smell of the talcum powder on her flesh after her bath. She came and woke me up. 'Albert says one of the boys is very sick,' she said. 'I think you'd better go down and see. He wouldn't get us up at this hour for nothing.'

'What time is it?'

'What does it matter?' Lerice is maddeningly logical.

I got up awkwardly as she watched me – how is it I always feel a fool when I have deserted her bed? After all, I know from the way she never looks at me when she talks to me at breakfast next day that she is hurt and humiliated at my not wanting her – and I went out, clumsy with sleep.

'Which of the boys is it?' I asked Albert as we followed the dance of my torch.

'He's too sick. Very sick,' he said.

'But who? Franz?' I remembered Franz had had a bad cough for the past week.

Albert did not answer; he had given me the path, and was walking along beside me in the tall dead grass. When the light of the torch caught his face, I saw that he looked acutely embarrassed. 'What's this all about?' I said.

He lowered his head under the glance of the light. 'It's not me, baas. I don't know. Petrus he send me.'

Irritated, I hurried him along to the huts. And there, on Petrus's iron bedstead, with its brick stilts, was a young man, dead. On his forehead there was still a light, cold sweat; his body was warm. The boys stood around as they do in the kitchen when it is discovered that someone has broken a dish – uncooperative, silent. Somebody's wife hung about in the shadows, her hands wrung together under her apron.

I had not seen a dead man since the war. This was very different. I felt like the others – extraneous, useless. 'What was the matter?' I asked.

The woman patted at her chest and shook her head to indicate the painful impossibility of breathing.

He must have died of pneumonia.

I turned to Petrus. 'Who was this boy? What was he doing here?' The light of a candle on the floor showed that Petrus was weeping. He followed me out the door.

When we were outside, in the dark, I waited for him to speak. But he didn't. 'Now, come on, Petrus, you must tell me who this boy was. Was he a friend of yours?'

'He's my brother, baas. He came from Rhodesia to look for work.'

The story startled Lerice and me a little. The young boy had walked down from Rhodesia to look for work in Johannesburg, had caught a chill from sleeping out along the way and had lain ill in his brother Petrus's hut since his arrival three days before. Our boys had been frightened to ask us for help for him because we had never been intended ever to know of his presence. Rhodesian natives are barred from entering the Union unless they have a permit; the young man was an illegal immigrant. No doubt our boys had managed the whole thing successfully several times before; a number of relatives must have walked the seven or eight hundred miles from poverty to the paradise of zoot suits, police raids and black slum townships that is their *Egoli*, City of Gold – the African name for Johannesburg. It was merely a matter of getting such a man to lie low on our farm until a job could be found with someone who would be glad to take the risk of prosecution for employing an illegal immigrant in exchange for the services of someone as yet untainted by the city.

Well, this was one who would never get up again.

'You would think they would have felt they could tell *us*,' said Lerice next morning. 'Once the man was ill. You would have thought at least –' When she is getting intense over something, she has a way of standing in the middle of a room as people do when they are shortly to leave on a journey, looking searchingly about her at the most familiar objects as if she had never seen them before. I had noticed that in Petrus's presence in the kitchen, earlier, she had had the air of being almost offended with him, almost hurt.

In any case, I really haven't the time or inclination any more to go into everything in our life that I know Lerice, from those alarmed and pressing eyes of hers, would like us to go into. She is the kind of woman who doesn't mind if she looks plain, or odd; I don't suppose she would even care if she knew how strange she looks when her whole face is out of proportion with urgent uncertainty. I said, 'Now I'm the one who'll have to do all the dirty work, I suppose.'

She was still staring at me, trying me out with those eyes – wasting her time, if she only knew.

'I'll have to notify the health authorities,' I said calmly. 'They can't just cart him off and bury him. After all, we don't really know what he died of.'

She simply stood there, as if she had given up – simply ceased to see me at all.

I don't know when I've been so irritated. 'It might have been something contagious,' I said. 'God knows.' There was no answer.

I am not enamoured of holding conversations with myself. I went out to shout to one of the boys to open the garage and get the car ready for my morning drive to town.

As I had expected, it turned out to be quite a business. I had to notify the police as well as the health authorities, and answer a lot of tedious questions: How was it I was ignorant of the boy's presence? If I did not supervise my native quarters, how did I know that that sort of thing didn't go on all the time? And when I flared up and told them that so long as my natives did their work, I didn't think it my right or concern to poke my nose into their private lives, I got from the coarse, dull-witted police sergeant one of those looks that come not from any thinking process going on in the brain but from that faculty common to all who are possessed by the master-race theory – a look of insanely inane certainty. He grinned at me with a mixture of scorn and delight at my stupidity.

Then I had to explain to Petrus why the health authorities had to take away the body for a post-mortem – and, in fact, what a post-mortem was. When I telephoned the health department some days later to find out the result, I was told that the cause of death was, as we had thought, pneumonia, and that the body had been suitably disposed of. I went out to where Petrus was mixing a mash for the fowls and told him that it was all right, there would be no trouble; his brother had died from that pain in his chest. Petrus put down the paraffin tin and said, 'When can we go to fetch him, baas?'

'To fetch him?'

'Will the baas please ask them when we must come?'

I went back inside and called Lerice, all over the house. She came down the stairs from the spare bedrooms, and I said, '*Now* what am I going to do? When I told Petrus, he just asked calmly when they could go and fetch the body. They think they're going to bury him themselves.'

'Well, go back and tell him,' said Lerice. 'You must tell him. Why didn't you tell him then?'

When I found Petrus again, he looked up politely. 'Look, Petrus,' I said. 'You can't go to fetch your brother. They've done it already – they've *buried* him, you understand?'

'Where?' he said slowly, dully, as if he thought that perhaps he was getting this wrong.

'You see, he was a stranger. They knew he wasn't from here, and they didn't know he had some of his people here so they thought they must bury him.' It was difficult to make a pauper's grave sound like a privilege.

'Please, baas, the baas must ask them.' But he did not mean that he wanted to know the burial place. He simply ignored the incomprehensible machinery I told him had set to work on his dead brother; he wanted the brother back.

'But, Petrus,' I said, 'how can I? Your brother is buried already. I can't ask them now.'

'Oh, baas!' he said. He stood with his bran-smeared hands uncurled at his sides, one corner of his mouth twitching.

'Good God, Petrus, they won't listen to me! They can't, anyway. I'm sorry, but I can't do it. You understand?'

He just kept on looking at me, out of his knowledge that white men have everything, can do anything; if they don't, it is because they won't.

And then, at dinner, Lerice started. 'You could at least phone,' she said.

'Christ, what d'you think I am? Am I supposed to bring the dead back to life?'

But I could not exaggerate my way out of this ridiculous responsibility that had been thrust on me. 'Phone them up,' she went on. 'And at least you'll be able to tell him you've done it and they've explained that it's impossible.'

She disappeared somewhere into the kitchen quarters after coffee. A little later she came back to tell me, 'The old father's coming down from Rhodesia to be at the funeral. He's got a permit and he's already on his way.'

Unfortunately, it was not impossible to get the body back. The authorities said that it was somewhat irregular, but that since the hygiene conditions had been fulfilled, they could not refuse permission for exhumation. I found out that, with the undertaker's charges, it would cost twenty pounds. Ah, I thought, that settles it. On five pounds a month, Petrus won't have twenty pounds – and just as well, since it couldn't do the dead any good. Certainly I should not offer it to him myself. Twenty pounds – or anything else within reason, for that matter – I would have spent without grudging it on doctors or medicines that might have helped the boy when he was alive. Once he was dead, I had no intention of encouraging Petrus to throw away, on a gesture, more than he spent to clothe his whole family in a year.

When I told him, in the kitchen that night, he said, 'Twenty pounds?'

I said, 'Yes, that's right, twenty pounds.'

For a moment, I had the feeling, from the look on his face,

that he was calculating. But when he spoke again I thought I must have imagined it. 'We must pay twenty pounds!' he said in the faraway voice in which a person speaks of something so unattainable it does not bear thinking about.

'All right, Petrus,' I said, and went back to the living room.

The next morning before I went to town, Petrus asked to see me. 'Please, baas,' he said, awkwardly, handing me a bundle of notes. They're so seldom on the giving rather than the receiving side, poor devils, they don't really know how to hand money to a white man. There it was, the twenty pounds, in ones and halves, some creased and folded until they were soft as dirty rags, others smooth and fairly new – Franz's money, I suppose, and Albert's, and Dora the cook's, and Jacob the gardener's, and God knows who else's besides, from all the farms and small holdings round about. I took it in irritation more than in astonishment, really – irritation at the waste, the uselessness of this sacrifice by people so poor. Just like the poor everywhere, I thought, who stint themselves the decencies of life in order to ensure themselves the decencies of death. So incomprehensible to people like Lerice and me, who regard life as something to be spent extravagantly and, if we think about death at all, regard it as the final bankruptcy.

The farm hands don't work on Saturday afternoon anyway, so it was a good day for the funeral. Petrus and his father had borrowed our donkey-cart to fetch the coffin from the city, where, Petrus told Lerice on their return, everything was 'nice' – the coffin waiting for them, already sealed up to save them from what must have been a rather unpleasant sight after two weeks' interment. (It had taken all that time for the authorities and the undertaker to make the final arrangements for moving the body.) All morning, the coffin lay in Petrus's hut, awaiting the trip to the little old burial ground, just outside the eastern boundary of our farm, that was a relic of the days when this was a real farming district rather than a fashionable rural estate. It was pure chance that I happened to be down there near the fence when the procession came past; once again Lerice had forgotten her promise to me and had made the house uninhabitable on a Saturday afternoon. I had come home and been infuriated to find her in a pair of filthy old slacks and with her hair uncombed since the night before, having all the varnish scraped from the living-room floor, if you please. So I had taken my No. 8 iron and gone off to practise my aproach shots. In my annoyance, I had forgotten about the funeral, and was reminded only when I saw the procession coming up the path along the outside of the fence towards me; from where I was standing, you can see the graves quite clearly, and that day the sun glinted on bits of broken pottery, a lopsided homemade cross, and jam-jars brown with rainwater and dead flowers.

I felt a little awkward, and did not know whether to go on hitting my golf ball or stop at least until the whole gathering was decently past. The donkey-cart creaks and screeches with every revolution of the wheels, and it came along in a slow, halting fashion somehow peculiarly suited to the two donkeys who drew it, their little potbellies rubbed and rough, their heads sunk between the shafts, and their ears flattened back with an air submissive and downcast; peculiarly suited, too, to the group of men and women who came along slowly behind. The patient ass. Watching, I thought, you can see now why the creature became a Biblical symbol. Then the procession drew level with me and stopped, so I had to put down my club. The coffin was taken down off the cart – it was a shiny, yellow-varnished wood, like cheap furniture – and the donkeys twitched their ears against the flies. Petrus, Franz, Albert and the old father from Rhodesia hoisted it on their shoulders and the procession moved on, on foot. It was really a very awkward moment. I stood there rather foolishly at the fence, quite still, and slowly they filed past, not looking up, the four men bent beneath the shiny wooden box, and the straggling troop of mourners. All of them were servants or neighbours' servants whom I knew as casual easygoing gossipers about our lands or kitchen. I heard the old man's breathing.

I had just bent to pick up my club again when there was a sort of jar in the flowing solemnity of their processional mood; I felt it at once, like a wave of heat along the air, or one of those sudden currents of cold catching at your legs in a placid stream. The old man's voice was muttering something; the people had stopped, confused, and they bumped into one another, some pressing to go on, others hissing them to be still. I could see that they were embarrassed, but they could not ignore the voice; it was much the way that the mumblings of a prophet, though not clear at first, arrest the mind. The corner of the coffin the old man carried was sagging at an angle; he seemed to be trying to get out from under the weight of it. Now Petrus expostulated with him.

The little boy who had been left to watch the donkeys dropped the reins and ran to see. I don't know why – unless it was for the same reason people crowd around someone who has fainted in a cinema – but I parted the wires of the fence and went through, after him.

Petrus lifted his eyes to me – to anybody – with distress and horror. The old man from Rhodesia had let go of the coffin entirely, and the three others, unable to support it on their own, had laid it on the ground, in the pathway. Already there was a film of dust lightly wavering up its shiny sides. I did not understand what the old man was saying; I hesitated to interfere. But now the whole seething group turned on my silence. The old man himself came over to me, with his hands outspread and shaking, and spoke directly to me, saying something that I could tell from the tone, without understanding the words, was shocking and extraordinary.

'What is it, Petrus? What's wrong?' I appealed.

Petrus threw up his hands, bowed his head in a series of hysterical shakes, then thrust his face up at me suddenly. 'He says, "My son was not so heavy."'

Silence. I could hear the old man breathing; he kept his mouth a little open, as old people do.

'My son was young and thin,' he said at last, in English.

Again silence. Then babble broke out. The old man thundered against everybody; his teeth were yellowed and few, and he had one of those fine, grizzled, sweeping moustaches one doesn't often see nowadays, which must have been grown in emulation of early Empire-builders. It seemed to frame all his utterances with a special validity. He shocked the assembly;

they thought he was mad, but they had to listen to him. With his own hands he began to prise the lid off the coffin and three of the men came forward to help him. Then he sat down on the ground; very old, very weak and unable to speak, he merely lifted a trembling hand towards what was there. He abdicated, he handed it over to them; he was no good any more.

They crowded round to look (and so did I), and now they forgot the nature of this surprise and the occasion of grief to which it belonged, and for a few minutes were carried up in the astonishment of the surprise itself. They gasped and flared noisily with excitement. I even noticed the little boy who had held the donkeys jumping up and down, almost weeping with rage because the backs of the grownups crowded him out of his view.

In the coffin was someone no one had seen before: a heavily built, rather light-skinned native with a neatly stitched scar on his forehead – perhaps from a blow in a brawl that had also dealt him some other, slower-working injury that had killed him.

I wrangled with the authorities for a week over that body. I had the feeling that they were shocked, in a laconic fashion, by their own mistake, but that in the confusion of their anonymous dead they were helpless to put it right. They said to me, 'We are trying to find out,' and 'We are still making inquiries.' It was as if at any moment they might conduct me into their mortuary and say, 'There! Lift up the sheets; look for him – your poultry boy's brother. There are so many black faces – surely one will do?'

And every evening when I got home, Petrus was waiting in the kitchen. 'Well, they're trying. They're still looking. The baas is seeing to it for you, Petrus,' I would tell him. 'God, half the time I should be in the office I'm driving around the back end of the town chasing after this affair,' I added aside, to Lerice, one night.

She and Petrus both kept their eyes turned on me as I spoke, and, oddly, for those moments they looked exactly alike, though it sounds impossible: my wife, with her high, white forehead and her attenuated Englishwoman's body, and the poultry boy, with his horny bare feet below khaki trousers tied at the knee with string and the peculiar rankness of his nervous sweat coming from his skin.

'What makes you so indignant, so determined about this now?' said Lerice suddenly.

I stared at her. 'It's a matter of principle. Why should they get away with a swindle? It's time these officials had a jolt from someone who'll bother to take the trouble.'

She said, 'Oh.' And as Petrus slowly opened the kitchen door to leave, sensing that the talk had gone beyond him, she turned away, too.

I continued to pass on assurances to Petrus every evening, but although what I said was the same and the voice in which I said it was the same, every evening it sounded weaker. At last, it became clear that we would never get Petrus's brother back, because nobody really knew where he was. Somewhere in a graveyard as uniform as a housing scheme, somewhere under a number that didn't belong to him, or in the medical school, perhaps, laboriously reduced to layers of muscle and strings of nerve? Goodness knows. He had no identity in this world anyway.

It was only then, and in a voice of shame, that Petrus asked me to try and get the money back.

'From the way he asks, you'd think he was robbing his dead brother,' I said to Lerice later. But as I've said, Lerice had got so intense about this business that she couldn't even appreciate a little ironic smile.

I tried to get the money; Lerice tried. We both telephoned and wrote and argued, but nothing came of it. It appeared that the main expense had been the undertaker, and after all he had done his job. So the whole thing was a complete waste, even more of a waste for the poor devils than I had thought it would be.

The old man from Rhodesia was about Lerice's father's size, so she gave him one of her father's old suits, and he went back home rather better off, for the winter, than he had come.

Which New Era Would That Be?

Jake Alexander, a big, fat coloured man, half Scottish, half African, was shaking a large pan of frying bacon on the gas stove in the back room of his Johannesburg printing shop when he became aware that someone was knocking on the door at the front of the shop. The sizzling fat and the voices of the five men in the back room with him almost blocked sounds from without, and the knocking was of the steady kind that might have been going on for quite a few minutes. He lifted the pan off the flame with one hand and with the other made an impatient silencing gesture, directed at the bacon as well as the voices. Interpreting the movement as one of caution, the men hurriedly picked up the tumblers and cups in which they had been taking their end-of-the-day brandy at their ease, and tossed the last of it down. Little yellow Klaas, whose hair was like ginger-coloured wire wool, stacked the cups and glasses swiftly and hid them behind the dirty curtain that covered a row of shelves.

'Who's that?' yelled Jake, wiping his greasy hands down his pants.

There was a sharp and playful tattoo, followed by an English voice: 'Me – Alister. For heaven's sake, Jake!'

The fat man put the pan back on the flame and tramped through the dark shop, past the idle presses, to the door, and flung it open. 'Mr Halford!' he said. 'Well, good to see you. Come in, man. In the back there, you can't hear a thing.' A young Englishman with gentle eyes, a stern mouth and flat, colourless hair which grew in an untidy, confused spiral from a double crown, stepped back to allow a young woman to enter ahead of him. Before he could introduce her, she held out her hand to Jake, smiling, and shook his firmly. 'Good evening. Jennifer Tetzel,' she said.

'Jennifer, this is Jake Alexander,' the young man managed to get in, over her shoulder.

The two had entered the building from the street through an archway lettered NEW ERA BUILDING. 'Which new era would that be?' the young woman had wondered aloud, brightly, while they were waiting in the dim hallway for the door to be opened, and Alister Halford had not known whether the reference was to the discovery of deep-level gold mining that had saved Johannesburg from the ephemeral fate of a mining camp in the nineties, or to the optimism after the settlement of labour troubles in the twenties, or to the recovery after the world went off the gold standard in the thirties – really, one had no idea of the age of these buildings in this run-down end of the town. Now, coming in out of the deserted hallway gloom, which smelled of dust and rotting wood – the smell of waiting – they were met by the live, cold tang of ink and the homely, lazy odour of bacon fat – the smell of acceptance. There was not much light in the deserted workshop. The host blundered to the wall and switched on a bright naked bulb, up in the ceiling. The three stood blinking at one another for a moment: a coloured man with the fat of the man-of-the-world upon him, grossly dressed – not out of poverty but obviously because he liked it that way – in a rayon sports shirt that gaped and showed two hairy stomach rolls hiding his navel in a lipless grin, the pants of a good suit misbuttoned and held up round the waist by a tie instead of a belt, and a pair of expensive sports shoes, worn without socks; a young Englishman in a worn greenish tweed suit with a neo-Edwardian cut to the waistcoat that labelled it a leftover from undergraduate days; a handsome white woman who, as the light fell upon her, was immediately recognizable to Jake Alexander.

He had never met her before but he knew the type well – had seen it over and over again at meetings of the Congress of Democrats, and other organizations where progressive whites met progressive blacks. These were the white women who, Jake knew, persisted in regarding themselves as your equal. That was even worse, he thought, than the parsons who persisted in regarding *you* as *their* equal. The parsons had had ten years at school and seven years at a university and theological school; you had carried sacks of vegetables from the market to white people's cars from the time you were eight years old until you were apprenticed to a printer, and your first woman, like your mother, had been a servant, whom you had visited in a backyard room, and your first gulp of whisky, like many of your other pleasures, had been stolen while a white man was not looking. Yet the good parson insisted that your picture of life was exactly the same as his own: *you* felt as *he* did. But these women – oh, Christ! – these women felt as *you* did. They were sure of it. They thought they understood the humiliation of the black man walking the streets only by the permission of a pass written out by a white person, and the guilt and swagger of the coloured man light-faced enough to slink, fugitive from his own skin, into the preserves – the cinemas, bars, libraries – marked 'EUROPEANS ONLY'. Yes, breathless with stout sensitivity, they insisted on walking the whole teeter-totter of the colour line. There was no escaping their understanding. They even insisted on feeling the resentment *you* must feel at their identifying themselves with your feelings . . .

Here was the black hair of a determined woman (last year they wore it pulled tightly back into an oddly perched knot; this year it was cropped and curly as a lap dog's), the round, bony brow unpowdered in order to show off the tan, the red mouth, the unrouged cheeks, the big, lively, handsome eyes, dramatically painted, that would look into yours with such intelligent, eager honesty – eager to mirror what Jake Alexander, a big, fat coloured man interested in women, money, brandy and boxing, was feeling. Who the hell wants a woman to look at you honestly, anyway? What has all this to do with a *woman* – with what men and women have for each other in their eyes? She was wearing a wide black skirt, a white cotton blouse baring a good deal of her breasts, and ear-rings that seemed to have been made by a blacksmith out of bits of scrap iron. On her feet she had sandals whose narrow thongs wound between her toes, and the nails of the toes were painted plum colour. By contrast, her hands were neglected-looking – sallow, unmanicured – and on one thin finger there swivelled a huge gold seal-ring. She was good-looking, he supposed with disgust.

He stood there, fat, greasy and grinning at the two visitors so lingeringly that his grin looked insolent. Finally he asked, 'What brings you this end of town, Mr Halford? Sight-seeing with the lady?'

The young Englishman gave Jake's arm a squeeze, where the short sleeve of the rayon shirt ended. 'Just thought I'd look you up, Jake,' he said, jolly.

'Come on in, come on in,' said Jake on a rising note, shambling ahead of them into the company of the back room. 'Here, what about a chair for the lady?' He swept a pile of handbills from the seat of a kitchen chair onto the dusty concrete floor, picked up the chair and planked it down again in the middle of the group of men who had risen awkwardly at the visitors' entrance. 'You know Maxie Ndube? And Temba?' Jake said, nodding at two of the men who surrounded him.

Alister Halford murmured with polite warmth his recognition of Maxie, a small, dainty-faced African in neat, businessman's dress, then said inquiringly and hesitantly to Temba, 'Have we? When?'

Temba was a coloured man – a mixture of the bloods of black slaves and white masters, blended long ago, in the days when the Cape of Good Hope was a port of refreshment for the Dutch East India Company. He was tall and pale, with a large Adam's apple, enormous black eyes, and the look of a musician in a jazz band; you could picture a trumpet lifted to the ceiling in those long yellow hands, that curved spine hunched forward to shield a low note. 'In Durban last year, Mr Halford, you remember?' he said eagerly. 'I'm sure we met – or perhaps I only saw you there.'

'Oh, at the Congress? Of course I remember you!' Halford apologized. 'You were in a delegation from the Cape?'

'Miss –?' Jake Alexander waved a hand between the young woman, Maxie, and Temba.

'Jennifer. Jennifer Tetzel,' she said again clearly, thrusting out her hand. There was a confused moment when both men reached for it at once and then hesitated, each giving way to the other. Finally the handshaking was accomplished, and the young woman seated herself confidently on the chair.

Jake continued, offhand, 'Oh, and of course Billy Boy –' Alister signalled briefly to a black man with sad, blood-shot eyes, who stood awkwardly, back a few steps, against some rolls of paper – 'and Klaas and Albert.' Klaas and Albert had in their mixed blood some strain of the Bushman, which gave them a batrachian yellowness and toughness, like one of those toads that (prehistoric as the Bushman is) are mythically believed to have survived into modern times (hardly more fantastically than the Bushman himself has survived) by spending centuries shut up in an air bubble in a rock. Like Billy Boy, Klaas and Albert had backed away, and, as if abasement against the rolls of paper, the wall or the window were a greeting in itself, the two little coloured men and the big African only stared back at the masculine nods of Alister and the bright smile of the young woman.

'You up from the Cape for anything special now?' Alister said to Temba as he made a place for himself on a corner of a table that was littered with photographic blocks, bits of type, poster proofs, a bottle of souring milk, a bow-tie, a pair of red braces and a number of empty Coca-Cola bottles.

'I've been living in Durban for a year. Just got the chance of a lift to Jo'burg,' said the gangling Temba.

Jake had set himself up easily, leaning against the front of the stove and facing Miss Jennifer Tetzel on her chair. He jerked his head towards Temba and said, 'Real banana boy.' Young white men brought up in the strong Anglo-Saxon tradition of the province of Natal are often referred to, and refer to themselves, as 'banana boys', even though fewer and fewer of them have any connection with the dwindling number of vast banana estates that once made their owners rich. Jake's broad face, where the bright-pink cheeks of a Highland complexion – inherited, along with his name, from his Scottish father – showed oddly through his coarse, beige skin, creased up in appreciation of his own joke. And Temba threw back his head and laughed, his Adam's apple bobbing, at the idea of himself as a cricket-playing white public-school boy.

'There's nothing like Cape Town, is there?' said the young

woman to him, her head charmingly on one side, as if this conviction were something she and he shared.

'Miss Tetzel's up here to look us over. She's from Cape Town,' Alister explained.

She turned to Temba with her beauty, her strong provocativeness, full on, as it were. 'So we're neighbours?'

Jake rolled one foot comfortably over the other and a spluttering laugh pursed out the pink inner membrane of his lips.

'Where did you live?' she went on, to Temba.

'Cape Flats,' he said. Cape Flats is a desolate coloured slum in the bush outside Cape Town.

'Me, too,' said the girl, casually.

Temba said politely, 'You're kidding,' and then looked down uncomfortably at his hands, as if they had been guilty of some clumsy movement. He had not meant to sound so familiar; the words were not the right ones.

'I've been there nearly ten months,' she said.

'Well, some people've got queer tastes,' Jake remarked, laughing, to no one in particular, as if she were not there.

'How's that?' Temba was asking her shyly, respectfully.

She mentioned the name of a social rehabilitation scheme that was in operation in the slum. 'I'm assistant director of the thing at the moment. It's connected with the sort of work I do at the university, you see, so they've given me fifteen months' leave from my usual job.'

Maxie noticed with amusement the way she used the word 'job', as if she were a plumber's mate; he and his educated African friends – journalists and schoolteachers – were careful to talk only of their 'professions'. 'Good works,' he said, smiling quietly.

She planted her feet comfortably before her, wriggling on the hard chair, and said to Temba with mannish frankness, 'It's a ghastly place. How in God's name did you survive living there? I don't think I can last out more than another few months, and I've always got my flat in Cape Town to escape to on Sundays, and so on.'

While Temba smiled, turning his protruding eyes aside slowly, Jake looked straight at her and said, 'Then why do you, lady, why *do* you?'

'Oh, I don't know. Because I don't see why anyone else – any one of the people who live there – should have to, I suppose.' She laughed before anyone else could at the feebleness, the philanthropic uselessness of what she was saying. 'Guilt, what-have-you...'

Maxie shrugged, as if at the mention of some expensive illness he had never been able to afford and whose symptoms he could not imagine.

There was a moment of silence; the two coloured men and the big black man standing back against the wall watched anxiously, as if some sort of signal might be expected, possibly from Jake Alexander, their boss, the man who, like themselves, was not white, yet who owned his own business and had a car and money and strange friends – sometimes even white people, such as these. The three of them were dressed in the ill-matched cast-off clothing that all humble workpeople who are not white wear in Johannesburg, and they had not lost the ability of rural people to stare, unembarrassed and unembarrassing.

Jake winked at Alister; it was one of his mannerisms – a bookie's wink, a stage comedian's wink. 'Well, how's it going, boy, how's it going?' he said. His turn of phrase was bar-room bonhomie; with luck, he *could* get into a bar, too. With a hat to cover his hair and his coat collar well up, and only a bit of greasy pink cheek showing, he had slipped into the bars of the shabbier Johannesburg hotels with Alister many times and got away with it. Alister, on the other hand, had got away with the same sort of thing narrowly several times, too, when he had accompanied Jake to a shebeen in a coloured location, where it was illegal for a white man to be, as well as illegal for anyone at all to have a drink; twice Alister had escaped a raid by jumping out of a window. Alister had been in South Africa only eighteen months, as correspondent for a newspaper in England, and because he was only two or three years away from undergraduate escapades such incidents seemed to give him a kind of nostalgic pleasure; he found them funny. Jake, for his part, had decided long ago (with the great help of the money he had made) that he would take the whole business of the colour bar as humorous. The combination of these two attitudes, stemming from such immeasurably different circumstances, had the effect of making their friendship less self-conscious than is usual between a white man and a coloured one.

'They tell me it's going to be a good thing on Saturday night?' said Alister, in the tone of questioning someone in the know. He was referring to a boxing match between two coloured heavyweights, one of whom was a protégé of Jake.

Jake grinned deprecatingly, like a fond mother. 'Well, Pikkie's a good boy,' he said. 'I tell you, it'll be something to see.' He danced about a little on his clumsy toes in pantomime of the way a boxer nimbles himself, and collapsed against the stove, his belly shaking with laughter at his breathlessness.

'Too much smoking, too many brandies, Jake,' said Alister.

'With me, it's too many women, boy.'

'We were just congratulating Jake,' said Maxie in his soft, precise voice, the indulgent, tongue-in-cheek tone of the protégé who is superior to his patron, for Maxie was one of Jake's boys, too – of a different kind. Though Jake had decided that for him being on the wrong side of a colour bar was ludicrous, he was as indulgent to those who took it seriously and politically, the way Maxie did, as he was to any up-and-coming youngster who, say, showed talent in the ring or wanted to go to America and become a singer. They could all make themselves free of Jake's pocket, and his printing shop, and his room in the lower end of the town, where the building had fallen below the standard of white people but was far superior to the kind of thing most coloureds and blacks were accustomed to.

'Congratulations on what?' the young white woman asked. She had a way of looking up around her, questioningly, from face to face, that came of long familiarity with being the centre of attention at parties.

'Yes, you can shake my hand, boy,' said Jake to Alister. 'I didn't see it, but these fellows tell me that my divorce went through. It's in the papers today.'

'Is that so? But from what I hear, you won't be a free man long,' Alister said teasingly.

Jake giggled, and pressed at one gold-filled tooth with a strong fingernail. 'You heard about the little parcel I'm expecting from Zululand?' he asked.

'Zululand?' said Alister. 'I thought your Lila came from Stellenbosch.'

Maxie and Temba laughed.

'Lila? *What* Lila?' said Jake with exaggerated innocence.

'You're behind the times,' said Maxie to Alister.

'You know I like them – well, sort of round,' said Jake. 'Don't care for the thin kind, in the long run.'

'But Lila had red hair!' Alister goaded him. He remembered the incongruously dyed, straightened hair on a fine coloured girl whose nostrils dilated in the manner of certain fleshy water-plants seeking prey.

Jennifer Tetzel got up and turned the gas off on the stove, behind Jake. 'That bacon'll be like charred string,' she said.

Jake did not move – merely looked at her lazily. 'This is not the way to talk with a lady around.' He grinned, unapologetic.

She smiled at him and sat down, shaking her ear-rings. 'Oh, I'm divorced myself. Are we keeping you people from your supper? Do go ahead and eat. Don't bother about us.'

Jake turned around, gave the shrunken rashers a mild shake and put the pan aside. 'Hell, no,' he said. 'Any time. But –' turning to Alister – 'won't you have something to eat?' He looked about, helpless and unconcerned, as if to indicate an absence of plates and a general careless lack of equipment such as white women would be accustomed to use when they ate. Alister said quickly, no, he had promised to take Jennifer to Moorjee's.

Of course, Jake should have known; a woman like that would *want* to be taken to eat at an Indian place in Vrededorp, even though she was white, and free to eat at the best hotel in town. He felt suddenly, after all, the old gulf opening between himself and Alister: what did *they* see in such women – bristling, sharp, all-seeing, knowing women, who talked like men, who wanted to show all the time that, apart from sex, they were exactly the same as men? He looked at Jennifer and her clothes, and thought of the way a white woman could look:

one of those big, soft, European women with curly yellow hair, with very high-heeled shoes that made them shake softly when they walked, with a strong scent, like hot flowers, coming up, it seemed, from their jutting breasts under the lace and pink and blue and all the other pretty things they wore – women with nothing resistant about them except, buried in white, boneless fingers, those red, pointed nails that scratched faintly at your palms.

'You should have been along with me at lunch today,' said Maxie to no one in particular. Or perhaps the soft voice, a vocal tiptoe, was aimed at Alister, who was familiar with Maxie's work as an organizer of African trade unions. The group in the room gave him their attention (Temba with the little encouraging grunt of one who has already heard the story), but Maxie paused a moment, smiling ruefully at what he was about to tell. Then he said, 'You know George Elson?' Alister nodded. The man was a white lawyer who had been arrested twice for his participation in anti-colour-bar movements.

'Oh, George? I've worked with George often in Cape Town,' put in Jennifer.

'Well,' continued Maxie,' George Elson and I went out to one of the industrial towns on the East Rand. We were interviewing the bosses, you see, not the men, and at the beginning it was all right, though, once or twice the girls in the offices thought I was George's driver – "Your boy can wait outside." ' He laughed, showing small, perfect teeth; everything about him was finely made – his straight-fingered dark hands, the curved African nostrils of his small nose, his little ears, which grew close to the sides of his delicate head. The others were silent, but the young woman laughed, too.

'We even got tea in one place,' Maxie went on. 'One of the girls came in with two cups and a tin mug. But old George took the mug.'

Jennifer Tetzel laughed again, knowingly.

'Then, just about lunch time, we came to this place I wanted to tell you about. Nice chap, the manager. Never blinked an eye at me, called me Mister. And after we'd talked, he said to

George, "Why not come home with me for lunch?" So of course George said, "Thanks, but I'm with my friend here." "Oh, that's O.K.," said the chap. "Bring him along." Well, we go along to this house, and the chap disappears into the kitchen, and then he comes back and we sit in the lounge and have a beer, and then the servant comes along and says lunch is ready. Just as we're walking into the dining room, the chap takes me by the arm and says, "I've had *your* lunch laid on a table on the stoep. You'll find it's all perfectly clean and nice, just what we're having ourselves." '

'Fantastic,' murmured Alister.

Maxie smiled and shrugged, looking around at them all. 'It's true.'

'After he'd asked you, and he'd sat having a drink with you?' Jennifer said closely, biting in her lower lip, as if this were a problem to be solved psychologically.

'Of course,' said Maxie.

Jake was shaking with laughter, like some obscene Silenus. There was no sound out of him, but saliva gleamed on his lips, and his belly, at the level of Jennifer Tetzel's eyes, was convulsed.

Temba said soberly, in the tone of one whose goodwill makes it difficult for him to believe in the unease of his situation, 'I certainly find it worse here than at the Cape. I can't remember, y'know, about buses. I keep getting put off European buses.'

Maxie pointed to Jake's heaving belly. 'Oh, I'll tell you a better one than that,' he said. 'Something that happened in the office one day. Now, the trouble with me is, apparently, I don't talk like a native.' This time everyone laughed, except Maxie himself, who, with the instinct of a good raconteur, kept a polite, modest, straight face.

'You know that's true,' interrupted the young white woman. 'You have none of the usual softening of the vowels of most Africans. And you haven't got an Afrikaans accent, as some Africans have, even if they get rid of the African thing.'

'Anyway, I'd had to phone a certain firm several times,' Maxie went on, 'and I'd got to know the voice of the girl at the other end, and she'd got to know mine. As a matter of fact, she must have liked the sound of me, because she was getting very friendly. We fooled about a bit, exchanged first names, like a couple of kids – hers was Peggy – and she said, eventually, "Aren't you ever going to come to the office yourself?"' Maxie paused a moment, and his tongue flicked at the side of his mouth in a brief, nervous gesture. When he spoke again, his voice was flat, like the voice of a man who is telling a joke and suddenly thinks that perhaps it is not such a good one after all. 'So I told her I'd be in next day, about four. I walked in, sure enough, just as I said I would. She was a pretty girl, blonde, you know, with very tidy hair – I guessed she'd just combed it to be ready for me. She looked up and said "Yes?" holding out her hand for the messenger's book or parcel she thought I'd brought. I took her hand and shook it and said, "Well, here I am, on time – I'm Maxie – Maxie Ndube."'

'What'd she do?' asked Temba eagerly.

The interruption seemed to restore Maxie's confidence in his story. He shrugged gaily. 'She almost dropped my hand, and then she pumped it like a mad thing, and her neck and ears went so red I thought she'd burn up. Honestly, her ears were absolutely shining. She tried to pretend she'd known all along, but I could see she was terrified someone would come from the inner office and see her shaking hands with a native. So I took pity on her and went away. Didn't even stay for my appointment with her boss. When I went back to keep the postponed appointment the next week, we pretended we'd never met.'

Temba was slapping his knee. 'God, I'd have loved to see her face!' he said.

Jake wiped away a tear from his fat cheek – his eyes were light blue, and produced tears easily when he laughed – and said, 'That'll teach you not to talk swanky, man. Why can't you talk like the rest of us?'

'Oh, I'll watch out on the "Missus" and "Baas" stuff in future,' said Maxie.

Jennifer Tetzel cut into their laughter with her cool, practical voice. 'Poor little girl, she probably liked you awfully, Maxie, and was really disappointed. You mustn't be too harsh on her. It's hard to be punished for not being black.'

The moment was one of astonishment rather than irritation. Even Jake, who had been sure that there could be no possible situation between white and black he could not find amusing, only looked quickly from the young woman to Maxie, in a hiatus between anger, which he had given up long ago, and laughter, which suddenly failed him. On his face was admiration more than anything else – sheer, grudging admiration. This one was the best yet. This one was the coolest ever.

'Is it?' said Maxie to Jennifer, pulling in the corners of his mouth and regarding her from under slightly raised eyebrows. Jake watched. Oh, she'd have a hard time with Maxie. Maxie wouldn't give up his suffering-tempered blackness so easily. You hadn't much hope of knowing what Maxie was feeling at any given moment, because Maxie not only never let you know but made you guess wrong. But this one was the best yet.

She looked back at Maxie, opening her eyes very wide, twisting her sandalled foot on the swivel of its ankle, smiling. 'Really, I assure you it is.'

Maxie bowed to her politely, giving way with a falling gesture of his hand.

Alister had slid from his perch on the crowded table, and now, prodding Jake playfully in the paunch, he said, 'We have to get along.'

Jake scratched his ear and said again, 'Sure you won't have something to eat?'

Alister shook his head. 'We had hoped you'd offer us a drink, but –'

Jake wheezed with laughter, but this time was sincerely concerned. 'Well, to tell you the truth, when we heard the knocking, we just swallowed the last of the bottle off, in case it was someone it shouldn't be. I haven't a drop in the place till tomorrow. Sorry, chappie. Must apologize to you, lady, but we black men've got to drink in secret. If we'd've known it was you two...'

Maxie and Temba had risen. The two wizened coloured men, Klaas and Albert, and the sombre black Billy Boy shuffled helplessly, hanging about.

Alister said, 'Next time, Jake, next time. We'll give you fair warning and you can lay it on.'

Jennifer shook hands with Temba and Maxie, called 'Good-bye! Good-bye!' to the others, as if they were somehow out of earshot in that small room. From the door, she suddenly said to Maxie, 'I feel I must tell you. About that other story – your first one, about the lunch. I don't believe it. I'm sorry, but I honestly don't. It's too illogical to hold water.'

It was the final self-immolation by honest understanding. There was absolutely no limit to which that understanding would not go. Even if she could not believe Maxie, she must keep her determined good faith with him by confessing her disbelief. She would go to the length of calling him a liar to show by frankness how much she respected him – to insinuate, perhaps, that she was *with him*, even in the need to invent something about a white man that she, because she herself was white, could not believe. It was her last bid for Maxie.

The small, perfectly-made man crossed his arms and smiled, watching her go. Maxie had no price.

Jake saw his guests out of the shop, and switched off the light after he had closed the door behind them. As he walked back through the dark, where his presses smelled metallic and cool, he heard, for a few moments, the clear voice of the white woman and the low, noncommittal English murmur of Alister, his friend, as they went out through the archway into the street.

He blinked a little as he came back to the light and the faces that confronted him in the back room. Klaas had taken the dirty glasses from behind the curtain and was holding them one by one under the tap in the sink. Billy Boy and Albert had come closer out of the shadows and were leaning their elbows on a roll of paper. Temba was sitting on the table, swinging his foot. Maxie had not moved, and stood just as he had, with his arms folded. No one spoke.

Jake began to whistle softly through the spaces between his front teeth, and he picked up the pan of bacon, looked at the twisted curls of meat, jellied now in cold white fat, and put it down again absently. He stood a moment, heavily, regarding them all, but no one responded. His eye encountered the chair that he had cleared for Jennifer Tetzel to sit on. Suddenly he kicked it, hard, so that it went flying on to its side. Then, rubbing his big hands together and bursting into loud whistling to accompany an impromptu series of dance steps, he said 'Now, boys!' and as they stirred, he planked the pan down on the ring and turned the gas up till it roared beneath it.

Enemies

When Mrs Clara Hansen travels, she keeps herself to herself. This is usually easy, for she has money, has been a baroness and a beauty and has survived dramatic suffering. The crushing presence of these states in her face and bearing is nearly always enough to stop the loose mouths of people who find themselves in her company. It is only the very stupid, the senile or the self-obsessed who blunder up to assail that face, withdrawn as a castle, across the common ground of a public dining room.

Last month, when Mrs Hansen left Cape Town for Johannesburg by train, an old lady occupying the adjoining compartment tried to make of her apologies, as she pressed past in the corridor loaded with string bags and paper parcels, an excuse [illegible]o open one of those pointless conversations between strangers [illegible]hich arise in the nervous moments of departure. Mrs Hansen [illegible]as giving last calm instructions to Alfred, her Malay chauffeur and manservant, whom she was leaving behind, and she [illegible]id not look up. Alfred had stowed her old calf cases from [illegible]urope firmly and within reach in her compartment, which, of [illegible]urs influence with the reservation office had ensured she [illegible]ould [illegible]e to herself all the way. He had watched her put aw[illegible] in a [illegible]ecial pocket in her handbag, her train ticket, a ticket for her [illegible]e luxe bed, a book of tickets for her meals. He had made sure that she had her two yellow sleeping pills and the red pills for that feeling of pressure in her head, lying in cottonwool in her silver pillbox. He himself had seen that her two pairs of spectacles, one for distance, one for reading, were in her overnight bag, and had noted that her lorgnette hung below the diamond bow on the bosom of her dress. He had taken down the folding table from its niche above the washbasin in the compartment, and placed on it the three magazines she had sent him to buy at the bookstall, along with the paper from Switzerland that, this week, had been kept aside, unread, for the journey.

For a full fifteen minutes before the train left, he and his employer were free to ignore the to-and-fro of voices and luggage, the heat and confusion. Mrs Hansen murmured down to him; Alfred, chauffeur's cap in hand, dusty sunlight the colour of beer dimming the oil shine of his black hair, looked up from the platform and made low assent. They used the half-sentences, the hesitations and the slight changes of tone or expression of people who speak the language of their association in the country of their own range of situation. It was hardly speech; now and then it sank away altogether into the minds of each, but the sounds of the station did not well up in its place. Alfred dangled the key of the car on his little finger. The old face beneath the toque noted it, and the lips, the infinitely weary corners of the eyes drooped in the indication of a smile. Would he really put the car away into the garage for six weeks after he'd seen that it was oiled and greased?

Unmindful of the finger, his face empty of the satisfaction of a month's wages in advance in his pocket, two friends waiting to be picked up in a house in the Malay quarter of the town, he said, 'I must make a note that I mustn't send Madam's letters on after the twenty-sixth.'

'No. Not later than the twenty-sixth.'

Did she know? With that face that looked as if it knew everything, could she know, too, about the two friends in the house in the Malay quarter?

She said – and neither of them listened – 'In case of need, you've always got Mr Van Dam.' Van Dam was her lawyer. This remark, like a stone thrown idly into a pool to pass the time, had fallen time and again between them into the widening hiatus of parting. They had never questioned or troubled to define its meaning. In ten years, what need had there ever been that Alfred couldn't deal with himself, from a burst pipe in the flat to a jammed fastener on Mrs Hansen's dress?

Alfred backed away from the ice-cream carton a vender

thrust under his nose; the last untidy lump of canvas luggage belonging to the woman next door thumped down like a dusty animal at Mrs Hansen's side; the final bell rang.

As the train ground past out of the station, Alfred stood quite still with his cap between his hands, watching Mrs Hansen. He always stood like that when he saw her off. And she remained at the window, as usual, smiling slightly, inclining her head slightly, as if in dismissal. Neither waved. Neither moved until the other was borne out of sight.

When the station was gone and Mrs Hansen turned slowly to enter her compartment to the quickening rhythm of the train, she met the gasping face of the old woman next door. Fat overflowed not only from her jowl to her neck, but from her ankles to her shoes. She looked like a pudding that had risen too high and run down the sides of the dish. She was sprinkling cologne onto a handkerchief and hitting with it at her face as if she were trying to kill something. 'Rush like that, it's no good for you,' she said. 'Something went wrong with my son-in-law's car, and what a job to get a taxi! *They* don't care – get you here today or tomorrow. I thought I'd never get up those steps.'

Mrs Hansen looked at her. 'When one is no longer young, one must always give oneself exactly twice as much time as one needs. I have learned that. I beg your pardon.' And she passed before the woman into her compartment.

The woman stopped her in the doorway. 'I wonder if they're serving tea yet? Shall we go along to the dining car?'

'I always have my tea brought to me in my compartment,' said Mrs Hansen, in the low, dead voice that had been considered a pity in her day but that now made young people who could have been her grandchildren ask if she had been an actress. And she slid the door shut.

Alone, she stood a moment in the secretive privacy, where everything swayed and veered in obedience to the gait of the train. She began to look anxiously over the stacked luggage, her lips moving, but she had grown too set to adjust her balance from moment to moment, and suddenly she found herself sitting down. The train had dumped her out of the way.

Good thing, too, she thought, chastising herself impatiently – counting the luggage, fussing, when in ten years Alfred's never forgotten anything. Old fool, she told herself, old fool. Her ageing self often seemed to her an enemy of her real self, the self that had never changed. The enemy was a stupid one, fortunately; she merely had to keep an eye on it in order to keep it outwitted. Other selves that had arisen in her life had been much worse; how terrible had been the struggle with some of *them*!

She sat down with her back to the engine, beside the window, and put on her reading glasses and took up the newspaper from Switzerland. But for some minutes she did not read. She heard again inside herself the words *alone*, *alone*, just the way she had heard them fifty-nine years ago when she was twelve years old and crossing France by herself for the first time. As she had sat there, bolt upright in the corner of a carriage, her green velvet fur-trimmed cloak around her, her hamper beside her, and the locket with the picture of her grandfather hidden in her hand, she had felt a swelling terror of exhilaration, the dark, drowning swirl of cutting loose, had tasted the strength to be brewed out of self-pity and the calm to be lashed together out of panic that belonged to other times and other journeys approaching her from the distance of her future. *Alone*, *alone*. This that her real self had known years before it happened to her – before she had lived the journey that took her from a lover, or those others that took her from the alienated faces of madness and death – that same self remembered years after those journeys had dropped behind into the past. Now she was alone, lonely, lone – whatever you liked to call it – all the time. There is nothing of the drama of an occasion about it, for me, she reminded herself dryly. Still, there was no denying it, *alone* was not the same as *lonely*; even the Old Fool could not blur the distinction of that. The blue silk coat quivered where Alfred had hung it, the bundle of magazines edged along the table, and somewhere above her head a loose strap tapped. She felt again aloneness as the carapace that did not shut her off but shielded her strong sense of survival – against it, and all else.

She opened the paper from Switzerland, and, with her left foot (the heat had made it a little swollen) up on the seat opposite, she began to read. She felt lulled and comfortable and was not even irritated by the thuds and dragging noises coming from the partition behind her head; it was clear that that was the woman next door – *she* must be fussing with her luggage. Presently a steward brought a tea tray, which Alfred had ordered before the train left. Mrs Hansen drew in her mouth with pleasure at the taste of the strong tea, as connoisseurs do when they drink old brandy, and read the afternoon away.

She took her dinner in the dining car because she had established in a long experience that it was not a meal that could be expected to travel train corridors and remain hot, and also because there was something shabby, something *petit bourgeois,* about taking meals in the stuffy cubicle in which you were also to sleep. She tidied her hair around the sides of her toque – it was a beautiful hat, one of four, always the same shape, that she had made for herself every second year in Vienna – took off her rings and washed her hands, and powdered her nose, pulling a critical, amused face at herself in the compact mirror. Then she put on her silk coat, picked up her handbag and went with upright dignity, despite the twitchings and lurchings of the train, along the corridors to the dining car. She seated herself at an empty table for two beside a window, and, of course, although it was early and there were many other seats vacant, the old woman from the compartment next door, entering five minutes later, came straight over and sat down opposite her.

Now it was impossible not to speak to the woman and Mrs Hansen listened to her with the distant patience of an adult giving half an ear to a child, and answered her when necessary, with a dry simplicity calculated to be far above her head. Of course, Old Fool was tempted to unbend, to lapse into the small boastings and rivalries usual between two old ladies. But Mrs Hansen would not allow it and certainly not with this woman – this acquaintance thrust upon her in a train. It was bad enough that, only the week before, Old Fool had led her into one of these pathetic pieces of senile nonsense, cleverly disguised – Old Fool could be wily enough – but, just the same, unmistakably the kind of thing that people found boring. It was about her teeth. At seventy-one they were still her own, which was a self-evident miracle. Yet she had allowed herself, at a dinner party given by some young friends who were obviously impressed by her, to tell a funny story (not quite true, either) about how, when she was a weekend guest in a house with an over-solicitous hostess, the jovial host had hoaxed his wife by impressing upon her the importance of providing a suitable receptacle for their guest's teeth when she took them out overnight. There was a glass beside the jug of water on the bedside table; the hostess appeared, embarrassedly, with another. 'But, my dear, what is the other glass for?' The denouement, laughter, etc. Disgusting. Good teeth as well as bad aches and pains must be kept to oneself; when one is young, one takes the first for granted, and does not know the existence of the others.

So it was that when the menu was held before the two women Mrs Hansen ignored the consternation into which it seemed to plunge her companion, forestalled the temptation to enter, by contributing her doctor's views, into age's passionate preoccupation with diet, and ordered fish.

'D'you think the fish'll be all right? I always wonder, on a train, you know...' said the woman from the next compartment.

Mrs Hansen merely confirmed her order to the waiter by lowering her eyes and settling her chin slightly. The woman decided to begin at the beginning, with soup. 'Can't go far wrong with soup, can you?'

'Don't wait, please,' said Mrs Hansen when the soup came.

The soup was watery, the woman said. Mrs Hansen smiled her tragic smile, indulgently. The woman decided that she'd keep Mrs Hansen company, and risk the fish, too. The fish lay beneath a pasty blanket of white sauce and while Mrs Hansen calmly pushed aside the sauce and ate, the woman said, 'There's nothing like the good, clean food cooked in your own kitchen.'

Mrs Hansen put a forkful of fish to her mouth and, when she had finished it, spoke at last. 'I'm afraid it's many years since I had my own kitchen for more than a month or two a year.'

'Well, of course, if you go about a lot, you get used to strange food, I suppose. I find I can't eat half the stuff they put in front of you in hotels. Last time I was away, there were some days I didn't know what to have at all for lunch. I was in one of the best hotels in Durban and all there was was this endless curry – curry this, curry that – and a lot of dried-up cold meats.'

Mrs Hansen shrugged. 'I always find enough for my needs. It does not matter much.'

'What can you do? I suppose this sauce is the wrong thing for me, but you've got to take what you get when you're travelling,' said the woman. She broke off a piece of bread and passed it swiftly around her plate to scoop up what was left of the sauce. 'Starchy,' she added.

Mrs Hansen ordered a cutlet, and, after a solemn study of the menu, the other woman asked for the item listed immediately below the fish – oxtail stew. While they were waiting she ate bread and butter and shifting her mouthful comfortably from one side of her mouth to the other, accomplished a shift of her attention, too, as if her jaw and her brain had some simple mechanical connection. 'You're not from here, I suppose?' she asked, looking at Mrs Hansen with the appraisal reserved for foreigners and the licence granted by the tacit acceptance of old age on both sides.

'I have lived in the Cape, on and off, for some years,' said Mrs Hansen. 'My second husband was Danish, but settled here.'

'I could have married again. I'm not boasting, I mean, but I did have the chance, if I'd've wanted to,' said the woman. 'Somehow, I couldn't face it, after losing my first – fifty-two, that's all, and you'd have taken a lease on his life. Ah, those doctors. No wonder I feel I can't trust them a minute.'

Mrs Hansen parted the jaws of her large, elegant black bag to take out a handkerchief; the stack of letters that she always had with her – new ones arriving to take the place of old with every airmail – lay exposed. Thin letters, fat letters, big envelopes, small ones; the torn edges of foreign stamps, the large, sloping, and small, crabbed hands of foreigners writing foreign tongues. The other woman looked down upon them like a tourist, curious, impersonally insolent, envious. 'Of course, if I'd been the sort to run about a lot, I suppose it might have been different. I might have met someone really *congenial*. But there's my daughters. A mother's responsibility is never over – that's what I say. When they're little, it's little troubles. When they're grown up, it's big ones. They're all nicely married, thank God, but you know, it's always something – one of them sick, or one of the grandchildren, bless them . . . I don't suppose you've got any children. Not even from your first, I mean?'

'No,' said Mrs Hansen. 'No.' And the lie, as always, came to her as a triumph against that arrogant boy (Old Fool persisted in thinking of him as a gentle-browed youth bent over a dachshund puppy, though he was a man of forty-five by now) whom truly she had made, as she had warned she would, no son of hers. When the lie was said it had the effect of leaving her breathless, as if she had just crowned a steep rise. Firmly and calmly, she leaned forward and poured herself a glass of water, as one who has deserved it.

'My, it does look fatty,' the other woman was saying over the oxtail, which had just been placed before her, 'My doctor'd have a fit if he knew I was eating this.' But eat it she did, and cutlet and roast turkey to follow. Mrs Hansen never knew whether or not her companion rounded off the meal with rhubarb pie (the woman had remarked, as she saw it carried past, that it looked soggy), because she herself had gone straight from cutlet to coffee, and, her meal finished, excused herself before the other was through the turkey course. Back in her compartment, she took off her toque at last and tied a grey chiffon scarf around her head. Then she took her red-and-gold Florentine leather cigarette case from her bag and settled down to smoke her nightly cigarette while she waited for the man to come and convert her seat into the de luxe bed Alfred had paid for in advance.

It seemed to Mrs Hansen that she did not sleep very well

during the early part of the night, though she did not quite know what it was that made her restless. She was awakened, time and again, apparently by some noise that had ceased by the time she was conscious enough to identify it. The third or fourth time this happened, she woke to silence and a sense of absolute cessation, as if the world had stopped turning. But it was only the train that had stopped. Mrs Hansen lay and listened. They must be at some deserted siding in the small hours; there were no lights shining in through the shuttered window, no footsteps, no talk. The voice of a cricket, like a fingernail screeching over glass, sounded, providing, beyond the old woman's closed eyes, beyond the dark compartment and the shutters, a landscape of grass, dark, and telephone poles.

Suddenly the train gave a terrific reverberating jerk, as if it had been given a violent push. All was still again. And in the stillness, Mrs Hansen became aware of groans coming from the other side of the partition against which she lay. The groans came, bumbling and nasal, through the wood and leather; they sounded like a dog with its head buried in a cushion, worrying at the feathers. Mrs Hansen breathed out once, hard, in annoyance, and turned over; the greedy old pig, now she was suffering agonies of indigestion from that oxtail, of course. The groans continued at intervals. Once there was a muffled tinkling sound, as if a spoon had been dropped. Mrs Hansen lay tense with irritation, waiting for the train to move on and drown the woman's noise. At last, with a shake that quickly settled into a fast clip, they were off again, lickety-lack, lickety-lack, past (Mrs Hansen could imagine) the endless telephone poles, the dark grass, the black-coated cricket. Under the dialogue of the train, she was an unwilling eavesdropper to the vulgar intimacies next door; then either the groans stopped or she fell asleep in spite of them, for she heard nothing till the steward woke her with the arrival of early-morning coffee.

Mrs Hansen sponged herself, dressed and had a quiet breakfast, undisturbed by anyone, in the dining car. The man sitting opposite her did not even ask her so much as to pass the salt. She was back in her compartment, reading, when the ticket examiner came in to take her ticket away (they would be in Johannesburg soon), and of course, she knew just where to lay her hand on it, in her bag. He leaned against the doorway while she got it out. 'Hear what happened?' he said.

'What happened?' she said uncertainly, screwing up her face because he spoke indistinctly, like most young South Africans.

'Next door,' he said. 'The lady next door, elderly lady. She died last night.'

'She died? That woman died?' She stood up and questioned him closely, as if he were irresponsible.

'Yes,' he said, checking the ticket on his list. 'The bed boy found her this morning, dead in her bed. She never answered when the steward came round with coffee, you see.'

'My God,' said Mrs Hansen. 'My God. So she died, eh?'

'Yes, lady.' He held out his hand for her ticket; he had the tale to tell all up and down the train.

With a gesture of futility, she gave it to him.

After he had gone, she sank down on the seat, beside the window, and watched the veld go by, the grasses streaming past in the sun like the long black tails of the widow birds blowing where they swung upon the fences. She had finished her paper and magazines. There was no sound but the sound of the hurrying train.

When they reached Johannesburg she had all her luggage trimly closed and ready for the porter from the hotel at which she was going to stay. She left the station with him within five minutes of the train's arrival, and was gone before the doctor, officials and, she supposed, newspaper reporters came to see the woman taken away from the compartment next door. What could I have said to them? she thought, pleased with her sensible escape. Could I tell them she died of greed? Better not to be mixed up in it.

And then she thought of something. Newspaper reporters. No doubt there would be a piece in the Cape papers tomorrow. ELDERLY WOMAN FOUND DEAD IN CAPE–JOHANNESBURG TRAIN.

As soon as she had signed the register at the hotel she asked for a telegram form. She paused a moment, leaning on the marble-topped reception desk, looking out over the heads of the clerks. Her eyes, which were still handsome, crinkled at the corners; her nostrils lifted; her mouth, which was still so shapely because of her teeth, turned its sad corners lower in her reluctant, calculating smile. She printed Alfred's name and the address of the flat in Cape Town, and then wrote quickly, in the fine hand she had mastered more than sixty years ago: 'It was not me. Clara Hansen.'

Happy Event

There were so many things in life you couldn't ever imagine yourself doing, Ella Plaistow told herself. Once or twice she had said it aloud, too, to Allan. But mostly it grew, forced its way up out of the silences that fell upon her like a restraining hand during those first few days after she had come home from the nursing home. It seemed to burst through her mouth in a sudden irresistible germination, the way a creeper shoots and uncurls into leaf and stem in one of those films which telescope plant growth into the space of a few terrifying vital seconds.

Silence followed it again. In her mind, if she had spoken inwardly, to herself; in the room, if she had spoken aloud. The silence that covers the endless inward activity of shuffling for a foothold, making out of a hundred-and-one past justifications and pressures the accommodations of a new position for oneself. It was true, of course. You start off as a child, pretending to think the blonde doll prettier than the brunette, so that your loved sister may fall into the trap of choosing the one you don't want for yourself. You go on by one day finding your own tongue glibly acquiescing to a discussion of your best friend's temperament with someone whom you know to be her disliked enemy. And before you know where you are, you have gone through all the sidlings and inveiglings of taking somebody's work for less than it is worth, throwing someone into an agony of jealousy for the sake of a moment's vanity, pretending not to see an old lover lest he should not seem impressive enough in the eyes of the new one. It is impossible to imagine yourself doing any of these; but once done ... Like ants teeming to repair a broken anthill, like white corpuscles rushing to a wound, all the forces that protect oneself from oneself have already begun their quick, sure, furtive, uneasy juggling for a new stance, a rearrangement for comfort into which amorphous life seems to have edged you.

'It's your *body* that objects,' said Allan. 'Remember that. That's all. There's some sort of physical protest that's got nothing to do with you at all, really. You must expect it. It'll pass off in a week or so.'

And of course he was quite right. She certainly didn't have any regrets. They had two children, a girl and a boy (the wrong way round, as they said – the girl was the elder – but it's dangerous to have everything too much the way you want it!) who were just old enough to be left with their grandmother. Allan's new partner was thoroughly reliable, the bond on the house was almost paid off; at last there was nothing to stop Allan and Ella: they had booked to go to Europe, in the spring of next year. So to have allowed themselves to be stopped by this –! To be, instead, this time next year, caught up in chemists' bills and napkins and wakeful nights all over again! No, they had brought up their babies, had loved and resented them and were content with them, and all through eight years had planned for this time when they would suddenly lift themselves clear of whatever it was that their lives had settled into, and land, free of it, lightly in another country.

Because it was something that Ella could never have dreamed she would ever do, in a week or two the trip to the nursing home slipped away into the unimportance of things that might never have happened. She was busy planning next winter's clothes for the children – it would be winter in South Africa while she and Allan were in spring in Europe – and getting the garden into shape because they hoped to let the house for the period they were to be away, and if they wanted a decent tenant the place must look attractive. She was just beginning to feel really strong again – undoubtedly that business had left her a little weak – and it was just as well, since she had so much to do, when, of course, servant trouble started.

The old house-cum-garden boy, Thomasi, began quarrelling with Lena, the native maid whom Ella had thought herself lucky to engage two months ago. Lena, a heavy, sullen, light-coloured Basuto, represented in her closed-in solemnity something that challenged irritation in Thomasi. Thomasi was a Basuto himself – Ella had the vague conviction that it was best to have servants who belonged to the same tribe, rather as she would have felt that it would be better to have two Siamese cats instead of one Siamese and one tabby, or two fan-tailed goldfish rather than one plain and one fancy. She always felt puzzled and rather peevish, then, when, as had happened often before, she found that her two Basutos or two Zulus or two Xhosas did not necessarily get on any better than one would have expected two Frenchmen to get on simply because both were French, or two Englishmen simply because both were English.

Now Thomasi, barely five feet tall and with that charming, ancient, prehuman look of little dark-skinned men with bandy legs, was maddened by the very presence of Lena, like an insect circling angrily around the impassive head of some great slow animal. He quarrelled with her over dusters, over the state of the kitchen sink, over the bones for the dog; he went about his work shaking his head and rumbling with volcanic mutterings.

'If you've got anything to say, come out and say it,' Ella said to him, irritated herself. 'What's the matter now?'

'That woman is too lazy, madam,' he said in his high, philosophical, exasperated voice.

It was difficult to think of old Thomasi as something quite like oneself, when he rose to his hind legs. (Yes, one had the feeling that this was *exactly* what happened when he got up from polishing the floor. Of course, if he had been dressed in a tailored American-drape hopsack instead of the regulation 'kitchen boy' outfit that was a cross between a small boy's cotton sailor suit and a set of underwear, he might not have looked any funnier than any of the small, middle-aged Johannesburg men behind their directors' desks.) 'Look, Thomasi, she does her work. I'm satisfied with her. I don't want you to go making trouble. I'm the missus, and she works for me, not you, you understand?'

Then, later in the day, Ella would relent. Having shown Thomasi the hand of authority, she could approach him on the other level of their association: that of common concern for the house that they had 'run' together for nearly six years, and whose needs and prides and inanimate quirks both understood perfectly.

'Thomasi?'

'Missus?' She might be strolling in the garden, pretending that she was not seeking him out. He would go on wielding the grass shears, widening and snapping like the sharp bill of some great bird imprisoned in his hands.

'What has she done?'

'Well, I tell her the dog he mustn't have the small bone. Yesterday I tell her. Now she doesn't say nothing when I tell her. This morning I see she give the chicken bone to the dog. All that small bone, you know, the missus keep for the cats. Now when I say why you give that bone to the dog, the dog he's going to get sick, she just look me ...'

The coffee cups left unwashed from the night before.

The iron left switched on while she went to her room after lunch.

And too many friends in her room at night, too many.

'I think she makes the kaffir beer,' said Thomasi.

But at this complaint Ella was ready to discredit all the others, again. This was Thomasi trying to cook something up. If the girl brewed kaffir beer in her room, Thomasi would be her first customer, not the informant seeking to get her into trouble.

'Listen, Thomasi, I don't want to hear any more of these tales and grumbles, you understand? I'll see if Lena works properly or not, and I don't want you interfering with her.'

As she would give her children a handful of sweets each to equalize some difference between them, Ella cleared out a cupboard that needed clearing anyway, and gave Thomasi an old shirt of Allan's, Lena a cheap blue satin nightgown that she had bought to take to the nursing home and that she somehow felt she didn't want to wear again. 'I must keep the peace,' she said to Allan. 'I'm not going to go training another new girl now. I must stick it out with this one until we go. She's a perfectly nice girl, really – a bit sulky, that's all, but you know what an old devil he can be when he wants to. I shouldn't be surprised if what's behind it is that he fancies her, and she's not interested. Shame, he looks such a little old wizened imp of a thing next to her, she's such a hulking, big-breasted Juno.'

But the gifts did not quiet for long whatever it was that inflamed Thomasi's malice. The following month, on a Monday morning, Ella found Thomasi alone in the kitchen, cooking the greasy, metallic-tasting fried eggs that were his idea of a white man's breakfast. Lena, he said, bearing his message from across that neat stretch of grass and crisscross washing line that was the no-man's-land between the lives of the white people in the house and the black people in their back-yard quarters, said she was sick this morning. She would do the washing tomorrow.

'Are those for the master...?' Ella indicated the eggs but lacked the courage to complain. 'What's wrong with Lena?'

Over the frying pan, Thomasi gave a great shrug of disbelief and contempt.

'What does she say?'

Thomasi turned around to the young woman in the soiled pink dressing-gown, the dark line of her plucked and dyed white-woman's eyebrows showing like pen strokes on the pastel of her fair-skinned face, unmade-up, faintly greasy with the patina of sleep. His brow drew in, intricately lined, over his little yellowish eyes; he said with exaggerated poise and indifference, 'I don't know how she's sick. I can't say how a person she's sick when there's noise in her room all night. When people is talking there, late. Sometime I think: She got someone staying there, or something? Talking, and late, late, a baby crying.'

Ella went out, over the stones and the grass, across the yard to the native girl's room. The grass was crisp with dew and the chill struck through the old sandals she liked to wear instead of slippers; long threads of spider-web danced between the clothes-line. She knocked on the door of the little brick room; the window was closed and curtained. She knocked again and called softly, 'Lena?'

'Ma'm?' The voice came after a pause.

Ella opened the door with difficulty – natives usually tampered with the doorknobs of their rooms, making them removable as an added protection against intruders – and, finding it would open only halfway, edged her way in. The room had a warm animal smell, like the inside of the cupboard where old Lixi, the tabby, lay with her kittens at her belly, purring and licking, purring and licking. The air in here had nothing to do with that other air, wet and sharp with morning, just outside: it was a creature air, created by breathing beings. Although the room was small, Lena in her bed seemed far away. The bed was raised high on bricks, and it was half-curtained, like a homemade four-poster. Some sort of design worked in red and purple thread trailed round the hems of the material. Lena lay, her head turned to the angle of her raised arm on the pillow. She seemed to be taking some communion of comfort from her own tender exposed armpit, close to her face.

'Are you sick, Lena?' said the white woman gently.

The black woman turned her head back and forth once, quickly, on the pillow. She swallowed and said, 'Yes.'

'What do you feel?' said Ella, still at the door, which she now saw could not open properly because of a cupboard made of boxes which was pushed half against it.

'My stomach, ma'am.' She moved under the fringed travelling rug that was her blanket.

'Do you think you've eaten something that's made you sick?' said Ella.

The girl did not answer. Ella saw her big slow eyes and the white of her teeth come out of the gloom.

'Sometime I've got a cold in my stomach,' the girl said at last.

'Is it pain?' said Ella.

'I can do the washing tomorrow,' said the voice from the great, hemmed-in agglomerate of the bed.

'Oh, it doesn't matter,' said Ella. 'I'll send Thomasi out with something for you to take. And do you want something to eat?'

'Only tea, thank you ma'm.'

'All right then.'

She felt the woman's slow eyes watching her out of that room, which curiously, despite its poverty, its soapbox cupboards fretted with cutout newspaper edgings, the broken china ducks and the sword-fern draped in stained crêpe paper (the ornaments and the fern were discards from the house), had something of the richly charged air of grand treasure-filled rooms of old houses heavy with association, rooms much used, thick with the overlaid echoes of human concourse. She thought, for some reason, of the kind of room in which one expects to find a Miss Havisham. And how ridiculous! These two whitewashed servants' rooms neatly placed out of the way between the dustbin and the garage! What had they to do with Dickens or flights of fancy or anything else, in fact, except clean, weatherproof and fairly decent places for the servants to sleep? They belonged to nothing and nobody, merely were thrown in along with the other conditions of work.

On the kitchen step Ella stopped and shook each foot like a cat; her feet were sopping. She made a little exclamation of irritation with herself.

And when she had dressed, she sent Thomasi out to the room with a dose of chlorodyne ready-mixed with water in one of the old kitchen-glasses. She got her younger child Pip ready for Allan to take to nursery school and saw that her daughter Kathie had some cake to take for her school lunch in place of the sandwiches Lena usually made.

'Darned nuisance, mmh?' Allan said (suppressing a belch, with distaste, after the eggs).

'Can't be helped, I suppose,' Ella said. 'I wouldn't mind so much if only it wasn't Monday. You know how it is when the washing isn't done on the right day. It puts the whole of the rest of the week out. Anyway, she should be all right by tomorrow.'

The next morning when Ella got up, Lena was already doing the washing. 'Girl appeared again?' called Allan from the bathroom. Ella came in, holding one of Pip's vests to her cheek to see if it was quite dry. 'She doesn't look too good, poor thing. She's moving terribly slowly between the tub and the line.'

'Well she's never exactly nimble is she?' murmured Allan, concentrating on the slight dent in his chin, always a tricky place to shave. They smiled at each other; when they smiled at each other these days, they had the conspiring look of children who have discovered where the Christmas presents are hidden: Europe, leisure and the freedom of the money they had saved up were unspoken between them.

Ella and Allan Plaistow lived in one of the pleasantest of Johannesburg suburbs: gently rolling country to the north of the city, where the rich had what amounted to country estates, and the impecunious possessors of good taste had small houses in an acre or two of half-cultivated garden. Some of the younger people, determined not to be forced back into real suburbia through lack of money, kept chickens or bred dogs to supplement the upkeep of their places, and one couple even had a small Jersey herd. Ella was one of their customers, quite sure she could taste the difference between their, and what she called 'city' milk.

One morning about a week after the native girl Lena had delayed Ella's wash-day, the milk delivery cart was bowling along the ruts it had made for itself along the track between the dairy and the houses in the Plaistows' direction, when the horse swerved and one wheel bowed down the tall grasses at the side of the track. There was a tinny clang; the wheel slithered against something. Big Charlie, the milk 'boy', growled softly at the horse, and climbed down to see. There, as if it had made a bed for itself in the long grass the way an animal turns round and round before sinking to rest, was a paraffin tin. Big Charlie stubbed at it once with his boot, as if to say, oh, well, if that's all ... But it gave back the resistance of a container that has something inside it; through his toes, there came to him the realization that this was not merely an empty tin. It was upside down, the top pressed to the ground. He saw an edge of blue material, stained with dew and earth, just showing. Still with his foot, he pushed hard – too hard, for whatever was inside was light – and the tin rocked over. There spilled out of it a small bundle, the naked decaying body of what had been a newborn child, rolled, carelessly as one might roll up old clothing, in a blue satin nightgown.

It did not seem for a moment to Big Charlie that the baby was dead. He gave a kind of aghast cluck, as at some gross neglect – one of his own five doubled up with a bellyache after eating berries, or the youngest with flies settling on his mouth because the mother had failed to wipe the milk that trickled down his chin from her abundance when she fed him – and knelt down to make haste to do whatever it was that the little creature needed. And then he saw that this was hardly a child at all; was now closer to those kittens he was sometimes ordered by his employers to drown in a bucket of water or closer still to one of those battered fledglings found lying beneath the mimosa trees the night after a bad summer storm.

So now he stood back and did not want to touch it. With his mouth lifted over his teeth in a superstitious horror at the coldness of what had been done, he took the crumpled satin in the tips of his fingers and folded it over the body again, then dropped the bundle back into the paraffin tin and lifted the tin on to the cart beside him.

As he drove, he looked down now and then, swiftly, in dismay to see it there still beside him. The bodice of the nightgown was uppermost and lifted in the firm currents of the morning air. It was inside out, and showed a sewn-on laundry label. Big Charlie could neither read or write so he did not know that it said in the neat letters devised for the nursing home, E. PLAISTOW.

That, of course, was how Ella came to find herself in court.

When she opened the door to the plainclothes detective that afternoon, she had the small momentary start, a kind of throb in some organ one didn't know one had, of all people who do not steal and who have paid their taxes: an alarm at the sight of a policeman that is perhaps rooted in the memory of childhood threats. The man was heavily built and large-footed and he had a very small, well-brushed moustache, smooth as the double flick of a paintbrush across his broad lip. He said in Afrikaans, '*Goeie middag. Mevrou Plaistow?*' And when she answered in English, he switched to slow, stilted English. She led him into the living room with a false air of calm and he sat on the edge of the sofa. When he told her that the Evans's milk boy had found a dead native baby in a paraffin tin on the veld, she made a polite noise of horror and even felt a small shudder, just back of her jaws, at the idea, but her face kept its look of strained patience: what had this gruesome happening to do with *her*? Then he told her that the child was found wrapped in a blue satin nightgown bearing her name, and she rose instantly from her chair in alarm, as if there had been a sudden jab inside her.

'*In my nightgown?*' she accused, standing over the man.

'Yes, I'm afraid so, lady.'

'But are you sure?' she said, withdrawing into anger and hauteur.

He opened a large brief-case he had brought with him and which she had imagined as much a part of his equipment as his official English or the rolled-gold signet ring on his little finger. Carefully he spread out the blue satin, which still kept, all refracted by creases, the sheen of satin, despite the earth stains and some others caused by something that had dried patchily – perhaps that birth fluid, *vernix caseosa*, in which a baby is coated when it slips into the world. The sight filled her with revulsion: 'Oh, put it away!' she said with difficulty.

'You recognize it?' he said – pronouncing the word as if it were spelled 'racognize'.

'It's mine all right,' she said. 'It's the one I gave to Lena a few weeks ago. But good God –?'

'It's a native girl, of course, the one you gave it to?' He had taken out his notebook.

Now all sorts of things were flooding into her mind. 'That's right! She was sick, she stayed in bed one day. The boy said he heard a baby cry in the night –' She appealed to the policeman: 'But it couldn't be!'

'Now if you'll just tal me, lady, what was the date when you gave the girl the nightgown...' Out of the disorder of her quicker mind, his own slow one stolidly sorted this recollection from that; her confused computation of dates and times through the measure of how much time had passed between the day Pip chipped a tooth at nursery school (that, she remembered distinctly, happened on the same day that she had given Thomasi a shirt and Lena the nightgown) and the morning the washing had not been done, became a statement. Then she went, haltingly because of her nervousness, into the kitchen to call Lena and Thomasi. 'Thomasi!' she called. And then, after a pause: 'Lena.' And she watched for her, coming across the yard.

But the two Africans met the fact of the policeman far more calmly than she herself had done. For Africans there is no stigma attached to any involvement with the forces of the law; the innumerable restrictions by which their lives are hedged from the day they are born make transgressions commonplace and punishment inevitable. To them a few days in prison is no more shaming than an attack of the measles. After all, there are few people who could go through a lifetime without at least once forgetting to carry the piece of paper which is their 'pass' to free movement about the town, or without getting drunk, or without sitting on a bench which looks just like every other bench but happens to be provided exclusively for the use of people with a pale skin. All these things keep Africans casually going in and out of prison, hardly the worse – since it is accepted that this is the ways things are – for a cold, buggy night in the cells or a kick from a warder.

Lena has not a pleasant face, thought Ella, but thought too that perhaps she was merely reading this into the face, now. The woman simply stood there, answering, in an obedient Afrikaans, the detective's questions about her identity. The detective had hitched his solid rump on to the kitchen table, and his manner had changed to the impatient one customarily used for Africans by all white persons in authority. The woman appeared weary, more than anything else; she did not look at the detective when he spoke to her or she answered. And she spoke coldly, as was her custom; just as she said, 'Yes madam no madam,' when Ella reproached her for some neglected chore. She was an untidy woman, too; now she had on her head a woollen *doek* again, instead of the maid's cap Ella provided for her to wear. Ella looked at her, from the *doek* to the coloured sandals with the cut thongs where they caught the toes; looked at her in a kind of fascination, and tried to fit with her the idea of the dead baby, rolled in a nightgown and thrust into a paraffin tin. It was neither credible nor did it inspire revulsion. Because she is not a *motherly* figure, Ella thought – that is it. One cannot imagine her mother to anything. She is the sort of woman, white or black, who is always the custodian of other people's children; she washes their faces and wipes their noses, but they throw their arms around somebody else's neck.

And just then the woman looked at her, suddenly, directly, without a flicker of escape, without dissimulation or appeal, not as a woman looks to another woman, or even a human being to another human being; looked at her out of those wide-set, even-lidded eyes and did not move a muscle of her face.

Oh, but I don't know her, I know nothing about her ... Ella recoiled, retracting to herself.

'She'll have to come along with me,' the detective was saying, and as the woman stood a moment, as if awaiting some permission, he told her in Afrikaans that she could go to her room if she wanted anything, but she must be quick.

Ella stood near the door watching her servant go slowly across the yard to the little brick room. Her own heart was pounding slowly. She felt a horrible conflict of agitation and shame – for what, she did not know. But if I go after her, she seemed to answer herself, what can I say to her? Behind Ella, the detective was questioning Thomasi, and Thomasi was enjoying it; she could hear from the quick, meaningful, confidential tones of Thomasi's voice that he was experiencing all the relish of a gossip who finds himself at last in the powerful position of being able to influence the lives of those who have forced him out into the cold of a vicarious recorder.

Ella said suddenly to the detective, 'Will you excuse me now, please –' and went away through the house to her bedroom. She was standing there still, some minutes later, when the detective called from the front door, 'Thank you very much, lady, hey? We'll let you know –' and she did not come out but called back, as if she were at some task she could not leave for a moment, 'I'm sorry – will you find your way out...'

But she could not forbear to bend apart the slats of the venetian blind in time to see the back of Lena, in one of those cheap short coats – jeep coats, they were called, beloved of suburban African girls – getting into the police car. It's unbelievable, she told herself; she didn't look any fatter than she does now... And she did the whole week's washing...

The moment Ella heard the car drive away, she went to telephone Allan. As she dialled, she noticed that her fingers were fumbling and damp. I'm really upset, she thought; I'm really upset about this thing.

By the time the court case came to be heard, the quiet, light-coloured Lena lying in her bed that day with her head turned to her arm for comfort, standing obediently before the questioning of the detective in the kitchen, was changed in Ella Plaistow's mind into the ghoulish creature who emerged out of discussion of the affair with friends and neighbours. A woman who could kill her own baby! A murderer, nothing less! It's quite awful to think that she handled Pip and Kathie, other women sympathized. It just shows you, you never know who you're taking into your home ... You never know, with *them* ... You can send them to a doctor to make sure you aren't harbouring someone who's diseased, but you've no way of finding out what sort of person a servant is. Well, Thomasi didn't like her from the first, you know, Ella always said at this point. Ah, Thomasi, someone would murmur, now he's a good old thing.

So that when Ella saw the woman Lena in court, there was something disquieting and unexpected about the ordinariness, the naturalness of her appearance: this was simply the woman who had stood so often at the stove in Ella's red-and-white kitchen. And where was the other, that creature who had abandoned her own newborn child to the cold of the veld?

Embarrassment precluded all other feelings, once the white woman found herself in the witness stand. Ella had never, she said again and again afterwards, felt such a fool in her whole life.

'You are, of course, a married woman?' said the magistrate.

'Yes,' said Ella.

'How long have you been married?'

'Eight years.'

'I see. And you have children?'

'Yes, two children.'

'Mrs Plaistow, am I to understand that you, a woman who has been married for eight years and has herself borne two children, were not aware that this woman in your employ was on the point of giving birth to a child?'

Of course, the man must have thought her quite moronic! But how to explain that one didn't go measuring one's servant's waistline, that she was a very big well-built woman in any case and that since she must have been well into her pregnancy when she started work, any further changes in her figure were not noticed?

He made such a *fool* of me, Ella protested; you can't imagine how *idiotic* I felt.

The case dragged on through two days. The woman herself said that the child had been born dead, and that since no one knew that she was pregnant, she had been 'frightened' and had hidden the body and then left it on the veld, but post-mortem findings showed strong evidence that the child might have lived some hours after birth, and had not died naturally. Then there was Thomasi's statement that he had heard an infant cry in the night.

'In your opinion, Doctor,' the magistrate asked the government medical officer, in an attempt to establish how much time had elapsed between the birth and death of the infant, 'would it be possible for a woman to resume her normal day's work thirty-six hours after confinement? This woman did her employer's household washing the following day.'

The doctor smiled slightly. 'Were the woman in question a European, I should, of course, say this would be most unlikely. Most unlikely. But of a native woman, I should say yes – yes, it would be possible.' In the silence of the court, the reasonableness, the validity of this statement had the air of clinching the matter. After all, everyone knew, out of a mixture of hearsay and personal observation, the physical stamina of the African. Hadn't everyone heard of at least one native who had walked around for three days with a fractured skull, merely complaining of a headache? And of one who had walked miles to a hospital, carrying, Van Gogh-like, in a piece of newspaper, his own ear – sliced off in a faction fight?

Lena got six months' hard labour. Her sentence coincided roughly with the time Ella and Allan spent in Europe, but though she was out of prison by the time they returned, she did not go back to work for them again.

The Smell of Death and Flowers

The party was an unusual one for Johannesburg. A young man called Derek Ross – out of sight behind the 'bar' at the moment – had white friends and black friends, Indian friends and friends of mixed blood, and sometimes he liked to invite them all to his flat at once. Most of them belonged to the minority that, through bohemianism, godliness, politics or a particularly sharp sense of human dignity, did not care about the difference in one another's skins. But there were always one or two – white ones – who came, like tourists, to see the sight, and to show that they did not care, and one or two black or brown or Indian ones who found themselves paralysed by the very ease with which the white guests accepted them.

One of the several groups that huddled to talk, like people sheltering beneath a cliff, on divans and hard borrowed chairs in the shadow of the dancers, was dominated by a man in a grey suit, Malcolm Barker. 'Why not pay the fine and have done with it, then?' he was saying.

The two people to whom he was talking were silent a moment, so that the haphazard noisiness of the room and the organized wail of the gramophone suddenly burst in irrelevantly upon the conversation. The pretty brunette said, in her quick, officious voice, 'Well, it wouldn't be the same for Jessica Malherbe. It's not quite the same thing, you see...' Her stiff, mascara'd lashes flickered an appeal – for confirmation, and for sympathy because of the impossibility of explaining – at a man whose gingerish whiskers and flattened, low-set ears made him look like an angry tomcat.

'It's a matter of principle,' he said to Malcom Barker.

'Oh, quite, I see,' Malcolm conceded. 'For someone like this Malherbe woman, paying the fine's one thing; sitting in prison for three weeks is another.'

The brunette rapidly crossed and then uncrossed her legs. 'It's not even quite that,' she said. 'Not the unpleasantness of being in prison. Not a sort of martyrdom on Jessica's part. Just the *principle*.' At that moment a black hand came out from the crush of dancers bumping round and pulled the woman to her feet; she went off, and as she danced she talked with staccato animation to her African partner, who kept his lids half lowered over his eyes while she followed his gentle shuffle. The ginger-whiskered man got up without a word and went swiftly through the dancers to the 'bar', a kitchen table covered with beer, brandy and gin bottles, at the other end of the small room.

'*Satyagraha*,' said Malcolm Barker, like the infidel pronouncing with satisfaction the holy word that the believers hesitate to defile.

A very large and plain African woman sitting next to him smiled at him hugely and eagerly out of shyness, not having the slightest idea what he had said.

He smiled back at her for a moment, as if to hyponotize the onrush of some frightening animal. Then, suddenly, he leaned over and asked in a special, loud, slow voice, 'What do you do? Are you a teacher?'

Before the woman could answer, Malcolm Barker's young sister-in-law, a girl who had been sitting silent, pink and cold as a porcelain figurine, on the window-sill behind his back, leaned her hand for balance on his chair and said urgently, near his ear, 'Has Jessica Malherbe really been in prison?'

'Yes, in Port Elizabeth. And in Durban, they tell me. And now she's one of the civil disobedience people – defiance campaign leaders who're going to walk into some native location forbidden to Europeans. Next Tuesday. So she'll land herself in prison again. – For Christ's sake, Joyce, what are you drinking that stuff for? I've told you that punch is the cheapest muck possible –'

But the girl was not listening to him any longer. Balanced delicately on her rather full, long neck, her fragile-looking face with the eyes and the fine, short line of nose of a Marie Laurençin painting was looking across the room with the intensity peculiar to the blank-faced. Hers was an essentially two-dimensional prettiness: flat, dazzlingly pastel-coloured, as if the mask of make-up on the unlined skin *were* the face; if one had turned her around, one would scarcely have been surprised to discover canvas. All her life she had suffered from this impression she made of not being quite real.

'She *looks* so nice,' she said now, her eyes still fixed on some point near the door. 'I mean she uses good perfume, and everything. You can't imagine it.'

Her brother-in-law made as if to take the tumbler of alcohol out of the girl's hand, impatiently, the way one might take a pair of scissors from a child, but without looking at him or at her hands she changed the glass from one hand to the other, out of his reach. 'At least the brandy's in a bottle with a recognizable label,' he said peevishly. 'I don't know why you don't stick to that.'

'I wonder if she had to eat the same food as the others,' said the girl.

'You'll feel like death tomorrow morning,' he said, 'and Madeline'll blame me. You are an obstinate little devil.'

A tall, untidy young man, whose blond head out-topped all others like a tousled palm-tree, approached with a slow, drunken smile and, with exaggerated courtesy, asked Joyce to dance. She unhurriedly drank down what was left in her glass, put the glass carefully on the window-sill and went off with him, her narrow waist upright and correct in his long arm. Her brother-in-law followed her with his eyes for a moment, then closed them suddenly, whether in boredom or in weariness one could not tell.

The young man was saying to the girl as they danced, 'You haven't left the side of your husband – or whatever he is – all night. What's the idea?'

'My brother-in-law,' she said. 'My sister couldn't come because the child's got a temperature.'

He squeezed her waist; it remained quite firm, like the crisp stem of a flower. 'Do I know your sister?' he asked. Every now and then his drunkenness came over him in a delightful swoon, so that his eyelids dropped heavily and he pretended that he was narrowing them shrewdly.

'Maybe. Madeline McCoy – Madeline Barker now. She's the

painter. She's the one who started that arts-and-crafts school for Africans.'

'Oh, yes. Yes, I know,' he said. Suddenly, he swung her away from him with one hand, executed a few loose-limbed steps around her, lost her in a collision with another couple, caught her to him again, and, with an affectionate squeeze, brought her up short against the barrier of people who were packed tight as a rugby scrum around the kitchen table where the drinks were. He pushed her through the crowd to the table.

'What d'you want, Roy, my boy?' said a little, very black-faced African, gleaming up at them.

'Barberton'll do for me.' The young man pressed a hand on the African's head, grinning.

'Ah, that stuff's no good. Sugar-water. Let me give you a dash of Pineapple. Just like mother makes.'

For a moment, the girl wondered if any of the bottles really did contain Pineapple or Barberton, two infamous brews made illegally in the blacks' locations. Pineapple, she knew, was made out of the fermented fruit and was supposed to be extraordinarily intoxicating; she had once read a newspaper report of a shebeen raid in which the Barberton still contained a lopped-off human foot – whether for additional flavour or the spice of witchcraft, it was not known.

But she was reassured at once. 'Don't worry,' said a good-looking blonde made up to look heavily sun-tanned, who was standing at the bar. 'No shebeen ever produced anything much more poisonous than this gin-punch thing of Derek's.' The host was attending to the needs of his guests at the bar, and she waved at him a glass containing the mixture the girl had been drinking over at the window.

'Not gin. It's arak – lovely,' said Derek. 'What'll you have, Joyce?'

'Joyce,' said the gangling young man with whom she had been dancing. 'Joyce. That's a nice name for her. Now tell her mine.'

'Roy Wilson. But you seem to know each other quite adequately without names,' said Derek. 'This is Joyce McCoy,

Roy – and, Joyce, these are Matt Shabalala, Brenda Shotley, Mahinder Singh, Martin Mathlongo.'

They smiled at the girl: the shiny-faced African, on a level with her shoulder; the blonde woman with the caked powder cracking on her cheeks; the handsome, scholarly-looking Indian with the high, bald dome; the ugly light-coloured man, just light enough for freckles to show thickly on his fleshy face.

She said to her host, 'I'll have the same again, Derek. Your punch.' And even before she had sipped the stuff, she felt a warmth expand and soften inside her, and she said the names over silently to herself – Matt Sha-ba-lala, Martin Math-longo, Ma-hinder Singh. Out of the corner of her eye, as she stood there, she could just see Jessica Malherbe, a short, plump, white woman in an elegant black frock, her hair glossy, like a bird's wing, as she turned her head under the light while she talked.

Then it happened, just when the girl was most ready for it, just when the time had come. The little African named Matt said, 'This is Miss Joyce McCoy – Eddie Ntwala,' and stood looking on with a smile while her hand went into the slim hand of a tall, light-skinned African with the tired, appraising, cynical eyes of a man who drinks too much in order to deaden the pain of his intelligence. She could tell from the way little Shabalala presented the man that he must be someone important and admired, a leader of some sort, whose every idiosyncrasy – the broken remains of handsome, smoke-darkened teeth when he smiled, the wrinkled tie hanging askew – bespoke to those who knew him his distinction in a thousand different situations. She smiled as if to say, 'Of course, Eddie Ntwala himself, I knew it,' and their hands parted and dropped.

The man did not seem to be looking at her – did not seem to be looking at the crowd or at Shabalala, either. There was a slight smile around his mouth, a public smile that would do for anybody. 'Dance?' he said, tapping her lightly on the shoulder. They turned to the floor together.

Eddie Ntwala danced well and unthinkingly, if without

much variation. Joyce's right hand was in his left, his right hand on the concavity of her back, just as if – well, just as if he were anyone else. And it was the first time – the first time in all her twenty-two years. Her head came just to the point of his lapel, and she could smell the faint odour of cigarette smoke in the cloth. When he turned his head and her head was in the path of his breath, there was the familiar smell of wine or brandy breathed down upon her by men at dances. He looked, of course, apart from his eyes – eyes that she had seen in other faces and wondered if she would ever be old enough to understand – exactly like any errand 'boy' or house 'boy'. He had the same close-cut wool on his head, the same smooth brown skin, the same rather nice high cheekbones, the same broad-nostrilled small nose. Only he had his arm around her and her hand in his and he was leading her through the conventional arabesques of polite dancing. She would not let herself formulate the words in her brain: I am dancing with a black man. But she allowed herself to question, with the careful detachment of scientific inquiry, quietly inside herself: 'Do I feel anything? What do I feel?' The man began to hum a snatch of the tune to which they were dancing, the way a person will do when he suddenly hears music out of some forgotten phase of his youth; while the hum reverberated through his chest, she slid her eyes almost painfully to the right, not moving her head, to see his very well-shaped hand – an almost feminine hand compared to the hands of most white men – dark brown against her own white one, the dark thumb and the pale one crossed, the dark fingers and the pale ones folded together. 'Is this exactly how I always dance?' she asked herself closely. 'Do I always hold my back exactly like this, do I relax just this much, hold myself in reserve to just this degree?'

She found she was dancing as she always danced.

I feel nothing, she thought. *I feel nothing.*

And all at once a relief, a mild elation, took possession of her, so that she could begin to talk to the man she was dancing with. In any case, she was not a girl who had much small talk; she knew that at least half the young men who, attracted by her exceptional prettiness, flocked to ask her to dance at parties never asked her again because they could not stand her vast minutes of silence. But now she said in her flat, small voice the few things she could say – remarks about the music and the pleasantness of the rainy night outside. He smiled at her with bored tolerance, plainly not listening to what she said. Then he said, as if to compensate for his inattention, 'You from England?'

She said, 'Yes. But I'm not English. I'm South African, but I've spent the last five years in England. I've only been back in South Africa since December. I used to know Derek when I was a little girl,' she added, feeling that she was obliged to explain her presence in what she suddenly felt was a group conscious of some distinction or privilege.

'England,' he said, smiling down past her rather than at her. 'Never been so happy anywhere.'

'London?' she said.

He nodded. 'Oh, I agree,' she said. 'I feel the same about it.'

'No, you don't, McCoy,' he said very slowly, smiling at her now. 'No, you don't.'

She was silenced at what instantly seemed her temerity.

He said, as they danced around again, 'The way you speak. Really English. Whites in S.A. can't speak that way.'

For a moment, one of the old, blank, impassively pretty-faced silences threatened to settle upon her, but the second glass of arak punch broke through it, and, almost animated, she answered lightly, 'Oh, I find I'm like a parrot. I pick up the accent of the people among whom I live in a matter of hours.'

He threw back his head and laughed, showing the gaps in his teeth. 'How will you speak tomorrow, McCoy?' he said, holding her back from him and shaking with laughter, his eyes swimming. 'Oh, how will you speak tomorrow, I wonder?'

She said, immensely daring, though it came out in her usual small, unassertive feminine voice, a voice gently toned for the utterance of banal pleasantries, 'Like you.'

'Let's have a drink,' he said, as if he had known her a long time – as if she were someone like Jessica Malherbe. And he took her back to the bar, leading her by the hand; she walked with her hand loosely swinging in his, just as she had done with young men at country-club dances. 'I promised to have one with Rajati,' he was saying, 'Where has he got to?'

'Is that the one I met?' said the girl. 'The one with the high, bald head?'

'An Indian?' he said. 'No, you mean Mahinder. This one's his cousin, Jessica Malherbe's husband.'

'She's married to an Indian?' The girl stopped dead in the middle of the dancers. 'Is she?' The idea went through her like a thrill. She felt startled as if by a sudden piece of good news about someone who was important to her. Jessica Malherbe – the name, the idea – seemed to have been circling about her life since before she left England. Even there, she had read about her in the papers: the daughter of a humble Afrikaner farmer, who had disowned her in the name of a stern Calvinist God for her anti-nationalism and her radical views; a girl from a backveld farm – such a farm as Joyce herself could remember seeing from a car window as a child – who had worked in a factory and educated herself and been sent by her trade union to study labour problems all over the world; a girl who negotiated with ministers of state; who, Joyce had learned that evening, had gone to prison for her principles. Jessica Malherbe, who was almost the first person the girl had met when she came in to the party this evening, and who turned out to look like any well-groomed English woman you might see in a London restaurant, wearing a pearl necklace and smelling of expensive perfume. An Indian! It was the final gesture. Magnificent. A world toppled with it – Jessica Malherbe's father's world. An Indian!

'Old Rajati,' Ntwala was saying. But they could not find him. The girl thought of the handsome, scholarly-looking Indian with the domed head, and suddenly she remembered that once, in Durban, she had talked across the counter of a shop with an Indian boy. She had been down in the Indian quarter with her sister, and they had entered a shop to buy a piece of silk. She had been the spokeswoman, and she had murmured across the counter to the boy and he had said, in a voice as low and gentle as her own, no, he was sorry, that length of silk was for a sari, and could not be cut. The boy had very beautiful, unseeing eyes, and it was as if they spoke to each other in a dream. The shop was small and deep-set. It smelled strongly of incense, the smell of the village church in which her grandfather had lain in state before his funeral, the scent of her mother's garden on a summer night – the smell of death and flowers, compounded, as the incident itself came to be, of ugliness and beauty, of attraction and repulsion. For just after she and her sister had left the little shop, they had found themselves being followed by an unpleasant man, whose presence first made them uneasily hold tightly to their handbags but who later, when they entered a busy shop in an attempt to get rid of him, crowded up against them and made an obscene advance. He had had a vaguely Eurasian face, they believed, but they could not have said whether he was white or Indian; in their disgust, he had scarcely seemed human to them at all.

She tried now, in the swarming noise of Derek's room, to hear again in her head the voice of the boy saying the words she remembered so exactly: 'No, I am sorry, that length of silk is for a sari, it cannot be cut.' But the tingle of the alcohol that she had been feeling in her hands for quite a long time became a kind of sizzling singing in her ears, like the sound of bubbles rising in aerated water, and all that she could convey to herself was the curious finality of the phrase: *can-not-be-cut, can-not-be-cut.*

She danced the next dance with Derek. 'You look sweet tonight, old thing,' he said, putting wet lips to her ear. 'Sweet.'

She said, 'Derek, which is Rajati?'

He let go her waist. 'Over there,' he said, but in an instant he clutched her again and was whirling her around and she saw only Mahinder Singh and Martin Mathlongo, the big, freckled coloured man, and the back of some man's dark neck with a businessman's thick roll of fat above the collar.

'Which?' she said, but this time he gestured towards a group in which there were white men only, and so she gave up.

The dance was cut short with a sudden wailing screech as

someone lifted the needle of the gramophone in the middle of the record, and it appeared that a man was about to speak. It turned out that it was to be a song and not a speech, for Martin Mathlongo, little Shabalala, two coloured women and a huge African woman with cork-soled green shoes grouped themselves with their arms hanging about one another's necks. When the room had quietened down, they sang. They sang with extraordinary beauty, the men's voices deep and tender, the women's high and passionate. They sang in some African language and when the song was done the girl asked Eddie Ntwala, next to whom she found herself standing, what they had been singing about. He said simply as a peasant, as if he had never danced with her, exchanging sophisticated banter, 'It's about a young man who passes and sees a girl working in her father's field.'

Roy Wilson giggled and gave him a comradely punch on the arm. 'Eddie's never seen a field in his life. Born and bred in Apex Location.'

Then Martin Mathlongo, with his spotted bow tie under his big, loose-mouthed, strong face, suddenly stood forward and began to sing 'Ol' Man River'. There was something insulting, defiant, yet shamefully supplicating in the way he sang the melodramatic, servile words, the way he kneeled and put out his big hands with their upturned pinkish palms. The dark faces in the room watched him, grinning as if at the antics of a monkey. The white faces looked drunk and withdrawn.

Joyce McCoy saw that, for the first time since she had been introduced to her that evening, she was near Jessica Malherbe. The girl was feeling a strong distress at the sight of the coloured man singing the blackface song, and when she saw Jessica Malherbe, she put – with a look, as it were – all this burden at the woman's feet. She put it all upon her, as if *she* could make it right, for on the woman's broad, neatly made-up face there was neither the sullen embarrassment of the other white faces nor the leering self-laceration of the black.

The girl felt the way she usually felt when she was about to cry, but this time it was the prelude to something different. She made her way with difficulty, for her legs were the drunkest part of her, murmuring politely, 'Excuse me,' as she had been taught to do for twenty-two years, past all the people who stood, in their liquor daze, stolid as cows in a stream. She went up to the trade-union leader, the veteran of political imprisonment, the glossy-haired woman who used good perfume. 'Miss Malherbe,' she said, and her blank, exquisite face might have been requesting an invitation to a garden party. 'Please. Miss Malherbe, I want to go with you next week. I want to march into the location.'

Next day, when Joyce was sober, she still wanted to go. As her brother-in-law had predicted, she felt sick from Derek's punch, and every time she inclined her head a great, heavy ball seemed to roll slowly from one side to the other inside her skull. The presence of this ball, which sometimes felt as if it were her brain itself, shrunken and hardened, rattling like a dried nut in its shell, made it difficult to concentrate, yet the thought that she would march into the location the following week was perfectly clear. As a matter of fact, it was obsessively clear.

She went to see Miss Malherbe at the headquarters of the Civil Disobedience Campaign, in order to say again what she had said the night before. Miss Malherbe did again just what *she* had done the night before – listened politely, was interested and sympathetic, thanked the girl and then gently explained that the movement could not allow anyone but bona fide members to take part in such actions. 'Then I'll become a member now,' said Joyce. She wore today a linen dress as pale as her own skin, and on the square of bare matching flesh at her neck hung a little necklace of small pearls – the sort of necklace that is given to a girl child and added to, pearl by pearl, a new one on every birthday. Well, said Miss Malherbe, she could join the movement, by all means – and would not that be enough? Her support would be much appreciated. But no, Joyce wanted to *do* something; she wanted to march with the others into the location. And before she left the office, she was formally enrolled.

When she had been a member for two days, she went to the

headquarters to see Jessica Malherbe again. This time, there were other people present; they smiled at her when she came in, as if they already had heard about her. Miss Malherbe explained to her the gravity of what she wanted to do. Did she realize that she might have to go to prison? Did she understand that it was the policy of the passive resisters to serve their prison sentences rather than to pay fines? Even if she did not mind for herself, what about her parents, her relatives? The girl said that she was over twenty-one; her only parent, her mother, was in England; she was responsible to no one.

She told her sister Madeline and her brother-in-law nothing. When Tuesday morning came, it was damp and cool. Joyce dressed with the consciousness of the performance of the ordinary that marks extraordinary days. Her stomach felt hollow; her hands were cold. She rode into town with her brother-in-law and all the way his car popped the fallen jacaranda flowers which were as thick on the street beneath the tyres as they were on the trees. After lunch, she took a tram to Fordsburg, a quarter where Indians and people of mixed blood, debarred from living anywhere better, lived alongside poor whites, and where, it had been decided, the defiers were to forgather. She had never been to this part of Johannesburg before, and she had the address of the house to which she was to go written in her tartan-silk-covered notebook in her minute, backward-sloping hand. She carried her white angora jacket over her arm and she had put on sensible flat sandals. I don't know why I keep thinking of this as if it were a lengthy expedition, requiring some sort of special equipment, she thought; actually it'll be all over in half an hour. Jessica Malherbe said we'd pay bail and be back in town by four-thirty.

The girl sat in the tram and did not look at the other passengers, and they did not look at her, although the contrast between them and her was startling. They were thin, yellow-limbed children with enormous sooty eyes; bleary-eyed, shuffling men, whom degeneracy had enfeebled into an appearance of indeterminate old age; heavy women with swollen legs, who were carrying newspaper parcels; young, almost-white factory girls whose dull, kinky hair was pinned up into a decent simulation of fashionable style, and on whose proud, pert faces rouge and lipstick had drawn a white girl's face.

She got off at the stop she had been told to and went slowly up the street, watching the numbers. It was difficult to find out how far she would have to walk, or even, for the first few minutes, whether she was walking in the right direction, because the numbers on the doorways were half obliterated, or ill-painted, or sometimes missing entirely. As in most poor quarters, houses and shops were mixed, and in fact some houses were being used as business premises, and some shops had rooms above, in which, obviously, the shopkeepers and their families lived. The street had a flower name but there were no trees and no gardens. Most of the shops had Indian firm-names amateurishly written on homemade wooden signboards or curlicued and flourished in signwriter's yellow and red across the lintel: Moonsammy Dadoo, Hardware, Ladies Smart Outfitting & General; K. P. Patel & Sons, Fruit Merchants; Vallabhir's Bargain Store. A shoemaker had enclosed the veranda of his small house as a workshop and had hung outside a huge black tin shoe of a style worn in the twenties.

The gutters smelled of rotting fruit. Thin *café-au-lait* children trailed smaller brothers and sisters; on the veranda of one of the little semidetached houses a lean coloured man in shirt-sleeves was shouting, in Afrikaans, at a fat woman who sat on the steps. An Indian woman in a sari and high-heeled European shoes was knocking at the door of the other half of the house. Farther on, a very small house, almost eclipsed by the tentacles of voracious-looking creepers, bore a polished brass plate with the name and consulting hours of a well-known Indian doctor.

The street was quiet enough; it had the dead, listless air of all places where people are making some sort of living in a small way. And so Joyce started when a sudden shriek of drunken laughter came from behind a rusty corrugated-iron wall that seemed to enclose a yard. Outside the wall, someone was sitting on a patch of the tough, gritty grass that sometimes scrabbles a hold for itself on worn city-pavements; as the girl passed, she saw that the person was one of the white women tramps whom she occasionally saw in the city crossing a street with the peculiar glassy purposefulness of the outcast.

She felt neither pity nor distaste at the sight. It was as if, dating from this day, her involvement in action against social injustice had purged her of sentimentality; she did not have to avert her gaze. She looked quite calmly at the woman's bare legs which were tanned with dirt and exposure, to the colour of leather. She felt only, in a detached way, a prim, angry sympathy for the young pale-brown girl who stood nursing a baby at the gate of the house just beyond, because she had to live next door to what was almost certainly a shebeen.

Then, ahead of her in the next block, she saw three cars parked outside a house and knew that that must be the place. She walked a little faster, but quite evenly, and when she reached it – No. 260, as she had been told – she found it was a small house of purplish brick with four steps leading from the pavement to the narrow veranda. A sword-fern in a paraffin tin, painted green, stood on either side of the front door, which had been left ajar, as the front door sometimes is in a house where there is a party. She went up the steps firmly over the dusty imprints of other feet and, leaning into the doorway a little, knocked on the fancy glass panel of the upper part of the door. She found herself looking straight down a passage that had a worn flowered linoleum on the floor. The head of a small Indian girl – low forehead and great eyes – appeared in a curtained archway halfway down the passage and disappeared again instantly.

Joyce McCoy knocked again. She could hear voices and above all the others, the tone of protest in a woman's voice.

A bald white man with thick glasses crossed the passage with quick, nervous steps and did not, she thought, see her. But he might have because, prompted perhaps by his entry to the room from which the voices came, the pretty brunette woman with the efficient manner, whom the girl remembered from the party, appeared suddenly with her hand outstretched and said enthusiastically, 'Come *in*, my dear. Come inside. Such a racket in there! You could have been knocking all day.'

The girl saw that the woman wore flimsy sandals and no

stockings, and that her toenails were painted. The girl did not know why details such as these intrigued her so much or seemed so remarkable. She smiled in greeting and followed the woman into the house.

Now she was really there; she heard her own footsteps taking her down the passage of a house in Fordsburg. There was a faintly spicy smell about the passage; on the wall she caught a glimpse of what appeared to be a photograph of an Indian girl in European bridal dress, the picture framed with fretted gold paper, like a cake frill. And then they were in a room where everyone smiled at her quickly but took no notice of her. Jessica Malherbe was there, in a blue linen suit, smoking a cigarette and saying something to the tall, tousle-headed Roy Wilson, who was writing down what she said. The bald man was talking low and earnestly to a slim woman who wore a man's wristwatch and had the hands of a man. The tiny African, Shabalala, wearing a pair of spectacles with thin tortoiseshell rims, was ticking a pencilled list. Three or four others, black and white, sat talking. The room was brisk with chatter.

Joyce lowered herself gingerly onto a dining-room chair whose legs were loose and swayed a little. And as she tried to conceal herself and sink into the composition of the room, she noticed a group sitting a little apart, near the windows in the shadow of the heavy curtains, and, from the arresting sight of them, saw the whole room as it was beneath the overlay of people. The group was made up of an old Indian woman and a slim Indian boy and another Indian child who were obviously her grandchildren. The woman sat with her feet apart, so that her lap, under the voluminous swathings of her sari, was broad, and in one nostril a jewel twinkled. Her hands were little and beringed – a fat woman's hands. Her forehead was low beneath the coarse black hair and the line of tinsel along the sari, and she looked out through the company of white men and women, Indian men in business suits, Africans in clerkly neatness, as if she were deaf or could not see. Yet when Joyce saw her eyes move, as cold and lacking in interest as the eyes of a tortoise, and her foot stir, asserting an inert force of life like the twitch in a muscle of some supine creature on a mudbank, the girl knew it was not deafness or blindness that kept the woman oblivious of the company but simply the knowledge that this house, this room, was her place. She was here before the visitors came; she would not move for them; she would be here when they had gone. And the children clung with their grandmother, knowing that she was the kind who could never be banished to the kitchen or some other backwater.

From the assertion of this silent group the girl became aware of the whole room (*their* room), of its furnishings: the hideous 'suite' upholstered in imitation velvet with a stamped design of triangles and sickles; the yellow, varnished table with the pink silk mat and the brass vase of paper roses; the easy chairs with circular apertures in the arms where coloured glass ashtrays were balanced; the crudely coloured photographs; the barbola vase; the green ruched-silk cushions; the standard lamp with more platforms for more glass ashtrays; the gilded plaster dog that stood at the door. An Indian went over and said something to the old woman with the proprietary, apologetic, irritating air of a son who wishes his mother would keep out of the way; as he turned his head, the girl saw something familiar in the angle and recognized him as the man the back of whose neck she had seen when she was trying to identify Jessica Malherbe's husband at the party. Now he came over to her, a squat, pleasant man, with a great deal of that shiny black Indian hair making his head look too big for his body. He said, 'My congratulations. My wife Jessica tells me you have insisted on identifying yourself with today's defiance. Well, how do you feel about it?'

She smiled at him with great difficulty; she really did not know why it was so difficult. She said, 'I'm sorry. We didn't meet that night. Just your cousin – I believe it is? – Mr Singh.' He was such a remarkably commonplace-looking Indian, Jessica Malherbe's husband, but Jessica Malherbe's husband after all – the man with the roll of fat at the back of his neck.

She said, 'You don't resemble Mr Singh in the least,' feeling that it was herself she offended by the obvious thought behind the comparison, and not this fat, amiable middle-aged man, who needed only to be in his shirt-sleeves to look like any well-to-do Indian merchant, or in a grubby white coat, and unshaven, to look like a fruit-and-vegetable hawker. He sat down beside her (she could see the head of the old woman just beyond his ear), and as he began to talk to her in his Cambridge-modulated voice, she began to notice something that she had not noticed before. It was curious, because surely it must have been there all the time; then again it might not have been – it might have been released by some movement of the group of the grandmother, the slender boy and the child, perhaps from their clothes – but quite suddenly she began to be aware of the odour of incense. Sweet and dry and smoky, like the odour of burning leaves – she began to smell it. Then she thought, it must be in the furniture, the curtains; the old woman burns it and it permeates the house and all the gewgaws from Birmingham, and Denver, Colorado, and American-occupied Japan. Then it did not remind her of burning leaves any longer. It was incense, strong and sweet. The smell of death and flowers. She remembered it with such immediacy that it came back literally, absolutely, the way a memory of words or a vision never can.

'Are you all right, Miss McCoy?' said the kindly Indian, interrupting himself because he saw that she was not listening and that her pretty, pale, impassive face was so white and withdrawn that she looked as if she might faint.

She stood up with a start that was like an inarticulate apology and went quickly from the room. She ran down the passage and opened a door and closed it behind her, but the odour was there, too, stronger than ever, in somebody's bedroom where a big double bed had an orange silk cover. She leaned with her back against the door, breathing it in and trembling with fear and with the terrible desire to be safe: to be safe from one of the kindly women who would come, any moment now, to see what was wrong; to be safe from the gathering up of her own nerve to face the journey in the car to the location, and the faces of her companions, who were not afraid, and the walk up the location street.

The very conventions of the life which, she felt, had insulated her in softness against the sharp, joyful brush of real life in action came up to save her now. If she was afraid, she was also polite. She had been polite so long that the colourless formula of good manners, which had stifled so much spontaneity in her, could also serve to stifle fear.

It would be so *terribly rude* simply to run away out of the house and go home, now.

That was the thought that saved her – the code of a well-brought-up child at a party – and it came to her again and again, slowing down her thudding heart, uncurling her clenched hands. *It would be terribly rude to run away now.* She knew with distress, somewhere at the back of her mind, that this was the wrong reason for staying, but it worked. Her manners had been with her longer and were stronger than her fear. Slowly the room ceased to sing so loudly about her, the bedspread stopped dancing up and down before her eyes, and she went slowly over to the mirror in the door of the wardrobe and straightened the belt of her dress, not meeting her own eyes. Then she opened the door and went down the passage and back again into the room where the others were gathered, and sat down in the chair she had left. It was only then that she noticed that the others were standing – had risen, ready to go.

'What about your jacket, my dear? Would you like to leave it?' the pretty brunette said, noticing her.

Jessica Malherbe was on her way to the door. She smiled at Joyce and said, 'I'd leave it, if I were you.'

'Yes, I think so, thank you.' She heard her own voice as if it were someone else's.

Outside there was the mild confusion of deciding who should go with whom and in which car. The girl found herself in the back of the car in which Jessica Malherbe sat beside the driver. The slim mannish woman got in; little Shabalala got in but was summoned to another car by an urgently waving hand. He got out again, and then came back and jumped in just as they were off. He was the only one who seemed excited. He sat forward, with his hands on his knees. Smiling widely at the girl, he said, 'Now we really are taking you for a ride, Miss McCoy.'

The cars drove through Fordsburg and skirted the city. Then they went out one of the main roads that connect the gold-mining towns of the Witwatersrand with each other and with Johannesburg. They passed mine dumps, pale grey and yellow; clusters of neat, ugly houses, provided for white mineworkers; patches of veld, where the rain of the night before glittered thinly in low places; a brickfield; a foundry; a little poultry farm. And then they turned into a muddy road along which they followed a native bus that swayed under its load of passengers, exhaust-pipe sputtering black smoke, canvas flaps over the windows wildly agitated. The bus thundered ahead through the location gates, but the three cars stopped outside. Jessica Malherbe got out first and stood pushing back the cuticles of the nails of her left hand as she talked in a business-like fashion to Roy Wilson. 'Of course, don't give the statement to the papers unless they ask for it. It would be more interesting to see *their* version first, and come along with our own afterwards. But they *may* ask –'

'There's a press car,' Shabalala said, hurrying up. 'There.'

'Looks like Brand, from the *Post*.'

'Can't be Dick Brand; he's transferred to Bloemfontein,' said the tall, mannish woman.

'Come here, Miss McCoy, you're the baby,' said Shabalala, straightening his tie and twitching his shoulders in case there was going to be a photograph. Obediently, the girl moved to the front.

But the press photographer waved his flash-bulb in protest. 'No, I want you walking.'

'Well, you better get us before we enter the gates or you'll find yourself arrested too,' said Jessica Malherbe, unconcerned. 'Look at that,' she added to the mannish woman, lifting her foot to show the heel of her white shoe, muddy already.

Lagersdorp Location, which they were entering and which Joyce McCoy had never seen before, was much like all such places. A high barbed-wire fence – more a symbol than a means of confinement, since, except for the part near the gates, it had comfortable gaps in many places – enclosed almost a square mile of dreary little dwellings to which the African population of the nearby town came home to sleep at night. There were mean houses and squalid tin shelters and, near the gates where the administrative offices were, one or two decent cottages which had been built by the white housing authorities 'experimentally' and never duplicated; they were occupied by the favourite African clerks of the white location-superintendent. There were very few shops, since every licence granted to a native shop in a location takes business away from the white stores in the town, and there were many churches, some built of mud and tin, some neo-Gothic and built of brick, representing a great many sects.

They began to walk, the seven men and women, towards the location gates. Jessica Malherbe and Roy Wilson were a little ahead, and the girl found herself between Shabalala and the bald white man with thick glasses. The flash-bulb made its brief sensation and the two or three picannins who were playing with tin hoops on the roadside looked up, astonished. A fat native woman selling oranges and roast mealies shouted speculatively to a passer-by in ragged trousers.

At the gateway, a fat black policeman sat on a soapbox and gossiped. He raised his hand to his cap as they passed. In Joyce McCoy, the numbness that had followed her nervous crisis began to be replaced by a calm embarrassment; as a child she had often wondered, seeing a circle of Salvation Army people playing a hymn out of tune on a street corner, how it would feel to stand there with them. Now she felt she knew. Little Shabalala ran a finger around the inside of his collar, and the girl thought, with a start of warmth, that he was feeling as she was; she did not know that he was thinking what he had promised himself he would not think about during this walk – that very likely the walk would cost him his job. People did not want to employ Africans who 'made trouble'. His wife, who was immensely proud of his education and his cleverness, had said nothing when she learned that he was going – had only gone, with studied consciousness, about her cooking. But after all Shabalala, like the girl – though neither he nor she could know it – was also saved by convention. In his case, it was a bold convention – that he was an amusing little man. He said to her as they began to walk up the road, inside the gateway, 'Feel the bump?'

'I beg your pardon?' she said, polite and conspiratorial.

A group of ragged children, their eyes alight with the tenacious beggarliness associated with the East rather than with Africa, were jumping and running around the white members of the party, which they thought was some committee come to judge a competition for the cleanest house, or a baby show. 'Penny, *missus*, penny, penny, *baas*!' they whined. Shabalala growled something at them playfully in their own language before he answered, with his delightful grin. 'The bump over the colour bar.'

Apart from the children, who dropped away desultorily like flying fish behind a boat, no one took much notice of the defiers. The African women carrying on their heads food they had bought in town or bundles of white people's washing, scarcely looked at them. African men on bicycles rode past preoccupied. But when the party came up parallel with the administration offices – built of red brick, and, along with the experimental cottages at the gate and the clinic next door, the only buildings of European standard in the location – a middle-aged white man in a suit worn shiny on the seat and the elbows (his slightly stooping body seemed to carry the shape of his office-chair and desk) came out and stopped Jessica Malherbe. Obediently, the whole group stopped; there was an air of quiet obstinacy about them. The man, who was the location-superintendent himself, evidently knew Jessica Malherbe and was awkward with the necessity of making this an official and not a personal encounter. 'You know that I must tell you it is prohibited for Europeans to enter Lagersdorp Location,' he said. The girl noticed that he carried his glasses in his left hand, dangling by one earpiece, as if he had been waiting for the arrival of the party and had jumped up from his desk nervously at last.

Jessica Malherbe smiled and there was in her smile something of the easy, informal amusement with which Afrikaners discount pomposity. 'Mr Dougal, good afternoon. Yes, of course, we know you have to give us official warning. How far do you think we'll get?'

The man's face relaxed. He shrugged and said, 'They're waiting for you.'

And suddenly the girl, Joyce McCoy, felt this – the sense of something lying in wait for them. The neat stereotyped faces of African clerks appeared at the windows of the administrative offices. As the party approached the clinic, the European doctor, in his white coat, looked out; two white nurses and an African nurse came out onto the veranda. And all the patient African women who were sitting about in the sun outside, suckling their babies and gossiping, sat silent while the party walked by – sat silent, and had in their eyes something of the look of the Indian grandmother, waiting at home in Fordsburg.

The party walked on up the street and on either side, in the little houses which had homemade verandas flanking the strip of worn, unpaved earth that was the pavement or whose front doors opened straight on to a foot or two of fenced garden where hens ran and pumpkins had been put to ripen, doors were open, and men and women stood, their children gathered in around them as if they sensed the approach of a storm. Yet the sun was hot on the heads of the party, walking slowly up the street. And they were silent, and the watchers were silent, or spoke to one another only in whispers, each bending his head to another's ear but keeping his eyes on the group passing up the street. Someone laughed, but it was only a drunk – a wizened little old man – returning from some shebeen. And ahead, at the corner of a crossroad, stood the police car, a black car, with the aerial from its radio-communication equipment a shining lash against all the shabbiness of the street. The rear doors opened and two heavy, smartly dressed policemen got out and slammed the doors behind them. They approached the party slowly, not hurrying themselves. When they drew abreast, one said, as if in reflex, 'Ah – good afternoon.' But the other cut in, in an emotionless official voice, 'You are all under arrest for illegal entry into Lagersdorp Location. If you'll just give us your names...'

Joyce stood waiting her turn, and her heart beat slowly and

evenly. She thought again as she had once before – how long ago was that party? – I feel *nothing*. It's all right. I feel *nothing*.

But as the policeman came to her and she spelled out her name for him, she looked up and saw the faces of the African onlookers who stood nearest her. Two men, a small boy and a woman, dressed in ill-matched cast-offs of European clothing which hung upon them without meaning, like coats spread on bushes, were looking at her. When she looked back, they met her gaze. And she felt, suddenly, not *nothing*, but what they were feeling at the sight of her, a white girl, taken – incomprehensibly, as they themselves were used to being taken – under the force of white men's wills, which dispensed and withdrew life, imprisoned and set free, fed or starved, like God himself.

Friday's Footprint

The hotel stood a hundred yards up from the bank of the river. On the lintel above the screen door at the entrance, small gilt letters read: J. P. Cunningham, Licensed to sell Malt, Wine and Spirituous Liquors; the initials had been painted in over others that had been painted out. Sitting in the office off the veranda at the old, high, pigeon-hole desk stuffed with papers, with the cardboard files stacked round her in record of twenty years, she turned her head now and then to the water. She did not see it, the sheeny, gnat-hazy surface of the tropical river; she rested her eyes a moment. And then she turned back to her invoices and accounts, or wrote out in her large, strong hand the lunch and dinner menus: *Potage of Green Peas, Crumbed Chop and Sauter Potatoes* – the language (to her an actual language) of hotel cooking, that was in fact the garbled remnant influence of the immigrant chef from Europe who had once stuck it out in the primitive kitchen for three months, on his way South to the scope and plush of a Johannesburg restaurant.

She spent most of the day in the office, all year. The only difference was that in winter she was comfortable, it was even cool enough for her to need to wear a cardigan, and in summer she had to sit with her legs spread under her skirt while the steady trickle of sweat crept down the inner sides of her thighs and collected behind her knees. When people came through the squealing screen-door onto the hotel veranda, and hung about in the unmistakable way of new arrivals (this only happened in winter, of course; nobody came to that part of Central Africa in the summer unless they were obliged to) she would sense rather than hear them, and she would make them wait a few minutes. Then she would get up from the desk slowly, grinding back her chair, pulling her dress down with one hand, and appear. She had never learned the obsequious yet superior manner of a hotel-keeper's wife; the truth was that she was shy, and, being a heavy forty-year-old woman she expressed this in lame brusqueness. Once the new guests had signed the register, she was quite likely to go back to her book-keeping without having shown them to their rooms or called a boy to carry their luggage. If they ventured to disturb her again in her office, she would say, astonished, 'Hasn't someone fixed you up? My husband, or the housekeeper? Oh Lord –' and she would go through the dingy company of the grass chairs in the lounge, and through the ping-pong room that smelled strongly of red floor-polish and cockroach repellent, to find help.

But usually people didn't mind their off-hand reception. By the time they arrived at the river village they had travelled two days from the last village over desert and dried-out salt pans; they had slept out under the crushing silence of a night sky that ignored them and held no human sound other than their own small rustlings. They were inclined to emerge from their jeeps feeling unreal. The sight of Mrs Cunningham, in her flowered print dress with a brooch on her big bosom, and her big, bright-skinned face looking clerically dazed beneath her thick permanent, was the known world, to them; Friday's footprint in the sand. And when she appeared in the bar, in the evening, they found out that she was quite nice, after all. She wore a ribbon in her large head of light curly hair, then, and like many fat women she looked suddenly not young but babyish. She did not drink – occasionally she would giggle experimentally over a glass of sweet sherry – and would sit reading a week-old Johannesburg paper that someone had brought up with him in his car.

A man served the drinks with light, spry movements that made everything he did seem like sleight of hand. Is that really Mrs Cunningham's *husband*, newcomers would ask, when they had struck up acquaintance with the three permanent guests – the veterinary officer, the meteorological officer and the post-master. The man behind the bar, who talked out of the curl of his upper lip, was small and slender and looked years younger than she did, although of course he was not – he was thirty-nine and only a year her junior. Outdoors, and in the daylight, his slenderness was the leanness of cured meat, his boy film-star face, with the satyr-shaped head of upstanding curly hair, the black, frown-framed eyes and forward-jutting mouth, was a monkey face, lined, watchful, always old.

Looking at him in the light of the bar, one of the permanent guests would explain, behind his glass, 'Her second husband, of course. Arthur Cunningham's dead. But this one's some sort of relative of her first husband, he's a Cunningham, too.'

Rita Cunningham did not always see nothing when she turned to look at the water. Sometimes (what times? she struggled to get herself to name – oh, times; when she had slept badly, or when – things – were not right) she saw the boat coming across the flooded river. She looked at the wide, shimmering, sluggish water where the waterlilies floated shining in the sun and she began to see, always at the same point, approaching the middle of the river from the other bank, the boat moving slowly under its heavy load. It was their biggest boat; it was carrying eight sewing machines and a black-japanned iron double bedstead as well as the usual stores, and Arthur and three store-boys were sitting on top of the cargo. As the boat reached the middle of the river, it turned over, men and cargo toppled, and the iron bed came down heavily on top of their flailing arms, their arms stuck through the bars as the bed sank, taking them down beneath it. That was all. There was a dazzle of sun on the water, where they had been; the waterlilies were thickest there.

She had not been there when it happened. She had been in Johannesburg on that yearly holiday that they all looked forward to so much. She had been sitting in the best seats on the stand at the Wanderers' Ground, the third day running, watching the international cricket test between South Africa and the visiting New Zealand team. Three of her children were with her – the little boy had the autographs of all the men in both teams; and Johnny was there. Johnny Cunningham, her husband's step-brother, who had worked with them at the hotel and the stores for the last few years, and who, as he did every year since he had begun to work for them, had driven her down to Johannesburg so that she could have a longer holiday than the time her husband, Arthur, could spare away from his work. The arrangement was always that Arthur came down to Johannesburg after his wife had been there for two weeks, and then Johnny Cunningham drove himself back to the hotel alone, to take care of things there.

Ever since she was a girl, she had loved cricket. At home, up in the territory, she'd have the radio going in the hotel office while she worked if there was a cricket commentary on, just as some people might like a little background music. She was happy, that day, high up in the stand in the shade. The grass was green, the figures of the players plaster-white. The sweet, short sound of the ball brought good-natured murmurs, roars of approval, dwindling growls of disappointment following it, from the crowd. There was the atmosphere of ease of people who are well enough off to take a day's holiday from the office and spend it drinking beer, idly watching a game and getting a red, warm look, so that they appear more like a bed of coarse, easy-growing flowers than a crowd of human faces. Every now and then a voice over the loudspeaker would announce some request or other – would the owner of car TJ 986339 please report to the ticket office at once; a lady's fob watch had been lost, and would anyone ... etc.; an urgent telegram, I repeat, an urgent telegram awaits Mr So-and-so ... The voice was addicted to the phrase 'I repeat', and there were mock groans here and there among the crowd every time the voice began to speak – she herself had exchanged a little shrug of amusement with someone in the row ahead who had turned in exasperation at the umpteenth 'I repeat' that day. And then, at exactly quarter past three in the afternoon, her own name was spoken by the voice. 'Will Mrs Rita Cunningham, of Olongwe, I repeat, Olongwe, please report to the main entrance immediately. This is an urgent message for Mrs Rita Cunningham. Will Mrs Cunningham please report...'

She turned to Johnny at once, surprised, pulling a face. 'I wouldn't know,' he said, giving a short, bored laugh. (He preferred a good fast rugby game, any time, but Arthur, wanting to give him a treat, had said to his wife, get a cricket ticket for Johnny, to, take Johnny along one of the days.) She said, smiling and confused, bridling, 'Somebody's making a silly ass of me, calling me out like this.' 'Awright,' he said, slapping down his box of cigarettes and getting up with the quickness of impatience, 'I'll go.' She hesitated a moment; she had suddenly thought of her fourth child, the naughty one, Margie, who had been left playing at the house of the Johannesburg relatives with whom the Cunninghams were staying. 'Oh, I'd better go. I suppose it must be Margie; I wonder what she's gone and done to herself now, the little devil.'

Johnny sat down again. 'Please yourself.' And she got up and made her way down the stand. As soon as she got to the entrance she saw her sister Ruth's car drawn up right at the gates where no one was allowed to park, and before she had seen her sister and her brother-in-law standing there, turned towards her, a throb of dread beat up once, in her throat.

'What happened? Did she run in the street –' she cried, rushing up to them. The man and the woman stared at her as if they were afraid of her. 'Not Margie,' said the man. 'It's not Margie. Come into the car.'

And in the car, outside the cricket ground, still within sound of the plonk of the ball and the voice of the crowd rising to it, they told her that a telegram had come saying that Arthur had been drowned that morning, bringing a boat-load of goods over the flooded river.

She did not cry until she got all the way back to the hotel on the bank of the river. She left the children behind, with her sister (the two elder girls went to boarding-school in Johannesburg, anyway), and Johnny Cunningham drove her home. Once, in the middle of a silence as vast as the waste of sand they were grinding through, she said, 'Who would ever have dreamt it would happen to him. The things he'd done in his time, and never come to any harm.' 'Don't tell me,' Johnny agreed, his pipe between his teeth.

In Johannesburg they had all said to each other, 'It'll hit her when she gets back.' But although she had believed the fact of her husband's death when she was away from the village, in the unreality of the city – once she saw and smelled the village again, once she stepped into the hotel, it all seemed nonsense. Nothing was changed. It was all there, wasn't it? The wildebeest skins pegged out to tan, the old horns half-buried in the sand, the plaster Johnny Walker on the counter in the bar; the river.

Two days later one of the store blacks came over to the hotel with some cheques for her to sign, and, standing in the office doorway with his old hat in his hand, said to her in a hoarse low voice, as if he wanted no one, not even the dead, to overhear, 'He was a good man, Missus, he was a very good man. Oh, missus.' She cried. While she wrote her name on the cheques and silently handed them back to the elderly black man, it came: strong pity for Arthur, who had been alive, as she was, and was now dead. When she was alone again she sat on at the desk staring at the spikes of invoices and the rubber stamps and the scratched and ink-stained wood, and she wept in pity for the pain of that strong, weathered man, filling his lungs with water with every breath under the weight of the iron bedstead. She wept at the cruel fact of death; perhaps that was not quite what her relatives in Johannesburg had meant when they had said that 'it would hit her when she got home' – but she wept, anyway.

Slowly, in short bursts of confidence that stopped abruptly or tailed off in embarrassment, people began to talk to her about the drowning. This one spared her this detail, another told her it and spared her something else; so it was that she had put together, out of what she had been told, that silent, unreal, orderly picture, scarcely supplemented at all by imagination, since she had very little, that she sometimes saw rise on the river and sink out of sight again.

The facts were simple and horrible. Arthur Cunningham had been doing what he had done dozens of times before; what everyone in the village had done time and again, whenever the river was flooded and the bridge was down. The bridge was either down, or under water, almost every year, at the height of the rainy season, and when this happened the only way to reach the village was by boat. That December day there was a pack of stuff to get across the river – all the food for the hotel and the store goods, that had come up North by truck. Arthur Cunningham was the sort of man who got things done himself; that was the only way to get them done. He went back and forth with the blacks four times, that morning, and they were making some headway. 'Come on, let's see if we c'n git things going,' he kept chivvying at the white assistants who were in charge of unloading the trucks, and were sweating with haste and the nervous exhaustion of working under his eye. 'I dunno, honestly, I've got my boat, I've got my team of boys, and what's happening? I'm waiting for you blokes. Don't tickle that stuff, there, man! For Christ's sake, get cracking. Get it on, get it on!'

The Africans took his manner – snarling, smiling, insulting in its assumption (true) that he could do everything his workers did but in half the time and twice as well – better than the white men. They laughed and grumbled back at him, and groaned under his swearing and his taunts. When the boat was fully loaded for the fifth trip, he noticed the black-japanned double bed, in its component parts but not assembled, propped against a grate. 'What about that thing?' he yelled. 'Don't keep leaving that behind for the next lot, you bloody fools. Get it on, get it on. That's a new bed for the Chief's new wife, that's an important order,' and he roared with laughter. He went up to a pimply little 22-year-old clerk, whose thin hair, tangled with the rims of his glasses, expressed wild timidity. 'You shouldn't be too young to know how important a nice comfortable big bed is? You expect the old Chief to wait till tomorrow? How'd'jou feel, if you were waiting for that beautiful bed for a beautiful new woman –' and while the young man peered at him, startled, Arthur Cunningham roared with laughter again.

'Mr Cunningham, the boat's full,' another white assistant called.

'Never mind, full! Put it on, man. I'm sick of seeing that bed lying here. Put it on!'

'I don't know how you'll get it over, it makes the whole load top-heavy.'

Arthur Cunningham walked up to his clerk. He was a man of middle height, with a chest and a belly, big, hard and resonant, like the body of a drum, and his thick hands and sandy-haired chest, which always showed in the open neck of his shirt, were blotched and wrinkled with resistance to and in tough protection against the sun. His face was red and he had even false teeth in a lipless mouth that was practical-looking rather than mean or unkind.

'Come on, Harris,' he said, as if he were taking charge of a child. 'Come on now, and no damn nonsense. Take hold here.' And he sent the man, tottering under the weight of the foot of the bed while he himself carried the head, down to the boat.

Rita had married him when she was twenty-three, and he was sixteen or seventeen years older than she was. He had looked almost exactly the same when she married him as he did the last time ever that she saw him, when he stood in the road with his hands on the sides of his belly and watched the car leave for Johannesburg. She was a virgin, she had never been in love, when she married him; he had met her on one of his trips down South, taken a fancy to her, and that was that. He always did whatever he liked and got whatever he wanted. Since she had never been made love to by a young man, she accepted his command of her in bed as the sum of love; his tastes in love-making, like everything else about him, were formed before she knew him, and he was as set in this way as he was in others. She never knew him, of course, because she had nothing of the deep need to possess his thoughts and plumb his feelings that comes of love.

He was as generous as his tongue was rough, which meant that his tongue took the edge off his generosity at least as often as his generosity took the sting out of his tongue. He had hunted and fished and traded all over Africa, and he had great contempt for travellers' tales. When safari parties stayed at his hotel, he criticized their weapons (What sort of contraption do you call that? I've shot round about fifty lion in my lifetime, without any telescopic sights, I can tell you), their camping equipment (I don't know what all this fuss is about water filters and whatnot. I've drunk water that was so filthy I've had to lean over and draw it into my mouth through a bit of rag, and been none the worse for it) and their general helplessness. But he also found experienced native guides for these people, and lent them the things they had forgotten to buy down South. He was conscious of having made a number of enemies, thinly scattered in that sparsely-populated territory, and was also conscious of his good standing, of the fact that everybody knew him, and of his ownership of the hotel, the two stores and whatever power there was in the village.

His step-mother had been an enemy of his, in that far-off childhood that he had overcome long ago, but he had had no grudge against his young step-brother, her son, who must have had his troubles, too, adopted into a house full of Cunninghams. Johnny'd been rolling around the world for ten years or so – America, Mexico, Australia – when he turned up in the territory one day, stony-broke and nowhere in particular to go. Arthur wasn't hard on him, though he chaffed him a bit, of course, and after the boy'd been loafing around the river and hotel for a month Arthur suggested that he might give a hand in one of the stores. Johnny took the hint in good part – 'Got to stop being a bum sometime, I suppose,' he said, and turned out to be a surprisingly good worker. Soon he was helping at the hotel, too – where, of course, he was living, anyway. And soon he was one of the family, doing whatever there was to be done.

Yet he kept himself to himself. 'I've got a feeling he'll just walk out, when he feels like it, same as he came,' Rita said to Arthur, with some resentment. She had a strong sense of loyalty and was always watchful of any attempt to take advantage of her husband, who had in such careless abundance so many things that other men wanted. 'Oh for Pete's sake, Rita, he's a bit of a natural sour-puss, that's all. He lives his life and we live ours. There's nothing wrong with the way he works, and nothing else about old Johnny interests me.'

The thing was, in a community the size of the village, and in the close life of the little hotel, that life of Johnny Cunningham's was lived, if in inner isolation, outwardly under their noses. He ate at table with them, usually speaking only when he was spoken to. When, along with the Cunningham couple, he got drawn into a party of hotel guests, he sat drinking with great ease but seldom bothered to contribute anything to the talk, and would leave the company with an abrupt, sardonic-sounding 'Excuse me' whenever he pleased. The only times he came 'out of his shell', as Rita used to put it to her husband, were on dance nights. He had arrived in the territory during the jive era, but his real triumphs on the floor came with the advent of rock-'n-roll. He learnt it from a film, originally – the lounge of the hotel was the local cinema, too, on Thursday nights – and he must have supplemented his self-teaching on the yearly holidays in Johannesburg. Anyway, he was expert, and on dance nights he would take up from her grass chair one of the five or six lumpy girls from the village at whom he never looked at any other time, let alone spoke to, and would transform her within the spell of his own rhythm. Sometimes he did this with women among the hotel guests, too. 'Look at old Johnny, giving it stick,' Arthur Cunningham would say, grinning, in the scornfully admiring tone of someone praising a performance he wouldn't stoop to, himself. There was something about Johnny, his mouth slightly open, the glimpse of saliva gleaming on his teeth, his head thrown back and his eyes narrowed while his body snaked on stooping legs and nimble feet, that couldn't be ignored. 'Well, he seems to be happy that way,' Rita would say with a laugh, embarrassed for the man.

Sometimes Johnny slept with one of these women guests (there was no bed that withheld its secrets from the old German housekeeper, who, in turn, insisted on relating all she knew to Rita Cunningham). It was tacitly accepted that there was some sort of connection between the rock-'n-roll performance and the assignation; who would ever notice Johnny at any other time? But in between these infrequent one-or two-night affairs, he took no interest in women, and it seemed clear that marriage was something that never entered his head. Arthur paid him quite well, but he seemed neither to save nor to have any money. He bet (by radio, using the meteorological officer's broadcast set) on all the big races in Cape Town,

Durban and Johannesburg, and he had bought three cars, all equally unsuitable for road conditions up in the territory, and tinkered them to death in Arthur's workshop.

When he came back to the hotel with Rita Cunningham after Arthur was drowned, he went on with his work as usual. But after a week, all the great bulk of work, all the decisions that had been Arthur's, could not be ignored any longer by considerate employees hoping to spare the widow. She said to Johnny at lunch, in her schoolgirlish way, 'Can you come to the office afterwards? I mean, there're some things we must fix up –' When she came into the office he was already there, standing about like a workman, staring at the calendar on the wall. 'Who's going to see that the store orders don't overlap, now?' she said. 'We've got to make that somebody's job. And somebody'll have to take over the costing of perishable goods, too, not old Johnson, Arthur always said he didn't have a clue about it.'

Johnny scratched his ear and said, 'D'jou want me to do it?'

They looked at each other for a moment, thinking it over. There was no sign on his face either of eagerness or reluctance.

'Well, if you could, Johnny, I think that's best...' And after a pause, she turned to something else. 'Who can we make responsible for the bar – the ordering and everything – D'you think we should try and get a man?'

He shrugged. 'If you like. You could advertise in Jo'burg, or p'raps in Rhodesia. You won't get anybody decent to come up here.'

'I know.' The distress of responsibility suddenly came upon her.

'You could try,' he said again.

'We'll get some old soak, I suppose, who can't keep a job anywhere else.'

'Sure,' he said with his sour smile.

'You don't think,' she said, 'I mean just for now ... Couldn't we manage it between us? I mean you could serve, and perhaps the Allgood boy from the garage could come at weekends to give a hand, and then you and I could do the ordering?'

'Sure,' he said, rocking from his heels to his toes and back again, and looking out of the window, 'I can do it, if you want to try.'

She still could not believe that the wheels of these practical needs were carrying her along, and with her, the hotel and the two stores. 'Oh yes,' she said, distracted, 'I think it'll be O.K., just for the time being, until I can . . .' She did not finish what she was saying because she did not know what it was for which the arrangement was to be a makeshift.

She took it for granted that she meant to sell the hotel and the two stores. Two of the children were at school in the South, already; the other two would have to follow when they had outgrown the village school, in a year or two. What was the point in her staying on, there, in a remote village, alone, seven hundred and fifty miles from her children or her relatives?

She talked, and she believed she acted, for the first six months after Arthur was drowned, as if the sale of the hotel and stores was imminent and inevitable. She even wrote to an agent in Johannesburg, and an old lawyer friend in Rhodesia, asking them their advice about what sort of price she could expect to get for her property and her businesses – Arthur had left everything to her.

Johnny had taken over most of Arthur's work. She, in her turn, had taken over some of Johnny's. Johnny drove back to Johannesburg to fetch the two younger children home, and the hotel and the stores went on as usual. One evening when she was doing some work in the office after dinner and giving half her attention to the talk of hotel matters with him, she added the usual proviso – 'it would do in the meantime.'

Johnny was hissing a tune through his teeth while he looked up the price of a certain brand of gin in a file of liquor wholesalers' invoices – he was sure he remembered Arthur had a cheaper way of buying it than he himself knew – and he stopped whistling but went on looking and said, 'What'll you do with yourself in Johannesburg, anyway, Rita? You'll have money and you won't need a job.'

She put down her pen and turned round, clutching at the straw of any comment on her position that would help her feel less adrift. 'Wha'd'you mean?'

'I suppose you'll buy a house somewhere near your sister and live there looking after the two little kids.'

'Oh, I don't know,' she parried, but faltering, 'I suppose I'd buy a house...'

'Well, what else could you do with yourself?'

He had made it all absolutely clear to her. It came over her with innocent dismay – she had not visualized it, thought about it for herself: the house in a Johannesburg suburb, the two children at school in the mornings, the two children in bed after seven each night, her sister saying, you must come down to us just whenever you like.

She got up slowly and turned, leaning her rump against the ridge of the desk behind her, frowning, unable to speak.

'You've got something here,' he said.

'But I always wanted to go. The summer ... it's so hot. We always said, one day, when the children...' All her appeals to herself failed. She said, 'But a woman ... it's silly – how can I carry on?'

He watched her with interest but would not save her with an interruption. He smoked and held his half-smoked cigarette between thumb and first finger, turned inward towards his palm. He laughed. 'You are carrying on,' he said. He made a pantomime gesture of magnificence, raising his eyebrows, waggling his head slowly and pulling down the corners of his mouth. 'All going strong. The whole caboodle. What you got to worry about?'

She found herself laughing, the way children laugh when they are teased out of tears.

In the next few weeks, a curious kind of pale happiness came over her. It was the happiness of relief from indecision, the happiness of confidence. She did not have to wonder if she could manage – she had been managing all the time! The confidence brought out something that had been in her all her life, dormant; she was capable, even a good business-woman. She began to take a firm hand with the children, with the hotel servants, with the assistants at the stores. She even wrote a letter to the liquor wholesaler, demanding, on a certain brand of gin, the same special discount that her late husband had squeezed out of him.

When the lawyer friend from Rhodesia, who was in charge of Arthur's estate, came up to consult with her, she discussed with him the possibility of offering Johnny – not a partnership, no – but some sort of share, perhaps a fourth share in the hotel and the stores. 'The only thing is, will he stay?' she said. 'Why shouldn't he stay?' said the lawyer, indicating the sound opportunity that was going to be offered to the man. 'Oh, I don't know,' she said. 'I always used to say to Arthur, I had the feeling he was the sort of man who would walk off, one day, same as he came.' In view of the steady work he had done – 'Oh I must be fair,' Rita hastened to agree with the lawyer, 'he *has* worked terribly hard, he's been wonderful, since it happened' – the lawyer saw no cause for concern on this point; in any case the contract, when he drew it up, would be a watertight one, and would protect her interests against any such contingency.

The lawyer went home to Rhodesia to draw up the contract that was never needed. In three months, she was married to Johnny. By the time the summer rainy season came round, and he was the one who was bringing the supplies across the river in the boat, this year, he was her husband and Arthur's initials were painted out and his were painted in, in their place, over the door.

To the meteorological officer, the veterinary officer and the postmaster – those permanent residents of the hotel who had known them both for years – and the people of the village, the marriage seemed quite sensible, really; a matter of convenience – though, of course, also rather funny – there were a number of jokes about it current in the village for a time. To her – well, it was not until after the marriage was an accomplished fact that she began to try to understand what it was, and what had brought it about.

At the end of that first winter after Arthur's death, Johnny had had an affair with one of the women in a safari party that was on its way home to the South. Rita knew about it, because, as usual, the housekeeper had told her. But on the day the party left (Rita knew which woman it was, a woman not young, but with a well-dieted and massaged slimness) Johnny came into the office after the two jeeps had left and plonked himself down in the old cane chair near the door. Rita turned her head at the creak of the cane, to ask him if he knew whether the cook had decided, for the lunch menu, on a substitute for the chops that had gone off, and his eyes, that had been closed in one of those moments of sleep that fall like a shutter on lively, enervated wakefulness, flew open. He yawned and grinned, and his one eye twitched, as if it winked at her of itself. 'Boy, that's that,' he said.

It was the first time, in the seven years he had been at the hotel, that he had ever, even obliquely, made any sort of comment on the existence of his private life or the state of his feelings. She blushed, like a wave of illness. He must have seen the red coming up over the skin of her neck and her ears and her face. But, stonily, he didn't mind her embarrassment or feel any of his own. And so, suddenly, there was intimacy; it existed between them as if it had always been there, taken for granted. They were alone together. They had an existence together apart from the hotel and the stores and the making of decisions about practical matters. He wouldn't have commented to her on his affair with a woman while Arthur was alive and she herself was a married woman. But now, well – it was in his careless face – she was simply a grown-up person, like any other, and she knew that babies weren't found under gooseberry bushes.

After that, whenever he came into the office, they were alone together. She felt him when she sat at her desk with her back to him; her arms tingled into goose-flesh and she seemed to feel a mocking eye (not his, she knew he was not looking at her) on a point exactly in the middle of the back of her neck. She did not know whether she had looked at him or not, before, but now she was aware of the effort of not looking at him, while he ate at table with her, or served in the bar, or simply ran, very lithe, across the sandy road.

And she began – it was an uncomfortable, shameful thing to her, something like the feeling she had had when she was adolescent – to be conscious of her big breasts. She would fold her arms across them when she stood talking to him. She hated them – jutting from her under-arm nearly to her waist, filling her dress – and the hidden nipples that were brown as an old bitch's teats since the children were born. She wanted to hide her legs, too – so thick and strong, the solid-fleshed, mottled calves with their bristly blond hairs, and the heavy bone of the ankles marked with bruises where, bare-legged, she constantly bumped them against her desk.

She said to him one morning after a dance night at the hotel – it simply came out of her mouth, 'That Mrs Burns seems to have taken a fancy to you.'

He gave a long, curly-mouthed yawn. He was looking into space, absent; and then he came to himself, briskly; and he smiled slowly, right at her. 'Uh, that. Does she?'

She began to feel terribly nervous. 'I mean I – I – thought she had her eye on you. The way she was laughing when she danced with you.' She laughed, jeering a little.

'She's a silly cow, all right,' he said. And as he went out of the bar, where they were checking the empties together, he put his hand experimentally on her neck, and tweaked her earlobe. It was an ambiguous caress; she did not know whether he was amused by her or if . . . he meant it, as she put it to herself.

He did not sleep with her until they were married; but, of course, they were married soon. He moved into the big bedroom with her, then, but he kept on his old, dingy rondavel outside the main building, for his clothes and his fishing tackle and the odds and ends of motor-car accessories he kept lying about, and he usually took his siesta in there, in the summer. She lay on her bed alone in the afternoon dark behind the curtains that glowed red with the light and heat that beat upon them from outside, and she looked at his empty bed. She would stare at that place where he lay, where he actually slept, there in the room with her, not a foot away, every night. She had for him a hundred small feelings more tender than any she had ever known, and yet included in them were what she had felt at other rare moments in her life: when she had seen a bird, winged by a shot, fall out of flight formation over the river; when she had first seen one of her own children, ugly, and crying at being born. Sometimes, at the beginning, she would go over in her mind the times when he had made love to her; even at her desk, with the big ledgers open in front of her, and the sound of one of the boys rubbing the veranda floor outside, her mind would let fall the figures she was collating and the dreamy recapitulation of a night would move in. He did not make love to her very often, of course – not after the first few weeks. (He would always pinch her, or feel her arm, when he thought of it, though.) Weeks went by and it was only on dance nights, when usually she went to their room long before him, that he would come in, moving lightly, breathing whisky in the dark, and come over to her as if by appointment. Often she heard him sigh as he came in. He always went through the business of love-making in silence; but to her, in whom a thousand piercing cries were deafening without a sound, it was accepted as part of the extraordinary clamour of her own silence.

As the months went by, he made love to her less and less often, and she waited for him. In tremendous shyness and secrecy, she was always waiting for him. And, oddly, when he did come to her again, next day she would feel ashamed. She began to go over and over things that had happened in the past; it was as if the ability to re-create in her mind a night's love-making had given her a power of imagination she had never had before, and she would examine in re-creation, detail by detail, scenes and conversations that were long over. She began always to have the sense of searching for something; searching slowly and carefully. That day at the cricket. A hundred times, she brought up for examination the way she had turned to look at Johnny, when the voice called her name; the way he had laughed, and said, please yourself. The silence between them in the car, driving back to the territory. The dance nights, long before that, when she had sat beside Arthur and watched Johnny dance. The times she had spoken distrustfully of him to Arthur. It began to seem to her that there was something of conspiracy about all these scenes. Guilt came slowly through them, a stain from deep down. She was beset by the impossibility of knowing – and then again she believed without a doubt – and then, once more, she absolved herself – was there *always* something between Johnny and her? Was it there, waiting, a gleaming eye in the dark, long before Arthur was drowned? All she could do was go over and over every shred of evidence of the past, again and again, reading now yes into it, now no.

She began to think about Arthur's drowning; she felt, crazily, that she and Johnny *knew* Arthur was drowning. They sat in the Wanderers' stand while they knew Arthur was drowning. While there, over there, right in front of the hotel, where she was looking, through the office window (not having to get up from the desk, simply turning her head) the boat with the eight sewing machines and the black-japanned double bed was coming over the water... The boat was turning over... The arms of the men (who was it who had taken care not to spare her that detail?) came through the iron bed-head; it took the men down with it – Arthur with his mouth suddenly stopped for ever with water.

She did not say one word to Johnny about all this. She would not have known how to put it into words, even to herself. It had no existence outside the terrifying freedom of her own mind, that she had stumbled down into by mistake, and that dwarfed the real world about her. Yet she changed, outwardly, protectively, to hide what only she knew was there – the shameful joy of loving. It was then that she started to talk about Johnny as 'he' and 'him', never referring to him by name, and to speak of him in the humorous, half-critical, half-nagging way of the wife who takes her husband for granted, no illusions and no nonsense about it. 'Have you seen my spouse around?' she would ask, or 'Where's that husband of mine?'

On dance nights, in the winter, he still astonished guests by his sudden emergence from taciturnity into rock-'n-roll. The housekeeper no longer told any tales of his brief ventures into the beds where other men's women slept, and so, of course, Rita presumed there weren't any. For herself, she learned to live with her guilt of loving, like some vague, chronic disorder. It was no good wrestling with it; she had come to understand that – for some reason she didn't understand – the fact, the plain fact that she had never committed the slightest disloyalty to Arthur all through their marriage, provided no cure of truth. She and Johnny never quarrelled, and if the hotel and the businesses didn't expand (Arthur was the one for making plans and money) at least they went on just as before. The summer heat, the winter cool, came and went again and again in the reassuring monotony that passes for security.

The torture of imagination died away in her almost entirely. She lost the power to create the past. Only the boat remained, sometimes rising up from her mind on the river through the commonplace of the day in the office, just as once her nights with Johnny had come between her and immediate reality.

One morning in the fourth winter of their marriage, they were sitting at table together in the hotel dining room, eating the leisurely and specially plentiful breakfast of a Sunday. The dining room was small and friendly; you could carry on a conversation from one table to the next. The meteorologist and the postmaster sat together at their table, a small one near the window, distinguished by the special sauce bottles and the bottles of vitamin pills and packet of crispbread that mark the table of the regular from that of the migrant guest in an hotel. The veterinary officer had gone off for a weekend's shooting. There were two tables of migrants in the room; one had the heads of three gloomy lion hunters bent together in low discussion over their coffee, the other held a jolly party who had come all the way from Cape Town, led by a couple who had been in the territory and stayed at the hotel twice or three times before. They had received a bundle of newspapers by post from the South the day before, and they were making them do in place of Sunday papers. Johnny was fond of the magazine sections of newspapers; he liked the memoirs of famous sportsmen or ex-spies that were always to be found in them, and he liked to do the crossword. He had borrowed the magazine section of a Johannesburg paper from one of the party and had done the crossword while he ate his bacon and fried liver and eggs. Now, while he drank a second or third cup of coffee, he found a psychological quiz, and got out his pencil again.

'He's like a kid doing his homework,' said Rita, sitting lazily in her chair, with her heavy legs apart and her shoulders rounded, smoking over her coffee. She spoke over her shoulder, to the people who had lent the paper, and smiled and jerked her head in the direction of her husband.

'Isn't he busy this morning?' one of the women agreed.

'Hardly been able to eat a thing, he's been so hard at it,' said the man who had been at the hotel before. And, except for the lion hunters, the whole dining room laughed.

'Just-a-minute,' Johnny said, lifting a finger but not looking up from his quiz. 'Just-a-minute – I got a set of questions to answer here. You're in this too, Rita. You got to answer, too, in this one.'

'Not me. You know I've got no brains. You don't get me doing one of those things on a Sunday morning.'

'Doesn't need brains,' he said, biting off the end of his sentence like a piece of thread. ' "How good a husband are you" – there you are –'

'As if he needs a quiz to tell him that' she said, at the Cape Town party, who at once began to laugh at the scepto-comical twist to her face. 'I'll answer that one, my boy.' And again they all laughed.

'Here's yours,' he said, feeling for his coffee cup behind the folded paper. ' "How good a wife are you?" –'

'Ah that's easy,' she said, pretending to show off. 'I'll answer that one, too.'

'You go ahead,' he said, with a look to the others, chin back, mouth pursed down. 'Here you are – "Do you buy your husband's toilet accessories, or does he choose his own?" '

'Come again?' she said. 'What they mean, toilet accessories?'

'His soap, and his razor and things,' called a man from the other table. 'Violet hair-oil to put on his hair!'

Johnny ran a hand through his upstanding curls and shrank down in his seat.

Even the postmaster, who was rather shy, twitched a smile.

'No, but seriously,' said Rita through the laughter. 'How can I choose a razor for a man? I ask you!'

'All they want to know is, do you or don't you?' said Johnny. 'Come on, now.'

'Well, if it's a razor, of course I don't,' Rita said, appealing to the room.

'Right! You don't. "No",' Johnny wrote.

'Hey – wait a minute, what about the soap? I do buy the soap. I buy the soap for every man in this hotel! Don't I get any credit for the soap –'

There were cries from the Cape Town table – 'Yes, that's not fair, Johnny, if she buys the soap.' 'She buys the soap for the whole bang shoot of us.'

Johnny put down the paper. 'Well, who's she supposed to be a good wife *to*, anyway?'

All ten questions for the wife were gone through in this manner, with interruptions, suggestions and laughter from the dining room in general. And then Johnny called for quiet while he answered his ten. He was urged to read them out, but he said no, he could tick off his yes's and no's straight off; if he didn't they'd all be sitting at breakfast until lunch time. When he had done, he counted up his wife's score and his own, and turned to another page to see the verdict.

'Come on, let's have it,' called the man from the Cape Town table. 'The suspense is horrible.'

Johnny was already skimming through the column. 'You really want to hear it?' he said. 'Well, I'm warning you ...'

'Oh, get on with it,' Rita said, with the possessive, irritated yet placid air of a wife, scratching a drop of dried egg-yolk off the print bosom of her dress.

'Well, here goes,' he said, in the tone of someone entering into fun of the thing. '"There is clearly something gravely wrong with your marriage. You should see a doctor or, better still, a psychiatrist,"' he paused for effect, and the laugh, '"and seek help, as soon as possible."'

The man from Cape Town laughed till the tears ran into the creases at the corners of his eyes. Everyone else laughed and talked at once: 'If that isn't the limit!' 'This psychology stuff!' 'Have you ever –!' 'Is there anything they *don't* think of in the papers these days!'

'There it is, my dear,' said Johnny, folding the paper in mock solemnity, and pulling a funereal yet careless face.

She laughed with them. She laughed looking down at her shaking body where the great cleft that ran between her breasts showed at the neck of her dress. She laughed and she heard, she alone heard, the catches and trips in her throat like the mad cries of some creature buried alive. The blood of a blush burned her whole body with agonizing slowness. When the laughter had died down she got up and, not looking at Johnny – for she knew how he looked, she knew that unembarrassed gaze – she said something appropriate and even funny, and with great skill went easily, comfortably sloppily, out of the dining room. She felt Johnny following behind her, as usual, but she did not fall back to have him keep up with her, and, as usual after breakfast, she heard him turn off, whistling, from the passage into the bar, where there was the aftermath of Saturday night to clear up.

She got to the office. At last she got to the office and sat down in her chair at the roll-top desk. The terrible blush of blood did not abate; it was as if something had burst inside her and was seeping up in a stain through all the layers of muscle and flesh and skin. She felt again, as she had before, a horrible awareness of her big breasts, her clumsy legs. She clenched her hand over the sharp point of a spike that held invoices and felt it press into her palm. Tears were burning hot on her face and her hands, the rolling lava of shame from that same source as the blush. And at last, Arthur! she called in a clenched, whimpering whisper, Arthur! grinding his name between her teeth, and she turned desperately to the water, to the middle of the river where the lilies were. She tried with all her being to conjure up once again out of the water *something*; the ghost of comfort, of support. But that boat, silent and unbidden, that she had so often seen before, would not come again.

The Night the Favourite Came Home

Duncan Miller and Freda Grant arrived at Roodekraal Mine the night the favourite came home. Freda was a South African herself, and Duncan had lived in the country on and off for many years, but when they walked into the house on the mine property where they were to be guests for the night, it was as if they had walked into some foreign village on the birthday of a local saint of whom they had never heard.

'Don't mind the racket, eh,' said their host, Alfred Ardendyck, coming across the lawn in a stream of bright light from the front door to greet them. 'Vera backed the winner today and the whole house's been celebrating since three o'clock. She promised the kids half-a-crown each and they just tearing around instead of going to bed. – Please to meet you, Mrs Miller. – Well, Dunkie, you old bastard – how's it, eh? – Come inside, Mrs Miller.' And he took Freda's overnight case from her and shepherded the couple up the steps and into the house.

Freda felt foolish rather than guilty at being called 'Mrs Miller'; Duncan had thought it simpler not to explain to a chap like Ardendyck that he and Freda, though they had lived and worked together for years, were not actually married, and never pretended to be. Ardendyck had been in the same hut with Duncan as a prisoner-of-war in Germany for three years of the war. Duncan had suddenly met him again, after thirteen years, one morning in a Johannesburg street, and in the course of the long talk in a bar that had followed, Duncan had promised that when one of their field trips took Freda and him up Alfred's way, in the Northern Transvaal, they would stop over at the Roodekraal Mine and spend the night at Alfred's house.

'This business of chaps one knew in the war,' Duncan had

said to her. 'It's like one's first girl. Afterwards you develop the faculty of natural selection, you seek out your own kind or the kind you aspire to be. But the first one's simply a girl. A prototype, one of those basic outline drawings that represent the female population in a comparative graph. In a prison camp, the chap who sleeps and lives next to you is simply a man, the prototype friend. Alfred was a good sort. I don't know what he's like at home, of course. I can only think of him in the simplest human terms – he used to play cards with the guards and swap the cigarettes he won off them with me, for my chocolate. I didn't know what he thought about.' And Duncan smiled at Freda, his glasses moving with a gleam; he was a small, lean, ugly man, with the smile of a shy girl. Only she, of all the people he had ever known, knew what *he* thought about; of that she was aware. No one else. Certainly not the little girl he had once been married to, when he was a student.

They entered the Ardendyck house past three gaping boys in short pyjamas that bared big pink legs and large feet. 'Garn you three, buzz off.' Their father gave them the verbal equivalent of an affectionate cuff, and, grumbling, they retreated just far enough up the passage to let the guests go by into the living room. Sobbing and shouting came from the radio, there was a hissing crescendo, as if a dragon were shut away somewhere, coming from the kitchen; a one-eyed spaniel lay, belly up, before the fire, and two guests, a grey-haired woman with pearl ear-rings weighing down her ears, and a skinny man with the open collar of his shirt showing his Adam's apple, turned in the composed expectancy of greeting. 'This's Bill Hamilton and over here's his wife, Cora, another one of these girls who cleaned up on the race this afternoon.' There was an air of placid triumph about Mrs Hamilton; she took, as if they were only her due, the polite exclamations of surprise and congratulation that Freda and Duncan immediately offered.

Freda was carrying a flowered drawstring plastic bag that held toilet bottles that couldn't be trusted not to leak in a suitcase, and of course, her books. She was being urged towards Mr Hamilton's swing chair, beside the fire, and at the same time was being asked by Alfred Ardendyck, 'What'll you have?

What you gonna have, eh, Mrs Miller?' She realized that she was not going to be shown to the room where she and Duncan were to sleep, and hastily sat down and stowed away her belongings beside her chair, like someone who has brought a musical instrument along to a party and is alert enough to discover at once that it is not to be a musical evening after all. She prided herself, in a quiet, solitary way, on the manner in which she adapted herself to her company; she could sit at a tribal beer drink (the work that she and Duncan did – research into the relation between malnutrition and African tribal life, on the one hand, and detribalized urban life on the other – sometimes brought them invitations of this kind) or among the black ties and crackling shirt-fronts at the formal dinner of some dull learned society, with equal naturalness. It was her form of humility; her way of showing that she knew and believed that her own particular way of life was not to be valued above other people's.

'What race meeting was this?' she said, taking her whisky and water from Alfred with a smile and turning conversationally to the grey-haired woman. The burst of laughter, the yell from Alfred Ardendyck, over at a cabinet whose front was let down like a drawbridge to bear a full load of whisky and brandy and gin bottles, orange squash and Coca-Cola and fancy glasses – this outburst made her memory wince to attention; her laughter came only a split second after theirs, as if her question really had been a joke. Who else in that room could have believed it to be anything else? There wasn't a child above the age of five, in South Africa, who didn't know about the Durban July Handicap. The first Saturday in July, when it was run, came round as regularly as Christmas, and was accorded nearly as much publicity. The newspapers spoke of 'the classic of the South African turf' and the posters announced, seasonally, S.A. IN GRIP OF JULY FEVER. She had seen the posters herself, of course, that morning, before they left Johannesburg, on every street corner. But her mind must have travelled over them harmlessly, like a magnet over a surface in which there is no particle with which it has affinity.

At this point a small boy, younger than the three who had hung about the front door, ran into the room and threw a half-eaten piece of toast into the fire. The bigger ones followed and stopped short, eyeing him from outside the orbit of grownups in which he had taken sanctuary. At the same time, a heavy woman came in forcefully, fresh from some sort of bustle, her legs – muscular and heavy-boned and shapely as a wrestler's – and great strong feet bearing crushingly down on black sandals with very high heels.

She was grinning as if she couldn't help it; the grin retained its personal, private and gleeful nature through the pleasantries of introduction. 'I've just been getting the kids' supper down their necks,' she said to Freda, standing with her hands on her hips as if looking round for the next thing that had to be done; dazed and exhilarated. 'They're nearly as bad as I am; and I don't know if I'm coming or going.' She giggled suddenly. Then she said, with grandeur, 'I won eighty-five pounds today!' And giggled again. 'So you must excuse me.'

'It must be a wonderful feeling,' said Freda. 'I mean it's a different sort of money. Not like money you've worked for. It's like magic.'

'*Go out now, Basil, man, go on out, all of you*,' said Mrs Ardendyck, tossing her head at her sons. They broke into a stir of grumbling exclamations, grunting, moaning, shrilling. 'Awh-h-h!' 'Mommy!' And they settled down again, perhaps a foot nearer the door, in attitudes of exaggerated protest, one hanging his arm thuggishly round the neck of his brother, another unplaiting the cord of his pyjama trousers. Mrs Ardendyck sat down on the sofa, beside the radiogram. She looked as if she would get up again at once; but instead she yelled, 'Alfred, you so-and-so, you've gone and pinched my drink.' Powerful as an ostrich's, her leg tipped against a little three-legged table, rocking the empty glass and full ashtray that stood on it.

'Don't be a clot, Vera, here's your drink on the mantelpiece, where you left it.'

She crossed her legs, leaned back in her chair and took the glass from him, eyeing it imperiously before she drank from it.

'Trouble with you women, you getting too big for your boots, after today,' said Bill Hamilton.

Mrs Ardendyck ran her freckled, square-fingered hands through closely-curly, brilliantined, bright hair. 'You'n my old man are so darned jealous you could spit blood. You are! You are!'

'But the money's all in the family, isn't it!' said Duncan. 'The husband can't lose if the wife wins, can he?'

Alfred gave a snorting laugh. 'That's what you think.'

'You should've seen him this afternoon,' said Mrs Ardendyck, a woman confident of the attention of her audience. 'Boy, you should have seen him. I was shouting Full House – it was just when they came round the second bend and until then the radio hadn't even mentioned that horse's name, he was right out of the running, he didn't get away at all, you know, and then suddenly he came up like that. There I was yelling Full House for all I was worth, and *he's* saying all the time, shut up, shut up, let's hear the race. Then Bojangles is mentioned for the first time. He nearly puts his hand over my mouth –'

'Ataboy!' said Bill Hamilton, while Alfred swaggered with laughter.

'Honest to God,' said Mrs Ardendyck. 'I'm telling you. He tries to do this' – she put her hand over her mouth; her shrewd hazel eyes signalled a furious pantomime of indignation. 'It's Bojangles, he yells – and I'm pulling his hand away all the time – it's Bojangles, lemme listen! And there we are struggling, and he's shouting Bojangles and I'm shouting Full House, and we never heard a thing over the radio. Not a thing! I'm telling you! Next thing is, the race's over and they waiting for the photo-finish. But I wasn't worried, you know.'

'She fancied Full House right from the beginning,' Alfred explained to Duncan. 'She said to me, the end of February it must have been, I want you to put something for me on Full House. And I thought she was crazy, man, I wanted to talk her out of it –' He began to replenish everyone's drinks. The noise of frying rose higher, and the smell of fat came into the warmth of the room and made the spaniel restless. The radio changed tempo and the eldest boy said 'Oh boy!' and began to jump about, pumping the arms of his brother. Mrs Ardendyck had settled down to discuss her success with Duncan and Freda. 'I had three separate bets on him, you know. I got him twenty-to-one, twelve-to-one and seven-to-one. I would have got him ten-to-one the last time, but Alfred, the clot, put off going to town to lay my money for me that day, and by the time he got round to it, the odds were down.'

'Vera just can't go wrong,' said Mrs Hamilton feebly. 'She fancies something, you can be sure your money's safe. Five of us were in with her.' She stayed Alfred's hand as he was about to put a brandy on the arm of her chair. 'No *thanks*. I'm still feeling what I had this afternoon.'

'Oh come on, Cora,' said Mrs Ardendyck. 'For Pete's sake. You only live once and you can only win the July once a year. Snap out of it man.'

'Here's how,' Alfred rounded up the room. 'To Bojangles and me, good losers –'

A peevish catcall from Mrs Hamilton and a yell from Mrs Ardendyck drowned his toast.

A large African woman had been looking coyly round the door, disappearing and coming back again, for the past ten minutes. Mrs Ardendyck had slipped into the technical jargon of punters with the expert's careless assumption that the layman cannot possibly be ignorant of whatever subject the expert's happens to be, and Freda was listening to her with the absolute attention of incomprehension. 'Emma wants you in the kitchen,' Alfred called to his wife, and she got up, her balance in question a moment on her high heels. 'I was going to turn out a smart dinner tonight, but once Full House was in I wasn't going to spend the afternoon in the kitchen. Not me. You don't blame me. All us girls in the syndicate had made a pact, we were going to meet at the club if we won. So there we were, on the phone to each other, and down to the club. It was a real party, Cora?'

Mrs Hamilton looked put out because she did not feel as she felt she ought to feel. 'I drank two brandies much too quickly. I don't like drinking in the afternoon at all.'

'Look at me,' said Mrs Ardendyck. 'On top of the world. You know what I do when I've had one too many? Two Alka-Seltzers and a tablespoon of glucose.' She slapped her middle. 'Don't feel a thing.'

'Emma *wants* you.'

She tousled Alfred's hair, making him spill some of his drink. 'Hell, no, Vera – You're tight, you know.' She crossed her goose-fleshed, quaking red arms in short sleeves and sneered at him; for a moment, the irritations, dissatisfactions and reproaches that twined and intertwined, making the strong and pliant stuff of everyday, showed through the swimming bright surface of celebration. Yesterday, before the race was won, and tomorrow, the day after the day the race was won, appeared briefly. Then Mrs Ardendyck did a few dance-steps in time to the samba that was coming from the radio and stopped short, indicating, with a jerk of her head and a grimace, the servant in the kitchen – 'You should have seen that one in there when the result was announced. I was doing a war-dance, man, and she ran in in a real state. Missus, are you sick, she said, Missus, are you sick. I reckon she thought I was potty or something. – Okay Emma, I'm coming,' she yelled, and went up the passage arguing with her sons, who followed her.

In a few minutes, Duncan and Freda and the Ardendycks went into the next room for dinner. The children had gone to bed and the Hamiltons, it appeared, had eaten before they came – 'Well, you know where the bottle is, Bill,' said Alfred with an expansive gesture, as those who were to dine filed out.

The food was the sort of food Freda and Duncan never cooked for themselves and that turned out to be much nicer than they remembered. There was a strong vegetable broth and liver and onions and a steamed pudding. Duncan kept taking off his glasses and resting them on the table a minute or two, while he looked at the world without them; something he always did when he had had a few drinks and was feeling at ease. Freda refused a whisky with her dinner because she had had two stiff ones already and she knew that if she had any more she would not feel equal to getting up at five o'clock next morning, as she and Duncan must do, if they were to keep to the schedule of their journey and their work.

Before the soup was drunk, there was a tattoo at the front door and Mrs Ardendyck said, triumphantly, 'The Mackenzies, I'll bet. She was in the syndicate with me, too. Going to get herself a new bedroom carpet. You'll see, the whole lot'll be over at our place before the night's out.'

A little woman with a round, excited face tied like a pudding in a silk scarf printed with pictures of Edinburgh Castle and the legend 'God Save The Queen', walked in carrying a covered dish. 'Ah brought you a few wee aspaaragus rolls, Vera. Ah've no ideer what they'll be like. Ah'm that worked up. I couldna even remember how many spoons of flour was needed.' All through the meal people kept arriving; Mrs Ardendyck kept up a two-way conversation, through the open door into the living room, where her guests were gathered, and with her table companions. 'Don't forget I want a helping of the sweets!' one of the men called, from the living room. 'We haven't reached the sweets stage yet, keep your hair on!' she shouted back. Alfred was telling Duncan about his job on the mine. Once Freda asked Mrs Ardendyck whether she had decided what to do with her winnings, and, ample and commanding at the head of the table, smiling at what she heard with that part of her attention that belonged to the room next door, she said, 'One thing, I'm definitely buying myself a bottle of some perfume I've seen. Grace Kelly's perfume. Ten pounds a bottle.'

Alfred turned at this. 'Like hell you are. You must be out of your mind, Vera.'

She ignored him and said to Freda with the disdainful air of a spoilt, petulant beauty, 'It's the only one I like, out of the lot. Too wonderful.'

The moment the last mouthful of pudding was eaten, Mrs Ardendyck scraped back her chair. 'C'mon dear,' she touched Freda on the shoulder – and with the touch noticed Freda, for a moment, the space of a rift in her elation, for perhaps the first time since Freda had come into the house, seeing, in that moment, shrewdly and bluntly, right through Freda's polite friendliness and attention. She continued rather gingerly, 'Let's go in to the others, Mrs Miller. Come on, folks.'

The living room was full. Canvas chairs had been brought in from the stoep and people were sitting on the little tables that were meant to hold glasses.

'Well, you girls certainly livened up the old club this afternoon.'

'How's it, Vera?'

'I'll say. Why did'n you come over and have a spot with us, Henry? We all called out to you but you weren't having any.'

'Next time we won't ask him, that's all.'

'Dreamt about anything for next week's double, Vera?'

'I'm sure to tell you.'

Duncan stood about with a group of men who leaned their weight against whatever support of wall or furniture offered, but Bill Hamilton had kept Freda's chair for her, and no one would hear of her giving it up. She protested quite strenuously, but giving it up, finding room for herself wherever she could, was a privilege of intimacy she was not to be accorded. The chair had got pushed closer to the fire and she sat wedged in, one cheek hectically flushed and the other turned to a man named Iggulden (she and Duncan had been introduced to everyone, as they came into the room). Iggulden drank his beer and said, 'I hear you people travel all over the show,' and they began to talk about the weather and the roads in various parts of the country, which was what travel meant, to him. Freda responded to him with ease and respect, for she knew that he was the kind of man who, though he might not share your enchantment with an historic ruin or your interest in a tribal dance, would not get petulant if you lost your way, and if the lorry stuck, would certainly be able to climb out and fix it. The man called across to his wife, a woman who sat bolt upright on a kitchen chair in the draught from the door, and had not ventured to take off her coat or embroidered woollen gloves, 'Sybil, here's someone who's been just about everywhere in the country.' But the woman seemed to reject the imputation of her interest as if it were something quite outlandish. She screwed up her face with wifely impatience. 'What?'

She looked at Freda; a smile, expressionless and laconic, came and ended abruptly as if the current had failed.

Freda's companion could not help having towards her the attitude of a man to an offering which has not been well received; he lost confidence in their conversation, and it died. For a little while Freda was on the periphery of a three-sided male conversation of which she was a shadowy fourth, but the men began to draw closer and closer round the point of the story one of them was telling, and when she laughed at the innocuously coarse climax, they became aware of her with such surprise and discomfiture that she felt she had been eavesdropping, and sat back in her chair.

Voices competed all round her like barkers on a fairground.

'... Grace Kelly's perfume. It was specially made for her by one of these blokes in France.'

'Man, no. I think I'll have a beer.'

'... but I wouldn't dare tell Alec's mother. She's always trying to get us to sign the pledge and she won't even take a bazaar ticket.'

'There's no more ginger ale. What'll you have with your brandy, Les – coke?'

'D'you know what time I was in town this morning? Quarter past eight. They were just taking the dust-sheets off in Bassett's ... the girls in the showroom always have a yap with me. Those black coats are lovely, I know, but I think it's too late in the season. Then I spent about an hour at the perfume counter. Here – and here – and here – Man, I just had it all over, I tell you ... yes, ten quid a bottle; it's the only one I'd have.'

One couple had brought a small boy and he had woken up the Ardendyck children; they burst in dodging and tumbling among the grownups and stayed, in the face of threats, until their presence was forgotten, when they would leap up on impulse and rush to some other part of the house, carrying off a dish of peanuts or a bottle of Coca-Cola. Someone had turned up the radio in the unconscious desire to provide the excitement of the opposition of one kind of blare against another. Duncan, kept by Alfred Ardendyck at his side, had the bewildered yet pleased look of the class swot who has suddenly been taken up by the gang.

Beneath the protection of the room's uproar, Freda was returned to her own private existence; she looked out at noise and knick-knacks and people – a room so full and at the same time so bare. There were no pictures, unless you counted those of embroidered wool, there were no books or papers. Her gaze went quietly over the curtains with their design of red and yellow cactus, the carpet with its beige and maroon scrolls, the mantelshelf with its population of china figurines, glass animals and miniature liquor bottles. There was no line, no object, no colour that spoke to her silently as she had so often found inanimate things do, even in the most unexpected and alien places. The title of a book she had read, a cup like one she had drunk out of in another place, a photograph, cut out of a newspaper and pinned on the wall, of something she had laughed at or admired – these were the things that leapt seas, made plain foreign tongues and gave into the stranger's hand the connecting thread of his own identity.

She got up and made her way across the room, murmuring good night at dazed, loosely animated faces wherever they happened to turn to her momentarily. 'Mrs Miller!' Alfred sang out. 'Come an' have a drink. This old Dunkie's been pulling a fast one. You better keep him in his place – Come on, have a whisky –' But he was so caught up among shouts of laughter, glasses thrust at him, the fragments of anecdotes and arguments whipping his burly centre like a top, that he did not even notice that she had not taken the drink, and he simply waved her good night, or perhaps was signalling across the room in a gesture meaning something quite other, and not intended for her, that she took as an appropriate one.

'I'm so sorry, but if I don't go to bed now, I know I'll never be able to get up in time tomorrow. You will forgive me –'

Mrs Ardendyck grinned into the apology with warm indifference, interrupted in the middle of an exchange in which the second half of each sentence was exploded in laughter and clutchings: 'All I could do was –' 'True as God, I couldn't –'

She got up and led Freda quickly down the long passage.

'There's the bathroom, lav. next door, I s'pose the kids've left the bath filthy. Here's the room.' She opened the door on a neat, dank spare room with a strip of mat between two beds covered with chintz. She cut short Freda's thanks, standing for a moment, hands on her hips, one foot turning on the pivot of its high heel. Her hair seemed to spring up from her head with a gaiety of its own, her neck was ruddy, her strong nose shone and the outer corners of her eyes were rheumy with laughter. 'Well, I hope you don't freeze, that's all,' she said jauntily, and she was gone.

Freda Grant stood, aware only of the small weight of the toilet bag hanging from her fingers. The chill of the room was like peace. But the noise came back, warmth to a numb limb; the clash of laughter against an engine-room hum of talk, the thumps and bumps and scrapes of movement. She lifted her overnight case – Alfred Ardendyck must have brought it into the room at some point – to the bed and took out her night things and Duncan's. She opened the toilet bag and, still standing in the middle of the room, slowly creamed her face. The children ran in a posse down the passage and up again, smothering giggles and thudding against walls and doors. While she was in the bathroom, one of them turned the handle of the door, which had no key, and she said in the indulgent, sporting voice she used for children, 'What is it?' – but there was only a spluttering sound and a clattering race away back to the party. She spread her coat over the bottom of the bed and wound her watch and put it on the stool that stood between the two beds, and slid her hand between the sheets: there was a good weight of blankets, after all – she would not be cold. A spatter of clapping followed laughter; some sort of performance must have been concluded at the party. She took a pot of handcream from the toilet bag and got into bed, taking note that she would have to get out of bed to switch off the light when she had finished reading – and then she discovered that she had no books.

She must have left the books in the living room beside her chair, or wherever they had been pushed by people's feet. She had a start of painful anxiety at the thought of the books, underfoot, sifting away somewhere inaccessible, lost in a crowd. She jumped out of bed at once, struggled into her dressing-gown and then stood about before the door. How could she go down the passage and hang about, hoping to catch Duncan's eye? How could she march in, before them all, to go scratching about under chairs for her books? But the sense of anxiety persisted. The books were not part of the essential library of reference and scientific books, or even the new books brought along for entertainment, that she and Duncan had left locked up with all their other equipment, in the jeep, but were simply her own personal things, her *Georgics,* a book of poems and a missionary's chronicle of early travels in Africa, that she kept with her always on field trips. If there were delays, if she and Duncan were stranded, she always knew that she had these, her hard tack, to sustain her.

No harm could come to them, of course. How could they be lost in a room? No one would touch them. No one would even look at them. They would be quite safe. All she had to do was to go into the living room in the morning, and pick them up. She had a vivid picture of the living room by the light of early day; the chairs cast like husks, the ashtrays, the bottle tops and dirty glasses. Under a thick lid of ash, the sleepy eye of the fire still alight. But the books, somehow the books were not there.

Suppose she should forget them, in the morning?

Irritated with herself, she closed down sharply on this fantasy. She took off her dressing-gown determinedly, folded it ready to pack away, and went to turn off the light. But with her hand on the switch she hesitated again, and suddenly went swiftly to the overnight case and felt for something in one of its worn silk pockets. She took out a small leather diary and, opening it at an empty page belonging to a month of the year that had already passed, she wrote, 'My books', and underscored what she had written. Then she looked about her, picked up the pot of cream and propped the open diary against it, on the bedside stool. She got into bed. She shifted the cream pot and the diary so that they faced her line of vision. Her lips moved slowly, shaping two words. Her hand went out almost secretly and she took up the diary and scrawled, this time in big, untidy block letters, MY BOOKS, and again underscored the words.

When she had turned out the light she pulled the covers up to her neck and closed her eyes and lay, all alone, listening to the party.

The Bridegroom

He came into his road camp that afternoon for the last time. It was neater than any house would ever be; the sand raked smooth in the clearing, the water drums under the tarpaulin, the flaps of his tent closed against the heat. Thirty yards away a black woman knelt, pounding mealies, and two or three children, grey with Kalahari dust, played with a skinny dog. Their shrillness was no more than a bird's piping in the great spaces in which the camp was lost.

Inside his tent, something of the chill of the night before always remained, stale but cool, like the air of a church. There was his iron bed with its clean pillowcase and big kaross. There was his table, his folding chair with the red canvas seat and the chest in which his clothes were put away. Standing on the chest was the alarm clock that woke him at five every morning and the photograph of the seventeen-year-old girl from Francistown whom he was going to marry. They had been there a long time, the girl and the alarm clock; in the morning when he opened his eyes, in the afternoon when he came off the job. But now this was the last time. He was leaving for Francistown in the Roads Department ten-tonner, in the morning; when he came back, the next week, he would be married and he would have with him the girl, and the caravan which the department provided for married men. He had his eye on her as he sat down on the bed and took off his boots; the smiling girl was like one of those faces cut out of a magazine. He began to shed his working overalls, a rind of khaki stiff with dust that held his shape as he discarded it, and he called, easily and softly, '*Ou Piet, ek wag.*' But the bony black man with his eyebrows raised like a clown's, in effort, and his bare feet shuffling under the weight, was already at the tent with a tin bath in which hot water made a twanging tune as it slopped from side to side.

When he had washed and put on a clean khaki shirt and a pair of worn grey trousers, and streaked back his hair with sweet-smelling pomade, he stepped out of his tent just as the lid of the horizon closed on the bloody eye of the sun. It was winter and the sun set shortly after five; the grey sand turned a fading pink, the low thorn scrub gave out spreading stains of lilac shadow that presently all ran together; then the surface of the desert showed pocked and pored, for a minute or two, like the surface of the moon through a telescope, while the sky remained light over the darkened earth and the clean crystal pebble of the evening star shone. The camp fires – his own and the black men's, over there – changed from near-invisible flickers of liquid colour to brilliant focuses of leaping tongues of light; it was dark. Every evening he sat like this through the short ceremony of the closing of the day, slowly filling his pipe, slowly easing his back round to the fire, yawning off the stiffness of his labour. Suddenly he gave a smothered giggle, to himself, of excitement. Her existence became real to him; he saw the face of the photograph, posed against a caravan door. He got up and began to pace about the camp, alert to promise. He kicked a log farther into the fire, he called an order to Piet, he walked up towards the tent and then changed his mind and strolled away again. In their own encampment at the edge of his, the road gang had taken up the exchange of laughing, talking, yelling and arguing that never failed them when their work was done. Black arms gestured under a thick foam of white soap, there was a gasp and splutter as a head broke the cold force of a bucketful of water, the gleaming bellies of iron cooking-pots were carried here and there in the talkative preparation of food. He did not understand much of what they were saying – he knew just enough Tswana to give them his orders, with help from Piet and one or two others who understood his own tongue, Afrikaans – but the sound of their voices belonged to this time of evening. One or other of the babies who always cried was keeping up a thin, ignored wail; the naked children were playing the chasing game that made the dog bark. He came back and sat down again at the fire, to finish his pipe.

After a certain interval (it was exact, though it was not timed by a watch but by long habit that had established the appropriate lapse of time between his bath, his pipe and his food) he called out, in Afrikaans, 'Have you forgotten my dinner, man?'

From across the patch of distorted darkness where the light of the two fires did not meet but flung wobbling shapes and opaque, overlapping radiances, came the hoarse, protesting laugh that was, better than the tribute to a new joke, the pleasure in constancy to an old one.

Then a few minutes later, 'Piet! I suppose you've burned everything, eh?'

'Baas?'

'Where's the food, man?'

In his own time the black man appeared with the folding table and an oil-lamp. He went back and forth between the dark and light, bringing pots and dishes and food, and nagging with deep satisfaction, in a mixture of English and Afrikaans. 'You want *koeksusters*, so I make *koeksusters*. You ask me this morning. So I got to make the oil nice and hot, I got to get everything ready ... It's little bit slow. Yes, I know. But I can't get everything quick-quick. You hurry tonight, you don't want wait, then it's better you have *koeksusters* on Saturday, then I'm got time in the afternoon, I do it nice ... Yes, I think next time it's better ...'

Piet was a good cook. 'I've taught my boy how to make everything,' the young man always told people, back in Francistown. 'He can even make *koeksusters*,' he had told the girl's mother, in one of those silences of the woman's disapproval it was so difficult to fill. He had had a hard time, trying to overcome the prejudice of the girl's parents against the sort of life he could offer her. He had managed to convince them that the life was not impossible, and they had given their consent to the marriage, but they still felt the life was unsuitable, and his desire to please and reassure them had made him anxious to see it with their eyes and forestall, by changes, their objections.

The girl was a farm girl and would not pine for town life, but at the same time he could not deny to her parents that living on a farm with her family around her, and neighbours only 30 or 40 miles away would be very different from living 220 miles from a town or village, alone with him in a road camp, 'surrounded by a gang of kaffirs all day', as her mother had said. He himself simply did not think at all about what the girl would do while he was out on the road; and as for the girl, until it was over, nothing could exist for her but the wedding, with her two little sisters in pink walking behind her, and her dress that she didn't recognize herself in being made at the dressmaker's, and the cake that was going to have a tiny china bride and groom in evening dress on the top.

He looked at the scored table and the rim of the open jam tin and the salt-cellar with a piece of brown paper tied neatly over the broken top, and said to Piet, 'You must do everything nice when the missus comes.'

'Baas?'

They looked at each other and it was not really necessary to say anything.

'You must make the table properly and do everything clean.'

'Always I make everything clean. Why you say now I must make clean –'

The young man bent his head over his food, dismissing him.

While he ate, his mind went automatically over the changes that would have to be made for the girl. He was not used to visualizing situations, but to dealing with what existed. It was like a lesson learned by rote; he knew the totality of what was needed, but if he found himself confronted by one of the component details, he foundered: he did not recognize it or know how to deal with it. The boys must keep out of the way. That was the main thing. Piet would have to come to the caravan quite a lot, to cook and clean. The boys – specially the boys who were responsible for the maintenance of the lorries and road-making equipment – were always coming with questions, what to do about this and that. They'd mess things up, otherwise. He spat out a piece of gristle he could not swallow; his mind went to something else. The women over there – they could do the washing for the girl. They were such a raw bunch of kaffirs, would they ever be able to do anything right? Twenty boys and about five of their women – you couldn't hide them under a thorn bush. They just mustn't hang around, that's all. They must just understand that they mustn't hang around. He looked keenly through the shadow-puppets of the half-dark on the margin of his fire's light; the voices, companionably quieter, now, intermittent over food, the echoing 'chut!' of wood being chopped, the thin film of a baby's wail through which all these sounded – they were on their own side. Yet he felt an odd, rankling suspicion.

His thoughts shuttled, as he ate, in a slow and painstaking way that he had never experienced before in his life – he was worrying. He sucked on a tooth; Piet, Piet, that kaffir talks such a hell of a lot. How's Piet going to stop talking, talking every time he comes near. If he talks to her. Man, it's sure he'll talk to her. He thought, in actual words, what he would say to Piet about this; the words were like those unsayable things people write on walls for others to see in private moments, but that are never spoken in their mouths.

Piet brought coffee and *koeksusters* and the young man did not look at him.

But the *koeksusters* were delicious, crisp, sticky and sweet, and as he felt the familiar substance and taste on his tongue, alternating with the hot bite of the coffee, he at once became occupied with the pure happiness of eating, as a child is fully occupied with a bag of sweets. *Koeksusters* never failed to give him this innocent, total pleasure. When first he had taken the job of overseer to the road gang, he had had strange, restless hours at night and on Sundays. It seemed that he was hungry. He ate but never felt satisfied. He walked about all the time, like a hungry creature. One Sunday he actually set out to walk (the Roads Department was very strict about the use of the ten-tonner for private purposes) the fourteen miles across the sand to the cattle-dipping post where the government cattle-officer and his wife, Afrikaners like himself and the only other white people between the road camp and Francistown, lived in their corrugated iron house. By a coincidence, they had decided to drive over and see him, that day, and they met him a little less than halfway, when he was already slowed and dazed by heat. But shortly after that Piet had taken over the cooking of his meals and the care of his person, and Piet had even learned to make *koeksusters*, according to instructions given to the young man by the cattle-officer's wife. The *koeksusters*, a childhood treat that he could indulge in whenever he liked, seemed to mark his settling down; the solitary camp became a personal way of life with its own special arrangements and indulgences.

'Ou Piet! Kêrel! What did you do to the *koeksusters*, hey?' he called out joyously.

A shout came that meant 'Right away.' The black man appeared, drying his hands on a rag, with the diffident, kidding manner of someone who knows he has excelled himself.

'Whatsa matter with the *koeksusters*, man?'

Piet shrugged. 'You must tell me. I don't know what's matter.'

'Here, bring me some more, man.' The young man shoved the empty plate at him, with a grin. And as the other went off, laughing, the young man called, 'You must always make them like that, see?'

He liked to drink at celebrations, at weddings or Christmas, but he wasn't a man who drank his brandy every day. He would have two brandies on a Saturday afternoon, when the week's work was over, and for the rest of the time the bottle that he brought from Francistown when he went to collect stores lay in the chest in his tent. But on this last night he got up from the fire on impulse and went over to the tent to fetch the bottle (one thing he didn't do, he didn't expect a kaffir to handle his drink for him; it was too much of a temptation to put in their way). He brought a glass with him, too, one of a set of six made of tinted, imitation cut-glass, and he poured himself a tot and stretched out his legs where he could feel the warmth of the fire through the soles of his boots. The nights were not cold, until the wind came up at two or three in the morning, but there was a clarifying chill to the air; now and then a figure came over from the black men's camp to put another log on the fire whose flames had dropped and become blue. The young man felt inside himself a similar low incandescence; he poured himself another brandy. The long yelping of the jackals prowled the sky without, like the wind about a house; there was no house, but the sounds beyond the light his fire tremblingly inflated into the dark – that jumble of meaningless voices, crying babies, coughs and hawking – had built walls to enclose and a roof to shelter. He was exposed, turning naked to space on the sphere of the world, but he was not aware of it.

The lilt of various kinds of small music began and died in the dark; threads of notes, blown and plucked, that disappeared under the voices. Presently a huge man whose thick black body had strained apart every seam in his ragged pants and shirt loped silently into the light and dropped just within it, not too near the fire. His feet, intimately crossed, were cracked and weathered like driftwood. He held to his mouth a one-stringed instrument shaped like a lyre, made out of a half-moon of bent wood with a ribbon of dried palm-leaf tied from tip to tip. His big lips rested gently on the strip and, while he blew, his one hand, by controlling the vibration of the palm-leaf, made of his breath a small, faint, perfect music. It was caught by the very limits of the capacity of the human ear; it was almost out of range. The first music men ever heard, when they began to stand upright among the rushes at the river, might have been like it. When it died away it was difficult to notice at what point it really had gone.

'Play that other one,' said the young man, in Tswana. Only the smoke from his pipe moved.

The pink-palmed hands settled down round the instrument. The thick, tender lips were wet once. The faint desolate voice spoke again, so lonely a music that it came to the player and listener as if they heard it inside themselves. This time the player took a short stick in his other hand, and, while he blew, scratched it back and forth inside the curve of the lyre, where the notches cut there produced a dry, shaking, slithering sound like the far-off movement of dancers' feet. There were two or three figures with more substance than the shadows, where the firelight merged with the darkness. They came and squatted. One of them had half a paraffin tin with a wooden neck and other attachments of gut and wire. When the lyre-player paused, lowering his piece of stick and leaf slowly, in ebb, from his mouth, and wiping his lips on the back of his hand, the other began to play. It was a thrumming, repetitive, banjo-tune. The young man's boot patted the sand in time to it and he took it up with handclaps once or twice. A thin, yellowish man in an old hat pushed his way to the front past sarcastic remarks and twittings and sat on his haunches with a little clay bowl between his feet. Over its mouth there was a keyboard of metal tongues. After some exchange, he played it and the others sang low and nasally, bringing a few more strollers to the fire. The music came to an end, pleasantly, and started up again, like a breath drawn. In one of the intervals the young man said, 'Let's have a look at that contraption of yours, isn't it a new one?' and the man to whom he signalled did not understand what was being said to him but handed over his paraffin-tin mandolin with pride and also with amusement at his own handiwork.

The young man turned it over, twanged it once, grinning and shaking his head. Two bits of string and an old jam tin and they'll make a whole band, man. He'd heard them playing some crazy-looking things. The circle of faces watched him with pleasure; they laughed and lazily remarked to each other; it was a funny-looking thing, all right, but it worked. The owner took it back and played it, clowning a little. The audience laughed and joked appreciatively; they were sitting close in to the fire now, painted by it. 'Next week,' the young man raised his voice gaily, 'next week when I come back, I bring radio with me, plenty real music. All the big white bands play over it –' Someone who had once worked in Johannesburg said 'Satchmo', and the others took it up, understanding that this was the word for what the white man was going to bring from town. Satchmo. Satch-mo. They tried it out, politely. 'Music, just like at a big white dance in town. Next week.' A friendly, appreciative silence fell, with them all resting back in the warmth of the fire and looking at him indulgently. A strange thing happened to him. He felt hot, over first his neck, then his ears and his face. It didn't matter, of course; by next week they would have forgotten. They wouldn't expect it. He shut down his mind on a picture of them, hanging round the caravan to listen, and him coming out on the steps to tell them –

He thought for a moment that he would give them the rest of the bottle of brandy. Hell, no, man, it was mad. If they got the taste for the stuff, they'd be pinching it all the time. He'd give Piet some sugar and yeast and things from the stores, for them to make beer with tomorrow when he was gone. He put his hands deep in his pockets and stretched out to the fire with his head sunk on his chest. The lyre-player picked up his flimsy piece of wood again, and slowly what the young man was feeling inside himself seemed to find a voice; up into the night beyond the fire it went, uncoiling from his breast and bringing ease. As if it had been made audible out of infinity and could be returned to infinity at any point, the lonely voice of the lyre went on and on. Nobody spoke, the barriers of tongues fell with silence. The whole dirty tide of worry and planning had gone out of the young man. The small, high moon, outshone by a spiky spread of cold stars, repeated the shape of the lyre. He sat for he was not aware how long, just as he had for so many other nights, with the stars at his head and the fire at his feet.

But at last the music stopped and time began again. There was tonight; there was tomorrow, when he was going to drive to Francistown. He stood up; the company fragmented. The lyre player blew his nose into his fingers. Dusty feet took their accustomed weight. They went off into their tents and he went off to his. Faint plangencies followed them. The young man gave a loud, ugly, animal yawn, the sort of unashamed personal noise a man can make when he lives alone. He walked very slowly across the sand; it was dark but he knew the way more surely than with his eyes. 'Piet! Hey!' he bawled as he reached his tent. 'You get up early tomorrow, eh? And I don't want to hear the lorry won't start. You get it going and then you call me. D'you hear?'

He was lighting the oil-lamp that Piet had left ready on the chest and as it came up softly it brought the whole interior of the tent with it; the chest, the bed, the clock, and the coy smiling face of the seventeen-year-old girl. He sat down on the bed, sliding his palms through the silky fur of the kaross. He drew a breath and held it for a moment, looking round purposefully. And then he picked up the photograph, folded the cardboard support back flat to the frame and put it in the chest with all his other things, ready for the journey.

The Last Kiss

When people become characters, they cease to be regarded as human; they are something to be pointed out, like the orange tree that President Kruger planted, the statue in the park, or the filling station that once was the first church hall. Mr Van As was a character, formed, as many characters are, by neglect. He was an Afrikaner who had started up as a cartage contractor before gold was discovered, when the town was a coal-mining village between black hills of coal dust on the high veld of the Transvaal. His donkey-drawn wagons moved the swaying household goods of the Cornish miners from the station to their cottages. Then there was gold; the shafts went down, the houses and shops went up. Mr Van As bought a team of dray horses and four wagons, and he moved machinery and equipment for the gold mines as well as smart new furniture for the influx of miners and tradespeople. He bought a large corrugated-iron shed and converted it into a storage place; he had an office, and an expensive trap for his personal use. His wagons, with VAN AS FOR CARTAGE painted across them in two-foot letters, were seen all over the village. He was an elder in the church. He built himself a house with white cake frill railings to the veranda, an ornamental turret, and an onion dome of corrugated iron – the first time that indispensable material, the very stuff of which the Witwatersrand was built, night-cold all winter, blazing noon-hot all summer, was made the soul as well as the substance of local architecture. Inside, neither plush nor ball fringe was spared, and there were mirrors in mahogany frames to multiply the heads of his wife and daughters.

As he became self-conscious of money and fine possessions, so the village, now a little town, became self-conscious too;

civic pride required a mayor and a gold chain for him to wear, and councillors for him to consult with. Van As was mayor, and wore the gold chain for three years running, and the first stone building in the town, a bank, still standing, has one of its stones inscribed: '15th July 1912. This foundation stone was laid by His Worship the Mayor, Councillor G. G. Van As.'

Years later, a photograph of him as he appeared at this time, in mayoral robes and chain, and with the tusk-like moustache that was the one thing he never lost, was discovered in the unsaleable rubbish cluttering a corner of one of the local auctioneers' sale-rooms, and was reproduced in the local paper; it looked about as credible as a picture of a manifestation of ectoplasm.

The town outgrew Van As. As he got older, it got younger, more vigorous and brash, became more and more of a show-off. He was all right for Masonic gatherings and Dutch Reformed Church bazaars and the Sons of England ball, but would he have done to open swimming galas, judge beauty queens, or welcome a visiting Hollywood film actress making an appearance in person? His English was not very good; his Afrikaans, though that was his mother tongue, was not much better. It had not been necessary to talk much at the beginning of the town; it had been enough to be solid and prosperous and wear the gold chain well. If he had lasted on into the rise of Afrikaner nationalism and the Nationalist government of South Africa, he certainly would not have done to welcome a minister of state on an official visit to celebrate the milling of the billionth ton of gold ore: one of those Nationalist ministers with their stern public faces, their apocalyptic manner, and the urbanity that coats politicians invisibly as the oil on a duck's back.

But he did not last even into the era of the motor-van. By the twenties, there were two other cartage contractors in the town, each with a motor removal-van, a lumbering, tin-hooded thing that kept furniture clean and dry in all weathers, and that had to be cranked up like a giant clockwork toy being wound. Van As's wife died in 1922 with the birth of their fourth or fifth daughter, and perhaps that was one of the reasons why he hesitated too long about exchanging his horse-drawn wagons for the new vans, and lost his lead in the cartage business. It was an unsettled year, anyway, on the Witwatersrand, with strikes and their attendant disruption of business life; liquor shops were closed for months and there was some glorious rioting in Johannesburg, when the streets ran with looted whisky and imported chocolates. People said – when they thought back on it – that it was with his wife's death that Van As began to go down; but then people like to pend the insidious slither of misfortune from some ill omen – it is part of the craving for order, for a fate to take their lives out of their hands. Mrs Van As turned her face to the wall and luck turned away with her; it makes a starting-point.

Van As continued to live in his grand house, with his eldest daughter, a girl of about eighteen, as housekeeper and mother to the rest. The weather-vane had not fallen down yet and the good plush furnishings were still in fine condition. But the valuable cartage contracts for new gold-mines opening up went to the men with the modern motor transport, and Van As For Cartage lost some of his old contracts, too, when they came up for renewal. He had begun to let go, it seemed, and there was no closing his hand on anything, after that. He had lent money; it was not paid back, and the securities proved worthless. It was many years since he had been mayor, almost as many since he had been dropped from the city council. He speculated on the wrong things and sold the cartage business. He was declared bankrupt.

It was perhaps the mark of his failure, his inability to adapt, that he and his immediate surroundings remained the same. He did not leave the ornate and dating house (it had been in his wife's name and was bequeathed to his daughters), he continued to wear the great tusky moustache that had once become the dignity of a city father. Nothing fades so quickly as what is unchanged. By the thirties, when the youngest child was ten years old and the eldest had provided grandchildren, the house was a landmark of positive antiquity for a town that young. The rusty weather-vane screeched drunkenly on windy days, the white railings had never been repainted, and looking in through the living-room window from the street you could see the moth-eaten plush, and the places where little balls were missing from the fringe on the pelmet. The Van Ases could not afford to change anything. The eldest daughter's husband got phthisis working underground on the mines, and had only his disability pension to get along on, so her family, too, came back to live under the old roof with the onion dome. Old Van As – already it seemed he had never been known as anything else – had a job in a produce store, the sort of job a bright youth may start with when he leaves school; if a middle-aged man has a job like that, people take it to mean that he is fit for nothing else.

It was about this time that a cinema went up on a vacant plot near the house (the old residential areas were being taken in by the expanding business-centre of the town and it was no longer fashionable to live within walking distance of the post office) and Van As took to dropping in there two or three nights a week. Did he develop a passion for seeing films? Nobody ever asked him. Not even his children. He went down the road to the cinema as some old men go to the pub, and are out of the way. The children were all busy trying to find space and importance for the growing paraphernalia of their interests; one had boy-friends, another played the piano and wanted to practise to enter a talent contest, a third collected butterflies and was trying for a scholarship.

Van As couldn't manage anything for them, so they had to manage for themselves.

He was no longer an elder of the church, of course; and church-going had been so much a part of the social position that he had lost that he didn't go to church any more, as if his presence would have embarrassed himself and God, just as the current mayor (a dentist who had made money on the stock market, had a house with a cocktail bar, and had instituted a publicity campaign for the town, with luminous signs that said: YOU ARE NOW ENTERING INDUSTRIAL NOORDDORP – WELCOME AND PROSPERITY) and his councillors would have been embarrassed if Van As had walked into the Council Chamber. In the forties, he lost his job at the produce store and for a while he was to be seen wandering about the town, looking long and steadily into shop windows, as if deliberating some important purchase. It was then that he began to be known as poor old Van As. But his enforced idleness did not last. The war was well under way by then, and the next thing was old Van As in uniform: he got a job in the recruiting office in Johannesburg. It was a mild sort of joke in the town. Some of the older city fathers who had continued to do well for themselves and who chose to regard his decline as a kind of eccentricity, poked him in the chest of his private's ill-fitting uniform and bellowed (it was well known that he seemed to have got rather deaf): 'Well, we've nothing to worry about now, eh, Van As? Hitler's had his chips, now.' And old Van As would wheeze and laugh, mumbling something unintelligible under his straggling moustache.

Week after week, he sat in his same seat in the cinema. It was one of the cheap seats two rows from the front, and often he had the whole row to himself because to sit there was to be grotesquely vis-à-vis the huge faces on the screen. All through the winter he was sunk to the ears – pale, sagging ears, tufted with albino bristles – in his army greatcoat. If he had brought along several thicknesses of newspaper and spread himself out on them on the floor, it would not have seemed too incongruous; he camped in the ugly little cinema with its red lights in brackets, like animal eyes, on the wall, and its wooden floorboards gritty with peanut shells, with the air of the homeless in a park.

Winter and summer, his presence was always known by his cough. At least two or three times in the course of a programme it would break out: the fully orchestrated cough of chronic bronchitis, beginning with a stifled wheeze like silent laughter, rising to a counterpoint of gulping, roaring, retching and then dying, through more wheezing, to silence. Old Van As's cough.

He coughed on the train, too, the early train that took him to his job at the recruiting office in Johannesburg every day. The morning air made him cough even more. Old Van As's here; ladies, going into Johannesburg to do the important shopping they couldn't trust to the local shops, and in those days of petrol rationing unable to travel in their cars, avoided the coach from which they heard that cough coming. It was unpleasant, coughing and spluttering in a railway carriage. Anyway it was embarrassing to find oneself shut up with poor old Van As sitting there calmly in that ridiculous uniform, poor old thing, at his time of life. What could one say to him? And one couldn't ignore him; after all, he wasn't just a tramp. No one had really spoken to him for *years* – it was so awkward. And the Van As girls were nice girls, actually; especially Essie (she had got her scholarship and was a nursery-school teacher) – thoroughly sensible and sweet with the children.

The high-school boys and girls who clambered onto the train every morning on their way to school in the next Witwatersrand town (Noorddorp's high school couldn't accommodate them all, before the new high schools were built) didn't notice old Van As or his cough. They filled his carriage and a number of others, willy-nilly, yelling and fooling, great, well-grown South African children whose legs and bodies defeated the purpose of school uniform so thoroughly that, on them, it was not modest and drab but robustly provocative, in the best vaudeville tradition. The girls' short serge gym-frocks showed inches of thigh above the black stockings straining to cover strong, curved legs and bulging calves; heavy breasts jutted under the tightly buttoned shirts. The enormous hairy legs of boys in football shorts that barely contained their muscular buttocks, stretched across the aisles; at fourteen or fifteen they weighed 170 pounds and had the terrifying belly-laugh that comes with newly-broken voices and new beards breaking erratically through adolescent pimples. They wrote four-letter words on the carriage doors. They stuck gum on the seats and pummelled and flirted, and were as unmindful of old Van As as they were of everyone else outside the violent and raucous orbit of their time of life.

The war ended and they left school and others grew up into their places and their ways, and old Van As was discharged from the army but continued to travel to Johannesburg every day, to another job. Nobody knew exactly what it was; some old man's small occupation. He was out of uniform, of course, but still, when it was cold, he wore his army greatcoat over his stained suit. And he still coughed.

Very rarely, the children would make some half-hearted attempt to bait the old man; it was really hardly worth the trouble, since he seemed to travel between invisible blinkers, simply sitting till he got there, sometimes dozing, scarcely even looking out of the window. Once someone had offered him a stone wrapped up in a sweet paper; but he had put up his hand, coughing by way of response, and shaken his head in innocent thanks and refusal. Months went by during which the boys and girls merely battered past him with their school cases and heavy feet, and he was forgotten. Then one of the boys got hold of one of those fake dog's messes made out of rubber, and when it had been tried in all the likely places and on all the likely people and seemed to have exhausted its potentialities of diversion, a girl who wanted to impress the boy snatched it up and planted it where the old man usually sat. Sure enough, he boarded the train at the coach two from the end, and sure enough he sat on the thing, but he never noticed it and there it stayed, while the girl sat with her hand over her mouth, her brass-bold eyes watching him for a move. Her friends pressed in on either side of her and the huddle shook with jeering laughter. For a while, the old man seemed to look at them rather than through them; his wrinkled eyelids flickered once or twice like a film clearing from the narrow apertures of his eyes. He might have been some harmless, slow-reacting creature in a zoo, dimly hearing the sound of pieces of thrown orange-peel bouncing off its hide.

Just before the train reached the station at which the children got off, the girl demanded, 'You sitting on something of mine.' It did not occur to the old man that she could be addressing him. 'You sitting on something of mine,' she said again, impatiently. He cupped his ear in surprise. 'I say there's something of mine you sitting on.' He shuffled fussily to his feet, looking all round him. The girl snatched the object, prancing, insolent, while her friends clutched each other in joy. But the old man had not even seen what the object represented, and he sank down heavily to his place again.

The next morning the misfired joke was forgotten; the same

girls were giggling and whispering over a *True Romances* paperback. They were unaware of him, but the old man sat looking at them.

A day or two later, by one of those simple chances that might so easily never have happened, the old man missed the train and took a later one. The girl who had played the joke (she looked exactly like the others, she might have been any one of them) missed the train, too, and caught the later one. That train was almost empty, since it was too late for workers or schoolchildren. By habit, the old man got into the second coach from the end; perhaps also out of habit, so did the girl. She flung down opposite him, panting and cross because she would be inexcusably late for school. She brought with her a smell of dusty serge, ink and the verdigris odour of her greasy yellow hair, which was curled every night but washed infrequently. She gave him the uninterested, ignoring look with which she regarded old people and little children, and became absorbed in a new *True Romances* she had bought herself. The sun shone directly in her eyes, and, without taking her attention from the magazine, she got up and bounced down on the other side of the compartment, on the seat beside him.

Ever since she had come into the empty compartment he had been looking at her, mildly, from his own distance, as if he both saw her and didn't see her. He sighed as she sat down beside him.

It was the old man with the cough, she told, the old man with the cough who was always on the seven-thirty. *Ô my God, man, the old pig, what a nerve, eh?* (These giant children spoke the coarse, slangy hybrid of English and Afrikaans that had grown up out of their situation as the progeny of half-educated parents in a bilingual country.) Her friends yelled with laughter until she lost her temper. Her teacher refused to listen to yet another wild tale. But the girl's father, who never knew where she was, what she was doing, or when she came home at night, roused to the promptings of some primitive tribal honour (he liked a fight, anyway) and swore, *vragtig*, he'd like to get his hands round that man's neck; he'd put the police on him.

So one day in 1951, when Van As was nearly seventy, he was arrested for kissing a schoolgirl in a train. One of the great robust schoolgirls with the spread thighs and the heavy breasts, female but not yet woman: the female of all erotic fantasy, from adolescence to senility, conjured up by glands, mindless, nameless, almost faceless.

Old Van As! That poor old thing, deaf as a post, with no teeth and the smelly old moustache. Ugh! People giggled with revulsion, grinned with disgust. Why, no woman had looked at him, surely he hadn't anything to do with one for twenty, thirty years. Since his wife died. He'd never married again or anything like that – of course not, old Van As! No one would dream of thinking of a woman in connection with him. What on earth got into him? The old devil, eh? Who would have thought it? Well, the old devil ... You know, the one who coughs so that you can't hear the film ... that's him ... harmless-looking old bird in an army greatcoat.

In the Johannesburg papers there was an inch of space saying that an elderly ex-soldier was alleged to have attempted criminal assault on a fourteen-year-old schoolgirl. The photograph of Van As in his mayoral robes and chain was taken out of the auctioneer's junk room and reproduced in the local paper, with the caption: 'FORMER MAYOR KISSES SCHOOLGIRL. G. G. Van As, once mayor of Noorddorp and city councillor for six years, appeared in the Magistrate's Court this week on the charge of kissing a fourteen-year-old schoolgirl, Anna Cornelia Jooste, 17 Dantry Road, Mooiklip.'

FOND OF HER DOLLS, SAYS MOTHER was one of the subheadings to the story. All at once, it seemed that a dirty, lecherous old man had frightened a tender little girl. His daughters (particularly Essie, who was so well known) could hardly hold up their heads. What a disgrace to them, what a nuisance to them he was, everyone said. Someone even whispered that it was a pity he'd lived on so long, his wife was dead nearly thirty years and he had no friends – not much good to himself or anyone.

His daughter Essie got a lawyer to defend him and he got off, of course: momentary loss of memory – some such plea. The salacious indignation of the town took a little longer to let him off. It was not so much what he had done – that was scarcely to be talked about; while the first kiss was something to make your eyes prick in the cinema, it was assumed that the last must be ridiculous and obscene – but that, for one crazy moment, he had stepped out of character, out of old Van As, the tusky moustache, the comic soldier, the cough in the cinema, and signalled.

It was as if the town's only statue, a shabby thing of an obscure general on a horse, standing in a dusty park and scrawled over by urchins, were to have been observed, bleeding.

The Gentle Art

In the heat of the day the huge, pale silky width of river put out your eyes, so that when you turned away from it everything else looked black and jumped. There was a one-roomed square reed-house on the bank, with a reed-mat door that rolled up and let down. Inside was a camp bed with an animal skin on it, and a table with an enamelled teapot, an assortment of flowered china cups, a tin of tea and a tin of powdered milk. There was a stool with a battery radio set that played all the time. The enormous trees of Africa, ant-eaten and ancient, hung still, over the hut; down on the margin of the river in the sun the black-and-lemon chequered skin of a crocodile made a bladder of air in the water, and, right on the verge, the body of the creature lay in its naked flesh, stripped, except for the head and jaws and the four gloves of skin left on its claws. The flesh looked pink, fresh and edible. The water stirred it like a breeze in feathers.

At night there was nothing – no river, no hut, no crocodile, no trees; only a vast soft moonless darkness that made the couple giggle with excitement as they bumped along the river track in the path of their headlights. 'Shall we ever find it?' said Vivien, and her husband knew that he must. 'This is it, all right,' he said. 'Do you think you're on the right path, Ricks?' she asked, ignoring him. Just then they heard the intimate, dramatic, triumphant, wheedling voice of the radio, finishing off a commercial in a squall of music; they were there, upon it, at the very hut. There was the dull red of a camp fire, an oil lamp came towards them, Ricks's torch leapt from branch to branch, figures emerged like actors coming onto a stage.

'We been waiting for you people since half past seven!' said a large blond man, half-challengingly.

Vivien broke into the exaggerated apologies of a woman anxious to make good in a world other than her own; at home in Johannesburg she was never punctual and disdained any reproach about it, but here in the bush she was abject at the thought that she might have kept the crocodile hunters waiting. She was sorry; she was terribly, terribly sorry, the hotel was so small, they couldn't upset regular meal hours by giving dinner a little earlier . . . She really was *terribly* sorry. 'I should jolly well think so,' said the blond man, no longer challenging, no longer even listening. Although the night was warm as milk he had a muffler round his neck, and his blue-eyed, red face wore the perpetual bright smile of short temper. The other man, in shorts and ribbed stockings, stood about with his hands on his hips. 'Ruddy motor's been kicking up hell,' he said. 'Jimmy and I've been friggin around with the damned thing best part of the afternoon.' In the light of the oil lamp he had piggy good looks; handsome turned-up nose, bristling moustache, narrow, blinking eyes.

A man's voice called, 'Davie? Davie, old man? You all ready?' and another oil lamp came out of the hut, circling with light a stripling and a woman. As they came nearer, the stripling became a forty-year-old man whose thin, hard body stored up nothing; simply acted as a conductor of energy. He was skinny and brown as an urchin, and he had dusty straight brown hair and large, deeply-recessed black eyes in a small, lined face. He looked like one of those small boys who look like old men, and the others watched him come towards them.

He was the host of the couple and the boss of the two men. Vivien followed his approach with parted lips; each time she saw him, since they had met by a miracle of accident on the river bank three days before, he materialized to her unbelievably out of all the stories she had heard about him. 'Mr Baird!' she called. 'Hullo there! I'm so terribly sorry . . .' and she went off into her elaborate obeisance of apology, all over again. 'That's all right, that's all right.' His voice was quick, light and friendly. 'Only I want you people to enjoy yourselves and see some action, that's the idea, isn't it? Haven't you got a coat along with you, Mr McEwen? It gets pretty chilly on the river at night, you want to wrap up ... Mike, can you spare a jersey or something for Mr McEwen? – Nothing of mine'd go near you, I'm afraid.'

Vivien spoke up for her husband, 'Oh Ricks's fine, Mr Baird, he's tough, really, he never wears a thing, even in winter. He spent his childhood running wild in Rhodesia, he's not really a soft city boy at all.' He was one of those huge, thick-set young men who have gone almost bald by the time they are twenty. He passed a hand over his head and said, 'Oh Vivien ...'

'He c'n have my coat,' said the smiling blond man, over his muffler.

Jimmy Baird turned to him with quick concern, 'No, no, Mike old man, you better hang on to that, you're not yourself yet. Give him one of your jerseys, there's a good chap.'

'I'm not comin',' said Mike, 'I don't need it.'

Vivien drew back, her head on one side. 'Not coming? Oh but you must, why, we wouldn't think of your staying behind alone.'

'He can keep me company,' said Mrs Baird. She stood beside her husband, her arms folded across her body that was young but made soft and comfortable with frequent childbearing. She had the air of the wife who, as usual, is walking down the garden path with her husband to see him off to work. Vivien turned to her. 'Mrs Baird! *You're* coming?'

'No, I think I'll just stay here. There's the children and everything.' She moved her head in the direction of a tent that was pitched in the shadowy darkness beside a truck.

'Aren't they asleep?'

'Yes, but the little one might wake up, and it's so close to the river ... I don't like the idea of one of them wandering round. It's strange, to the little one, we usually leave her at home, you see, it's her first time camping out up here with her Daddy.'

Jimmy Baird, talking, giving orders, making suggestions all the time, disappeared into Mike's reed hut – this was Mike's headquarters, of the three that belonged to Jimmy Baird's river concession – and came out shaking himself into a pair of overalls.

'Doesn't he look wonderful?' said Vivien. 'Doesn't your

husband look wonderful, Mrs Baird! That's how I like a man to look, as if he's really got a job to do. It drives me mad to see poor Ricks shut up in a blue suit in town. Isn't that a wonderful outfit, Ricks? – Is that the sort of thing you had on the night the hippo overturned the boat, Mr Baird? I can imagine it's not too easy to swim in that, unless you're a terrifically strong swimmer.'

But Jimmy Baird was not so easily to be led to repeat, first-hand, as she longed to hear it, the story of one of his exploits famous in the territory; one of the stories out of which she had built up her idea of what such men are like. That idea had had to go through some modification already; she had always loathed 'tiny men' – that was, any man under the standard of six-foot-one which she had set when she married Ricks. But although her picture of a man had shrunk to fit Jimmy Baird, three days ago, other aspects of it had not changed. Everything he said and did she saw as a manifestation of the qualities she read into his exploits and that she admired most – ruthlessness, recklessness, animal courage.

She said to Mrs Baird, 'I still can't believe this really is the famous Jimmy Baird. Oh yes, you know it. Your husband is the most talked-about man in the territory, wherever we've been on this trip up here, it's been Jimmy Baird, Jimmy Baird. And now we're actually going crocodile-hunting with him!'

'*Ag*, yes.' Mrs Baird came from South Africa and had the usual offhand careless way of speaking, putting in a word of Afrikaans here and there; tongue-tied and yet easy, shy and yet forthright. 'The Bairds have lived in the territory for donkey's years. Everybody knows them.'

'We're off now, girl,' said Jimmy Baird, coming up to her and putting his arm round her.

Out on the river, the boat kicked and roared and puttered into silence again under the experimenting hands of Davie; he brought it back into the submerged reeds with a skidding rush. 'Right-o,' he yelled.

'Enjoy yourself,' said Mrs Baird.

'It's awful your not being able to come. Are you sure you won't – But I suppose you've been dozens of times before –' said Vivien.

Mrs Baird held her arms and looked round the limit of the camp fire's light as if it were a room. 'I don't like water,' she said. 'They say if you don't like it, that's a warning to keep away from it.'

At the last moment, the man Mike got into the boat with them after all. He wore an old army overcoat in addition to his muffler – Ricks put the borrowed sweater round his shoulders as a concession to Jimmy Baird's insistence. Davie handed Vivien into the boat, while she called out, 'Now where do you want me to sit. Don't let us be in the way, please.' The light of an oil lamp ran over their faces like liquid; the boat grated heavily in the mud. Two Africans, enclosed in a sullen cocoon of silence, pushed and shoved beneath the shouts of the men in the boat. 'Ricks, you're too heavy,' said Vivien, laughing excitedly. They began to argue about the distribution of weight, changing places with each other. 'No – wait –' Jimmy Baird rolled up the legs of his overalls, kicked off his shoes and jumped out of the boat. 'That's it – that's it –' his strong thin hands spread in a straining grip on the prow, his head was lifted with effort. With one last concerted shove, along with the Africans, he freed the boat and jumped in.

They saw the two black men, for a moment, gasping, leaning forward with hands hanging where the boat had been wrenched from their grasp; they heard the reeds hissing away on either side; they felt the sky open, enormous, above them. The black water took them; between one moment and the next, they left the downward pull of the land and were afloat on an element that made nothing of their weight. 'Oh!' said Vivien, like a child on a swing. 'Oh, it's lovely.' And at once remembered that she was on a crocodile hunt, and fell silent.

They were drifting without sound or sensation in the dark. Far away already, there was the small glowing centre that was the camp fire, throwing up a fading orbit of light that caught the trees architecturally, here a branch, there the column of a trunk, like the planes of a lost temple half-hidden in the jungle. They were out in deep water; the middle of the river offered them to the sky.

The oil lamps had been left on shore and Mike, who was to steer, switched on the long, stiff, powerful beam of a portable searchlight. It shot through the dark and plucked out of nothing the reeds of the opposite bank, rose like a firework steeply into the sky, plunged, shortening, down into the water. 'O.K.,' said Mike, and Davie started up the engine at the first kick. They began to cleave smoothly up river at a steady pace.

'Now we let the light travel all over the show, like this,' Jimmy Baird was explaining. 'Along the reeds and so on, specially when we get farther up, in the shallows, and we watch out to pick up the eyes of a croc. You can see them quite distinctly, you'll see, Mrs McEwen, you can pick them up quite a way off, and then when you do you just make straight for them, keep the light on them all the time. They're like rabbits, you know, in the headlights of a car. They seem to be fascinated by the glare or something; so long's you keep the light full on them they don't move. Then we go right close up, right up, and shoot them at about two yards. – Bit lower down Mike, that's it. – There you are Mrs McEwen, you can see the mudbank over there, that's the sort of place the old croc likes, nice and soft for his belly.'

'Two yards!' said Ricks.

Jimmy Baird turned sympathetically. He was standing up in the boat with his gun in his hand. 'Yes. Two yards or even less. It's not sport, you see, Mr McEwen. You must get them, and you must kill first shot. Then we usually give them another one, anyway, just to make sure. It's pretty nasty if you get one coming alive in the boat. We've had some scares, eh, Mike?'

'I'll say,' said the blond man, bright-eyed, grinning into the night.

'Yes,' said Jimmy Baird. 'You must be quite sure they're knocked right out. – Can you see, Mrs McEwen? I'm sorry to be standing right here half in front of you like this. But I promise I'll skip out of the way the moment there's anything to see. Are you comfy? Wait a minute – there ought to be a cushion down here –' 'Oh no, please, I'm wonderful,' protested Vivien, rapt. 'Davie,' Jimmy Baird called to him, 'isn't there that old leather cushion down there?' 'Oh please, Mr Baird, don't worry – I am – perfect – here!'

'Over there,' said Mike's voice drily.

Jimmy Baird, excusing himself, slipped past Vivien and came up behind her so that he could direct her. 'There you are! Yes, there he is, fair-sized chappie, I should say. See those red eyes?'

The long beam of light led across the dark to a small reedy island. Vivien half-rose from the box she had been huddled on; 'Where,' she whispered urgently, 'where?'

'There, there,' Jimmy Baird said soothingly. 'There he is...'

Ricks said, 'I've got it. Like two little bits of coal! I'll be damned!'

'Oh *where*!' Vivien was desperate.

Jimmy Baird took her hand and pointed: 'Straight ahead, my dear. Got him?'

Then she saw, low down in the dank tangle, two glowing red points. The boat bore down upon them. Nobody spoke except Jimmy. He kept up a quiet running commentary, a soothing incantation to keep the crocodile unmoving. But as they reached the reeds, there was a movement quicker than a blink. 'He's gone!' said Jimmy. 'There he goes.'

The boat kicked, turned, made for open water again.

'I saw him!' said Vivien. 'I saw his tail!'

'Never mind, lots more to come,' said Jimmy Baird, promising.

'I think you'll find 'em a bit shy, down this way,' said Davie. 'We been giving 'em hell the last week, Jimmy. I think we ought to go right up a bit.'

'O.K. Davie, if you think so,' said Jimmy politely.

In a few minutes they caught another pair of eyes in the beam of the searchlight; but again the unseen creature got away without even a splash. To the two visitors, the unlikelihood of the whole business – that men could earn a living on a tropical river, at night, shooting crocodiles in order to sell their skins – seemed the answer. They could not believe that they themselves really were *there*; so it did not seem strange that there was no crocodile lying dead in the boat. Then Jimmy Baird said in his encouraging, friendly voice, 'On the right, Davie, please.' As the boat swerved neatly and closed in, Vivien said, 'Oh yes, I see it,' although she could see nothing.

'It's a babe, I'm afraid – yes, just a babe,' said Jimmy, who had explained earlier that they did not shoot crocodiles below a certain minimum size, though they took them as big as they came. 'You can see how close together the eyes are; that's a little head, that one.' The boat nosed into the reeds and the engine cut out. Suddenly Jimmy Baird said, 'Bring her right in, Davie! Right up!' and as the boat shot by the mud bank where the light had settled, he leant swiftly out of the boat and with a movement of incredible balance and strength, like a circus performer, he brought up in his hands a struggling two-foot-long crocodile.

Vivien was so astonished that she looked quickly round the boat, from one to another, as if she were afraid she had been fooled. 'There you are,' said Jimmy Baird, with both small hard hands rigid as steel round the long snout of the frantic creature. 'Now you can have a good look at him, Mrs McEwen. – Ah-ah, you wicked one,' he added to the crocodile in the special voice of admonishment you would use for a young child. 'Look at him, look at him trying to lever himself loose with his tail.' The crocodile had slapped his strong tail round the man's slender right forearm and was using a wrestler's muscular pressure to free himself.

The young woman put out a hand. 'Go on,' said Jimmy Baird. 'He's all right, the little blighter,' and she touched the creature's cool, hard back, a horny hide of leather medallions, fresh, strange, alive; from a life unknown to the touch of humans, beneath the dark river. In the light of the searchlight turned upon the creature and the faces of those round it, she saw the scissor jaws – parted a little as the man moved his grip a shade back towards the throat – with the ugly, uneven rows of razor-jagged teeth. In the light, she met the eyes; slits of pale, brilliant green, brilliant as fire; in their beast's innocence of such things, they held, for humans, the projection of hate, cunning and evil. There was a moment when the eyes saw her, of all the others. She felt that the thing knew her, as God knew her; there was an incomparable thrill of fear.

The creature suddenly bellowed hoarsely with the yell of an infuriated and desperate baby; and they all laughed.

'Ma-ma! Ma-ma!'

'Jesus, how he'd like one of your fingers!'

'Could he really?' asked Vivien.

'You bet,' said Mike. 'Just like that. Clean as a whistle.'

Jimmy Baird bent over the water, with care. Then his hands sprang back like a released trap. 'That's the last we'll see of him,' he said wiping his wet hands down his overalls.

Vivien was excited and boastful. 'Oh I'm sure you'll get him. You'll get him next year, when he's bigger.'

Davie was using a pole to shove the boat off from the mud bank.

'They live a long time . . . Their lives are slower than ours. Probably he'll be lying here in the sun long after I've finished banging away up and down this river or anywhere else,' said Jimmy Baird. His face was serene, in the light, then the light left him and went out over the darkness again.

'We should have put a mark on him,' Vivien went on joyfully. 'Couldn't we have branded him, or something, so that you'd know him if you caught him?'

Mike turned with his perpetual ill-tempered grin. 'We got six hundred last season and we didn't know any of 'em by name.'

'Sure you're O.K., Mike?' Jimmy Baird asked, and touched him on the shoulder.

'Fine, fine,' he said, looking out into the dark with his eyes wide open, like a blind man.

'Isn't he well tonight?' said Vivien.

'He's had a nasty temperature all day,' said Jimmy Baird, concernedly. 'Bit of malaria – he says it's flu, old Mike.'

In an hour the haze had cleared from the sky and, although there was only a thin new moon, the stars were bright; their faint silvering, that is put out by the glow of cities in countries where there are cities, came out in a night silence hundreds of miles away from even the most distant sound of a train. The mere touch of light lay on the water, a membrane upon the darkness; touched the reeds; penetrated nothing of the great massed mansions of wild fig trees on the banks. There were low calls and whoops, a snatch of far-off human laughter from the jackals – the behind-the-hand noises of the river's secret life. Awe invaded the heart and took the tongue of Vivien McEwen; at the same time, she wanted to giggle, like a child watching an adventure film. Where the right bank of the river opened out on what must have been treeless scrub, small glowing points jumped about; it looked as if, out there in the waste where no one lived, someone were throwing cigarette-butts away in the dark. Jimmy Baird explained that they were the eyes of spring-hares, who had a big warren just there.

'Slow down, Davie, old man, perhaps we can spot them.'

The searchlight swivelled obediently and made slow sweeps on the bank, but it was too far away; they could see nothing but the light itself, the colour of strong tea, reaching out.

They went on and twice they entered a water-maze, where the river closed in to alleys and lanes and passages enclosed by high walls of reeds, but to the crocodile hunters these were the streets of their own neighbourhood. They glided by narrow mud-bars where heavy wet bodies had made a resting-place like the place in long grass where a dog has made a bed. The propeller was lifted clear of the water, bearded with debris, and their progress was silent, as Davie poled them along. Jimmy Baird held back the reeds that came to splatter and hit at Vivien's face. This was a closely inhabited place, like a ghetto or a souk, it had the atmosphere of an interior, of the particular quality and kind of life lived there. It was a closed saurian world of mud, dankness, sun, unmeasured time.

The boat emerged again, into the broad main flow and the power of the engine coming to life like a great fish carrying them along on its back. The big blond Mike sat hunched in his place, his face turned smiling into the dark, not following the purposeful wandering of the light his hands directed. There were stretches where he whistled, piercingly and professionally, tunes that had gone round in people's heads exhaustively, then died, like spinning tops, of their own repetition, over the past twenty years. When the young woman heard a tune that was recent enough to have pleasant associations for her, she asked him what it was called. 'I wooden know,' he said, not looking at her. 'I pick 'em up from the radio.' The searchlight pushed aside the darkness from the reeds, first on this side, then on that; occasionally, as you might lift your eyes from a trying task in order to rest them with a change of focus, it ran lightly over the bank, discovering trees, caves of undergrowth, sudden clearings, and the crook of the terrible finger, grey and fifteen feet high, of an ant-heap.

'What d'you think?' Davie called.

'Well, yes, I suppose we should think about getting back, you know, Davie,' said Jimmy Baird, and paused to consider a moment. 'What d'you say, Mike?' It seemed that it was not out of an inability to make up his own mind about things that he consulted his companions with great care, on every point, but rather out of a fear that, always knowing exactly what he wanted to do, he might impose his will thoughtlessly.

'Nothing up here tonight,' said Mike, as if someone were arguing with him. 'This's where I got those two big fellers yesterday.'

'Oh we'll raise something yet,' said Jimmy Baird. 'We'll go back down slowly and see what we can find. I must say, this's been disappointing for you so far, Mrs McEwen – are you sure you're warm enough? Hands not too cold?' He added to Mike, 'You missing your tea-time tonight, Mike, eh? – Mike always pumps up the old primus and gives us a cuppa tea round about this time, it makes all the difference, you know, specially when it's cold – you just long for that cuppa tea.'

Mike looked at his watch. 'Half past ten. Yes, just about time.'

'We'll have something hot when we get back, to make up,' promised Jimmy Baird. Vivien and her husband protested that they were not thirsty, needed nothing.

Davie, who could not always follow what was being said, because of his closeness to the noise of the motor, suddenly called out, 'Mike! D'jou forget the tea tonight? S'half past ten.'

'He didn't bring the primus.'

'Well, of all the lousy chumps ...'

'We're not working,' said Mike. 'That's why I didn't think of it, man, just fooling around.'

While the discussion about tea was going on, Jimmy Baird,

still talking, spotted a crocodile with that third eye of alertness that was constantly awake in him. He had been telling Vivien and her husband how Dave and Mike always argued over the cups – Davie had a flowered china cup, the last of three he had brought with him from town life two years ago, and he didn't want Mike to risk it on the river. 'I must say, it is a very pretty cup, Royal Doulton or something posh like that –' he was saying, when he suddenly changed his manner beneath his voice, which went on in exactly the same tone: 'On the left there, Davie. Come on, now –' and he bent down and picked up his gun. 'Excuse me, Mrs McEwen,' he said with concern, because he had brushed her shoulder as he moved – and he was looking at the two red eyes fifty yards ahead, and he was loading the gun that he insisted must always be kept unloaded the moment it was not in use. Mike thrust the light into the hands of Ricks McEwen, saying, 'Keep that dead steady, eh?' and picked up the gaff.

With the numb swiftness of a piece of surgery it was accomplished; Vivien seemed to hear Jimmy Baird's voice through ether, kind and confident, the voice of the doctor doing what has to be done, without the futility of pity and with the mercy of skill.

'Right up, now, quickly, Davie.'

The boat bore down fast on the reeds and the two pencil-torch eyes glowed nearer, and there it was, in the space of a second, the horny-looking, greenish-black forehead with the frontal ridges over the eyes above the water, and the nostrils breaking the water again at the end of the lumpy snout – there it was, gazing, in the eternity of a split second, not three feet away, and Jimmy Baird's calm, compassionate voice saying 'Right,' and the gun swiftly on his shoulder and the crack beside her where he stood. Then the pale gaze coming from the dark forehead exploded; it blew up as if from within, and where the gaze had been there was a soft pink mess of brain with the scarlet wetness of blood and the mother-of-pearl sheen of muscle. There was violent threshing of the water, and although the crocodile was dead – had been completely alive one second and quite dead the next – Jimmy Baird shot it again and the great gaff swooped down and hooked it out of the pull of the river. The men heaved it aboard. 'All over. O.K. O.K. Let's get him down here, that's it.' Jimmy Baird saw the creature laid out carefully on the bottom of the boat, out of the way, but so that Vivien and Ricks could see it well. It was about five feet long, less than half-grown. The broad, soft-looking belly part, which was the part for which it had been hunted, was beautifully marked in lozenge-shaped plates, cream-coloured with tinges of black, that were perfectly articulated as the segments of a tortoise-shell. The lizard legs and the belly twitched occasionally, as if the blown communications had left some unfinished message of impulse.

Vivien McEwen was on her feet. 'Oh my God,' she cried, grinning, laughing. 'What a man! Wasn't that wonderful, Ricks? Did you ever see anything like it! What a man! Oh Mr Baird, that was terrific. Terrific!' She was in such a state of excitement that she was unsteady, like a drunk; the boat rocked and her husband had to hold her elbow. 'That's the most wonderful thing I've ever seen,' she appealed from one to the other. 'Wasn't that splendid? Oh my God, what do you think of him? – The way he simply goes up and blazes the hell out of that thing – Those eyes! Staring at you! Crash – Whoom – Finished!'

Mike took a look at the crocodile. 'Just a teenager, eh, Jimmy?'

'Well, not too bad, Mike, he'll pay for the petrol.'

Ricks McEwen said, as one man to another, 'You certainly don't give yourself time to fumble. Hardly a chance to aim, even.'

Jimmy Baird gave him his attention. 'You're so close, you don't have to aim, really. It's instantaneous, you know. The old croc doesn't suffer at all. I don't like to kill. I haven't shot a buck, for instance, since just after the war. But I often think these old crocs have a better end than most of us will ever have. We come up so close, you see, it's only a second...'

'Ricks, look at this!'

Davie had taken a spanner and knocked off one of the crocodile's teeth for the young woman. She was a dark woman, rather plain, with a very small head; the scarf she had worn over it had fallen back and now, bared, with its smooth brown hair in a bun, her head emerged rather reptilian itself – the little black moles, one beside her left eye, one beside the corner of her mouth and two on her cheek, added to the suggestion. She might have come out of the night river, a creature cunningly marked for concealment in the ambiguous shifting, blotchy light-and-dark of reeds and water. 'Just look,' her teeth and small eyes shone in the light 'Imagine that crunching into your leg! And if he breaks this one, he's got another inside!' She showed her husband how the big mossy yellowed tooth held a spare one wedged within it.

At last they all settled themselves in the boat again, and Davie poled off from the mudbank where a cloud of blood, suspended in the shallows, was slowly threading away into the mass of water.

Vivien McEwen sat back, plumping herself with sighs of triumph. She could not control her excited laughter; it rippled over with everything she said. 'Ricks? Ricks? How do you feel about Johannesburg now?' She wrapped the crocodile tooth carefully in a handkerchief and put it in among the cigarettes and cosmetics that made a perfumed jumble in her handbag.

'Oh fine, Vivien, fine.'

Her brow wrinkled, she drew her head back on her shoulder with intensity, as she confided to Mike, 'This'll make my poor husband just impossible. He loathes cities, anyway. This is a life for a *man*.'

Jimmy Baird had unloaded the gun and put it away and was squatting next to Ricks McEwen. He took out his pipe and began to fill it, but McEwen said, 'Oh come on, try some of this.' 'May I really? That's jolly nice.' Jimmy Baird took the proffered pouch, a pigskin-and-suède affair that Vivien had had made for her husband last Christmas.

The two men sat feeding the tobacco into their pipes and tamping it down. The light of matches opened and closed on their faces, and a spasm of muscle made the dead beast at their feet nudge suddenly at their shoes. 'Sometimes when I've got five or six big crocs in one night, I look at them spread out on the river bank and I think, that's a thousand years of life, lying there. It seems kind of awful, a thousand years of life,' Jimmy Baird said.

The night river closed away behind them. It went back where it came from; from the world of sleep, of eternity and darkness, the place before birth, after death – all those ideas with which the flowing continuity of dark water is bound up. And the boat came back; brought them within sight of the light of the camp fire and the shapes it touched, and then back to the camp itself, existence itself, a fire, the reed house, the smell of food and a human figure. A moment, between boat and bank, when each one of them saw the dark water beneath him, wriggling with light from the oil lamp an African held – and then they were on land, lively and stretching. 'Are you all ready for us, my girlie?' said Jimmy Baird, putting his arm round his wife and looking at her tenderly. 'Yes, yes, there's coffee there, and sandwiches,' she said, making as if to put him away but staying within his arm. Mike stamped around, hunching his shoulders and hitting the fist of one hand in the palm of the other, and Davie kicked the big logs closer into the fire so that sparks flew. 'I didn't see you coming, you know,' she said smiling. 'You gave me quite a scare. You can't see beyond the light of the fire, when you're sitting there in it.'

Vivien McEwen was glowing, even panting a little, 'Ah Mrs Baird,' she said, 'your husband! It was sensational! I thought I'd die! Oh you should've been there! You should've been there, really!' She stood dramatically, as if the other woman, who was smiling at her kindly with a polite smile, might catch alight from her. 'I'll bring you a cup of coffee, eh,' said Jimmy Baird's wife, and as Vivien, who had followed her to the table, stood beside her while she poured the coffee out of a big enamel jug, Vivien looked at her and suddenly said, curious, 'What did you do, all the time we were gone? Did you read or something?'

'I waited,' said Mrs Baird.

'Yes, but I mean how did you pass the time,' Vivien said. She had taken the cup and, although the coffee was boiling hot, was taking quick, darting sips at it.

The other woman looked up from the coffee jug a moment,

apologetic because her visitor hadn't caught what she had said.

'I waited,' she said.

For a moment, Vivien looked as if, this time, she really hadn't heard. Then she gave the woman a big, brilliant, dazed smile, and wandered off back to the company of the men.

Something For The Time Being

He thought of it as discussing things with her, but the truth was that she did not help him out at all. She said nothing, while she ran her hand up the ridge of bone behind the rim of her child-sized yellow-brown ear, and raked her fingers tenderly into her hairline along the back of her neck as if feeling out some symptom in herself. Yet her listening was very demanding; when he stopped at the end of a supposition or a suggestion, her silence made the stop inconclusive. He had to take up again what he had said, carry it – where?

'Ve vant to give you a tsance, but you von't let us,' he mimicked; and made a loud glottal click, half-angry, resentfully amused. He knew it wasn't because Kalzin Brothers were Jews that he had lost his job at last, but just because he had lost it, Mr Solly's accent suddenly presented to him the irresistibly vulnerable. He had come out of prison nine days before, after spending three months as an awaiting-trial prisoner in a political case that had just been quashed – he was one of those who would not accept bail. He had been in prison three or four times since 1952; his wife Ella and the Kalzin Brothers were used to it. Until now, his employers had always given him his job back when he came out. They were importers of china and glass and he was head packer in a team of black men who ran the dispatch department. 'Well, what the hell, I'll get something else,' he said. 'Hey?'

She stopped the self-absorbed examination of the surface of her skin for a slow moment and shrugged, looking at him.

He smiled.

Her gaze loosened hold like hands falling away from grasp. The ends of her nails pressed at small imperfections in the skin of her neck. He drank his tea and tore off pieces of bread to dip in it; then he noticed the tin of sardines she had opened and sopped up the pale matrix of oil in which ragged flecks of silver were suspended. She offered him more tea, without speaking.

They lived in one room of a decent, three-roomed house belonging to someone else; it was better for her that way, since he was often likely to have to be away for long stretches. She worked in a factory that made knitted socks; there was no one at home to look after their one child, a girl, and the child lived with a grandmother in a dusty, peaceful village a day's train-journey from the city.

He said, dismissing it as of no importance, 'I wonder what chance they meant? You can imagine. I don't suppose they were going to give me an office with my name on it.' He spoke as if she would appreciate the joke. She had known when she married him that he was a political man; she had been proud of him because he didn't merely want something for himself, like the other young men she knew, but everything, and for *the people*. It had excited her, under his influence, to change her awareness of herself as a young black girl to awareness of herself as belonging to the people. She knew that everything wasn't like something – a hand-out, a wangled privilege, a trinket you could hold. She would never get something from him.

Her hand went on searching over her skin as if it must come soon, come anxiously, to the flaw, the sickness, the evidence of what was wrong with her; for on this Saturday afternoon all these things that she knew had deserted her. She had lost her wits. All that she could understand was the one room, the child growing up far away in the mud house, and the fact that you couldn't keep a job if you kept being away from work for weeks at a time.

'I think I'd better look up Flora Donaldson,' he said. Flora Donaldson was a white woman who had set up an office to help political prisoners. 'Sooner the better. Perhaps she'll dig up something for me by Monday. It's the beginning of the month.'

He got on all right with those people. Ella had met Flora Donaldson once; she was a pretty white woman who looked just like any white woman who would automatically send a black face round to the back door, but she didn't seem to know that she was white and you were black.

He pulled the curtain that hung across one corner of the room and took out his suit. It was a thin suit, of the kind associated with holidaymakers in American clothing advertisements, and when he was dressed in it, with a sharp-brimmed grey hat tilted slightly back on his small head, he looked a wiry, boyish figure, rather like one of those boy-men who sing and shake before a microphone, and whose clothes admirers try to touch as a talisman.

He kissed her good-bye, obliging her to put down, the lowering of a defence, the piece of sewing she held. She had cleared away the dishes from the table and set up the sewing-machine, and he saw that the shapes of cut material that lay on the table were the parts of a small girl's dress.

She spoke suddenly. 'And when the next lot gets tired of you?'

'When that lot gets tired of me, I'll get another job again, that's all.'

She nodded, very slowly, and her hand crept back to her neck.

'Who was that?' Madge Chadders asked.

Her husband had been out into the hall to answer the telephone.

'Flora Donaldson. I wish you'd explain to these people exactly what sort of factory I've got. It's so embarrassing. She's trying to find a job for some chap, he's a skilled packer. There's no skilled packing done in my workshop, no skilled jobs at all done by black men. What on earth can I offer the fellow? She says he's desperate and anything will do.'

Madge had the broken pieces of a bowl on a newspaper spread on the Persian carpet. 'Mind the glue, darling! There, just next to your foot. Well, anything is better than nothing. I suppose it's someone who was in the Soganiland sedition case. Three months awaiting trial taken out of their lives, and now they're chucked back to fend for themselves.'

William Chadders had not had any black friends or mixed

with coloured people on any but master–servant terms until he married Madge, but his views on the immorality and absurdity of the colour bar were sound; sounder, she often felt, than her own, for they were backed by the impersonal authority of a familiarity with the views of great thinkers, saints and philosophers, with history, political economy, sociology and anthropology. She knew only what she felt. And she always did something, at once, to express what she felt. She never measured the smallness of her personal protest against the establishment she opposed; she marched with Flora and eight hundred black women in a demonstration against African women being forced to carry passes; outside the university where she had once been a student, she stood between sandwich-boards bearing messages of mourning because a Bill had been passed closing the university, for the future, to all but white students; she had living in the house for three months a young African who wanted to write and hadn't the peace or space to get on with it in a location. She did not stop to consider the varying degree of usefulness of the things she did, and if others pointed this out to her and suggested that she might make up her mind to throw her weight on the side either of politics or philanthropy, she was not resentful but answered candidly that there was so little it was possible to do that she simply took any and every chance to get off her chest her disgust at the colour bar. When she had married William Chadders, her friends had thought that her protestant activities would stop; they underestimated not only Madge, but also William, who, although he was a wealthy businessman, subscribed to the view of absolute personal freedom as strictly as any bohemian. Besides he was not fool enough to want to change in any way the person who had enchanted him just as she was.

She reacted upon him, rather than he upon her; she, of course, would not hesitate to go ahead and change anybody. (But why not? she would have said, astonished. If it's to the good?) The attitude she sought to change would occur to her as something of independent existence, she would not see it as a cell in the organism of personality, whose whole structure would have to regroup itself round the change. She had the boldness of being unaware of these consequences.

William did not carry a banner in the streets, of course; he worked up there, among his first principles and historical precedents and economic necessities, but now they were translated from theory to practice of an anonymous, large-scale and behind-the-scenes sort – he was the brains and part of the money in a scheme to get Africans some economic power besides consumer power, through the setting up of an all-African trust company and investment corporation. A number of Madge's political friends, both white and black (like her activities, her friends were mixed, some political, some do-gooders), thought this was putting the middle-class cart before the proletarian horse, but most of the African leaders welcomed the attempt as an essential backing to popular movements on other levels – something to count on outside the unpredictability of mobs. Sometimes it amused Madge to think that William, making a point at a meeting in a boardroom, fifteen floors above life in the streets, might achieve in five minutes something of more value than she did in all her days of turning her hand to anything – from sorting old clothes to roneo-ing a manifesto or driving people during a bus boycott. Yet this did not knock the meaning out of her own life, for her; she knew that she had to see, touch and talk to people in order to care about them, that's all there was to it.

Before she and her husband dressed to go out that evening she finished sticking together the broken Chinese bowl and showed it to him with satisfaction. To her, it was whole again. But it was one of a set, that had belonged together, and whose unity had illustrated certain philosophical concepts. William had bought them long ago, in London; for him, the whole set was damaged for ever.

He said nothing to her, but he was thinking of the bowls when she said to him as they drove off, 'Will you see that chap, on Monday, yourself?'

He changed gear deliberately, attempting to follow her out of his preoccupation. But she said, 'The man Flora's sending. What was his name?'

He opened his hand on the steering wheel, indicating that the name escaped him.

'See him yourself?'

'I'll have to leave it to the works manager to find something for him to do,' he said.

'Yes, I know. But see him yourself, too?'

Her anxious voice made him feel very fond of her. He turned and smiled at her suspiciously. 'Why?'

She was embarrassed at his indulgent manner. She said, frank and wheedling, 'Just to show him. You know. That you know about him and it's not much of a job.'

'All right,' he said. 'I'll see him myself.'

He met her in town straight from the office on Monday and they went to the opening of an exhibition of paintings and on to dinner and to see a play, with friends. He had not been home at all, until they returned after midnight. It was a summer night and they sat for a few minutes on their terrace, where it was still mild with the warmth of the day's sun coming from the walls in the darkness, and drank lime juice and water to quench the thirst that wine and the stuffy theatre had given them. Madge made gasps and groans of pleasure at the release from the pressures of company and noise. Then she lay quiet for a while, her voice lifting now and then in fragments of unrelated comment on the evening – the occasional chirp of a bird that has already put its head under its wing for the night.

By the time they went in, they were free of the evening. Her black dress, her ear-rings and her bracelets felt like fancy-dress; she shed the character and sat on the bedroom carpet, and, passing her, he said, 'Oh – that chap of Flora's came today, but I don't think he'll last. I explained to him that I didn't have the sort of job he was looking for.'

'Well, that's all right, then,' she said enquiringly. 'What more could you do?'

'Yes,' he said, deprecating. 'But I could see he didn't like the idea much. It's a cleaner's job; nothing for him. He's an intelligent chap. I didn't like having to offer it to him.'

She was moving about her dressing table, piling out upon it

the contents of her handbag. 'Then I'm sure he'll understand. It'll give him something for the time being, anyway, darling. You can't help it if you don't need the sort of work he does.'

'Huh, he won't last. I could see that. He accepted it, but only with his head. He'll get fed up. Probably won't turn up tomorrow. I had to speak to him about his Congress button, too. The works manager came to me.'

'What about his Congress button?' she said.

He was unbuttoning his shirt and his eyes were on the unread evening paper that lay folded on the bed. 'He was wearing one,' he said inattentively.

'I know, but what did you have to speak to him about it for?'

'He was wearing it in the workshop all day.'

'Well, what about it?' She was sitting at her dressing-table, legs spread, as if she had sat heavily and suddenly. She was not looking at him, but at her own face.

He gave the paper a push and drew his pyjamas from under the pillow. Vulnerable and naked, he said authoritatively, 'You can't wear a button like that among the men in the workshop.'

'Good heavens,' she said, almost in relief, laughing, backing away from the edge of tension, chivvying him out of a piece of stuffiness. 'And why can't you?'

'You can't have someone clearly representing a political organization like Congress.'

'But he's not there *representing* anything, he's there as a workman?' Her mouth was still twitching with something between amusement and nerves.

'Exactly.'

'Then why can't he wear a button that signifies his allegiance to an organization in his private life outside the workshop? There's no rule about not wearing tie-pins or club buttons or anything, in the workshop, is there?'

'No, there isn't, but that's not quite the same thing.'

'My dear William,' she said, 'it is exactly the same. It's nothing to do with the works manager whether the man wears a Rotary button, or an Elvis Presley button, or an African National Congress button. It's damn all his business.'

'No, Madge, I'm sorry,' William said, patient, 'but it's not the same. I can give the man a job because I feel sympathetic towards the struggle he's in, but I can't put him in the workshop as a Congress man. I mean that wouldn't be fair to Fowler. That I can't do to Fowler.' He was smiling as he went towards the bathroom, but his profile, as he turned into the doorway, was incisive.

She sat on at her dressing-table, pulling a comb through her hair, dragging it down through knots. Then she rested her face on her palms, caught sight of herself and became aware, against her fingers, of the curving shelf of bone, like the lip of a strong shell, under each eye. Everyone has his own intimations of mortality. For her, the feel of the bone beneath the face, in any living creature, brought her the message of the skull. Once hollowed out of this, outside the world, too. For what it's worth. It's worth a lot, the world, she affirmed, as she always did, life rising at once in her as a fish opens its jaws to a fly. It's worth a lot; and she sighed and got up with the sigh.

She went into the bathroom and sat down on the edge of the bath. He was lying there in the water, his chin relaxed on his chest, and he smiled at her. She said, 'You mean you don't want Fowler to know.'

'Oh,' he said, seeing where they were again. 'What is it I don't want Fowler to know?'

'You don't want your partner to know that you slip black men with political ideas into your workshop. Cheeky kaffir agitators. Specially a man who's been in jail for getting people to defy the government! – What was his name; you never said?'

'Daniel something. I don't know. Mongoma or Ngoma. Something like that.'

A line like a cut appeared between her eyebrows. 'Why can't you remember his name?' Then she went on at once, 'You don't want Fowler to know what you think, do you? That's it? You want to pretend you're like him, you don't mind the native in his place. You want to pretend that to please Fowler. You don't want Fowler to think you're cracked or Communist or whatever it is that good-natured, kind, jolly rich people like old Fowler think about people like us.'

'I couldn't have less interest in what Fowler thinks outside our boardroom. And inside it, he never thinks about anything but how to sell more earth-moving gear.'

'I don't mind the native in his place. You want him to think you go along with all that.' She spoke aloud, but she seemed to be telling herself rather than him.

'Fowler and I run a factory. Our only common interest is the efficient running of that factory. Our *only* one. The factory depends on a stable, satisfied black labour-force, and that we've got. Right, you and I know that the whole black wage standard is too low, right, we know that they haven't a legal union to speak for them, right, we know that the conditions they live under make it impossible for them really to be stable. All that. But the fact is, so far as accepted standards go in this crazy country, they're a stable, satisfied labour-force with better working conditions than most. So long as I'm a partner in a business that lives by them, I can't officially admit an element that represents dissatisfaction with their lot.'

'A green badge with a map of Africa on it,' she said.

'If you make up your mind not to understand, you don't, and there it is,' he said indulgently.

'You give him a job but you make him hide his Congress button.'

He began to soap himself. She wanted everything to stop while she inquired into things, she could not go on while a remark was unexplained or a problem unsettled, but he represented a principle she subscribed to but found so hard to follow, that life must go on, trivially, commonplace, the trailing hem of the only power worth clinging to. She smoothed the film of her nightgown over the shape of her knees, over and over, and presently she said, in exactly the flat tone of statement that she had used before, the flat tone that was the height of belligerence in her, 'He can say and do what he likes, he can call for strikes and boycotts and anything he likes, outside the factory, but he mustn't wear his Congress button at work.'

He was standing up, washing his body that was full of scars;

she knew them all, from the place on his left breast where a piece of shrapnel had gone in, all the way back to the place under his arm where he had torn himself on barbed wire as a child. 'Yes, of course, anything he likes.'

'Anything except his self-respect,' she grumbled to herself. 'Pretend, pretend. Pretend he doesn't belong to a political organization. Pretend he doesn't want to be a man. Pretend he hasn't been to prison for what he believes.' Suddenly she spoke to her husband: 'You'll let him have anything except the one thing worth giving.'

They stood in uncomfortable proximity to each other, in the smallness of the bathroom. They were at once aware of each other as people who live in intimacy are only when hostility returns each to the confines of himself. He felt himself naked before her, where he had stepped out onto the towelling mat, and he took a towel and slowly covered himself, pushing the free end in round his waist. She felt herself an intrusion and, in silence, went out.

Her hands were tingling as if she were coming round from a faint. She walked up and down the bedroom floor like someone waiting to be summoned, called to account. I'll forget about it, she kept thinking, very fast, I'll forget about it again. Take a sip of water. Read another chapter. Don't call a halt. Let things flow, cover up, go on.

But when he came into the room with his wet hair combed and his stranger's face, and he said, 'You're angry,' it came from her lips, a black bird in the room, before she could understand what she had released – 'I'm not angry. I'm beginning to get to know you.'

Ella Mngoma knew he was going to a meeting that evening and didn't expect him home early. She put the paraffin lamp on the table so that she could see to finish the child's dress. It was done, buttons and all, by the time he came in at half past ten.

'Well, now we'll see what happens. I've got them to accept, *in principle*, that in future we won't take bail. You should have seen Ben Tsolo's face when I said that we lent the government our money interest-free when we paid bail. That really hit him. That was language he understood.' He laughed, and did not seem to want to sit down, the heat of the meeting still upon him. '*In principle.* Yes, it's easy to accept in principle. We'll see.'

She pumped the primus and set a pot of stew to warm up for him. 'Ah, that's nice.' He saw the dress. 'Finished already?' And she nodded vociferously in pleasure; but at once she noticed his forefinger run lightly along the braid round the neck, and the traces of failure that were always at the bottom of her cup tasted on her tongue again. Probably he was not even aware of it, or perhaps his instinct for what was true – the plumb line, the coin with the right ring – led him absently to it, but the fact was that she had botched the neck.

She had an almost Oriental delicacy about not badgering him and she waited until he had washed and sat down to eat before she asked, 'How did the job go?'

'Oh that,' he said. 'It went.' He was eating quickly, moving his tongue strongly round his mouth to marshal the bits of meat that escaped his teeth. She was sitting with him, feeling, in spite of herself, the rest of satisfaction in her evening's work. 'Didn't you get it?'

'It got *me*. But I got loose again, all right.'

She watched his face to see what he meant. 'They don't want you to come back tomorrow?'

He shook his head, no, no, no, to stem the irritation of her suppositions. He finished his mouthful and said, 'Everything very nice. Boss takes me into his office, apologizes for the pay, he knows it's not the sort of job I should have and so forth. So I go off and clean up in the assembly shop. Then at lunchtime he calls me into the office again: they don't want me to wear my A.N.C. badge at work. Flora Donaldson's sympathetic white man, who's going to do me the great favour of paying me three pounds a week.' He laughed. 'Well, there you are.'

She kept on looking at him. Her eyes widened and her mouth tightened; she was trying to prime herself to speak, or was trying not to cry. The idea of tears exasperated him and he held her with a firm, almost belligerently inquiring gaze.

Her hand went up round the back of her neck under her collar, anxiously exploratory. 'Don't do that!' he said. 'You're like a monkey catching lice.'

She took her hand down swiftly and broke into trembling, like a sweat. She began to breathe hysterically. 'You couldn't put it in your pocket, for the day,' she said wildly, grimacing at the bitterness of malice towards him.

He jumped up from the table. 'Christ! I knew you'd say it! I've been waiting for you to say it. You've been wanting to say it for five years. Well, now it's out. Out with it. Spit it out!' She began to scream softly as if he were hitting her. The impulse to cruelty left him and he sat down before his dirty plate, where the battered spoon lay among bits of gristle and potato-eyes. Presently he spoke. 'You come out and you think there's everybody waiting for you. The truth is, there isn't anybody. You think straight in prison because you've got nothing to lose. Nobody thinks straight, outside. They don't want to hear you. What are you all going to do with me, Ella? Send me back to prison as quickly as possible? Perhaps I'll get a banishment order next time. That'd do. That's what you've got for me. I must keep myself busy with that kind of thing.'

He went over to her and said, in a kindly voice, kneading her shoulder with spread fingers, 'Don't cry. Don't cry. You're just like any other woman.'

A Company of Laughing Faces

When Kathy Hack was seventeen her mother took her to Ingaza Beach for the Christmas Holidays. The Hacks lived in the citrus-farming district of the Eastern Transvaal, and Kathy was an only child; 'Mr Hack wouldn't let me risk my life again,' her mother confided at once, when ladies remarked, as they always did, that it was a lonely life when there was only one. Mrs Hack usually added that she and her daughter were like sisters anyway; and it was true that since Kathy had left school a year ago she had led her mother's life, going about with her to the meetings and afternoon teas that occupied the ladies of the community. The community was one of retired businessmen and mining officials from Johannesburg who had acquired fruit farms to give some semblance of productivity to their leisure. They wore a lot of white linen and created a country-club atmosphere in the village where they came to shop. Mr Hack had the chemist's shop there, but he too was in semi-retirement and he spent most of his afternoons on the golf course or in the club.

The village itself was like a holiday place, with its dazzling white buildings and one wide street smelling of flowers; tropical trees threw shade and petals, and bougainvillaea climbed over the hotel. It was not a rest that Mrs Hack sought at the coast but a measure of gaiety and young company for Kathy. Naturally, there were few people under forty-five in the village and most of them had grown-up children who were married or away working or studying in the cities. Mrs Hack couldn't be expected to part with Kathy – after all, she *is* the only one, she would explain – but, of course, she felt, the child must get out among youngsters once in a while. So she packed up and went on the two-day journey to the coast for Kathy's sake.

They travelled first class and Mrs Hack had jokingly threatened Mr Van Meulen, the stationmaster, with dire consequences if he didn't see to it that they had a carriage to themselves. Yet though she had insisted that she wanted to read her book in peace and not be bothered with talking to some woman, the main-line train had hardly pulled out of Johannesburg station before she and Kathy edged their way along the corridors to the dining car, and over tea Mrs Hack at once got into conversation with the woman at the next table. There they sat for most of the afternoon; Kathy looking out of the window through the mist of human warmth and teapot steam in which she had drawn her name with her forefinger and wiped a porthole with her fist, her mother talking gaily and comfortingly behind her. '... yes, a wonderful place for youngsters, they tell me. The kids really enjoy themselves there ... Well, of course, everything they want, dancing every night. Plenty of youngsters of their own age, that's the thing ... *I* don't mind, I mean I'm quite content to chat for half an hour and go off to my bed ...'

Kathy herself could not imagine what it would be like, this launching into the life of people her own age that her mother had in store for her; but her mother knew all about it and the idea was lit up inside the girl like a room made ready, with everything pulled straight and waiting ... Soon – very soon now, when they got there, when it all began to happen – life would set up in the room. She would know she was young. (When she was a little girl, she had often asked, But what is it like to *be* grown-up? She was too grown-up now to be able to ask, But what do you mean by 'being young', 'oh, to be young' – what is it I ought to feel?) Into the lit-up room would come the young people her own age who would convey the secret quality of being that age; the dancing; the fun. She had the vaguest idea of what this fun would be; she had danced, of course, at the monthly dances at the club, her ear on a level with the strange breathing-noises of middle-aged partners who were winded by whisky. And the fun, the fun? When she tried to think of it she saw a blur, a company of laughing faces, the faces among balloons in a Mardi Gras film, the crowd of bright-skinned, bright-eyed faces like glazed fruits, reaching for a bottle of Coca-Cola on a roadside hoarding.

The journey passed to the sound of her mother's voice. When she was not talking, she looked up from time to time from her knitting, and smiled at Kathy as if to remind her. But Kathy needed no reminder; she thought of the seven new dresses and the three new pairs of shorts in the trunk in the van.

When she rattled up the dusty carriage shutters in the morning and saw the sea, all the old wild joy of childhood gushed in on her for a moment – the sight came to her as the curl of the water along her ankles and the particular sensation, through her hands, of a wooden spade lifting a wedge of wet sand. But it was gone at once. It was the past. For the rest of the day, she watched the sea approach and depart, approach and depart as the train swung towards and away from the shore through green bush and sugar cane, and she was no more aware of it than her mother, who, without stirring, had given the token recognition that Kathy had heard from her year after year as a child: 'Ah, I can smell the sea.'

The hotel was full of mothers with their daughters. The young men, mostly students, had come in groups of two or three on their own. The mothers kept 'well out of the way' as Mrs Hack enthusiastically put it; kept, in fact, to their own comfortable adult preserve – the veranda and the card room – and their own adult timetable – an early, quiet breakfast before the young people, who had been out till all hours, came in to make the dining room restless; a walk or a chat, followed by a quick bathe and a quick retreat from the hot beach back to the cool of the hotel; a long sleep in the afternoon; bridge in the evening. Any young person who appeared among them longer than to snatch a kiss and fling a casual good-bye between one activity and the next was treated with tolerant smiles and jolly remarks that did not conceal a feeling that she really ought to run off – she was there to enjoy herself wasn't she? For the first few days Kathy withstood this attitude stolidly; she knew no one and it seemed natural that she should accompany her mother. But her mother made friends at once, and Kathy became a hanger-on, something her schoolgirl ethics had taught her to despise. She no longer followed her mother to the veranda. 'Well, where are you off to, darling?' 'Up to change.' She and her mother paused in the foyer; her mother was smiling, as if she caught a glimpse of the vista of the morning's youthful pleasures. 'Well, don't be too late for lunch. All the best salads go first.' 'No, I won't.' Kathy went evenly up the stairs, under her mother's eyes.

In her room, that she shared with her mother, she undressed slowly and put on the new bathing suit. And the new Italian straw hat. And the new sandals. And the new bright wrap, printed with sea horses. The disguise worked perfectly; she saw in the mirror a young woman like all the others: she felt the blessed thrill of belonging. This was the world for which she had been brought up, and now, sure enough, when the time had come, she looked the part. Yet it was a marvel to her, just as it must be to the novice when she puts her medieval hood over her shaved head and suddenly is a nun.

She went down to the beach and lay all morning close by, but not part of, the groups of boys and girls who crowded it for two hundred yards, lying in great ragged circles that were constantly broken up and re-formed by chasing and yelling, and the restless to-and-fro of those who were always getting themselves covered with sand in order to make going into the water worth while, or coming back out of the sea to fling a wet head down in someone's warm lap. Nobody spoke to her except two huge louts who tripped over her ankles and exclaimed a hoarse, 'Gee, I'm sorry'; but she was not exactly lonely – she had the satisfaction of knowing that at least she was where she ought to be, down there on the beach with the young people.

Every day she wore another of the new dresses or the small tight shorts – properly, equipment rather than clothes – with which she had been provided. The weather was sufficiently steamy hot to be described by her mother, sitting deep in the shade of the veranda, as glorious. When, at certain moments, there was that pause that comes in the breathing of the sea, music from the beach tearoom wreathed up to the hotel, and at night when the dance was in full swing down there the volume of music and voices joined the volume of the sea's sound itself, so that, lying in bed in the dark, you could imagine yourself under the sea, with the waters sending swaying sound-waves of sunken bells and the cries of drowned men ringing out from depth to depth long after they themselves have touched bottom in silence.

She exchanged smiles with other girls, on the stairs; she made a fourth at tennis; but these encounters left her again, just exactly where they had taken her up – she scarcely remembered the mumbled exchange of names, and their owners disappeared back into the anonymous crowd of sprawled bare legs and sandals that filled the hotel. After three days, a young man asked her to go dancing with him at the Coconut Grove, a rickety bungalow on piles above the lagoon. There was to be a party of eight or more – she didn't know. The idea pleased her mother; it was just the sort of evening she liked to contemplate for Kathy. A jolly group of youngsters and no nonsense about going off in 'couples'.

The young man was in his father's wholesale tea business; 'Are you at varsity?' he asked her, but seemed to have no interest in her life once that query was settled. The manner of dancing at the Coconut Grove was energetic and the thump of feet beat a continuous talc-like dust out of the wooden boards. It made the lights twinkle, as they do at twilight. Dutifully, every now and then the face of Kathy's escort, who was called Manny and was fair, with a spongy nose and small farapart teeth in a wide grin, would appear close to her through the bright dust and he would dance with her. He danced with every girl in turn, picking them out and returning them to the pool again with obvious enjoyment and a happy absence of discrimination. In the intervals, Kathy was asked to dance by other boys in the party; sometimes a bold one from some other party would came up, run his eye over the girls and choose one at random, just to demonstrate an easy confidence. Kathy felt helpless. Here and there there were girls who did not belong to the pool, boys who did not rove in predatory search simply because it was necessary to have a girl to dance with. A boy and a girl sat with hands loosely linked, and got up to dance time and again without losing this tenuous hold of each other. They talked, too. There was a lot of guffawing and some verbal sparring at the table where Kathy sat, but she found that she had scarcely spoken at all, the whole evening. When she got home and crept into bed in the dark in order not to waken her mother, she was breathless from dancing all night, but she felt that she had been running a long way, alone, with only the snatches of remembered voices in her ears.

She did everything everyone else did, now, waking up each day as if to a task. She had forgotten the anticipation of this holiday that she had had; that belonged to another life. It was gone, just as surely as what the sea used to be was gone. The sea was a shock of immersion in cold water, nothing more, in the hot sandy morning of sticky bodies, cigarette smoke, giggling, and ragging. Yet inside her was something distressing, akin to the thickness of not being able to taste when you have a cold. She longed to break through the muffle of automatism with which she carried through the motions of pleasure. There remained in her a desperate anxiety to succeed in being young, to grasp, not merely fraudulently to do, what was expected of her.

People came and went, in the life of the hotel, and their going was not noticed much. They were replaced by others much like them or who became like them, as those who enter into the performance of a rite inhabit a personality and a set of actions preserved in changeless continuity by the rite itself. She was lying on the beach one morning in a crowd when a young man dropped down beside her, turning his head quickly to see if he had puffed sand into her face, but not speaking to her. She had seen him once or twice before; he had been living at the hotel for two or three days. He was one of those young men of the type who are noticed; he no sooner settled down, lazily smoking, addressing some girl with exaggerated endearments and supreme indifference, than he would suddenly get up again and drop in on some other group. There he would be seen in the same sort of ease and intimacy; the first group would feel both slighted and yet admiring. He was not dependent upon anyone; he gave or withheld his presence as he pleased, and the mood of any gathering lifted a little when he was there, simply because his being there was always unexpected. He had brought to perfection the art, fashionable among the boys that year, of leading a girl to believe that he had singled her out for his attention, 'fallen for her', and then, the second she acknowledged this, destroying her self-confidence by one look or sentence that made it seem she had stupidly imagined the whole thing.

Kathy was not surprised that he did not speak to her; she knew only too well she did not belong to that special order of girls and boys among whom life was really shared out, although outwardly the whole crowd might appear to participate. It was going to be a very hot day; already the sea was a deep, hard blue and the sky was taking on the gauzy look of a mirage. The young man – his back half-turned to her – had on a damp pair of bathing trunks and on a level with her eyes, as she lay, she could see a map-line of salt emerging white against the blue material as the moisture dried out of it. He got into some kind of argument and his gestures released from his body the smell of oil. The argument died down and then, in relief at a new distraction, there was a general move up to the beach tearoom where the crowd went every day to drink variously coloured bubbly drinks and to dance, in their bathing suits, to the music of a gramophone. It was the usual straggling procession; 'Aren't you fellows coming?' – the nasal, complaining voice of a girl. 'Just a sec, what's happened to my glasses...' 'All right, don't *drag* me, man –' 'Look what you've done!' 'I don't want any more blisters, thank you very much, not after last night...' Kathy lay watching them troop off, taking her time about following. Suddenly there was a space of sand in front of her, kicked up and tousled, but empty. She felt the sun, that had been kept off her right shoulder by the presence of the young man, strike her; he had got up to follow the others. She lay as if she had not heard when suddenly he was standing above her and had said, shortly, 'Come for a walk.' Her eyes moved anxiously. 'Come for a walk,' he said, taking out of his mouth the empty pipe that he was sucking. She sat up; going for a walk might have been something she had never done before, was not sure if she could do.

'I know you like walking.'

She remembered that when she and some others had limped into the hotel from a hike the previous afternoon, he had been standing at the reception desk, looking up something in a directory. 'All right,' she said, subdued, and got up.

They walked quite briskly along the beach together. It was much cooler down at the water's edge. It was cooler away from the crowded part of the beach, too; soon they had left it behind. Each time she opened her mouth to speak, a mouthful of refreshing air came in. He did not bother with small talk – not even to the extent of an exchange of names. (Perhaps, despite his air of sophistication, he was not really old enough to have acquired any small talk. Kathy had a little stock, like premature grey hairs, that she had found quite useless at Ingaza Beach.) He was one of those people whose conversation is an interior monologue now and then made audible to others. There was a ship stuck like a tag out at sea, cut in half by the horizon, and he speculated about it, its size in relation to the distance, interrupting himself with thrown-away remarks, sceptical of his own speculation, that sometimes were left unfinished. He mentioned something an anonymous 'they' had done 'in the lab'; she said, taking the opportunity to take part in the conversation, 'What do you do?'

'Going to be a chemist,' he said.

She laughed with pleasure. 'So's my father!'

He passed over the revelation and went on comparing the performance of an MG sports on standard commercial petrol with the performance of the same model on a special experimental mixture. 'It's a lot of tripe, anyway,' he said suddenly, abandoning the plaything of the subject. 'Crazy fellows tearing up the place. What for?' As he walked he made a rhythmical clicking sound with his tongue on the roof of his mouth, in time to some tune that must have been going round in his head. She chattered intermittently and politely, but the only part of her consciousness that was acute was some small marginal awareness that along this stretch of gleaming, sloppy sand he was walking without making any attempt to avoid treading on the dozens of small spiral-shell creatures who sucked themselves down into the ooze at the shadow of an approach.

They came to the headland of rock that ended the beach. The rocks were red and smooth, the backs of centuries-warm, benign beasts; then a gaping black seam, all crenellated with turban-shells as small and rough as crumbs, ran through a rocky platform that tilted into the gnashing, hissing sea. A small boy was fishing down there, and he turned and looked after them for a few moments, perhaps expecting them to come to see what he had caught. But when they got to the seam, Kathy's companion stopped, noticed her; something seemed to occur to him; there was the merest suggestion of a pause, a reflex of a smile softened the corner of his mouth. He picked her up in his arms, not without effort, and carried her across. As he set her on her feet she saw his unconcerned eyes, and they changed, in her gaze, to the patronizing, preoccupied expression of a grown-up who has swung a child in the air. The next time they came to a small obstacle he stopped again, jerked his head in dry command and picked her up again, though she could quite easily have stepped across the gap herself. This time they laughed, and she examined her arm when he had put her down. 'It's awful, to be grabbed like that, without warning.' She felt suddenly at ease and wanted to linger at the rock pools, poking about in the tepid water for seaweed and the starfish that felt, as she ventured to tell him, exactly like a cat's tongue. 'I wouldn't know,' he said, not unkindly. 'I haven't got a cat. Let's go.' And they turned back towards the beach. But at anything that could possibly be interpreted as an obstacle he swung her carelessly into his arms and carried her to safety. He did not laugh again, and so she did not either; it seemed to be some very serious game of chivalry. When they were down off the rocks, she ran into the water and butted into a wave and then came flying up to him with the usual shudders and squeals of complaint at the cold. He ran his palm down her bare back and said with distaste, 'Ugh. What did you do that for.'

And so they went back to the inhabited part of the beach and continued along the path up to the hotel, slowly returning to that state of anonymity, that proximity without contact, that belonged to the crowd. It was true, in fact, that she still did not know his name, and did not like to ask. Yet as they passed the beach tearoom and heard the shuffle of bare sandy feet accompanying the wail and fall of a howling song, she had a sudden friendly vision of the dancers.

After lunch was the only time when the young people were in possession of the veranda. The grown-ups had gone up to sleep. There was an unwritten law against afternoon sleep for the young people; to admit a desire for sleep would have been to lose at once your fitness to be one of the young crowd: 'Are you crazy?' The enervation of exposure to the long hot day went on without remission.

It was so hot, even in the shade of the veranda, that the heat seemed to increase gravity; legs spread with more than their usual weight on the grass chairs, feet rested heavily as the monolithic feet of certain sculptures. The young man sat beside Kathy, constantly relighting his pipe; she did not know whether he was bored with her or seeking out her company, but presently he spoke to her monosyllabically, and his laconicism was that of long familiarity. They dawdled down into the garden, where the heat was hardly any worse. There was bougainvillaea, as there was at home in the Eastern Transvaal – a huge, harsh shock of purple, papery flowers that had neither scent nor texture, only the stained-glass colour through which the light shone violently. Three boys passed with swinging rackets and screwed-up eyes, on their way to the tennis courts. Someone called, 'Have you seen Micky and them?'

Then the veranda and garden were deserted. He lay with closed eyes on the prickly grass and stroked her hand – without being aware of it, she felt. She had never been caressed before, but she was not alarmed because it seemed to her such a simple gesture, like stroking a cat or a dog. She and her mother were great readers of novels and she knew, of course, that there were a large number of caresses – hair, and eyes and arms and even breasts – and an immense variety of feelings that would be attached to them. But this simple caress sympathized with her in the heat; she was so hot that she could not breathe with her lips closed and there was on her face a smile of actual suffering. The buzz of a fly round her head, the movement of a leggy red ant on the red earth beneath the grass made her aware that there were no voices, no people about; only the double presence of herself and the unknown person breathing beside her. He propped himself on his elbow and quickly put his half-open lips on her mouth. He gave her no time for surprise or shyness, but held her there, with his wet warm mouth; her instinct to resist the kiss with some part of herself – inhibition, inexperience – died away with the first ripple of its impulse, was smoothed and lost in the melting, boundaryless quality of physical being in the hot afternoon. The salt taste that was in the kiss – it was the sweat on his lip or on hers; his cheek, with its stipple of roughness beneath the surface, stuck to her cheek as the two surfaces of her own skin stuck together wherever they met. When he stood up she rose obediently. The air seemed to swing together, between them. He put his arm across her shoulder – it was heavy and uncomfortable, and bent her head – and began to walk her along the path towards the side of the hotel.

'Come on,' he said, barely aloud, as he took his arm away at the dark archway of an entrance. The sudden shade made her draw a deep breath. She stopped. 'Where are you going?' He gave her a little urging push. 'Inside,' he said, looking at her. The abrupt change from light to dark affected her vision; she was seeing whorls and spots, her heart was plodding. Somewhere there was a moment's stay of uneasiness, but a great unfolding impulse, the blind turn of a daisy towards the sun, made her go calmly with him along the corridor, under his influence: her first whiff of the heady drug of another's will.

In a corridor of dark doors he looked quickly to left and right and then opened a door softly and motioned her in. He slipped in behind her and pushed home the old-fashioned bolt. Once it was done, she gave him a quick smile of adventure and complicity. The room was a bare little room, not like the one she shared with her mother. This was the old wing of the hotel, and it was certain that the push-up-and-down window did not have a view of the sea, although dingy striped curtains were drawn across it, anyway. The room smelled faintly of worn shoes and the rather cold, stale, male smells of dead cigarette-ends and ironed shirts; it was amazing that it could exist, so dim and forgotten, in the core of the hotel that took the brunt of a blazing sun. Yet she scarcely saw it; there was no chance to look round in the mood of curiosity that came upon her, like a movement down to earth. He stood close in front of her, their bare thighs touching beneath their shorts, and kissed her and kissed her. His mouth was different then, it was cool, and she could feel it, delightfully, separate from her own. She became aware of the most extraordinary sensation; her little breasts, that she had never thought of as having any sort of assertion of life of their own, were suddenly inhabited by two struggling trees of feeling, one thrusting up, uncurling, spreading, towards each nipple. And from his lips, it came, this sensation! From his lips! This person she had spoken to for the first time that morning. How pale and slow were the emotions engendered, over years of childhood, by other people, compared to this! You lost the sea, yes, but you found this. When he stopped kissing her she followed his mouth like a calf nuzzling for milk.

Suddenly he thrust his heavy knee between hers. It was a movement so aggressive that he might have hit her. She gave an exclamation of surprise and backed away, in his arms. It was the sort of exclamation that, in the context of situations she was familiar with, automatically brought a solicitous apology – an equally startled 'I'm sorry! Did I hurt you!' But this time there was no apology. The man was fighting with her; *he did not care* that the big bone of his knee had bruised hers. They struggled clumsily, and she was pushed backwards and landed up sitting on the bed. He stood in front of her, flushed and burning-eyed, contained in an orbit of attraction strong as the colour of a flower, and he said in a matter-of-fact, reserved voice, 'It's all right. I know what I'm doing. There'll be nothing for you to worry about.' He went over to the chest of drawers, while she sat on the bed. Like a patient in a doctor's waiting room: the idea swept into her head. She got up and unbolted the door. 'Oh no,' she said, a whole horror of prosaicness enveloping her, 'I'm going now.' The back of the stranger's neck turned abruptly away from her. He faced her, smiling exasperatedly, with a sneer at himself. 'I thought so. I thought that would happen.' He came over and the kisses that she tried to avoid smeared her face. 'What the hell did you come in here for then, hey? Why did you come?' In disgust, he let her go.

She ran out of the hotel and through the garden down to the beach. The glare from the sea hit her, left and right, on both sides of her face; her face that felt battered out of shape by the experience of her own passion. She could not go back to her room because of her mother; the idea of her mother made her furious. She was not thinking at all of what had happened, but was filled with the idea of *her mother*, lying there asleep in the room with a novel dropped open on the bed. She stumbled off over the heavy sand towards the rocks. Down there, there was nobody but the figure of a small boy, digging things out of the wet sand and putting them in a tin. She would have run from anyone, but he did not count; as she drew level with him, ten yards off, he screwed up one eye against the sun and gave her a crooked smile. He waved the tin. 'I'm going to try them for bait,' he said. 'See these little things?' She nodded and walked on. Presently the child caught up with her, slackening his pace conversationally. But they walked on over the sand that the ebbing tide had laid smooth as a tennis court, and he did not speak. He thudded his heels into the firmness.

At last he said, 'That was me, fishing on the rocks over there this morning.'

She said with an effort, 'Oh, was it? I didn't recognize you.' Then, after a moment: 'Did you catch anything?'

'Nothing much. It wasn't a good day.' He picked a spiral shell out of his tin and the creature within put out a little undulating body like a flag. 'I'm going to try these. No harm in trying.'

He was about nine years old, thin and hard, his hair and face covered with a fine powder of salt – even his eyelashes held it. He was at exactly the stage of equidistant remoteness: he had forgotten his mother's lap, and had no inkling of the breaking voice and growing beard to come. She picked one of the spirals out of the tin, and the creature came out and furled and unfurled itself about her fingers. He picked one of the biggest. 'I'll bet this one'd win if we raced them,' he said. They went nearer the water and set the creatures down when the boy gave the word 'Go!' When the creatures disappeared under the sand, they dug them out with their toes. Progressing in this fashion, they came to the rocks, and began wading about in the pools. He showed her a tiny hermit crab that had blue eyes; she thought it the most charming thing she had ever seen and poked about until she found one like it for herself. They laid out on the rock five different colours of starfish, and discussed possible methods of drying them; he wanted to take back some sort of collection for the natural history class at his school. After a time, he picked up his tin and said, with a responsible sigh, 'Well, I better get on with my fishing.' From the point of a particularly high rock, he turned to wave at her.

She walked along the water's edge back to the hotel. In the room, her mother was spraying cologne down the front of her dress. 'Darling, you'll get boiled alive, going to the beach at this hour.' 'No,' said Kathy, 'I'm used to it now.' When her mother had left the room, Kathy went to the dressing-table to brush her hair, and running her tongue over her dry lips, tasted not the salt of the sea, but of sweat; it came to her as a dull reminder. She went into the bathroom and washed her face.

Christmas was distorted, as by a thick lens, by swollen, rippling heat. The colours of paper caps ran on sweating foreheads. The men ate flaming pudding in their shirtsleeves. Flies settled on the tinsel snow of the Christmas tree.

Dancing in the same room on Christmas Eve, Kathy and the young man ignored each other with newly acquired adult complicity. Night after night Kathy danced, and did not lack partners. Though it was not for Mrs Hack to say it, the new dresses *were* a great success. There was no girl who looked nicer. 'K. is having the time of her life,' wrote Mrs Hack to her husband. 'Very much in the swing. She's come out of herself completely.'

Certainly Kathy was no longer waiting for a sign; she had discovered that this was what it was to be young, of course, just exactly this life in the crowd that she had been living all along, silly little ass that she was, without knowing it. There it was. And once you'd got into it, well, you just went on. You clapped and booed with the others at the Sunday-night talent contests, you pretended to kick sand in the boys' faces when they whistled at your legs; squashed into an overloaded car, you yelled songs as you drove, and knew that you couldn't have any trouble with a chap (on whose knees you found yourself) getting too fresh, although he could hold your hand adoringly. The thickness of skin required for all this came just as the required sun-tan did; and everyone was teak-brown, sallow-brown, homogenized into a new leathery race by the rigorous daily exposure to the fierce sun. The only need she had, these days, it seemed, was to be where the gang was; then the question of what to do and how to feel solved itself. The crowd was flat or the crowd was gay; they wanted to organize a beauty contest or trail to the beach at midnight for a watermelon feast.

One afternoon someone got up a hike to a small resort a few miles up the coast. This was the sort of jaunt in which brothers and sisters who really were still too young to qualify for the crowd were allowed to join; there were even a few children who tagged along. The place itself was strange, with a half-hidden waterfall, like a crystal rope, and great tiers of overhanging rock stretching out farther and farther, higher and higher, over a black lagoon; the sun never reached the water. On the other side, where the sea ran into the lagoon at high tide, there was open beach, and there the restless migration from Ingaza Beach settled. Even there, the sand was cool; Kathy felt it soothing to her feet as she struggled out of the shorts and shirt she had worn over her bathing suit while she walked. She swam steadily about, dipping to swim underwater when the surface began to explode all over the place with the impact of the bodies of the boys who soon clambered up the easier reaches of rock and dived from them. People swam close under the wide roof of rock and looked up; hanging plants grew there, and the whole undersurface was chalky, against its rust-streaked blackness, with the droppings of swallows that threaded in and out the ledges like bats. Kathy called to someone from there and her voice came ringing down at her: '... al-l-low!' Soon the swimmers were back on the sand, wet and restless, to eat chocolate and smoke. Cold drinks were brought down by an Indian waiter from the little hotel overlooking the beach; two girls buried a boy up to the neck in sand; somebody came out of the water with a bleeding toe, cut on a rock. People went off exploring, there was always a noisy crowd clowning in the water and there were always a few others lying about talking on the sand. Kathy was in such a group when one of the young men came up with his hands on his hips, lips drawn back from his teeth thoughtfully, and asked, 'Have you seen the Bute kid around here?' 'What kid?' someone said. 'Kid about ten, in green trunks. Libby Bute's kid brother.' 'Oh, I know the one you mean. I don't know – all the little boys were playing around on the rocks over there, just now.' The young man scanned the beach, nodding. 'Nobody knows where he's got to.'

'The kids were all together over there, only a minute ago.'

'I know. But he can't be found. Kids say they don't know where he is. He might have gone fishing. But Libby says he would have told her. He was supposed to tell her if he went off on his own.'

Kathy was making holes in the sand with her forefinger. 'Is that the little boy who goes fishing up on the rocks at the end of our beach?'

'Mm. Libby's kid brother.'

Kathy got up and looked round at the people, the lagoon, as if she were trying to reinterpret what she had seen before. 'I didn't know he was here. I don't remember seeing him. With those kids who were fooling around with the birds' nests?'

'That's right. He was there.' The young man made a little movement with his shoulders and wandered off to approach some people farther along. Kathy and her companions went on to talk of something else. But suddenly there was a stir on the beach: a growing stir. People were getting up; others were coming out of the water. The young man hurried past again; 'He's not found,' they caught from him in passing. People began moving about from one knot to another, gathering suppositions, hoping for news they'd missed. Centre of an awkward, solicitous, bossy circle was Libby Bute herself, a dark girl with long hands and a bad skin, wavering uncertainly between annoyance and fear. 'I suppose the little tyke's gone off to fish somewhere, without a word. I don't know. Doesn't mean a thing that he didn't have his fishing stuff with him, he's always got a bit of string and a couple of pins.' Nobody said anything. 'He'll turn up,' she said; and then looked round at them all.

An hour later, when the sun was already beginning to drop from its afternoon zenith, he was not found. Everyone was searching for him with a strange concentration, as if, in the mind of each one, an answer, the remembrance of where he was, lay undisturbed, if only one could get at it. Before there was time for dread, like doubt, like dew, to form coldly, Kathy Hack came face to face with him. She was crawling along the first ledge of rock because she had an idea he might have got it into his head to climb into what appeared to be a sort of cave behind the waterfall, and be stuck there, unable to get out and unable to make himself heard. She glanced down into the water and saw a glimmer of light below the surface. She leant over between her haunches and he was looking at her, not more than a foot below the water, where, shallow over his face, it showed golden above its peat-coloured depths. The water was very deep there, but he had not gone far. He lay held up by the just-submerged rock that had struck the back of his head as he had fallen backwards into the lagoon. What she felt was not shock, but recognition. It was as if he had had a finger to his lips, holding the two of them there, so that she might not give him away. The water moved but did not move him; only his little bit of short hair was faintly obedient, leaning the way of the current, as the green beard of the rock did. He was as absorbed as he must have been in whatever it was he was doing when he fell. She looked at him, looked at him, for a minute, and then she clambered back to the shore and went on with the search. In a little while, someone else found him and Libby Bute lay screaming on the beach, saliva and sand clinging round her mouth.

Two days later, when it was all over, and more than nine pounds had been collected among the hotel guests for a wreath, and the body was on the train to Johannesburg, Kathy said to her mother, 'I'd like to go home.' Their holiday had another week to run. 'Oh I know,' said Mrs Hack with quick sympathy. 'I feel the same myself. I can't get that poor little soul out of my mind. But life has to go on, darling, one can't take the whole world's troubles on one's shoulders. Life brings you enough troubles of your own, believe me.' 'It's not that at all,' said Kathy. 'I don't like this place.'

Mrs Hack was just feeling herself nicely settled and would have liked another week. But she felt that there was the proof of some sort of undeniable superiority in her daughter's great sensitivity; a superiority they ought not to forgo. She told the hotel proprietor and the other mothers that she had to leave; that was all there was to it: Kathy was far too much upset by the death of the little stranger to be able simply to go ahead with the same zest for holiday pleasures that she had enjoyed up till now. Many young people could do it, of course; but not Kathy. She wasn't made that way, and what was she, her mother, to do about it?

In the train going home they did not have a carriage to themselves and very soon Mrs Hack was explaining to their lady travelling companion – in a low voice, between almost closed teeth, in order not to upset Kathy – how the marvellous holiday had been ruined by this awful thing that had happened.

The girl heard, but felt no impulse to tell her mother – knew, in fact, that she would never have the need to tell anyone the knowledge that had held her secure since the moment she looked down into the lagoon: the sight, there, was the one real happening of the holiday, the one truth and the one beauty.

Not For Publication

It is not generally known – and it is never mentioned in the official biographies – that the Prime Minister spent the first eleven years of his life, as soon as he could be trusted not to get under a car, leading his uncle about the streets. His uncle was not really blind, but nearly, and he was certainly mad. He walked with his right hand on the boy's left shoulder; they kept moving part of the day, but they also had a pitch on the cold side of the street, between the legless man near the post office who sold bootlaces and copper bracelets, and the one with the doll's hand growing out of one elbow, whose pitch was outside the Y.W.C.A. That was where Adelaide Graham-Grigg found the boy, and later he explained to her, 'If you sit in the sun they don't give you anything.'

Miss Graham-Grigg was not looking for Praise Basetse. She was in Johannesburg on one of her visits from a British Protectorate, seeing friends, pulling strings and pursuing, on the side, her private study of following up the fate of those people of the tribe who had crossed the border and lost themselves, sometimes over several generations, in the city. As she felt down through the papers and letters in her bag to find a sixpence for the old man's hat, she heard him mumble something to the boy in the tribe's tongue – which was not in itself anything very significant in this city where many African languages could be heard. But these sounds formed in her ear as words: it was the language that she had learnt to understand a little. She asked, in English, using only the traditional form of address in the tribe's tongue, whether the old man was a tribesman. But he was mumbling the blessings that the clink of a coin started up like a kick to a worn and useless mechanism. The boy spoke to him, nudged him; he had already learnt in a rough way to be a businessman. Then the old man protested, no, no, he had come a long time from that tribe. A long, long time. He was Johannesburg. She saw that he confused the question with some routine interrogation at the pass offices, where a man from another territory was always in danger of being endorsed out to some forgotten 'home'. She spoke to the boy, asking him if he came from the Protectorate. He shook his head terrifiedly; once before he had been ordered off the streets by a welfare organization. 'But your father? Your mother?' Miss Graham-Grigg said, smiling. She discovered that the old man had come from the Protectorate, from the very village she had made her own, and that his children and grandchildren continued to speak the language as their mother tongue, among themselves, down to the second generation born in the alien city.

Now the pair were no longer beggars to be ousted from her conscience by a coin: they were members of the tribe. She found out what township they went to ground in after the day's begging, interviewed the family, established for them the old man's right to a pension in his adopted country, and above all, did something for the boy. She never succeeded in finding out exactly who he was – she gathered he must have been the illegitimate child of one of the girls in the family, his parentage concealed so that she might go on with her schooling. Anyway, he was a descendant of the tribe, a displaced tribesman, and he could not be left to go on begging in the streets.

That was as far as Miss Graham-Grigg's thoughts for him went, in the beginning. Nobody wanted him particularly, and she met with no opposition from the family when she proposed to take him back to the Protectorate and put him to school. He went with her just as he had gone through the streets of Johannesburg each day under the weight of the old man's hand.

The boy had never been to school before. He could not write, but Miss Graham-Grigg was astonished to discover that he could read quite fluently. Sitting beside her in her little car in the khaki shorts and shirt she had bought him, stripped of the protection of his smelly rags and scrubbed bare to her questions, he told her that he had learnt from the newspaper vender whose pitch was on the corner: from the posters that changed several times a day, and then from the front pages of the newspapers and magazines spread there. Good God, what had he not learnt on the street! Everything from his skin out unfamiliar to him, and even that smelling strangely different – this detachment, she realized, made the child talk as he could never have done when he was himself. Without differentiation, he related the commonplaces of his life; he had also learnt from the legless, copper-bracelet man how to make *dagga* cigarettes and smoke them for a nice feeling. She asked him what he thought he would have done when he got older, if he had had to keep on walking with his uncle, and he said that he had wanted to belong to one of the gangs of boys, some little older than himself, who were very good at making money. They got money from white people's pockets and handbags without their even knowing it, and if the police came they began to play penny whistles and sing. She said with a smile, 'Well, you can forget all about the street, now. You don't have to think about it ever again.' And he said, 'Yes, med-dam,' and she knew she had no idea what he was thinking – how could she? All she could offer were more unfamiliarities, the unfamiliarities of generalized encouragement, saying, 'And soon you will know how to write.'

She had noticed that he was hatefully ashamed of not being able to write. When he had had to admit it, the face that he turned open and victimized to her every time she spoke had the squinting grimace – teeth showing and a grown-up cut between the faint, child's eyebrows – of profound humiliation. Humiliation terrified Adelaide Graham-Grigg as the spectacle of savage anger terrifies others. That was one of the things she held against the missionaries: how they stressed Christ's submission to humiliation, and so had conditioned the people of Africa to humiliation by the white man.

Praise went to the secular school that Miss Graham-Grigg's committee of friends of the tribe in London had helped pay to set up in the village in opposition to the mission school. The sole qualified teacher was a young man who had received his training in South Africa and now had been brought back to serve his people; but it was a beginning. As Adelaide Graham-Grigg often said to the Chief, shining-eyed as any proud daughter, 'By the time independence comes we'll be free not only of the British government, but of the church as well.' And he always giggled a little embarrassedly, although he knew her so well and was old enough to be her father, because her own father was both a former British M.P. and the son of a bishop.

It was true that everything was a beginning; that was the beauty of it – of the smooth mud houses, red earth, flies and heat that visitors from England wondered she could bear to live with for months on end – while their palaces and cathedrals and streets, choked on a thousand years of used-up endeavour, were an ending. Even Praise was a beginning; one day the tribe would be economically strong enough to gather its exiles home, and it would no longer be necessary for its sons to sell their labour over that border. But it soon became clear that Praise was also exceptional. The business of learning to read from newspaper headlines was not merely a piece of gutter wit; it proved to have been the irrepressible urge of real intelligence. In six weeks the boy could write, and from the start he could spell perfectly, while boys of sixteen and eighteen never succeeded in mastering English orthography. His arithmetic was so good that he had to be taught with the Standard Three class instead of the beginners; he grasped at once what a map was; and in his spare time showed a remarkable aptitude for understanding the workings of various mechanisms, from water-pumps to motorcycle engines. In eighteen months he had completed the Standard Five syllabus, only a year behind the average age of a city white child with all the background advantage of a literate home.

There was as yet no other child in the tribe's school who was ready for Standard Six. It was difficult to see what could be done, now, but send Praise back over the border to school. So Miss Graham-Grigg decided it would have to be Father Audry. There was nothing else for it. The only alternative was the mission school, those damned Jesuits who'd been sitting in the Protectorate since the days when the white imperialists were on the grab, taking the tribes under their 'protection' – and the children the boy would be in class with there wouldn't provide any sort of stimulation, either. So it would have to be Father Audry, and South Africa. He was a priest, too, an Anglican one, but his school was a place where at least, along with the pious pap, a black child could get an education as good as a white child's.

When Praise came out into the veld with the other boys his eyes screwed up against the size: the land ran away all round, and there was no other side to be seen; only the sudden appearance of the sky, that was even bigger. The wind made him snuff like a dog. He stood helpless as the country men he had seen caught by changing traffic lights in the middle of a street. The bits of space between buildings came together, ballooned uninterruptedly over him, he was lost; but there were clouds as big as the buildings had been, and even though space was vaster than any city, it was peopled by birds. If you ran for ten minutes into the veld the village was gone; but down low on the ground thousands of ants knew their way between their hard mounds that stood up endlessly as the land.

He went to herd cattle with the other boys early in the mornings and after school. He taught them some gambling games they had never heard of. He told them about the city they had never seen. The money in the old man's hat seemed a lot to them, who had never got more than a few pennies when the mail train stopped for water at the halt five miles away; so the sum grew in his own estimation too, and he exaggerated it a bit. In any case, he *was* forgetting about the city, in a way; not Miss Graham-Grigg's way, but in the manner of a child, who makes, like a wasp building with its own spittle, his private context within the circumstance of his surroundings, so that the space around him was reduced to the village, the pan where the cattle were taken to drink, the halt where the train went by; whatever particular patch of sand or rough grass astir with ants the boys rolled on, heads together, among the white egrets and the cattle. He learnt from the others what roots and leaves were good to chew, and how to set wire traps for spring-hares. Though Miss Graham-Grigg had said he need not, he went to church with the children on Sundays.

He did not live where she did, in one of the Chief's houses, but with the family of one of the other boys; but he was at her house often. She asked him to copy letters for her. She cut things out of the newspapers she got and gave them to him to read; they were about aeroplanes, and dams being built, and the way the people lived in other countries. 'Now you'll be able to tell the boys all about the Volta Dam, that is also in Africa – far from here – but still, in Africa,' she said, with that sudden smile that reddened her face. She had a gramophone and she played records for him. Not only music, but people reading our poems, so that he knew that the poems in the school reader were not just short lines of words, but more like songs. She gave him tea with plenty of sugar and she asked him to help her to learn the language of the tribe, to talk to her in it. He was not allowed to call her *madam* or *missus*, as he did the white women who had put money in the hat, but had to learn to say *Miss Graham-Grigg*.

Although he had never known any white women before except as high-heeled shoes passing quickly in the street, he did not think that all white women must be like her; in the light of what he had seen white people, in their cars, their wealth, their distance, to be, he understood nothing that she did. She looked like them, with her blue eyes, blond hair and skin that was not one colour but many: brown where the sun burned it, red when she blushed – but she lived here in the Chief's houses, drove him in his car, and sometimes slept out in the fields with the women when they were harvesting kaffircorn far from the village. He did not know why she had brought him there or why she should be kind to him. But he could not ask her, any more than he would have asked her why she went out and slept in the fields when she had a gramophone and a lovely gas lamp (he had been able to repair it for her) in her room. If, when they were talking together, the talk came anywhere near the pitch outside the post office, she became slowly very red, and they went past it, either by falling silent or (on her part) talking and laughing rather fast.

That was why he was amazed the day she told him that he was going back to Johannesburg. As soon as she had said it she blushed darkly for it, her eyes pleading confusion: so it was really from her that the vision of the pitch outside the post office came again. But she was already speaking: '... to school. To a really good boarding-school. Father Audry's school, about nine miles from town. You must get your chance at a good school, Praise. We really can't teach you properly any longer. Maybe you'll be the teacher here yourself, one day. There'll be a high school, and you'll be the headmaster.'

She succeeded in making him smile, but she looked sad, uncertain. He went on smiling because he couldn't tell her about the initiation school that he was about to begin with the other boys of his age-group. Perhaps someone would tell her. The other women. Even the Chief. But you couldn't fool her with smiling.

'You'll be sorry to leave Tebedi and Joseph and the rest.'

He stood there, smiling.

'Praise, I don't think you understand about yourself – about your brain.' She gave a little sobbing giggle, prodded at her own head. 'You've got an awfully good one. More in there than other boys – you know? It's something special – it would be such a waste. Lots of people would like to be clever like you, but it's not easy, when you are the clever one.'

He went on smiling. He did not want her face looking into his any more and so he fixed his eyes on her feet, white feet in sandals with the veins standing out over the ankles like the feet of Christ dangling above his head in the church.

Adelaide Graham-Grigg had met Father Audry before, of course. All those white people who do not accept the colour bar in southern Africa seem to know each other, however different the bases of their rejection. She had sat with him on some committee or other in London a few years earlier, along with a couple of exiled white South African leftists and a black nationalist leader. Anyway, everyone knew him – from the newspapers, if nowhere else: he had been warned, in a public speech by the Prime Minister of the South African Republic,

Dr Verwoerd, that the interference of a churchman in political matters would not be tolerated. He continued to speak his mind, and (as the newspapers quoted him) 'to obey the commands of God before the dictates of the State'. He had close friends among African and Indian leaders, and it was said that he even got on well with certain ministers of the Dutch Reformed Church, that, in fact, *he* was behind some of the dissidents who now and then questioned Divine Sanction for the colour bar – such was the presence of his restless, black-cassocked figure, stammering eloquence, and jagged handsome face.

He had aged since she saw him last; he was less handsome. But he had still what he would have as long as he lived: the unconscious bearing of a natural prince among men that makes a celebrated actor, a political leader, a successful lover; an object of attraction and envy who, whatever his generosity of spirit, is careless of one cruelty for which other people will never forgive him – the distinction, the luck with which he was born.

He was tired and closed his eyes in a grimace straining at concentration when he talked to her, yet in spite of this, she felt the dimness of the candle of her being within his radius. Everything was right with him; nothing was quite right with her. She was only thirty-six but she had never looked any younger. Her eyes were the bright shy eyes of a young woman, but her feet and hands with their ridged nails had the look of tension and suffering of extremities that would never caress: she saw it, she saw it, she knew in his presence that they were deprived for ever.

Her humiliation gave her force. She said, 'I must tell you we want him back in the tribe – I mean, there are terribly few with enough education even for administration. Within the next few years we'll desperately need more and more educated men ... We shouldn't want him to be allowed to think of becoming a priest.'

Father Audry smiled at what he knew he was expected to come out with: that if the boy chose the way of the Lord, etc.

He said, 'What you want is someone who will turn out to be an able politician without challenging the tribal system.'

They both laughed, but, again, he had unconsciously taken the advantage of admitting their deeply divergent views; he believed the chiefs must go, while she, of course, saw no reason why Africans shouldn't develop their own tribal democracy instead of taking over the Western pattern.

'Well, he's a little young for us to be worrying about that now, don't you think?' He smiled. There were a great many papers on his desk, and she had the sense of pressure of his preoccupation with other things. 'What about the Lemeribe Mission? What's the teaching like these days – I used to know Father Chalmon when he was there –'

'I wouldn't send him to those people,' she said spiritedly, implying that he knew her views on missionaries and their role in Africa. In this atmosphere of candour, they discussed Praise's background. Father Audry suggested that the boy should be encouraged to resume relations with his family, once he was back within reach of Johannesburg.

'They're pretty awful.'

'It would be best for him to acknowledge what he was, if he is to accept what he is to become.' He got up with a swish of his black skirts and strode, stooping in the opened door, to call, 'Simon, bring the boy.' Miss Graham-Grigg was smiling excitedly towards the doorway, all the will to love pacing behind the bars of her glance.

Praise entered in the navy-blue shorts and white shirt of his new school uniform. The woman's kindness, the man's attention, got him in the eyes like the sun striking off the pan where the cattle had been taken to drink. Father Audry came from England, Miss Graham-Grigg had told him, like herself. That was what they were, these two white people who were not like any white people he had seen to be. What they were was being English. From far off; six thousand miles from here, as he knew from his geography book.

Praise did very well at the new school. He sang in the choir in the big church on Sundays; his body, that was to have been made a man's out in the bush, was hidden under the white robes. The boys smoked in the lavatories and once there was a girl who came and lay down for them in a storm-water ditch behind the workshops. He knew all about these things from before, on the streets and in the location where he had slept in one room with a whole family. But he did not tell the boys about the initiation. The women had not said anything to Miss Graham-Grigg. The Chief hadn't, either. Soon when Praise thought about it he realized that by now it must be over. Those boys must have come back from the bush. Miss Graham-Grigg had said that after a year, when Christmas came, she would fetch him for the summer holidays. She did come and see him twice that first year, when she was down in Johannesburg, but he couldn't go back with her at Christmas because Father Audry had him in the Nativity play and was giving him personal coaching in Latin and algebra. Father Audry didn't actually teach in the school at all – it was 'his' school simply because he had begun it, and it was run by the order of which he was Father Provincial – but the reports of the boy's progress were so astonishing that, as he said to Miss Graham-Grigg, one felt one must give him all the mental stimulation one could.

'I begin to believe we may be able to sit him for his matric when he is just sixteen.' Father Audry made the pronouncement with the air of doing so at the risk of sounding ridiculous. Miss Graham-Grigg always had her hair done when she got to Johannesburg, she was looking pretty and gay. 'D'you think he could do a Cambridge entrance? My committee in London would set up a scholarship, I'm sure – investment in a future prime minister for the Protectorate!'

When Praise was sent for, she said she hardly knew him; he hadn't grown much, but he looked so *grown-up*, with his long trousers and glasses. 'You really needn't wear them when you're not working,' said Father Audry. 'Well, I suppose if you take 'em on and off you keep leaving them about, eh?' They both stood back, smiling, letting the phenomenon embody in the boy.

Praise saw that she had never been reminded by anyone

about the initiation. She began to give him news of his friends, Tebedi and Joseph and the others, but when he heard their names they seemed to belong to people he couldn't see in his mind.

Father Audry talked to him sometimes about what Father called his 'family', and when first he came to the school he had been told to write to them. It was a well-written, well-spelled letter in English, exactly the letter he presented as a school exercise when one was required in class. They didn't answer. Then Father Audry must have made private efforts to get in touch with them, because the old woman, a couple of children who had been babies when he left and one of his grown-up 'sisters' came to the school on a visiting day. They had to be pointed out to him among the other boys' visitors; he would not have known them, nor they him. He said, 'Where's my uncle?' – because he would have known him at once; he had never grown out of the slight stoop of the left shoulder where the weight of the old man's hand had impressed the young bone. But the old man was dead. Father Audry came up and put a long arm round the bent shoulder and another long arm round one of the small children and said from one to the other, 'Are you going to work hard and learn a lot like your brother?' And the small black child stared up into the nostrils filled with strong hair, the tufted eyebrows, the red mouth surrounded by the pale jowl dark-pored with beard beneath the skin, and then down, torn by fascination, to the string of beads that hung from the leather belt.

They did not come again but Praise did not much miss visitors because he spent more and more time with Father Audry. When he was not actually being coached, he was set to work to prepare his lessons or do his reading in the Father's study, where he could concentrate as one could not hope to do up at the school. Father Audry taught him chess as a form of mental gymnastics, and was jubilant the first time Praise beat him. Praise went up to the house for a game nearly every evening after supper. He tried to teach the other boys, but after the first ten minutes of explanation of moves, someone would bring out the cards or dice and they would all play one of the old games that were played in the streets and yards and locations. Johannesburg was only nine miles away; you could see the lights.

Father Audry rediscovered what Miss Graham-Grigg had found – that Praise listened attentively to music, serious music. One day Father Audry handed the boy the flute that had lain for years in its velvet-lined box that bore still the little silver name-plate: Rowland Audry. He watched while Praise gave the preliminary swaying wriggle and assumed the bent-kneed stance of all the urchin performers Father Audry had seen, and then tried to blow down it in the shy, fierce attack of penny-whistle music. Father Audry took it out of his hands. 'It's what you've just heard there.' Bach's unaccompanied flute sonata lay on the record-player. Praise smiled and frowned, giving his glasses a lift with his nose – a habit he was developing. 'But you'll soon learn to play it the right way round,' said Father Audry, and with the lack of self-consciousness that comes from the habit of privilege, put the flute to his mouth and played what he remembered after ten years.

He taught Praise not only how to play the flute but also the elements of musical composition, so that he should not simply play by ear, or simply listen with pleasure, but also understand what it was that he heard. The flute-playing was much more of a success with the boys than the chess had been, and on Saturday nights, when they sometimes made up concerts, he was allowed to take it to the hostel and play it for them. Once he played in a show for white people, in Johannesburg; but the boys could not come to that; he could only tell them about the big hall at the university, the jazz band, the African singers and dancers with their red lips and straightened hair, like white women.

The one thing that dissatisfied Father Audry was that the boy had not filled out and grown as much as one would have expected. He made it a rule that Praise must spend more time on physical exercise – the school couldn't afford a proper gymnasium but there was some equipment outdoors. The trouble was that the boy had so little time; even with his exceptional ability, it was not going to be easy for a boy with his lack of background to matriculate at sixteen. Brother George, his form master, was certain he could be made to bring it off; there was a specially strong reason why everyone wanted him to do it since Father Audry had established that he would be eligible for an open scholarship that no black boy had ever won before – what a triumph that would be, for the boy, for the school, for all the African boys who were considered fit only for the inferior standard of 'Bantu education'! Perhaps some day this beggar child from the streets of Johannesburg might even become the first black South African to be a Rhodes Scholar. This was what Father Audry jokingly referred to as Brother George's 'sin of pride'. But who knew? It was not inconceivable. So far as the boy's physique was concerned – what Brother George said was probably true: 'You can't feed up for those years in the streets.'

From the beginning of the first term of the year he was fifteen Praise had to be coached, pressed on, and to work as even he had never worked before. His teachers gave him tremendous support; he seemed borne along on it by either arm so that he never looked up from his books. To encourage him, Father Audry arranged for him to compete in certain inter-school scholastic contests that were really intended for the white Anglican schools – a spelling bee, a debate, a quiz contest. He sat on the platform in the polished halls of huge white schools and gave his correct answers in the African-accented English that the boys who surrounded him knew only as the accent of servants and delivery men.

Brother George often asked him if he were tired. But he was not tired. He only wanted to be left with his books. The boys in the hostel seemed to know this; they never asked him to play cards any more, and even when they shared smokes together in the lavatory, they passed him his drag in silence. He specially did not want Father Audry to come in with a glass of hot milk. He would rest his cheek against the pages of the books, now and then, alone in the study; that was all. The damp stone smell of the books was all he needed. Where he had once had to force himself to return again and again to the pages of things he did not grasp, gazing in blankness at the print until meaning assembled itself, he now had to force himself when it was necessary to leave the swarming facts outside which he no longer seemed to understand anything. Sometimes he could not work for minutes at a time because he was thinking that Father Audry would come in with the milk. When he did come, it was never actually so bad. But Praise couldn't look at his face. Once or twice when he had gone out again, Praise shed a few tears. He found himself praying, smiling with the tears and trembling, rubbing at the scalding water that ran down inside his nose and blotched on the books.

One Saturday afternoon when Father Audry had been entertaining guests at lunch he came into the study and suggested that the boy should get some fresh air – go out and join the football game for an hour or so. But Praise was struggling with geometry problems from the previous year's matriculation paper that, to Brother George's dismay, he had suddenly got all wrong, that morning.

Father Audry could imagine what Brother George was thinking: was this an example of the phenomenon he had met with so often with African boys of a lesser calibre – the inability, through lack of an assumed cultural background, to perform a piece of work well known to them, once it was presented in a slightly different manner outside one of their own textbooks? Nonsense, of course, in this case; everyone was over-anxious about the boy. Right from the start he'd shown that there was nothing mechanistic about his thought processes; he had a brain, not just a set of conditioned reflexes.

'Off you go. You'll manage better when you've taken a few knocks on the field.'

But desperation had settled on the boy's face like obstinacy. 'I must, I must,' he said, putting his palms down over the books.

'Good. Then let's see if we can tackle it together.'

The black skirt swishing past the shiny shoes brought a smell of cigars. Praise kept his eyes on the black beads; the leather belt they hung from creaked as the big figure sat down. Father Audry took the chair on the opposite side of the table and switched the exercise book round towards himself. He scrubbed at the thick eyebrows till they stood out tangled, drew the hand down over his great nose and then screwed his eyes closed a moment, mouth strangely open and lips drawn back in a familiar grimace. There was a jump, like a single painful hiccup, in Praise's body. The Father was explaining the problem gently, in his offhand English voice.

He said, 'Praise? D'you follow?' – the boy seemed sluggish, almost deaf, as if the voice reached him as the light of a star reaches the earth from something already dead.

Father Audrey put out his fine hand, in question or compassion. But the boy leapt up, dodging a blow. 'Sir – no. Sir – no.'

It was clearly hysteria; he had never addressed Father Audry as anything but 'Father'. It was some frightening retrogression, a reversion to the subconscious, a place of symbols and collective memory. He spoke for others, out of another time. Father Audry stood up but saw in alarm that by the boy's retreat he was made his pursuer, and he let him go blundering in clumsy panic out of the room.

Brother George was sent to comfort the boy. In half an hour Praise was down on the football field, running and laughing. But Father Audry took some days to get over the inci[illegible] kept thinking how when the boy had backed away [illegible] almost gone after him. The ugliness of the instinct [illegible] him; who would have thought how, at the mercy of [illegible] stinct to prey, the fox, the wild dog long for the innocen[illegible] the gentle rabbit, and the lamb. No one had shown fear of [illegible] ever before in his life. He had never given a thought [illegible] people who were not like himself; those from whom [illegible] for turn away. He felt at last a repugnant and resent[illegible] that he them, the dripping-jawed hunters. He even tho[illegible] [illegible]ut it was inwould like to go into retreat fo[illegible] a few days, convenient – he had so many obligations. Finally, the matter-of-factness of the boy, Praise, was the thing that restored normality. So far as the boy was concerned, one would have thought that nothing had happened. The next day he seemed to have forgotten all about it; a good thing. And so Father Audry's own inner disruption, denied by the boy's calm, sank away. He allowed the whole affair the one acknowledgement of writing to Miss Graham-Grigg – surely that was not making too much of it – to suggest that the boy was feeling the tension of his final great effort, and that a visit from her, etc.; but she was still away in England – some family troubles had kept her there for months, and in fact she had not been to see her protégé for more than a year.

Praise worked steadily on the last lap. Brother George and Father Audry watched him continually. He was doing extremely well and seemed quite overcome with the weight of pride and pleasure when Father Audry presented him with a new black fountain-pen: this was the pen with which he was to write the matriculation exam. On a Monday afternoon Father Audry, who had been in conference with the bishop all morning, looked in on his study, where every afternoon the boy would be seen sitting at the table that had been moved in for him. But there was no one there. The books were on the table. A chute of sunlight landed on the seat of the chair.

Praise was not found again. The school was searched; and then the police were informed; the boys questioned; there were special prayers said in the mornings and evenings. He had not taken anything with him except the fountain-pen.

When everything had been done there was nothing but silence; nobody mentioned the boy's name. But Father Audry was conducting investigations on his own. Every now and then he would get an idea that would bring a sudden hopeful relief. He wrote to Adelaide Graham-Grigg: '... what worries me – believe the boy may have been on the verge of a nervous breakdown. I am hunting everywhere ...'; was it possible that he might make his way to the Protectorate? She was acting as confidential secretary to the Chief, now, but she wrote to say that if the boy turned up she would try to make time to deal with the situation. Father Audry even sought out, at last, the 'family' – the people with whom Miss Graham-Grigg had discovered Praise living as a beggar. They had been moved to a new township and it took some time to trace them. He found Number 28b, Block E, in the appropriate ethnic group. He was accustomed to going in and out of African homes and he explained his visit to the old woman in matter-of-fact terms at once, since he knew how suspicious of questioning the people would be. There were no interior doors in these houses and a woman in the inner room who was dressing moved out of the visitor's line of vision as he sat down. She heard all that passed between Father Audry and the old woman and presently she came in with mild interest. Out of a silence the old woman was saying, 'My-my-my-my!' – she shook her head down into her bosom in a stylized expression of commiseration; they had not seen the boy. 'And he spoke so nice, everything was so nice in the school.' But they knew nothing about the boy, nothing at all. The younger woman remarked, 'Maybe he's with those boys who sleep in the old empty cars there in town – you know? – there by the beer hall?'

A Chip of Glass Ruby

When the duplicating machine was brought into the house, Bamjee said, 'Isn't it enough that you've got the Indians' troubles on your back?' Mrs Bamjee said, with a smile that showed the gap of a missing tooth but was confident all the same, 'What's the difference, Yusuf? We've all got the same troubles.'

'Don't tell me that. We don't have to carry passes; let the natives protest against passes on their own, there are millions of them. Let them go ahead with it.'

The nine Bamjee and Pahad children were present at this exchange as they were always; in the small house that held them all there was no room for privacy for the discussion of matters they were too young to hear, and so they had never been too young to hear anything. Only their sister and half-sister, Girlie, was missing; she was the eldest, and married. The children looked expectantly, unalarmed and interested, at Bamjee, who had neither left the room nor settled down again to the task of rolling his own cigarettes, which had been interrupted by the arrival of the duplicator. He had looked at the thing that had come hidden in a wash-basket and conveyed in a black man's taxi, and the children turned on it too, their black eyes surrounded by thick lashes like those still, open flowers with hairy tentacles that close on whatever touches them.

'A fine thing to have on the table where we eat,' was all he said at last. They smelled the machine among them; a smell of cold black grease. He went out, heavily on tiptoe, in his troubled way.

'It's going to go nicely on the sideboard!' Mrs Bamjee was busy making a place by removing the two pink glass vases filled with plastic carnations and the hand-painted velvet runner with the picture of the Taj Mahal.

After supper she began to run off leaflets on the machine. The family lived in that room – the three other rooms in the house were full of beds – and they were all there. The older children shared a bottle of ink while they did their homework, and the two little ones pushed a couple of empty milk-bottles in and out the chair-legs. The three-year-old fell asleep and was carted away by one of the girls. They all drifted off to bed eventually; Bamjee himself went before the older children – he was a fruit-and-vegetable hawker and was up at half past four every morning to get to the market by five. 'Not long now,' said Mrs Bamjee. The older children looked up and smiled at him. He turned his back on her. She still wore the traditional clothing of a Moslem woman, and her body, which was scraggy and unimportant as a dress on a peg when it was not host to a child, was wrapped in the trailing rags of a cheap sari and her thin black plait was greased. When she was a girl, in the Transvaal town where they lived still, her mother fixed a chip of glass ruby in her nostril; but she had abandoned that adornment as too old-style, even for her, long ago.

She was up until long after midnight, turning out leaflets. She did it as if she might have been pounding chillies.

Bamjee did not have to ask what the leaflets were. He had read the papers. All the past week Africans had been destroying their passes and then presenting themselves for arrest. Their leaders were jailed on charges of incitement, campaign offices were raided – someone must be helping the few minor leaders who were left to keep the campaign going without offices or equipment. What was it the leaflets would say – 'Don't go to work tomorrow', 'Day of Protest', 'Burn Your Pass for Freedom'? He didn't want to see.

He was used to coming home and finding his wife sitting at the table deep in discussion with strangers or people whose names were familiar by repute. Some were prominent Indians, like the lawyer, Dr Abdul Mohammed Khan, or the big businessman, Mr Moonsamy Patel, and he was flattered, in a suspicious way, to meet them in his house. As he came home from work next day he met Dr Khan coming out of the house and Dr Khan – a highly educated man – said to him, 'A wonderful woman.' But Bamjee had never caught his wife out in any presumption; she behaved properly, as any Moslem woman should, and once her business with such gentlemen was over would never, for instance, have sat down to eat with them. He found her now back in the kitchen, setting about the preparation of dinner and carrying on a conversation on several different wave-lengths with the children. 'It's really a shame if you're tired of lentils, Jimmy, because that's what you're getting – Amina, hurry up, get a pot of water going – don't worry, I'll mend that in a minute, just bring the yellow cotton, and there's a needle in the cigarette box on the sideboard.'

'Was that Dr Khan leaving?' said Bamjee.

'Yes, there's going to be a stay-at-home on Monday. Desai's ill, and he's got to get the word around by himself. Bob Jali was up all last night printing leaflets, but he's gone to have a tooth out.' She had always treated Bamjee as if it were only a mannerism that made him appear uninterested in politics, the way some woman will persist in interpreting her husband's bad temper as an endearing gruffness hiding boundless goodwill, and she talked to him of these things just as she passed on to him neighbours' or family gossip.

'What for do you want to get mixed up with these killings and stonings and I don't know what? Congress should keep out of it. Isn't it enough with the Group Areas?'

She laughed. 'Now, Yusuf, you know you don't believe that. Look how you said the same thing when the Group Areas started in Natal. You said we should begin to worry when we get moved out of our own houses here in the Transvaal. And then your own mother lost her house in Noorddorp, and there you are; you saw that nobody's safe. Oh, Girlie was here this afternoon, she says Ismail's brother's engaged – that's nice, isn't it? His mother will be pleased; she was worried.'

'Why was she worried?' asked Jimmy, who was fifteen, and old enough to patronize his mother.

'Well, she wanted to see him settled. There's a party on Sunday week at Ismail's place – you'd better give me your suit to give to the cleaners tomorrow, Yusuf.'

One of the girls presented herself at once. 'I'll have nothing to wear, Ma.'

Mrs Bamjee scratched her sallow face. 'Perhaps Girlie will lend you her pink, eh? Run over to Girlie's place now and say I say will she lend it to you.'

The sound of commonplaces often does service as security, and Bamjee, going to sit in the armchair with the shiny armrests that was wedged between the table and the sideboard, lapsed into an unthinking doze that, like all times of dreamlike ordinariness during those weeks, was filled with uneasy jerks and starts back into reality. The next morning, as soon as he got to market, he heard that Dr Khan had been arrested. But that night Mrs Bamjee sat up making a new dress for her daughter; the sight disarmed Bamjee, reassured him again, against his will, so that the resentment he had been making ready all day faded into a morose and accusing silence. Heaven knew, of course, who came and went in the house during the day. Twice in that week of riots, raids and arrests, he found black women in the house when he came home; plain ordinary native women in doeks, drinking tea. This was not a thing other Indian women would have in their homes, he thought bitterly; but then his wife was not like other people, in a way he could not put his finger on, except to say what it was not: not scandalous, not punishable, not rebellious. It was, like the attraction that had led him to marry her, Pahad's widow with five children, something he could not see clearly.

When the Special Branch knocked steadily on the door in the small hours of Thursday morning he did not wake up, for his return to consciousness was always set in his mind to half past four, and that was more than an hour away. Mrs Bamjee got up herself, struggled into Jimmy's raincoat which was hanging over a chair and went to the front door. The clock on the wall – a wedding present when she married Pahad – showed three o'clock when she snapped on the light, and she knew at once who it was on the other side of the door. Although she was not surprised, her hands shook like a very old person's as she undid the locks and the complicated catch on the wire burglar-proofing. And then she opened the door and they were there – two coloured policemen in plain clothes. 'Zanip Bamjee?'

'Yes.'

As they talked, Bamjee woke up in the sudden terror of having overslept. Then he became conscious of men's voices. He heaved himself out of bed in the dark and went to the window, which, like the front door, was covered with a heavy mesh of thick wire against intruders from the dingy lane it looked upon. Bewildered, he appeared in the room, where the policemen were searching through a soapbox of papers beside the duplicating machine. 'Yusuf, it's for me,' Mrs Bamjee said.

At once, the snap of a trap, realization came. He stood there in an old shirt before the two policemen, and the woman was going off to prison because of the natives. 'There you are!' he shouted, standing away from her. 'That's what you've got for it. Didn't I tell you? Didn't I? That's the end of it now. That's the finish. That's what it's come to.' She listened with her head at the slightest tilt to one side, as if to ward off a blow, or in compassion.

Jimmy, Pahad's son, appeared at the door with a suitcase; two or three of the girls were behind him. 'Here, Ma, you take my green jersey.' 'I've found your clean blouse.' Bamjee had to keep moving out of their way as they helped their mother to make ready. It was like the preparation for one of the family festivals his wife made such a fuss over; wherever he put himself, they bumped into him. Even the two policemen mumbled, 'Excuse me,' and pushed past into the rest of the house to continue their search. They took with them a tome that Nehru had written in prison; it had been bought from a persevering travelling salesman and kept, for years, on the mantelpiece. 'Oh, don't take that, please,' Mrs Bamjee said suddenly, clinging to the arm of the man who had picked it up.

The man held it away from her.

'What does it matter, Ma?'

It was true that no one in the house had ever read it; but she said, 'It's for my children.'

'Ma, leave it.' Jimmy, who was squat and plump, looked like a merchant advising a client against a roll of silk she had set her heart on. She went into the bedroom and got dressed. When she came out in her old yellow sari with a brown coat over it, the faces of the children were behind her like faces on the platform at a railway station. They kissed her good-bye. The policemen did not hurry her, but she seemed to be in a hurry just the same.

'What am I going to do?' Bamjee accused them all.

The policemen looked away patiently.

'It'll be all right. Girlie will help. The big children can manage. And Yusuf –' The children crowded in around her; two of the younger ones had awakened and appeared, asking shrill questions.

'Come on,' said the policemen.

'I want to speak to my husband.' She broke away and came back to him, and the movement of her sari hid them from the rest of the room for a moment. His face hardened in suspicious anticipation against the request to give some message to the next fool who would take up her pamphleteering until he, too, was arrested. 'On Sunday,' she said. 'Take them on Sunday.' He did not know what she was talking about. 'The engagement party,' she whispered, low and urgent. 'They shouldn't miss it. Ismail will be offended.'

They listened to the car drive away. Jimmy bolted and barred the front door, and then at once opened it again; he put on the raincoat that his mother had taken off. 'Going to tell Girlie,' he said. The children went back to bed. Their father did not say a word to any of them; their talk, the crying of the younger ones and the argumentative voices of the older, went on in the bedrooms. He found himself alone; he felt the night all around him. And then he happened to meet the clock face and saw with a terrible sense of unfamiliarity that this was not the secret night but an hour he should have recognized: the time he always got up. He pulled on his trousers and his dirty white hawker's coat and wound his grey muffler up to the stubble on his chin and went to work.

The duplicating machine was gone from the sideboard. The

policemen had taken it with them, along with the pamphlets and the conference reports and the stack of old newspapers that had collected on top of the wardrobe in the bedroom – not the thick dailies of the white men but the thin, impermanent-looking papers that spoke up, sometimes interrupted by suppression or lack of money, for the rest. It was all gone. When he had married her and moved in with her and her five children, into what had been the Pahad and became the Bamjee house, he had not recognized the humble, harmless and apparently useless routine tasks – the minutes of meetings being written up on the dining-room table at night, the government blue books that were read while the latest baby was suckled, the employment of the fingers of the older children in the fashioning of crinkle-paper Congress rosettes – as activity intended to move mountains. For years and years he had not noticed it, and now it was gone.

The house was quiet. The children kept to their lairs, crowded on the beds with the doors shut. He sat and looked at the sideboard, where the plastic carnations and the mat with the picture of the Taj Mahal were in place. For the first few weeks he never spoke of her. There was the feeling, in the house, that he had wept and raged at her, that boulders of reproach had thundered down upon her absence, and yet he had said not one word. He had not been to inquire where she was; Jimmy and Girlie had gone to Mohammed Ebrahim, the lawyer, and when he found out that their mother had been taken – when she was arrested, at least – to a prison in the next town, they had stood about outside the big prison door for hours while they waited to be told where she had been moved from there. At last they had discovered that she was fifty miles away, in Pretoria. Jimmy asked Bamjee for five shillings to help Girlie pay the train fare to Pretoria, once she had been interviewed by the police and had been given a permit to visit her mother; he put three two-shilling pieces on the table for Jimmy to pick up, and the boy, looking at him keenly, did not know whether the extra shilling meant anything, or whether it was merely that Bamjee had no change.

It was only when relations and neighbours came to the

house that Bamjee would suddenly begin to talk. He had never been so expansive in his life as he was in the company of these visitors, many of them come on a polite call rather in the nature of a visit of condolence. 'Ah, yes, yes, you can see how I am – you see what has been done to me. Nine children, and I am on the cart all day. I get home at seven or eight. What are you to do? What can people like us do?'

'Poor Mrs Bamjee. Such a kind lady.'

'Well, you see for yourself. They walk in here in the middle of the night and leave a houseful of children. I'm out on the cart all day, I've got a living to earn.' Standing about in his shirt sleeves, he became quite animated; he would call for the girls to bring fruit drinks for the visitors. When they were gone, it was as if he, who was orthodox if not devout and never drank liquor, had been drunk and abruptly sobered up; he looked dazed and could not have gone over in his mind what he had been saying. And as he cooled, the lump of resentment and wrongedness stopped his throat again.

Bamjee found one of the little boys the centre of a self-important group of championing brothers and sisters in the room one evening, 'They've been cruel to Ahmed.'

'What has he done?' said the father.

'Nothing! Nothing!' The little girl stood twisting her handkerchief excitedly.

An older one, thin as her mother, took over, silencing the others with a gesture of her skinny hand. 'They did it at school today. They made an example of him.'

'What is an example?' said Bamjee impatiently.

'The teacher made him come up and stand in front of the whole class, and he told them, "You see this boy? His mother's in jail because she likes the natives so much. She wants the Indians to be the same as natives."'

'It's terrible,' he said. His hands fell to his sides. 'Did she ever think of this?'

'That's why Ma's *there*,' said Jimmy, putting aside his comic and emptying out his schoolbooks upon the table. 'That's all the kids need to know. Ma's there because things like this happen. Petersen's a coloured teacher, and it's his black blood that's brought him trouble all his life, I suppose. He hates anyone who says everybody's the same because that takes away from him his bit of whiteness that's all he's got. What d'you expect? It's nothing to make too much fuss about.'

'Of course, you are fifteen and you know everything,' Bamjee mumbled at him.

'I don't say that. But I know Ma, anyway.' The boy laughed.

There was a hunger strike among the political prisoners, and Bamjee could not bring himself to ask Girlie if her mother was starving herself too. He would not ask; and yet he saw in the young woman's face the gradual weakening of her mother. When the strike had gone on for nearly a week one of the elder children burst into tears at the table and could not eat. Bamjee pushed his own plate away in rage.

Sometimes he spoke out loud to himself while he was driving the vegetable lorry. 'What for?' Again and again: 'What for?' She was not a modern woman who cut her hair and wore short skirts. He had married a good plain Moslem woman who bore children and stamped her own chillies. He had a sudden vision of her at the duplicating machine, that night just before she was taken away, and he felt himself maddened, baffled and hopeless. He had become the ghost of a victim, hanging about the scene of a crime whose motive he could not understand and had not had time to learn.

The hunger strike at the prison went into the second week. Alone in the rattling cab of his lorry, he said things that he heard as if spoken by someone else, and his heart burned in fierce agreement with them. 'For a crowd of natives who'll smash our shops and kill us in our houses when their time comes.' 'She will starve herself to death there.' 'She will die there.' 'Devils who will burn and kill us.' He fell into bed each night like a stone, and dragged himself up in the mornings as a beast of burden is beaten to its feet.

One of these mornings, Girlie appeared very early, while he was wolfing bread and strong tea – alternate sensations of dry solidity and stinging heat – at the kitchen table. Her real name was Fatima, of course, but she had adopted the silly modern name along with the clothes of the young factory girls among whom she worked. She was expecting her first baby in a week or two, and her small face, her cut and curled hair and the sooty arches drawn over her eyebrows did not seem to belong to her thrust-out body under a clean smock. She wore mauve lipstick and was smiling her cocky little white girl's smile, foolish and bold, not like an Indian girl's at all.

'What's the matter?' he said.

She smiled again. 'Don't you know? I told Bobby he must get me up in time this morning. I wanted to be sure I wouldn't miss you today.'

'I don't know what you're talking about.'

She came over and put her arm up around his unwilling neck and kissed the grey bristles at the side of his mouth. 'Many happy returns! Don't you know it's your birthday?'

'No,' he said. 'I didn't know, didn't think –' He broke the pause by swiftly picking up the bread and giving his attention desperately to eating and drinking. His mouth was busy, but his eyes looked at her, intensely black. She said nothing, but stood there with him. She would not speak, and at last he said, swallowing a piece of bread that tore at his throat as it went down, 'I don't remember these things.'

The girl nodded, the Woolworth baubles in her ears swinging. 'That's the first thing she told me when I saw her yesterday – don't forget it's Bajie's birthday tomorrow.'

He shrugged over it. 'It means a lot to children. But that's how she is. Whether it's one of the old cousins or the neighbour's grandmother, she always knows when the birthday is. What importance is my birthday, while she's sitting there in a prison? I don't understand how she can do the things she does when her mind is always full of woman's nonsense at the same time – that's what I don't understand with her.'

'Oh, but don't you see?' the girl said. 'It's because she doesn't want anybody to be left out. It's because she always remembers; remembers everything – people without somewhere to live, hungry kids, boys who can't get educated – remembers all the time. That's how Ma is.'

'Nobody else is like that.' It was half a complaint.

'No, nobody else,' said his stepdaughter.

She sat herself down at the table, resting her belly. He put his head in his hands. 'I'm getting old' – but he was overcome by something much more curious, by an answer. He knew why he had desired her, the ugly widow with five children; he knew what way it was in which she was not like the others; it was there, like the fact of the belly that lay between him and her daughter.

Good Climate, Friendly Inhabitants

In the office at the garage eight hours a day I wear mauve linen overalls – those snappy uniforms they make for girls who aren't really nurses. I'm forty-nine but I could be twenty-five except for my face and my legs. I've got that very fair skin and my legs have gone mottled, like Roquefort cheese. My hair used to look pretty as chickens' fluff, but now it's been bleached and permed too many times. I wouldn't admit this to anyone else, but to myself I admit everything. Perhaps I'll get one of those wigs everyone's wearing. You don't have to be short of hair, any more, to wear a wig.

I've been years at the garage – service station, as it's been called since it was rebuilt all steel and glass. That's at the front, where the petrol pumps are; you still can't go into the workshop without getting grease on your things. But I don't have much call to go there. Between doing the books you'll see me hanging about in front for a breath of air, smoking a cigarette and keeping an eye on the boys. Not the mechanics – they're all white chaps of course (bunch of ducktails they are, too, most of them) – but the petrol attendants. One boy's been with the firm twenty-three years – sometimes you'd think he owns the place; gets my goat. On the whole they're not a bad lot of natives, though you get a cheeky bastard now and then, or a thief, but he doesn't last long, with us.

We're just off the Greensleeves suburban shopping centre with the terrace restaurant and the fountain, and you get a very nice class of person coming up and down. I'm quite friends with some of the people from the luxury flats round about; they wouldn't pass without a word to me when they're walking their dogs or going to the shops. And of course you get to know a lot of the regular petrol customers, too. We've got two Rolls and any amount of sports cars who never go anywhere else. And I only have to walk down the block to Maison Claude when I get my hair done, or in to Mr Levine at the Greensleeves Pharmacy if I feel a cold coming on.

I've got a flat in one of the old buildings that are still left, back in town. Not too grand, but for ten quid a month and right on the bus route ... I was married once and I've got a lovely kid – married since she was seventeen and living in Rhodesia; I couldn't stop her. She's very happy with him and they've got twin boys, real little toughies! I've seen them once.

There's a woman friend I go to the early flicks with every Friday, and the Versfelds' where I have a standing invitation for Sunday lunch. I think they depend on me, poor old things; they never see anybody. That's the trouble when you work alone in an office, like I do, you don't make friends at your work. Nobody to talk to but those duckies in the workshop, and what can I have in common with a lot of louts in black leather jackets? No respect, either, you should hear the things they come out with. I'd sooner talk to the blacks, that's the truth, though I know it sounds a strange thing to say. At least they call you missus. Even old Madala knows he can't come into my office without taking his cap off, though heaven help you if you ask that boy to run up to the Greek for a packet of smokes, or round to the Swiss Confectionery. I had a dust-up with him once over it, the old monkey-face, but the manager didn't seem to want to get rid of him, he's been here so long. So he just keeps out of my way and he has his half-crown from me at Christmas, same as the other boys. But you get more sense out of the boss-boy, Jack, than you can out of some whites, believe me, and he can make you laugh, too, in his way – of course they're like children, you see them yelling with laughter over something in their own language, noisy lot of devils; I don't suppose we'd think it funny at all if we knew what it was all about. This Jack used to get a lot of phone calls (I complained to the manager on the quiet and he's put a stop to it, now) and the natives on the other end used to be asking to speak to Mpanza and Makiwane and I don't know what all, and when I'd say there wasn't anyone of that name working here they'd come out with it and ask for Jack. So I said to him one day, why do you people have a hundred and one names, why don't these uncles and aunts and brothers-in-law come out with your name straight away and stop wasting my time?' He said, 'Here I'm Jack because Mpanza Makiwane is not a name, and there I'm Mpanza Makiwane because Jack is not a name, but I'm the only one who knows who I am wherever I am.' I couldn't help laughing. He hardly ever calls you missus, I notice, but it doesn't sound cheeky, the way he speaks. Before they were allowed to buy drink for themselves, he used to ask me to buy a bottle of brandy for him once a week and I didn't see any harm.

Even if things are not too bright, no use grumbling. I don't believe in getting old before my time. Now and then it's happened that some man's taken a fancy to me at the garage. Every time he comes to fill up he finds some excuse to talk to me; if a chap likes me, I begin to feel it just like I did when I was seventeen, so that even if he was just sitting in his car looking at me through the glass of the office, I would know that he was waiting for me to come out. Eventually he'd ask me to the hotel for a drink after work. Usually that was as far as it went. I don't know what happens to these blokes, they are married, I suppose, though their wives don't still wear a perfect size fourteen, like I do. They enjoy talking to another woman once in a while, but they quickly get nervous. They are businessmen and well off; one sent me a present, but it was one of those old-fashioned compacts, we used to call them flapjacks, meant for loose powder, and I use the solid kind everyone uses now.

Of course you get some funny types, and, as I say, I'm alone there in the front most of the time, with only the boys, the manager is at head office in town, and the other white men are all at the back. Little while ago a fellow came into my office wanting to pay for his petrol with Rhodesian money. Well, Jack, the boss-boy, came first to tell me that this fellow had given him Rhodesian money. I sent back to say we didn't take it. I looked through the glass and saw a big, expensive American car, not very new, and one of those men you recognize at once as the kind who move about a lot – he was poking out his cheek with his tongue, looking round the station and out into the busy street like, in his head, he was trying to work out his way around in a new town. Some people kick up hell with a native if he refuses them something, but this one didn't seem to; the next thing was he got the boy to bring him to me. 'Boss says he must talk to you,' Jack said, and turned on his heel. But I said, you wait here. I know Johannesburg; my cash-box was there in the open safe. The fellow was young. He had that very tanned skin that has been sunburnt day after day, the tan you see on lifesavers at the beach. His hair was the thick streaky blond kind, waste on men. He says, 'Miss, can't you help me out for half an hour?' Well, I'd had my hair done, it's true, but I don't kid myself you could think of me as a miss unless you saw my figure, from behind. He went on, 'I've just driven down and I haven't had a chance to change my money. Just take this while I get hold of this chap I know and get him to cash a cheque for me.'

I told him there was a bank up the road but he made some excuse. 'I've got to tell my friend I'm in town anyway. Here, I'll leave this – it's a gold one.' And he took the big fancy watch off his arm. 'Go on, please, do me a favour.' Somehow when he smiled he looked not so young, harder. The smile was on the side of his mouth. Anyway, I suddenly said okay, then, and the native boy turned and went out of the office, but I knew it was all right about my cash, and this fellow asked me which was the quickest way to get to Kensington and I came out from behind my desk and looked it up with him on the wall map. I thought he was a fellow of about twenty-nine or thirty; he was so lean, with a snakeskin belt around his hips and a clean white open-neck shirt.

He was back on the dot. I took the money for the petrol and said, here's your watch, pushing it across the counter. I'd seen, the moment he'd gone and I'd picked up the watch to put it in the safe, that it wasn't gold: one of those Jap fakes that men take out of their pockets and try to sell you on streetcorners. But I didn't say anything, because maybe he'd been had? I gave him the benefit of the doubt. What'd it matter? He'd paid for his petrol, anyway. He thanked me and said he supposed he'd better push off and find some hotel. I said the usual sort of thing, was he here on a visit and so on, and he said, yes, he didn't know how long, perhaps a couple of weeks, it all depended, and he'd like somewhere central. We had quite a little chat – you know how it is, you always feel friendly if you've done someone a favour and it's all worked out okay – and I mentioned a couple of hotels. But it's difficult if you don't know what sort of place a person wants, you may send him somewhere too expensive, or on the other hand you might recommend one of the small places that he'd consider just a joint, such as the New Park, near where I live.

A few days later I'd been down to the shops at lunch hour and when I came by where some of the boys were squatting over their lunch in the sun, Jack said, 'That man came again.' Thinks I can read his mind; what man, I said, but they never learn. 'The other day, with the money that was no good.' Oh, you mean the Rhodesian, I said. Jack didn't answer but went on tearing chunks of bread out of half a loaf and stuffing them into his mouth. One of the other boys began telling, in their own language with bits of English thrown in, what I could guess was the story of how the man had tried to pay with money that was no good; big joke, you know; but Jack didn't take any notice, I suppose he'd heard it once too often.

I went into my office to fetch a smoke, and when I was enjoying it outside in the sun Jack came over to the tap near me. I heard him drinking from his hand, and then he said, 'He went and looked in the office window.' Didn't he buy petrol? I said. 'He pulled up at the pump but then he didn't buy, he said he will come back later.' Well, that's all right, what're you getting excited about, we sell people as much petrol as they like, I said. I felt uncomfortable. I don't know why; you'd think I'd been giving away petrol at the garage's expense or something.

'You can't come from Rhodesia on those tyres,' Jack said. No? I said. 'Did you look at those tyres?' Why should *I* look at tyres? 'No-no, you look at those tyres on that old car. You can't drive six hundred miles or so on those tyres. Worn out!

Down to the tread!' But who cares where he came from, I said, it's his business. 'But he had that money,' Jack said to me. He shrugged and I shrugged; I went back into my office. As I say, sometimes you find yourself talking to that boy as if he was a white person.

Just before five that same afternoon the fellow came back. I don't know how it was, I happened to look up like I knew the car was going to be there. He was taking petrol and paying for it, this time; old Madala was serving him. I don't know what got into me, curiosity maybe, but I got up and came to my door and said, how's Jo'burg treating you? 'Ah, hell, I've had bad luck,' he says. 'The place I was staying had another booking for my room from today. I was supposed to go to my friend in Berea, but now his wife's brother has come. I don't mind paying for a decent place, but you take one look at some of them ... Don't you know somewhere?' Well yes, I said, I was telling you that day. And I mentioned the Victoria, but he said he'd tried there, so then I told him about the New Park, near me. He listened, but looking round all the time, his mind was somewhere else. He said, 'They'll tell me they're full, it'll be the same story.' I told him that Mrs Douglas who runs the place is a nice woman – she would be sure to fix him up. 'You couldn't ask her?' he said. I said well, all right, from my place she was only round the corner, I'd pop in on my way home from work and tell her he'd be getting in touch with her.

When he heard that he said he'd give me a lift in his car, and so I took him to Mrs Douglas myself, and she gave him a room. As we walked out of the hotel together he seemed wrapped up in his own affairs again, but on the pavement he suddenly suggested a drink. I thought he meant we'd go into the hotel lounge, but he said, 'I've got a bottle of gin in the car,' and he brought it up to my place. He was telling me about the time he was in the Congo a few years ago, fighting for that native chief, whats's-name – Tshombe – against the Irishmen who were sent out there to put old whats's-name down. The stories he told about Elisabethville! He was paid so much he could live like a king. We only had two gins each out the bottle, but when I wanted him to take it along with him, he said, 'I'll come in for it sometime when I get a chance.' He didn't say anything, but I got the idea he had come up to Jo'burg about a job.

I was frying a slice of liver next evening when he turned up at the door. The bottle was still standing where it'd been left. You feel uncomfortable when the place's full of the smell of frying and anyone can tell you're about to eat. I gave him the bottle but he didn't take it; he said he was on his way to Vereeniging to see someone, he would just have a quick drink. I had to offer him something to eat, with me. He was one of those people who eat without noticing what it is. He never took in the flat, either; I mean he didn't look round at my things the way it's natural you do in someone else's home. And there was a lovely photo of my kid on the built-in fixture round the electric fire. I said to him while we were eating, is it a job you've come down for? He smiled the way youngsters smile at an older person who won't understand, anyway. 'On business.' But you could see that he was not a man who had an office, who wore a suit and sat in a chair. He was like one of those men you see in films, you know, the stranger in town who doesn't look as if he lives anywhere. Somebody in a film, thin and burned red as a brick and not saying much. I mean he did talk but it was never really anything about himself, only about things he'd seen happen. He never asked me anything about myself, either. It was queer; because of this, after I'd seen him a few times, it was just the same as if we were people who know each other so well they don't talk about themselves any more.

Another funny thing was, all the time he was coming in and out the flat, I was talking about him with the boy – with Jack. I don't believe in discussing white people with natives, as a rule, I mean, whatever I think of a white, it encourages disrespect if you talk about it to a black. I've never said anything in front of the boys about the behaviour of that crowd of ducktails in the workshop, for instance. And of course I wouldn't be likely to discuss my private life with a native boy. Jack didn't know that this fellow was coming to the flat, but he'd heard me say I'd fix up about the New Park Hotel, and he'd seen me take a lift home that afternoon. The boy's remark about the tyres seemed to stick in my mind; I said to him: That man came all the way from the Congo.

'In that car?' Jack said; he's got such a serious face, for a native. The car goes all right, I said, he's driving all over with it now.

'Why doesn't he bring it in for retreads?'

I said he was just on holiday, he wouldn't have it done here.

The fellow didn't appear for five or six days and I thought he'd moved on, or made friends, as people do in this town. There was still about two fingers left in his bottle. I don't drink when I'm on my own. Then he turned up at the garage just at the time I knock off. Again I meant to look at the tyres for myself, but I forgot. He took me home just like it had been an arranged thing; you know, a grown-up son calling for his mother not because he wants to, but because he has to. We hardly spoke in the car. I went out for pies, which wasn't much of a dinner to offer anyone, but, as I say, he didn't know what he was eating, and he didn't want the gin, he had some cans of beer in the car. He leaned his chair back with all the weight on two legs and said, 'I think I must clear out of this lousy dump, I don't know what you've got to be to get along here with these sharks.' I said, you kids give up too easy, have you still not landed a job? 'A job!' he said. 'They owe me *money*, I'm trying to get *money* out of them.' What's it all about, I said, what money? He didn't take any notice, as if I wouldn't understand. 'Smart alecks and swindlers. I been here nearly three lousy weeks, now.' I said, everybody who comes here finds Jo'burg tough compared with their home.

He'd had his head tipped back and he lifted it straight and looked at me. 'I'm not such a kid.' No? I said, feeling a bit awkward because he never talked about himself before. He was looking at me all the time, you'd have thought he was going to find his age written on my face. 'I'm thirty-seven,' he said. 'Did you know that? Thirty-seven. Not so much younger.'

Forty-nine. It was true, not so much. But he looked so young, with that hair always slicked back longish behind the ears as if he'd just come out of the shower, and that brown neck in the open-neck shirt. Lean men wear well, you can't tell. He did have false teeth, though, that was why his mouth made him look hard. I supposed he could have been thirty-seven; I didn't know, I didn't know.

It was like the scars on his body. There were scars on his back and other scars on his stomach, and my heart was in my mouth for him when I saw them, still pink and raw-looking, but he said that the ones on his back were from strokes he'd had in a boys' home as a kid and the others were from the fighting in Katanga.

I know nobody would believe me, they would think I was just trying to make excuses for myself, but in the morning everything seemed just the same, I didn't feel I knew him any better. It was just like it was that first day when he came in with his Rhodesian money. He said, 'Leave me the key. I might as well use the place while you're out all day.' But what about the hotel, I said. 'I've taken my things,' he says. I said, you mean you've moved out? And something in his face, the bored sort of look, made me ask, you've told Mrs Douglas? 'She's found out by now,' he said, it was unusual for him to smile. You mean you went without paying? I said. 'Look, I told you I can't get my money out of those bastards.'

Well, what could I do? I'd taken him to Mrs Douglas myself. The woman'd given him a room on my recommendation. I had to go over to the New Park and spin her some yarn about him having to leave suddenly and that he'd left the money for me to pay. What else could I do? Of course I didn't tell *him*.

But I told Jack. That's the funny thing about it. I told Jack that the man had disappeared, run off without paying my friend who ran the hotel where he was staying. The boy clicked his tongue the way they do, and laughed. And I said that was what you got for trying to help people. Yes, he said, Johannesburg was full of people like that, but you learn to know their faces, even if they were nice faces.

I said, you think that man had a nice face?

'You see he has a nice face,' the boy said.

I was afraid I'd find the fellow there when I got home, and he was there. I said to him, that's my daughter, and showed him the photo, but he took no interest, not even when I said she lived in Gwelo and perhaps he knew the town himself. I said why didn't he go back to Rhodesia to his job but he said Central Africa was finished, he wasn't going to be pushed around by a lot of blacks running the show – from what he told me, it's awful, you can't keep them out of hotels or anything.

Later on he went out to get some smokes and I suddenly thought, I'll lock the door and I won't let him into the flat again. I had made up my mind to do it. But when I saw his shadow on the other side of the frosty glass I just got up and opened it, and I felt like a fool, what was there to be afraid of? He was such a clean, good-looking fellow standing there; and anybody can be down on his luck. I sometimes wonder what'll happen to me – in some years, of course – if I can't work any more and I'm alone here, and nobody comes. Every Sunday you read in the paper about women dead alone in flats, no one discovers it for days.

He smoked night and day, like the world had some bad smell that he had to keep out of his nose. He was smoking in the bed at the weekend and I made a remark about Princess Margaret when she was here as a kid in 1947 – I was looking at a story about the Royal Family, in the Sunday paper. He said he supposed he'd seen her, it was the year he went to the boys' home and they were taken to watch the procession.

One of the few things he'd told me about himself was that he was eight when he was sent to the home; I lay there and worked out that if he was thirty-seven, he should have been twenty in 1947, not eight years old.

But by then I found it hard to believe that he was only twenty-five. You could always get rid of a boy of twenty-five. He wouldn't have the strength inside to make you afraid to try it.

I'd've felt safer if someone had known about him and me but of course I couldn't talk to anyone. Imagine the Versfelds. Or the woman I go out with on Fridays, I don't think she's had a cup of tea with a man since her husband died! I remarked to Jack, the boss-boy, how old did he think the man had been, the one with the Rhodesian money who cheated the hotel? He said, 'He's still here?' I said no, no, I just wondered. 'He's young, that one,' he said, but I should have remembered that half the time natives don't know their own age, it doesn't matter to them the way it does to us. I said to him, wha'd'you call young? He jerked his head back at the workshop. 'Same like the mechanics.' That bunch of kids! But this fellow wasn't cocky like them, wrestling with each other all over the place, calling after girls, fancying themselves the Beatles when they sing in the washroom. The people he used to go off to see about things – I never saw any of them. If he had friends, they never came round. If only *somebody* else had known he was in the flat!

Then he said he was having the car overhauled because he was going off to Durban. He said he had to leave the next Saturday. So I felt much better; I also felt bad, in a way, because there I'd been, thinking I'd have to find some way to make him go. He put his hand on my waist, in the daylight, and smiled right out at me and said, 'Sorry; got to push on and get moving sometime, you know,' and it was true that in a way he was right, I couldn't think what it'd be like without him, though I was always afraid he would stay. Oh he was nice to me then, I can tell you; he could be nice if he wanted to, it was like a trick that he could do, so real you couldn't believe it when it stopped just like that. I told him he should've brought the car into our place, I'd've seen to it that they did a proper job on it, but no, a friend of his was doing it free, in his own workshop.

Saturday came, he didn't go. The car wasn't ready. He sat about most of the week, disappeared for a night, but was there again in the morning. I'd given him a couple of quid to keep him going. I said to him, what are you mucking about with that car in somebody's back yard for? Take it to a decent garage. Then – I'll never forget it – cool as anything, a bit irritated, he said, 'Forget it. I haven't got the car any more.' I said, wha'd'you mean, you mean you've sold it? – I suppose because in the back of my mind I'd been thinking, why doesn't he sell it, he needs money. And he said, 'That's right. It's sold,' but I knew he was lying, he couldn't be bothered to think of anything else to say. Once he'd said the car was sold, he said he was waiting for the money; he did pay me back three quid, but he borrowed again a day or so later. He'd keep his back to me when I came into the flat and he wouldn't answer when I spoke to him; and then just when he turned on me with that closed, half-asleep face and I'd think, this is it, now this is it – I can't explain how finished, done-for I felt, I only know that he had on his face exactly the same look I remember on the face of a man, once, who was drowning some kittens one after the other in a bucket of water – just as I knew it was coming, he would burst out laughing at me. It was the only time he laughed. He would laugh until, nearly crying, I would begin to laugh too. And we would pretend it was kidding, and he would be nice to me, oh, he would be nice to me.

I used to sit in my office at the garage and look round at the car adverts and the maps on the wall and my elephant ear growing in the oil drum and that was the only place I felt: but this is nonsense, what's got into me? The flat, and him in it – they didn't seem real. Then I'd go home at five and there it would all be.

I said to Jack, what's a '59 Chrysler worth? He took his time, he was cleaning his hands on some cotton waste. He said, 'With those tyres, nobody will pay much.'

Just to show him that he mustn't get too free with a white person, I asked him to send up to Mr Levine for a headache powder for me. I joked, I'm getting a bit like old Madala there, I feel so tired today.

D'you know what that boy said to me then? They've got more feeling than whites sometimes, that's the truth. He said, 'When my children grow up they must work for me. Why don't you live there in Rhodesia with your daughter? The child must look after the mother. Why must you stay here alone in this town?'

Of course I wasn't going to explain to him that I like my independence. I always say I hope when I get old I die before I become a burden on anybody. But that afternoon I did something I should've done long ago, I said to the boy, if ever I don't turn up to work, you must tell them in the workshop to send someone to my flat to look for me. And I wrote down the address. Days could go by before anyone'd find what had become of me; it's not right.

When I got home that same evening, the fellow wasn't there. He'd gone. Not a word, not a note; nothing. Every time I heard the lift rattling I thought, here he is. But he didn't come. When I was home on Saturday afternoon I couldn't stand it any longer and I went up to the Versfelds and asked the old lady if I couldn't sleep there a few days, I said my flat was being painted and the smell turned my stomach. I thought, if he comes to the garage, there are people around, at least there are the boys. I was smoking nearly as much as *he* used to and I couldn't sleep. I had to ask Mr Levine to give me something. The slightest sound and I was in a cold sweat. At the end of the week I had to go back to the flat, and I bought a chain for the door and made a heavy curtain so's you couldn't see anyone standing there. I didn't go out, once I'd got in from work – not even to the early flicks – so I wouldn't have to come back into the building at night. You know how it is when you're nervous, the funniest things comfort you: I'd just tell myself, well, if I shouldn't turn up to work in the morning, the boy'd send someone to see.

Then slowly I was beginning to forget about it. I kept the curtain and the chain and I stayed at home, but when you get used to something, no matter what it is, you don't think about it all the time, any more, though you still believe you do. I hadn't been to Maison Claude for about two weeks and my hair was a sight. Claude advised a soft perm and so it happened that I took a couple of hours off in the afternoon to get it done. The boss-boy Jack says to me when I come back, 'He was here.'

I didn't know what to do, I couldn't help staring quickly all round. When, I said. 'Now-now, while you were out.' I had the feeling I couldn't get away. I knew he would come up to me with that closed, half-asleep face – burned as a good-looker lifesaver, burned like one of those tramps who are starving and lousy and pickled with cheap booze but have a horrible healthy look that comes from having nowhere to go out of the sun. I don't know what that boy must have thought of me, my face. He said, 'I told him you're gone. You don't work here any more. You went to Rhodesia to your daughter. I don't know which place.' And he put his nose back in one of the newspapers he's always reading whenever things are slack; I think he fancies himself quite the educated man and he likes to read about all these blacks who are becoming prime ministers and so on in other countries these days. I never remark on it; if you take any notice of things like that with them, you begin to give them big ideas about themselves.

That fellow's never bothered me again. I never breathed a word to anybody about it – as I say, that's the trouble when you work alone in an office like I do, there's no one you can speak to. It just shows you, a woman on her own has always got to look out; it's not only that it's not safe to walk about alone at night because of the natives, this whole town is full of people you can't trust.

The African Magician

Ships always assemble the same cast and this one was no exception. The passengers were not, of course, the ones you would meet on any of those liners described as floating hotels that take tourists to and fro between places where they never stay long enough to see the bad season come. But, as if supplied by some theatrical agency unmindful of a change of style in the roles available in the world, these passengers setting off up the Congo River instead of across an ocean were those you might have met at any time as long as the colonial era lasted, travelling between the country in Europe where they were born and the country across the sea where its flag also flew. There was the old hand who inevitably trapped my husband by the hour; released at last, he would come to me deeply under the man's deadly fascination. '... twenty-two years ... prospecting for minerals for the government ... torpedoed going back to Belgium in the war ... Free French ... two and a half years in a Russian prison camp ... he still carries his card signed by de Gaulle ...'

'Oh I know, I know, I don't want to see it.'

But when the old hand interrupted his evening stroll round the deck to sit down where we sat, outside our cabin, no measure of aloofness, head bent to book, would prevent him from cornering my eye at some point and growling with a pally wink, 'Two more year and I sit and drink beer and look at the girls in Brussels. Best beer, best girls in the world.' When he saw us, leaning together over the rail but lost from each other and ourselves in the sight of the towering, indifferent fecundity of the wilderness that the river cleaved from height to depth, he would pause, hang about and then thrust the observation between our heads – 'Lot of bloomin' nothing, eh?

Country full of nothing. Bush, bush, trees, trees. Put you two metres in there and you won't come out never.' His mind ran down towards some constant, smug yet uncertain vision of his retirement that must have been with him all the twenty-two years. 'Bush, nothing.'

There were sanitary officers, a police officer, a motor mechanic, agricultural officers and research workers, returning with their wives and children from home leave in Belgium. The women looked as if they had been carved out of lard and were in the various stages of reproduction – about to give birth, or looking after small fat children who might have been believed to be in danger of melting. There was a priest who sat among the women in the row of deck-chairs all day, reading paperbacks; he was a big elderly man with a forward-thrust, intelligent jaw, and when he stood up slowly and leant upon the rail, his hard belly lifting his cassock gave him the sudden appearance of an odd affinity with the women around him. There was a newly-married couple, of course – that look of a pair tied up for a three-legged race who haven't mastered the gait yet. The husband was ordinary enough but the girl was unexpected, among the browsing herd setting to over the first meal aboard. She was very tall, the same size as her husband, and her long thin naked legs in shorts showed the tense tendon, fleshless, on each inner thigh as she walked. On the extreme thinness and elongation of the rest of her – half pathetic, half elegant – was balanced a very wide square jaw. In profile the face was pretty; full on, the extraordinary width of her blemished forehead, her thick black eyebrows above grey eyes, her very big straight mouth with pale lips, was a distortion of unusual beauty. Her style could have been Vogue model or beatnik. In fact she was a Belgian country girl who had hit naturally, by an accident of physique and a natural sluttishness, upon what I knew only as a statement of artifice of one kind or another.

The 'white' boat, broad and tiered top-heavy upon the water like a Mississippi paddle-steamer, had powerful Diesel engines beating in her flat floor, and we pushed two barges covered with cars, jeeps and tanks of beer, and another passenger boat, painted drab but soon fluttering with the flags of the third class's washing. There was a lot of life going on down there at the other boat; you could look down the length of the two barges from the deck in front of our cabin and see it – barbering, cooking, a continual swarming and clambering from deck to deck that often overflowed onto the barges. Jars of palm wine passed between our galley and crew's quarters, and their galley. A tin basin full of manioc spinach appeared at intervals moving along in the air from the bowels of the boat beneath our feet; then we saw the straight, easygoing body of the black beauty on whose turban it was balanced. She went down the street of the barges with languor, winding easily between the tethered cars, stopping to disparage a basket of dried fish that had just been dumped aboard from a visiting canoe, or to parry some flattering and insulting suggestion from a member of the crew lounging off duty, and finally disappeared into the boat at the other end.

The police officer's wife noticed a scribble chalked on the barge below us. 'My God, take a look at that, will you!' It did not consist, as messages publicly addressed to no one in particular usually do, of curses or declarations of love, but hailed, in misspelt French and the uneven script of some loiterer in Léopoldville harbour, the coming of the country's independence of white man's rule, that was only two months away. 'They are mad, truly. They think they can run a country.' She was a gay one, strongly made-up, with a small waist and wide jelly-hips in bright skirts, and she had the kind of roving alertness that put her on chatting terms with the whole boat within twenty-four hours. In case I had missed the point, she turned to me and said in English, 'They are just like monkeys, you know. We've taught them a few tricks. Really, they are monkeys out from *there*.' And she gestured at the forest that we were passing before night and day, while we looked and while we slept.

Our passengers were all white, not because of a colour bar, but because even those few black people who could afford the first class thought it a waste of money. Yet except for the Belgian captain, who never came down among us from his quarters on the top deck, the entire crew was black, and we were kept fed and clean by a small band of Congolese men. They managed this with an almost mysterious ease. There were only three stewards and a barman visible, and often, five minutes before the bell rang for a meal, I would see them sitting on their haunches on the barge below us, barefoot and in dirty shorts, murmuring their perpetual tide of gossip. But however promptly you presented yourself at table, they were there before you, in mildewed white cotton suits and forage caps decorated with the shipping company's badge. Only their bare feet provided a link with the idlers of a few minutes before. The idlers never looked up and did not notice a greeting from the decks above them; but the stewards were grinning and persuasive, pressing food on you, running to get your wine with a happy, speedy slither that implied a joking reference to your thirst. When we stopped at river stations and the great refrigerated hold was opened, we recognized the same three, grunting as they tossed the weight of half a frozen ox from hand to hand; once I remarked to George, who waited on us and even took it upon himself to wake us in time for breakfast, pounding on our cabin door and calling 'Chop! Chop!' – 'You were working hard this afternoon, eh?'

But he looked at me blankly. 'Madame?'

'Yes, unloading. I saw you unloading meat.'

'It wasn't me,' he said.

'Not you, in the green shirt?'

He shook his head vehemently. It appeared as if I had insulted him by the suggestion. And yet it was he, all right, his gruff laugh and small moustache and splayed toes. 'No, no, not me.' Wasn't it a known fact that to white people all black faces look alike? How could I argue with him?

In the evenings the priest put on grey flannel trousers and smoked a big cigar; you would have said then that he was a big businessman, successful and yet retaining some residue of sensitivity in the form of sadness – my husband found out that he was in fact the financial administrator of a remote and very large complex of mission schools. I was often aware of him, without actually seeing him, when I was in our cabin at night:

he liked to stand alone on the deserted bend of the deck, outside. The honeymoon couple (as we thought of the newly-married pair, although their honeymoon was over and he was taking her to the inland administrative post where he worked) formed the habit of coming there too, during the hot hours when everyone was resting after lunch. He, with his fair curly hair and rather snouty, good-looking face, would stand looking out at the leap and glitter of the water, but she could see nothing but him, he was blown up to fill the screen of her vision, and in this exaggerated projection every detail, every hair and pore held her attention like the features of a landscape. Fascinated, she concentrated on squeezing blackheads from his chin. I used to come noisily out of the cabin, hoping to drive this idyll away. But they were not aware of me; she was not aware of the presence of another woman, like herself, recognizing the ugliness of some intimacies when seen, as they never should be, as a spectator. 'Why must they choose our deck?' I was indignant.

My husband was amused. 'Come on, what's the matter with love?' He lay on his bed grinning, picking at a tooth with a match.

'That's not love. I wouldn't mind nearly so much if I found them copulating on the deck.'

'Oh wouldn't you? That's because you never have.'

The thing was that I could not help expecting something of that face – the girl's face. As I have said, it was not a fraud in the ways that it might have been – a matter of fashion in faces or ideas. She had come by it honestly, so to speak, and I could not believe that it was not the outward sign of some remarkable quality, not, perhaps, an obvious one, like a talent, but some bony honesty of mind or freshness of spirit. It disappointed me to see that face, surfeit as a baby's bleary with milk, with the simplest relationship with a commonplace man. I was reluctant to admit that her intensity at table was merely a ruthless desire to get the choice bits of every dish shovelled onto his plate. I felt irritated when I came upon her sitting placidly cobbling the torn ribbon of a vulgar frilly petticoat made of rainbow-coloured net: it was simply a face, that was all, clapped on the same old bundle of well-conformed instincts and the same few feelings. Yet every time I saw it I could not suppress a twinge of hopeful disbelief; this was part of the mild preoccupation with a collection of lives you will never touch on again that makes a voyage so restful.

Our first stop was in the middle of the night and next morning we woke to find the ivory sellers aboard. They came from the forest and the expressions on their faces were made difficult to read by distracting patterns of tattooing, but they wore white cotton vests from a trading store. Out of cardboard school cases they spread ivory toothpicks, paper-knives and bracelets on the narrow deck, and squatted among them. Nearly all the Belgians had seen this tourist bric-à-brac many times before, but they gathered round, asking prices challengingly, and then putting the stuff down and walking away. A few women, sheepish about it, bought bracelets and shook them on their wrists as if deciding they were not so bad, after all. One of the agricultural officers whose child, learning to walk, hampered his father's left leg like a manacle, said, 'Have you locked your door? You want to, while these fellows are about. They'll take anything.'

The vender outside our cabin hadn't taken anything but I don't think he had sold anything, either. Just before lunchtime he packed his cardboard case again and went off down to the public thoroughfare of the barges, where a pirogue was tied, trailing alongside in the water like a narrow floating leaf. He did not seem downcast; but then, as I have remarked, it was difficult to tell, with those rows of nicks running in curved lines across his forehead and the sharp cuts tightening the skin under the eyes.

People brought all sorts of things aboard to sell, and they were all sorts of people, too, for we were following the river a thousand miles through the homes of many tribes. Sometimes old hags with breasts like bellpulls and children with dusty bellies sprang up on the dark river-bank and yelled '*'depen-DANCE!*' The young men and girls of the same village would swim out ahead of our convoy and drift past us with darting, uplifted eyes, begging for jam tins from the galley. Those men who managed to scramble aboard, to our eyes dressed in their sleek wet blackness, hid their penises between their closed thighs with exactly that instinct that must have come to Adam when he was cast out of the Garden. The gesture put them, although they lived alone in the forest among the wild creatures, apart from the animal life they shared, just as it had done to him, for himself and them, for ever.

The pirogues came with live turtles and with fish, with cloudy beer and wine made from bananas, palm nuts or sorghum, and with the smoked meat of hippopotamus and crocodile. The venders did a good trade with our crew and the passengers down at the third-class boat; the laughter, the exclamations and the argument of bargaining were with us all day, heard but not understood, like voices in the next room. At stopping places, the people who were nourished on these ingredients of a witches' brew poured ashore across the single plank flung down for them, very human in contour, the flesh of the children sweet, the men and women strong and sometimes handsome. We, thank God, were fed on veal and ham and Brussels sprouts brought frozen from Europe.

When our convoy put off some contribution to the shore instead of taking on some of its fruits, the contribution was usually something outlandish and bulky. A product of heavy industry, some chunk of machinery or road-making tractor, set down in a country that has not been industrialized, looks as strange as a space-ship from Mars might, set down in a city. A strip of landing-stage with a tin shed, a hut or two, not quite native and not quite a white man's house, a row of empty oil drums, and a crane standing like some monster waterbird on three legs above the water: the crane came into action with the rattle of chains playing out and there, hanging in the air ready to land where its like had never been seen, where, in fact, there was nothing that could prepare one for the look of it, were the immense steel angles of something gleaming with grey paint and intricate with dials where red arrows quivered. Cars and jeeps went ashore this way, too, dangling, but they seemed more agile, adaptable and accepted, and no sooner were they ashore than some missionary or trader jumped in and they went scrambling away up the bank and disappeared.

We stopped, one day, long enough for us to be able to go ashore and wander round a bit; it was quite a place – white provincial offices in a garden with marigolds on a newly cleared space of raw red earth, a glass and steel hospital in the latest contemporary architecture, an avenue of old palms along the waterfront leading to a weathered red brick cathedral. And when the taxi we had hired drove a mile out along the single road that led away into the forest, all this was hidden by the forest as if already it were one of those ancient lost cities that are sometimes found in a rich humus grave, dead under the rotting green, teeming culture of life. Another day we stopped only long enough for us to go ashore but stay within sight of the boat. There was nothing much to see; it was Sunday and a few Portuguese traders and their fat wives in flowered dresses were sitting on the veranda of a house drinking lemonade; opposite, a tin store sold sewing machines and cigarettes. A crumbling white fort, streaked with livid moss and being pushed apart by the swelling roots of trees like the muscles of Samson, remained from the days eighty years ago when the Arab slave-traders built it. The native village that they had raided and burned, incidentally providing a convenient place for the fort, had left no trace except, perhaps, the beginning of the line of continuity that leads men always to build where others, enemies or vanquished, have lived before them.

Someone came aboard at this brief stopping-place, just as, at the stop in the ivory country behind us, the ivory venders had.

At dinner that evening we found slips of paper with a typewritten announcement on our tables. There was to be an entertainment at 8 p.m. in the bar. Gentlemen, 80 francs, Ladies, 70 francs. There was a stir of amusement in the dining room. I thought, for a moment, of a Donkey Derby or Bingo game. My husband said, 'A choir, I'll bet. Girls singing mission-school hymns. They must have been practising down at the other boat.'

'What's this?' I asked George.

'You will like it,' he said.

'But what is it, a show or what?'

'Very good,' he said. 'You will see. A man who does things you have never seen. Very clever.' When we had finished eating the sweet course he came skidding back to hit at our swiftly-cleared table with a napkin, scattering crumbs. 'You are coming to the bar?' – he made sure. It was a kindly but firm command. We began to have that obscure anxiousness to see the thing a success that descends upon one at school concerts and amateur theatricals. Oh yes, we were coming, all right. We usually took coffee on deck, but this time we carried our cups straight into the lounge, where the bar occupied one wall and the fans in the low panelled ceiling did not dispel the trapped heat of the day but blew down upon the leather chairs a perpetual emanation of radio music coming from loudspeakers set in grilles overhead. We were almost the first there; we thought we might as well take good seats at one of the tables right in front of the space that had been cleared before the bar. The senior administrator and his daughter, who sat in the bar every night playing tric-trac, got up and went out. There were perhaps fourteen or fifteen of us, including the honeymoon couple, who had looked in several times, grinning vaguely, and at last had decided to come. 'What a lot of mean bastards, eh?' said my husband admiringly. It did seem a surprising restraint that could resist an unspecified local entertainment offered in the middle of a green nowhere. The barman, a handsome young Bacongo from Léopoldville, leaned an elbow on the counter and stared at us. George came in from the dining-room and bent his head to talk closely to him; he remained, hunched against the counter, smiling at the room with the reassuring, confident smile that the compère sends out into the proscenium whether it is addressed to faces set close as a growth of pinhead mould, or a blankness of empty seats.

At last the entertainment began. It was, of course, a magician, as we had understood from George it must be. The man walked in suddenly from the deck – perhaps he had been waiting there behind the stacked deck-chairs for the right moment.

He wore a white shirt and grey trousers and carried an attaché case. He had an assistant with him, a very black, dreamy squat chap, most likely picked up as a volunteer from among the passengers down at the third-class boat. He spent most of the performance sitting astride a chair with his chin on his arms on the high back.

There was a hesitant spatter of clapping as the magician came in but he did not acknowledge it and it quickly died out. He went to business at once; out of the attaché case, that was rather untidily filled, came bits of white paper, scissors, a bunch of paper flowers and strings of crumpled flags. His first trick was a card trick, an old one that most of us had seen many times before, and one or two of us could have done himself. There were a few giggles and only one person attempted to clap; but the magician had already gone on to his next illusion, which involved the string of pennants and a hat. Then there was the egg that emerged from his ear. Then the fifty-franc note that was torn up before our eyes and made whole again, not exactly before them, but almost.

Between each item of his performance there was an interval when he turned his back protectively to us and made some preparation hidden beneath a length of black cloth. Once he spoke to the barman, and was given a glass. He did not seem to be aware of the significance of applause when he got it, and he went through his revelations without a word of patter, not even the universally understood exclamations like *Abracadabra!* or *Hey Presto!* gestures without which it is impossible to imagine a magician bringing anything off. He did not smile and we saw his small, filed white teeth in his smooth black face only when his upper lip lifted in concentration; his eyes, though they met ours openly, were inner-focused. He went through what was clearly his limited repertoire, learned God knows where or from whom (perhaps even by some extraordinary correspondence course?), without mishap, but only just. When he crunched up the glass and ate it, for instance, he did not wear the look of eye-rolling agony that is this trick's professional accompaniment and makes even the most sceptical audience hold its breath in sympathy – he looked fearful and anxious, his face twitching like the face of someone crawling through a barbed-wire fence. After half an hour he turned away at the conclusion of a trick and began folding up the string of flags, and we assumed that there would now be an interval before the second part of the performance. But at once the assistant got up from his chair and came round the room with a plate, preceded by George, who handed out all over again the slips of paper that we had found on our tables at dinner: *An entertainment,* 8 *p.m., in the bar. Gentlemen,* 80 *francs, Ladies,* 70 *francs.* The performance was over. The audience, who had felt flat anyway, was done down. One of the Belgian ladies demurred, smiling, 'Seventy francs for this!' – although the local currency wasn't worth much.

Tomorrow morning, at ten o'clock, George announced proudly to each table, there would be a repeat performance, same prices for adults, 30 francs for children. We could all see the magician again then.

'It's too much, too expensive.' One of the Belgians spoke up for us all. 'You can't charge eighty francs for only half an hour. Is this all he knows?'

There were murmurs of half-interested assent; some people were inclined to go off to bed, anyway. The objection was explained to George, and his organizer's pride died slowly, wonderingly, out of his manner. Suddenly he waggled a reassuring palm of the hand; it would be all right, he would make it all right, and his idiotic assurance based on what we could not imagine – eventual return of our money? another performance free? – was so sweeping that everybody handed over their 70 and 80 francs doggedly, as a condition he expected us to fulfil.

Then he went to the magician and began to talk to him in a low, fast, serious voice, not without a tinge of scorn and exasperation, whether directed towards the magician or towards us we did not know, because none of us understood the language being spoken. The barman leaned over to hear and the assistant stood stolidly in the little huddle.

Only two members of the audience had gone to bed, after all; the rest of us sat there, amused, but with a certain thread of tension livening us up. It was clear that most of the people did not like to be done down, it was a matter they prided themselves on – not to be done down, even by blacks, whom they didn't expect to have the same standards about these things and whom they thought of as thievish anyway. Our attitude – that of my husband and myself – was secretly different, though the difference could not show outwardly. Tempted though we were to treat the whole evening as a joke and a rather naive extortion of 150 francs from our pockets, we had the priggish feeling that it was perhaps patronizing and a kind of insult to make special allowances for these people, simply because they were black. If they chose, as they had, to enter into activity governed by Western values, whether it was conjuring or running a twentieth-century state, they must be done the justice of being expected to fulfil their chosen standards. For the sake of the magician himself and our relation to him as an audience, he must himself give us his 150 francs' worth. We finished our glasses of beer (we had picked up the habit) while the urgent discussion between George, the barman and the magician went on.

The magician seemed adamant. Almost before George had begun to speak, he was shaking his head, and he did not stop packing away the stuff of his illusions – the cards, the paper flowers, the egg. He drew his lips back from his teeth and answered in the hard tone of flat refusal, again and again. But George and the barman closed in on him verbally, a stream of words that flowed round and spilled over challenges. Quite suddenly the magician gave in, must have given in, on what sounded like a disclaimer of all responsibility, a warning and a reluctant submission more in the nature of a challenge itself.

George turned to us with a happy grin. He bowed and threw up his hands. 'I have told him too short. Now he makes some more for you. Some magic.' And he laughed, lifting his eyebrows and inclining his head so that his white forage cap nearly fell off, implying that the whole business was simply a miracle to him, as it must be to us.

The magician bowed too. And we clapped him; it was sporting, on both sides. The newly-married girl rested her head a moment on the snouty young man's shoulder and yawned in his ear. Then we were all attention. The assistant, who had taken the opportunity to subside into his chair again, was summoned by the magician and made to stand before him. Then the magician ran a hand along inside the waistband of his trousers, tucking in his shirt in a brief, final and somehow preparatory gesture, and began to make passes with his hands in front of the assistant's face. The assistant blinked, like a sleepy dog worried by a fly. His was a dense, coaly face, bunched towards the front with a strong jutting jaw, puffy lips, and a broad nose with a single tattoo mark like a line of ink drawn down it. He had long, woolly eyelashes and they seemed to sway over his eyes. The magician's black hands were thin and the yellow-pink palms looked almost translucent; he might not have had the words, but he had the gestures, all right, and his hands curled like serpents and fluttered like birds. The assistant began to dance. He shuffled away from the magician, the length of the bar, the slither and hesitation from one foot to another, neck retracted and arms bent at elbows like a runner, that Africans can do as soon as they learn to walk, and that they can always do, drunk or sober, even when they are so old that they can scarcely walk. A subdued but generous laughter went up. We were all ready to give the magician good-natured encouragement now that he was trying. The magician continued to stand, his hands fallen now at his sides, his slim body modest and relaxed, hanging from his shoulders in its shabby clean shirt and too-big grey trousers. He kept his eyes quietly on the assistant and the man turned and came back to him, singing now as well as dancing, and in a young *girl's* voice. And here we all laughed without any prompting wish to seem appreciative. As a hypnotist the magician had the sense of timing that he lacked so conspicuously when performing tricks, and before the laughter stopped he had said something curtly to the assistant, and the man went over to the bar counter and picking up an empty glass jug that stood there, drank it off in deep, gasping gulps as if he had been wandering for days in a desert. He was returned to his inanimate self by one movement of the magician's hands before his face; he looked at us all without surprise and then, finding himself the focus of an attention that did not even arouse him to any curiosity, sat down in his chair again and yawned.

'Let's see what he can do with someone else, not his own man!' one of the Belgians called out good-humouredly, signalling for the barman at the same time. 'Yes, come on, someone else.' 'Ask him to try someone he doesn't know.'

'You want it, yes?' George was grinning. He pointed a finger at the magician.

'You, George, let's see if he can do you!'

'No, one of *us*.' A shiny, tubby-faced man in cocoa research, who had towards the blacks the chaffing, half-scornful ease of one of those who knew them well, swung round in his chair. 'That's an idea, eh? Let him have a go at one of us, and see how he gets on.' 'Yes, yes.' There was a positive chorus of rising assent; even the honeymooners joined in. Someone said, 'But what about the language? How can he suggest things in our minds if we don't know the same language?' – but she was dismissed, and George explained to the magician what was wanted.

He made no protest; in a swift movement he walked away towards the bar a few steps and then turned to face us, at bay. I noticed that his nostrils – he had a fine nose – moved in and out once or twice as if he were taking slow deep breaths.

We were waiting, I suppose, for him to call upon one of us, one of the men, of course – the cocoa man and some others were ready for the right moment, a rough equivalent of the familiar: Will any kind gentleman or lady please step up on to the stage? But oddly it did not come. Over the giggles and nudges and half-sentences, an expectancy fell. We sat looking at the awkward young black man, searching slowly along our faces, and we did not know when the performance had begun. Fidgeting died out, looking at him, and our eyes surrounded him closely. He was still as any prey run to ground. And then while we were looking at him, waiting for him to choose one of us, we became aware of a sudden smooth movement in our ranks. My attention was distracted to the right, and I saw the girl – the honeymoon girl, my girl with the face – get up with a little exclamation, a faint wondering *tst!* ... of remembering something, and walk calmly, without brushing against anyone, over to the magician. She stood directly before him, quite still, her tall rounded shoulders drooping naturally and thrusting forward a little her head, that was raised to him, almost on a level with his own. He did not move; he did not gaze; his eyes blinked quietly. She put up her long arms and, standing just their length from him, brought her hands to rest on his shoulders. Her cropped head dropped before him to her chest.

It was the most extraordinary gesture. None of us could see her face; there was nothing but the gesture. God knows where it came from – *he* could not have put it into her will, it was not in any hypnotist's repertoire, and she, surely, could not have had the place for something so other, in her female, placidly sensual nature. I don't think I have ever seen such a gesture before, but I knew – they knew – we all knew what it meant. It was nothing to do with what exists between men and women. She had never made such a gesture to her husband, or any man. She had never stood like that before her father – none of us has. How can I explain? One of the disciples might have come before Christ like that. There was the peace of absolute trust in it. It stirred a needle of fear in me – more than that, for a moment I was horribly afraid; and how can I explain that, either? For it was beautiful, and I have lived in Africa all my life and I know them, *us,* the white people. To see it was beautiful would make us dangerous.

The husband sat hunched back in his chair in what was to me a most unexpected reaction – his fist pushed his cheek out of shape and he was frozenly withdrawn, like a parent witnessing a suddenly volunteered performance by a child who, so far as he knew, had neither talent nor ambition. But the cocoa expert, who had dealt with the blacks so long, acted quickly and jumped up calling, authoritative, loud, but only just controlled, 'Hey! No, no, we want him to try his magic with the men, tell him not the ladies. No, no, he must take a man.'

The room was released as if it had struck a blow. And at the same moment the magician, before George had begun to translate sharply at him, understood without understanding words and passed his hand across the lower part of his own face in an almost servile movement that bumped the arms of the girl without deliberately touching her, and released her instantly from the gesture. At once she laughed and was dazed, and as her husband came to her as if to escort an invalid, I heard her saying pleasedly, 'It's wonderful! You should try! Like a dreamy feeling ... really!'

She had missed the sight of the gesture; she was the only person at ease in the room.

There was no performance next morning. I suppose the first audience had been too disappointingly small. When my husband asked mildly after the magician, at lunch, George said inattentively, 'He has gone.' We had not made a stop anywhere, but of course pirogues were constantly coming and going between us and the shore.

The boat began to take on the look of striking camp; we were due at Stanleyville in two days and some of the Belgians were getting off at the big agricultural research station where we would call a few hours before Stanleyville. Tin trunks with neat lettering began to appear outside the cabins. The honeymoon couple spent hours down on the second barge, cleaning their car – they had rags and a bucket, and they let the bucket down into the Congo and then sloshed the brown water over the metal that was too hot to touch. The old hand changed a tyre on his jeep and announced that he had room for two passengers going from Stanleyville north, towards the Sudan. Only my husband and I and the priest made no preparations: we two had the meagre luggage of air travellers, and the single briefcase of papers for the congress on tropical diseases that we were going to attend, and he was in no hurry to be first off the boat at Stanleyville since, he explained, he would have to wait there several weeks, perhaps, before a car went his way – the mission could not send all that distance specially to fetch him. He had run out of reading matter and allowed himself a cigar in broad daylight as we leaned on the rail together on the morning of our last day aboard, watching passengers struggling ashore from the third-class boat against the stream of visitors and people selling things, coming up the gangplank. We had stopped, with the usual lack of ceremony at such places, at some point in a mile-long village of huts thatched with banana leaves and surrounded by banana plantations that stretched along the river bank. The 'white' boat and the barges stood out in the water at an angle from the shore; the link with it was a tenuous one. But babies and goats and bicycles passed over it, and among them I saw the magician. He looked like any other young black clerk, with his white shirt and grey trousers, and the attaché case. All Africa carries an attaché case now; and what I knew was in that one might not be more extraordinary than what might be in some of the others.

Some Monday For Sure

My sister's husband, Josias, used to work on the railways but then he got this job where they make dynamite for the mines. He was the one who sits out on that little iron seat clamped to the back of the big red truck, with a red flag in his hand. The idea is that if you drive up too near the truck or look as if you're going to crash into it, he waves the flag to warn you off. You've seen those trucks often on the Main Reef Road between Johannesburg and the mining towns – they carry the stuff and have DANGER – EXPLOSIVES painted on them. The man sits there, with an iron chain looped across his little seat to keep him from being thrown into the road, and he clutches his flag like a kid with a balloon. That's how Josias was, too. Of course, if you didn't take any notice of the warning and went on and crashed into the truck, he would be the first to be blown to high heaven and hell, but he always just sits there, this chap, as if he has no idea when he was born or that he might not die in a bed an old man of eighty. As if the dust in his eyes and the racket of the truck are going to last for ever.

My sister knew she had a good man but she never said anything about being afraid of this job. She only grumbled in winter, when he was stuck out there in the cold and used to get a cough (she's a nurse), and in summer when it rained all day and she said he would land up with rheumatism, crippled, and then who would give him work? The dynamite people? I don't think it ever came into her head that any day, every day, he could be blown up instead of coming home in the evening. Anyway, you wouldn't have thought so by the way she took it when he told us what it was he was going to have to do.

I was working down at a garage in town, that time, at the petrol pumps, and I was eating before he came in because I was on night shift. Emma had the water ready for him and he had a wash without saying much, as usual, but then he didn't speak when they sat down to eat, either, and when his fingers went into the mealie meal he seemed to forget what it was he was holding and not to be able to shape it into a mouthful. Emma must have thought he felt too dry to eat, because she got up and brought him a jam tin of the beer she had made for Saturday. He drank it and then sat back and looked from her to me, but she said, 'Why don't you eat?' and he began to, slowly. She said, 'What's the matter with you?' He got up and yawned and yawned, showing those brown chipped teeth that remind me of the big ape at the Johannesburg zoo that I saw once when I went with the school. He went into the other room of the house, where he and Emma slept, and he came back with his pipe. He filled it carefully, the way a poor man does; I saw, as soon as I went to work at the filling station, how the white men fill their pipes, stuffing the tobacco in, picking out any bits they don't like the look of, shoving the tin half-shut back into the glove-box of the car. 'I'm going down to Sela's place,' said Emma. 'I can go with Willie on his way to work if you don't want to come.'

'No. Not tonight. You stay here.' Josias always speaks like this, the short words of a schoolmaster or a boss-boy, but if you hear the way he says them, you know he is not really ordering you around at all, he is only asking you.

'No, I told her I'm coming,' Emma said, in the voice of a woman having her own way in a little thing.

'Tomorrow.' Josias began to yawn again, looking at us with wet eyes. 'Go to bed,' Emma said. 'I won't be late.'

'No, no, I want to ...' He blew a sigh. 'When he's gone, man –' He moved his pipe at me. 'I'll tell you later.'

Emma laughed. 'What can you tell me that Willie can't hear.' I've lived with them ever since they were married. Emma always was the one who looked after me, even before, when I was a little kid. It was true that whatever happened to us happened to us together. He looked at me; I suppose he saw that I was a man, now: I was in my blue overalls with *Shell* on the pocket and everything.

He said, 'They want me to do something ... a job with the truck.'

Josias used to turn out regularly to political meetings and he took part in a few protests before everything went underground, but he had never been more than one of the crowd. We had Mandela and the rest of the leaders, cut out of the paper, hanging on the wall, but he had never known, personally, any of them. Of course there were his friends Ndhlovu and Seb Masinde who said they had gone underground and who occasionally came late at night for a meal or slept in my bed for a few hours.

'They want to stop the truck on the road –'

'Stop it?' Emma was like somebody stepping into cold dark water; with every word that was said she went deeper. 'But how can you do it – when? Where will they do it?' She was wild, as if she must go out and prevent it all happening right then.

I felt that cold water of Emma's rising round the belly because Emma and I often had the same feelings, but I caught also, in Josias's not looking at me, a signal Emma couldn't know. Something in me jumped at it like catching a swinging rope. 'They want the stuff inside...?'

Nobody said anything.

I said, 'What a lot of big bangs you could make with that, man,' and then shut up before Josias needed to tell me to.

'So what're you going to do?' Emma's mouth stayed open after she had spoken, the lips pulled back.

'They'll tell me everything. I just have to give them the best place on the road – that'll be the Free State road, the others're too busy ... and ... the time when we pass...'

'You'll be dead.' Emma's head was shuddering and her whole body shook; I've never seen anybody give up like that. He was dead already, she saw it with her eyes and she was kicking and screaming without knowing how to show it to him. She looked like she wanted to kill Josias herself, for being dead. 'That'll be the finish, for sure. He's got a gun, the white man in front, hasn't he, you told me. And the one with him? They'll kill you. You'll go to prison. They'll take you to

Pretoria jail and hang you by the rope ... Yes, he's got the gun, you told me, didn't you – many times you told me –'

'The others've got guns too. How d'you think they can hold us up? They've got guns and they'll come all round him. It's all worked out –'

'The one in front will shoot you, I know it, don't tell me, I know what I say ...' Emma went up and down and around till I thought she would push the walls down – they wouldn't have needed much pushing, in that house in Alexandra Township – and I was scared of her. I don't mean for what she would do to me if I got in her way, or to Josias, but for what might happen to her: something like taking a fit or screaming that none of us would be able to forget.

I don't think Josias was sure about doing the job before but he wanted to do it now. 'No shooting. Nobody will shoot me. Nobody will know that I know anything. Nobody will tell them anything. I'm held up just the same like the others! Same as the white man in front! Who can shoot me? They can shoot me for that?'

'Someone else can go, I don't want it, do you hear? You will stay at home, I will say you are sick ... You will be killed, they will shoot you ... Josias, I'm telling you, I don't want ... I won't ...'

I was waiting my chance to speak, all the time, and I felt Josias was waiting to talk to someone who had caught the signal. I said quickly, while she went on and on, 'But even on that road there are some cars?'

'Roadblocks,' he said, looking at the floor. 'They've got the signs, the ones you see when a road's being dug up, and there'll be some men with picks. After the truck goes through they'll block the road so that any other cars turn off onto the old road there by Kalmansdrif. The same thing on the other side, two miles on. There where the farm road goes down to Nek Halt.'

'Hell, man! Did you have to pick that part of the road?'

'I know it like this yard. Don't I?'

Emma stood there, between the two of us, while we discussed the whole business. We didn't have to worry about anyone hearing, not only because Emma kept the window wired up in that kitchen, but also because the yard the house was in was a real Alexandra Township one, full of babies yelling and people shouting, night and day, not to mention the transistors playing in the houses all round. Emma was looking at us all the time and out of the corner of my eye I could see her big front going up and down fast in the neck of her dress.

'... so they're going to tie you up as well as the others?'

He drew on his pipe to answer me.

We thought for a moment and then grinned at each other; it was the first time for Josias, that whole evening.

Emma began collecting the dishes under our noses. She dragged the tin bath of hot water from the stove and washed up. 'I said I'm taking my day off on Wednesday. I suppose this is going to be next week.' Suddenly, yet talking as if carrying on where she let up, she was quite different.

'I don't know.'

'Well, I have to know because I suppose I must be at home.'

'What must you be at home for?' said Josias.

'If the police come I don't want them talking to *him*,' she said, looking at us both without wanting to see us.

'The police –' said Josias, and jerked his head to send them running, while I laughed, to show her.

'And I want to know what I must say.'

'What must you say? Why? They can get my statement from me when they find us tied up. In the night I'll be back here myself.'

'Oh yes,' she said, scraping the mealie meal he hadn't eaten back into the pot. She did everything as usual; she wanted to show us nothing was going to wait because of this big thing, she must wash the dishes and put ash on the fire. 'You'll be back, oh yes. – Are you going to sit here all night, Willie? – Oh yes, you'll be back.'

And then, I think, for a moment Josias saw himself dead, too; he didn't answer when I took my cap and said, so long, from the door.

I knew it must be a Monday. I notice that women quite often

don't remember ordinary things like this, I don't know what they think about – for instance, Emma didn't catch on that it must be Monday, next Monday or the one after, some Monday for sure, because Monday was the day that we knew Josias went with the truck to the Free State mines. It was Friday when he told us and all day Saturday I had a terrible feeling that it was going to be *that* Monday, and it would be all over before I could – what? I didn't know, man. I felt I must at least see where it was going to happen. Sunday I was off work and I took my bicycle and rode into town before there was even anybody in the streets and went to the big station and found that although there wasn't a train on Sundays that would take me all the way, I could get one that would take me about thirty miles. I had to pay to put the bike in the luggage van as well as for my ticket, but I'd got my wages on Friday. I got off at the nearest halt to Kalmansdrif and then I asked people along the road the best way. It was a long ride, more than two hours. I came out on the main road from the sand road just at the turn-off Josias had told me about. It was just like he said: a tin sign KALMANSDRIF pointing down the road I'd come from. And the nice blue tarred road, smooth, straight ahead: was I glad to get on to it! I hadn't taken much notice of the country so far, while I was sweating along, but from then on I woke up and saw everything. I've only got to think about it to see it again now. The veld is flat round about there, it was the end of winter, so the grass was dry. Quite far away and very far apart, there was a hill and then another, sticking up in the middle of nothing, pink colour, and with its point cut off like the neck of a bottle. Ride and ride, these hills never got any nearer and there were none beside the road. It all looked empty and the sky much bigger than the ground, but there were some people there. It's funny you don't notice them like you do in town. All our people, of course; there were barbed-wire fences, so it must have been white farmers' land, but they've got the water and their houses are far off the road and you can usually see them only by the big dark trees that hide them. Our people had mud houses and there would be three or four in the same place made bare by goats and people's feet. Often the huts were near a kind of crack in the ground, where the little kids played and where, I suppose, in summer, there was water. Even now the women were managing to do washing in some places. I saw children run to the road to jig about and stamp when cars passed, but the men and women took no interest in what was up there. It was funny to think that I was just like them, now, men and women who are always busy inside themselves with jobs, plans, thinking about how to get money or how to talk to someone about something important, instead of like the children, as I used to be only a few years ago, taking in each small thing around them as it happens.

Still, there were people living pretty near the road. What would they do if they saw the dynamite truck held up and a fight going on? (I couldn't think of it, then, in any other way except like I'd seen hold-ups in Westerns, although I've seen plenty of fighting, all my life, among the Location gangs and drunks – I was ashamed not to be able to forget those kid-stuff Westerns at a time like this.) Would they go running away to the white farmer? Would somebody jump on a bike and go for the police? Or if there was no bike, what about a horse? I saw someone riding a horse.

I rode slowly to the next turn-off, the one where a farm road goes down to Nek Halt. There it was, just like Josias said. Here was where the other roadblock would be. But when he spoke about it there was nothing inbetween! No people, no houses, no flat veld with hills on it! It had been just one of those things grown-ups see worked out in their heads: while all the time, here it was, a real place where people had cooking fires, I could hear a herdboy yelling at a dirty bundle of sheep, a big bird I've never seen in town balanced on the barbed-wire fence right in front of me ... I got off my bike and it flew away.

I sat a minute on the side of the road. I'd had a cold drink in an Indian shop in the dorp where I'd got off the train, but I was dry again inside my mouth, while plenty of water came out of my skin, I can tell you. I rode back down the road looking for the exact place I would choose if I was Josias. There was a stretch where there was only one kraal with two houses, and that quite a way back from the road. Also there was a dip where the road went over a donga. Old stumps of trees and nothing but cows' business down there; men could hide. I got off again and had a good look round.

But I wondered about the people, up top. I don't know why it was, I wanted to know about those people just as though I was going to have to go and live with them or something. I left the bike down in the donga and crossed the road behind a Cadillac going so fast the air smacked together after it, and I began to trek over the veld to the houses. I know most of our people live like this, in the veld, but I'd never been into houses like that before. I was born in some Location (I don't know which one, I must ask Emma one day) and Emma and I lived in Moroka with our grandmother. Our mother worked in town and she used to come and see us sometimes, but we never saw our father and Emma thinks perhaps we didn't have the same father, because she remembers a man before I was born, and after I was born she didn't see him again. I don't really remember anyone, from when I was a little kid, except Emma. Emma dragging me along so fast my arm almost came off my body, because we had nearly been caught by the Indian while stealing peaches from his lorry: we did that every day.

We lived in one room with our grandmother but it was a tin house with a number and later on there was a streetlight at the corner. These houses I was coming to had a pattern all over them marked into the mud they were built of. There was a mound of dried cows' business, as tall as I was, stacked up in a pattern, too. And then the usual junk our people have, just like in the Location: old tins, broken things collected from white people's rubbish heaps. The fowls ran sideways from my feet and two old men let their talking die away into ahas and ehês as I came up. I greeted them the right way to greet old men and they nodded and went on ehêing and ahaing to show that they had been greeted properly. One of them had very clean ragged trousers tied with string and he sat on the ground, but the other, sitting on a bucket-seat that must have been taken from some scrapyard car, was dressed in a way I've never seen – from the old days, I suppose. He wore a black suit with very wide trousers, laced boots, a stiff white collar and black tie, and on top of it all, a broken old hat. It was Sunday, of course, so I suppose he was all dressed up. I've heard that these people who work for farmers wear sacks most of the time. The old ones didn't ask me what I wanted there. They just peered at me with their eyes gone the colour of soapy water because they were so old. And I didn't know what to say because I hadn't thought what I was going to say, I'd just walked. Then a little kid slipped out of the dark doorway quick as a cockroach. I thought perhaps everyone else was out because it was Sunday but then a voice called from inside the other house, and when the child didn't answer, called again, and a woman came to the doorway.

I said my bicycle had a puncture and could I have some water.

She said something into the house and in a minute a girl, about fifteen she must've been, edged past her carrying a paraffin tin and went off to fetch water. Like all the girls that age, she never looked at you. Her body shook under an ugly old dress and she almost hobbled in her hurry to get away. Her head was tied up in a rag-doek right down to the eyes the way old-fashioned people do, otherwise she would have been quite pretty, like any other girl. When she had gone a little way the kid went pumping after her, panting, yelling, opening his skinny legs wide as scissors over stones and antheaps, and then he caught up with her and you could see that right away she was quite different, I knew how it was, she yelled at him, you heard her laughter as she chased him with the tin, whirled around from out of his clutching hands, struggled with him; they were together like Emma and I used to be when we got away from the old lady, and from the school, and everybody. And Emma was also one of our girls who have the big strong comfortable bodies of mothers even when they're still kids, maybe it comes from always lugging the smaller one round on their backs.

A man came out of the house behind the woman and was friendly. His hair had the dusty look of someone who's been sleeping off drink. In fact, he was still a bit heavy with it.

'You coming from Jo'burg?'

But I wasn't going to be caught out being careless at all, Josias could count on me for that.

'Vereeniging.'

He thought there was something funny there – nobody dresses like a Jo'burger, you could always spot us a mile off – but he was too full to follow it up.

He stood stretching his sticky eyelids open and then he fastened on me the way some people will do: 'Can't you get me work there where you are?'

'What kind of work?'

He waved a hand describing me. 'You got a good work.'

' 'Sall right.'

'Where you working now?'

'Garden boy.'

He tittered, 'Look like you work in town,' shook his head.

I was surprised to find the woman handing me a tin of beer, and I squatted on the ground to drink it. It's mad to say that a mud house can be pretty, but those patterns made in the mud looked nice. They must have been done with a sharp stone or stick when the mud was smooth and wet, the shapes of things like big leaves and moons filled in with lines that went all one way in this shape, another way in that, so that as you looked at the walls in the sun, some shapes were dark and some were light, and if you moved the light ones went dark and the dark ones got light instead. The girl came back with the heavy tin of water on her head making her neck thick. I washed out the jam tin I'd had the beer in and filled it with water. When I thanked them, the old men stirred and ahaed and ehêd again. The man made as if to walk a bit with me, but I was lucky, he didn't go more than a few yards. 'No good,' he said. 'Every morning, five o'clock, and the pay – very small.'

How I would have hated to be him, a man already married and with big children, working all his life in the fields wearing sacks. When you think like this about someone he seems something you could never possibly be, as if it's his fault, and not just the chance of where he happened to be born. At the same time I had a crazy feeling I wanted to tell him something wonderful, something he'd never dreamed could happen, something he'd fall on his knees and thank me for. I wanted to say, 'Soon you'll be the farmer yourself and you'll have shoes like me and your girl will get water from your windmill. Because on Monday, or another Monday, the truck will stop down there and all the stuff will be taken away and they – Josias, me; even you, yes – we'll win for ever.' But instead all I said was, 'Who did that on your house?' He didn't understand and I made a drawing in the air with my hand. 'The women,' he said, not interested.

Down in the donga I sat a while and then threw away the tin and rode off without looking up again to where the kraal was.

It wasn't that Monday. Emma and Josias go to bed very early and of course they were asleep by the time I got home late on Sunday night – Emma thought I'd been with the boys I used to go around with at weekends. But Josias got up at half past four every morning, then, because it was a long way from the Location to where the dynamite factory was, and although I didn't usually even hear him making the fire in the kitchen which was also where I was sleeping, that morning I was awake the moment he got out of bed next door. When he came into the kitchen I was sitting up in my blankets and I whispered loudly, 'I went there yesterday. I saw the turn-off and everything. Down there by the donga, ay? Is that the place?'

He looked at me, a bit dazed. He nodded. Then: 'Wha'd' you mean you went there?'

'I could see that's the only good place. I went up to the house, too, just to see . . . the people are all right. Not many. When it's not Sunday there may be nobody there but the old man – there were two, I think one was just a visitor. The man and the women will be over in the fields somewhere, and that must be quite far, because you can't see the mealies from the road . . .' I could feel myself being listened to carefully, getting in with him (and if with him, with *them*) while I was talking, and I knew exactly what I was saying, absolutely clearly, just as I would know exactly what I was doing. He began to question me; but like I was an older man or a clever one; he didn't know what to say. He drank his tea while I told him all about it. He was thinking. Just before he left he said, 'I shouldn't've told you.'

I ran after him, outside, into the yard. It was still dark. I blurted in the same whisper we'd been using, 'Not today, is it?' I couldn't see his face properly but I knew he didn't know whether to answer or not. 'Not today.' I was so happy I couldn't go to sleep again.

In the evening Josias managed to make some excuse to come out with me alone for a bit. He said, 'I told them you were a hundred-per-cent. It's just the same as if I know.' 'Of course, no difference. I just haven't had much of a chance to do anything...' I didn't carry on: '... because I was too young'; we didn't want to bring Emma into it. And anyway, no one but a real kid is too young any more. Look at the boys who are up for sabotage. I said, 'Have they got them all?'

He hunched his shoulders.

'I mean, even the ones for the picks and spades...?'

He wouldn't say anything, but I knew I could ask. 'Oh, boetie, man, even just to keep a lookout, there on the road...'

I know he didn't want it but once they knew I knew, and that I'd been there and everything, they were keen to use me. At least that's what I think. I never went to any meetings or anything where it was planned, and beforehand I only met the two others who were with me at the turn-off in the end, and we were told exactly what we had to do by Seb Masinde. Of course, Josias and I never said a word to Emma. The Monday that we did it was three weeks later and I can tell you, although a lot's happened to me since then, I'll never forget the moment when we flagged the truck through with Josias sitting there on the back in his little seat. Josias! I wanted to laugh and shout there in the veld; I didn't feel scared – what was there to be scared of, he'd been sitting on a load of dynamite every day of his life for years now, so what's the odds. We had one of those tins of fire and a bucket of tar and the real ROAD CLOSED signs from the P.W.D. and everything went smooth at our end. It was at the Nek Halt end that the trouble started when one of these A.A patrol bikes had to come along (Josias says it was something new, they'd never met a patrol on that road that time of day, before) and get suspicious about the block there. In the meantime the truck was stopped all right but someone was shot and Josias tried to get the gun from the white man up in front of the truck and there was a hell of a fight and they had to make a getaway with the stuff in a car and van back through our block, instead of taking over the truck and driving it to a hiding place to offload. More than half the stuff had to be left behind in the truck. Still, they got clean away with what they did get and it was never found by the police. Whenever I read in the papers here that something's been blown up back at home, I wonder if it's still one of our bangs. Two of our people got picked up right away and some more later and the whole thing was all over the papers with speeches by the chief of Special Branch about a master plot and everything. But Josias got away okay. We three chaps at the road block just ran into the veld to where there were bikes hidden. We went to a place we'd been told in Rustenburg district for a week and then we were told to get over to Bechuanaland. It wasn't so bad; we had no money but around Rustenburg it was easy to pinch pawpaws and oranges off the farms... Oh, I sent a message to Emma that I was all right; and at that time it didn't seem true that I couldn't go home again.

But in Bechuanaland it was different. We had no money, and you don't find food on trees in that dry place. They said they would send us money; it didn't come. But Josias was there too, and we stuck together; people hid us and we kept going. Planes arrived and took away the big shots and the white refugees but although we were told we'd go too, it never came off. We had no money to pay for ourselves. There were plenty others like us in the beginning. At last we just walked, right up Bechuanaland and through Northern Rhodesia to Mbeya, that's over the border in Tanganyika, where we were headed for. A long walk; took Josias and me months. We met up with a chap who'd been given a bit of money and from there sometimes we went by bus. No one asks questions when you're nobody special and you walk, like all the other African people themselves, or take the buses, that the whites never use; it's only if you've got the money for cars or to arrive at the airports that all these things happen that you read about: getting sent back over the border, refused permits and so on. So we got here, to Tanganyika at last, down to this town of Dar es Salaam where we'd been told we'd be going.

There's a refugee camp here and they give you a shilling or two a day until you get work. But it's out of town, for one thing, and we soon left there and found a room down in the shanty town. There are some nice buildings, of course, in the real town – nothing like Johannesburg or Durban, though – and that used to be the white town, the whites who are left still live there, but the Africans with big jobs in the government and so on live there too. Some of our leaders who are refugees like us live in these houses and have big cars; everyone knows they're important men, here, not like at home where if you're black you're just rubbish for the Locations. The people down where we lived are very poor and it's hard to get work because they haven't got enough work for themselves, but I've got my Standard Seven and I managed to get a small job as a clerk. Josias never found steady work. But that didn't matter so much because the big thing was that Emma was able to come to join us after five months, and she and I earn the money. She's a nurse, you see, and Africanization started in the hospitals and the government was short of nurses. So Emma got the chance to come up with a party of them sent for specially from South Africa and Rhodesia. We were very lucky because it's impossible for people to get their families up here. She came in a plane paid for by the government, and she and the other girls had their photograph taken for the newspaper as they got off at the airport. That day she came we took her to the beach, where everyone can bathe, no restrictions, and for a cool drink in one of the hotels (she'd never been in a hotel before), and we walked up and down the road along the bay where everyone walks and where you can see the ships coming in and going out so near that the men out there wave to you. Whenever we bumped into anyone else from home they would stop and ask her about home, and how everything was. Josias and I couldn't stop grinning to hear us all, in the middle of Dar, talking away in our language about the things we know. That day it was like it had happened already: the time when we are home again and everything is our way.

Well, that's nearly three years ago, since Emma came. Josias has been sent away now and there's only Emma and me. That was always the idea, to send us away for training. Some go to Ethiopia and some go to Algeria and all over the show and by the time they come back there won't be anything Verwoerd's men know in the way of handling guns and so on that they won't know better. That's for a start. I'm supposed to go too, but some of us have been waiting a long time. In the meantime I go to work and I walk about this place in the evenings and I buy myself a glass of beer in a bar when I've got money. Emma and I have still got the flat we had before Josias left and two nurses from the hospital pay us for the other bedroom. Emma still works at the hospital but I don't know how much longer. Most days now since Josias's gone she wants me to walk up to fetch her from the hospital when she comes off duty, and when I get under the trees on the drive I see her staring out looking for me as if I'll never turn up ever again. Every day it's like that. When I come up she smiles and looks like she used to for a minute but by the time we're ten yards on the road she's shaking and shaking her head until the tears come, and saying over and over, 'A person can't stand it, a person can't stand it.' She said right from the beginning that the hospitals here are not like the hospitals at home, where the nurses have to know their job. She's got a whole ward in her charge and now she says they're worse and worse and she can't trust anyone to do anything for her. And the staff don't like having strangers working with them anyway. She tells me every day like she's telling me for the first time. Of course it's true that some of the people don't like us being here. You know how it is, people haven't got enough jobs to go round, themselves. But I don't take much notice; I'll be sent off one of these days and until then I've got to eat and that's that.

The flat is nice with a real bathroom and we are paying off the table and six chairs she liked so much, but when we walk in, her face is terrible. She keeps saying the place will never be straight. At home there was only a tap in the yard for all the houses but she never said it there. She doesn't sit down for more than a minute without getting up at once again, but you can't get her to go out, even on these evenings when it's so hot you can't breathe. I go down to the market to buy the food now, she says she can't stand it. When I asked why – because at the beginning she used to like the market, where you can pick a live fowl for yourself, quite cheap – she said those little rotten tomatoes they grow here, and dirty people all shouting and she can't understand. She doesn't sleep, half the time, at night, either, and lately she wakes me up. It happened only last night. She was standing there in the dark and she said, 'I felt bad.' I said, 'I'll make you some tea,' though what good could tea do. 'There must be something the matter with me,' she says. 'I must go to the doctor tomorrow.'

'Is it pains again, or what?'

She shakes her head slowly, over and over, and I know she's going to cry again. 'A place where there's no one. I get up and look out the window and it's just like I'm not awake. And every day, every day. I can't ever wake up and be out of it. I always see this town.'

Of course it's hard for her. I've picked up Swahili and I can get around all right; I mean I can always talk to anyone if I feel like it, but she hasn't learnt more than *ahsante* – she could've picked it up just as easily, but she *can't*, if you know what I mean. It's just a noise to her, like dogs barking or those black crows in the palm trees. When anyone does come here to see her – someone else from home, usually, or perhaps I bring the Rhodesian who works where I do – she only sits there and whatever anyone talks about she doesn't listen until she can sigh and say, 'Heavy, heavy. Yes, for a woman alone. No friends, nobody. For a woman alone, I can tell you.'

Last night I said to her, 'It would be worse if you were at home, you wouldn't have seen Josias or me for a long time.'

But she said, 'Yes, it would be bad. Sela and everybody. And the old crowd at the hospital – but just the same, it would be bad. D'you remember how we used to go right into Jo'burg on my Saturday off? The people – ay! Even when you were twelve you used to be scared you'd lose me.'

'I wasn't scared, you were the one was scared to get run over sometimes.' But in the Location when we stole fruit, and sweets from the shops, Emma could always grab me out of the way of trouble, Emma always saved me. The same Emma. And yet it's not the same. And what could I do for her?

I suppose she wants to be back there now. But still she wouldn't be the same. I don't often get the feeling she knows what I'm thinking about, any more, or that I know what she's thinking, but she said, 'You and he go off, you come back or perhaps you don't come back, you know what you must do. But for a woman? What shall I do there in my life? What shall I do here? What time is this for a woman?'

It's hard for her. Emma. She'll say all that often now, I know. She tells me everything so many times. Well, I don't mind it when I fetch her from the hospital and I don't mind going to the market. But straight after we've eaten, now, in the evenings, I let her go through it once and then I'm off. To walk in the streets when it gets a bit cooler in the dark. I don't know why it is, but I'm thinking so bloody hard about getting out there in the streets that I push down my food as fast as I can without her noticing. I'm so keen to get going I feel queer, kind of tight and excited. Just until I can get out and not hear. I wouldn't even mind skipping the meal. In the streets in the evening everyone is out. On the grass along the bay the fat Indians in their white suits with their wives in those fancy coloured clothes. Men and their girls holding hands. Old watchmen like beggars, sleeping in the doorways of the shut shops. Up and down people walk, walk, just sliding one foot after the other because now and then, like somebody lifting a blanket, there's air from the sea. She should come out for a bit of air in the evening, man. It's an old, old place this, they say. Not the buildings, I mean; but the place. They say ships were coming here before even a place like London was a town. She thought the bay was so nice, that first day. The lights from the ships run all over the water and the palms show up a long time even after it gets dark. There's a smell I've smelled ever since we've been here – three years! I don't mean the smells in the shanty town; a special warm night-smell. You can even smell it at three in the morning. I've smelled it when I was standing about with Emma, by the window; it's as hot in the middle of the night here as it is in the middle of the day, at home – funny, when you look at the stars and the dark. Well, I'll be going off soon. It can't be long now. Now that Josias is gone. You've just got to wait your time; they haven't forgotten about you. Dar es Salaam. Dar. Sometimes I walk with another chap from home, he says some things, makes you laugh! He says the old watchmen who sleep in the doorways get their wives to come there with them. Well, I haven't seen it. He says we're definitely going with the next lot. Dar es Salaam. Dar. One day I suppose I'll remember it and tell my wife I stayed three years there, once. I walk and walk, along the bay, past the shops and hotels and the German church and the big bank, and through the mud streets between old shacks and stalls. It's dark there and full of other walking shapes as I wander past light coming from the cracks in the walls, where the people are in their homes.

Abroad

Manie Swemmer talked for years about going up to Northern Rhodesia for a look around. His two boys, Thys and Willie, were there, and besides, he'd worked up there himself in the old days, the early thirties.

He knew the world a bit although he was born in Bontebokspruit. His grandmother had been a Scots woman, Agnes Swan, and there was a pack of relatives in Scotland; he hadn't got that far, but in a sergeant's mess in Alex just before Sidi Rezegh, when he was with the South African First Division, he had met a Douglas Swan who must have been a cousin – there was quite a resemblance about the eyes.

Yes, he thought of going up, when he could get away. He had been working for the Barends brothers, the last five years, he had put up the Volkskas Bank and the extensions to the mill as well as the new waiting-rooms for Europeans and non-Europeans at the station. The town was going ahead. Before that, he worked for the Provincial Public Works Department, and had even had a spell in Pretoria, at the steel works. That was after the motor business went bust; when he came back from the war he had sold his share of the family land to his uncle, and gone into the motor business with the money. Fortunately – as Manie Swemmer said to the people he had known all his life, in the bar of Buks Jacobs's hotel on Saturdays after work – although he'd had no real training there wasn't much in the practical field he couldn't do. If he'd had certificates, he wouldn't have been working for a salary from Abel and Johnnie Barends today, that was for sure, but there you are. People still depended on him; if he wanted to take his car and drive up North, he needed three weeks, and who could Abel find to take his place and manage his gang of boys on the site?

He often said he'd like to drive up. It was a long way but he didn't mind the open road and he'd done it years ago when it was strip roads if you were lucky, and plain murder the rest of the way. His old '57 Studebaker would make it; he looked after her himself, and there were many people in the town – including Buks Jacobs from the hotel with his new Volkswagen combi – who wouldn't have anybody else touch their cars. Manie spent most of his Saturday afternoons under somebody's; he had no one at home (the boys' mother, born Helena Thys, had died of a diseased kidney, leaving him to bring up the two little chaps all alone) and he did it more out of friendship than for anything else.

On Sundays, when he was always expected at the Gysbert Swemmers', he had remarked that he'd like to go up and have a look around. And there were his boys, of course. His cousin Gysbert said, 'Let them come down and visit you.' But they were busy making their way; Thys was on the mines, but didn't like it, Willie had left the brewery and was looking for an opening down in the capital. After the British Government gave the natives the country and the name was change to Zambia, Gysbert said, 'Man, you don't want to go there now. What for? After you waited so long.'

But he had moved around the world a bit: Gysbert might run three hundred head of cattle, and was making a good thing out of tobacco and chillies as well as mealies on the old Swemmer farm where they had all grown up, but Gysbert had never been farther than a holiday in Cape Town. Gysbert had not joined up during the war, Gysbert sat in their grandfather's chair at Sunday dinner and served roast mutton and sweet potatoes and rice to his wife and family, including Manie, and Gysbert's mother, Tante Adela. Tante Adela had her little plot on the farm where she grew cotton, and after lunch she sat in the dark *voorkamer*, beside the big radio and record player combination, and stuffed her cotton into the cushion-covers she cut from sheets of plastic foam. There was coffee on the stoep, handed round by pregnant daughters and daughters-in-law, and there were grandchildren whose mouths exploded huge bubbles of gum before Oom Manie and made him laugh. Gysbert even still drank *mampoer*, home-made peach brandy sent from the Cape, but Manie couldn't stand the stuff and never drank any spirits but Senator Brandy – Buks Jacobs, at the hotel, would set it up without asking.

At the end of the Sunday Manie Swemmer would drive home from the old family farm that was all Gysbert knew, past the fields shuffling and spreading a hand of mealies, then tobacco, and then chilli bushes blended by distance, like roof-tiles, into red-rose-yellows. Past the tractor and the thresher with its beard of torn husks, and down into the dip over the dried-up river bed, where they used to try and catch leguaans, as youngsters. Past the cattle nibbling among the thorn bushes and wild willow. Through the gates opened by picannins running with the kaffir dogs, from the kraal. Past the boys and their women squatting around paraffin tins of beer and pap, and the Indian store, old Y. S. Mia's, boarded up for Sunday, and all the hundred-and-one relations those people have, collected on the stoep of the bright pink house next to the store. At that time in the late afternoon the shadow of the hilly range had taken up the dam; Manie looked, always, for the glittering circles belched by fish. He fished there, in summer, still; the thorn trees they used to play under were dead, but stood around the water.

The town did not really leave the lands behind. His house in Pretorius Street was the same as the farm-houses, a tin roof, a polished stoep on stumpy cement pillars darkening the rooms round two sides, paint the colour of the muddy river halfway up the outside walls and on the woodwork. Inside there was flowered linoleum and sword-fern in a painted kaffir pot that rocked a little on its uneven base as he walked in. The dining table and six chairs he and Helena had bought when they got married, and Tante Adela's plastic-foam cushions, covering the places on the sofa where the kids had bounced the springs almost through. He had a good old boy, Jeremiah, looking after him. The plot was quite big and was laid out in rows of beetroot, onions and cabbage behind a quince hedge. Jeremiah had his mealie patch down at his *khaya*. There were half-a-dozen Rhode Island Reds in the *hok*, and as for the tomatoes, half the town ate presents of Manie Swemmer's tomatoes.

He'd never really cleared out his sons' room, though once there'd been a young chappie from the railways looking for somewhere to rent. But Willie was only sixteen when he went up North to have a look round – that's how kids are, his brother Thys had gone up and it was natural – he might want to come back home again sometime. The beds were there, and Willie's collection of bottle-tops. On the netted-in stoep round the back there was his motorbike, minus wheels. Manie Swemmer often thought of writing to ask Willie what he ought to do with the bike; but the boys didn't answer letters often. In fact, Willie was better than Thys; Thys hadn't written for about eighteen months, by the time the place had gone and changed its name from Northern Rhodesia to Zambia. Not that the change would frighten Manie Swemmer if he decided to make the trip. After all, it wasn't as if he were going to drag a woman up there. And it might be different for people with young daughters. But for someone like him, well, what did he have to worry about except himself?

One September, when the new abattoir was just about off his hands, he told the Barends brothers that he was taking leave. 'No, not down to Durban – I'm pushing off up there for a couple of weeks –' His rising eyebrows and backward jerk of the head indicated the back of the hotel bar, the mountain range, the border.

'Gambia, Zambia! These fancy names. With the new kaffir government. Doctor or Professor or whatever-he-calls-himself Kaunda,' said Carel Janse van Vuuren, the local solicitor, who had been articled in Johannesburg, making it clear by his amusement that he, too, knew something of the world.

'Tell your sons to come home here, man. *Hulle is ons mense.*' Dawie Mulder was hoping to be nominated as a candidate for the next provincial elections and liked to put a patriotic edge on his remarks.

'Oh they know their home, all right, don't you worry,' Manie Swemmer said, in English, because some of the regulars on the commercial travellers' run, old Joe Zeff and Edgar Bloch, two nice Jewish chappies, had set up the beers for the group. 'They'll settle down when they've had their fling, I'm not worried.'

'Up in this, uh, Northern Rhodesia – I hear the natives don't bother the white people on the mines, eh?' said Zeff. 'I mean you don't have to worry, they won't walk into your house or anything – after all, it's not a joke, you have a big kaffir coming and sitting down next to us here? It's all you're short of.'

Sampie Jacobs, the proprietor's wife and a business woman who could buy and sell any man in Bontebokspruit, if it came to money matters, said, 'Willie was a bea-utiful child. When he was a little toddler! Eyes like saucers, and blue!' She hung the fly-swatter on its hook, and mentally catching somebody out, scratched at some fragment of food dried fast to a glass. 'If Helena could have seen him' – she reminded Manie Swemmer of the pimple-eroded youth who had bought an electric guitar on credit and gone away leaving his father to meet the instalments.

'They'll settle down! Thys is earning good money up there now, though, man. You couldn't earn money like that here! Not a youngster.'

'Twenty-six – no, twenty-seven, by now,' said Sampie Jacobs. 'But Willie. Willie's not twenty-one.'

Buks Jacobs said, 'Well, you can have it for me, Oom Manie.'

'Man, I nearly died of malaria up there in thirty-two,' Manie Swemmer said, putting a fist on the counter. 'Good Lord, I knew the place when it was nothing but a railhead and a couple of mine shafts in the bush. There was an Irish doctor, that time. Fitzgerald was his name, he got my boss-boy to sponge me down every hour...'

On the third day of the journey, in the evening, the train drew into the capital, Lusaka. Manie Swemmer had taken the train, after all; it would have been different if there had been someone to drive up with him. But the train was more restful and, with this trip in the back of his mind all the time, it was some years since he'd taken a holiday. He was alone in the second-class compartment until the Bechuanaland border, wondering if Abel Barends wouldn't make a mess, now, of that gang of boys it had taken years to get into shape, a decent gang of boys but they had to know where they were with you, the native doesn't like to be messed around, either. He mouthed aloud to himself what he had meant to say to Abel, 'Don't let me come back and find you've taken on a lot of black scum from the location.' But then the train stopped at a small station and he got up to lean on the let-down window; and slowly the last villages of the Transvaal were paused at and passed, and as he looked out at them with his pipe in his mouth and the steam letting fly from beneath the carriage, Barends and the building gang sank to the bottom of his mind. Once or twice, when the train moved on again, he checked his post office savings book (he had transferred money to Lusaka) and the indigestion pills he had put in with his shaving things. He had his bedding ticket (everything under control, he had joked, smiling to show how easy it was if you knew how, to Gysbert and his wife and Sampie Jacobs, who had seen him on to the train) and a respectful coloured boy made up a nice bunk for him and was grateful for his five-cent tip. By the time the train reached Mafeking after dinner, he felt something from the past that he had forgotten entirely, although he talked about it often: the jubilant lightness of moving on, not a stranger among strangers, but a new person discovered among new faces. He felt as if he had been travelling for ever and could go on for ever. Through Rhodesia the hills, the bush, the smell of a certain shrub came back to him across thirty years. It was like the veld at home, only different. The balancing rocks, the white-barked figs that split them and held them in tight-spread roots, the flat-topped trees turning red with spring – yes, he remembered that – the bush becoming tangled forest down over the rivers, the old baobabs and the kaffir-orange trees with their green billiard-balls sticking out all over, the huge vleis with, far off, a couple of palms craning up looking at you. Two more days slid past the windows. He bought a set of table mats from a picannin at a siding; nicely made, the reeds dyed pink and black – he saw Sampie Jacobs putting them under her flower arrangements in the hotel lounge, far, far away, far, far ahead. When the train reached the Rhodesian–Zambian border there was a slight nervous bracing of his manner; he laid out his open passport – HERMANUS STEFANUS SWEMMER, national of the Republic of South Africa. The young Englishman and the black man dressed exactly like him, white socks, gold shoulder tabs, smart cap, the lot, said, 'Thank you Sir', the black one scribbled and stamped.

Well, he was in.

As the train neared Lusaka he began to get anxious. About Willie. About what he would say to Willie. After all, five years. Willie's twenty-first was coming up in December. He forgot that he was drawing into Lusaka through the dark, he forgot that he was travelling, he thought: Willie, Willie. There were no outskirts to Lusaka, even now. A few lights at a level crossing or two, bicycles, native women with bundles – and they were in the station. The huge black sky let down a trail of rough bright stars as close as the lights of a city. Bells rang and the train, standing behind Manie Swemmer, stamped backwards. People sauntered and yelled past him; white people, Indians, natives in moulded plastic shoes.

Willie said, 'Hell, where were you?'

Tall. Sideburns. A black leather jacket zipped up to where the button was missing at the neck of the shirt. The same; and Manie Swemmer had forgotten. Never sent a snap of himself, and naturally you'd expect him to have changed in five years.

They spoke in English. 'I was just beginning to wonder did the letter get lost. I was just going to take a taxi. Well how's it! Quite a trip, eh? Since Wednesday, man!' Manie knew how to behave; he had his hands on the kid's biceps, he was pushing him and shaking him. Willie was grinning down the side of his mouth. He stood there while his father talked about the train, and why he hadn't driven up, and what Gysbert said, that backvelder tied to Tante Adela's apron, and the good dinner the dining-car had put up. 'Give us your things,' Willie said. 'What's this?' The mats were tied up in a bit of newspaper. 'Presents, man. I can't go back empty-handed.' 'Just hang on here a minute, ay, Dad, I'mna get some smokes.' Held his shoulders too high when he ran; that was always his fault, when he did athletics at Bontebokspruit High. Willie. Couldn't believe it. Suddenly, Manie Swemmer landed in Lusaka, knew he was there, and exhilaration spread through his breast like some pleasurable form of heartburn.

Willie opened the pack and shook out a cigarette, tenting his hands round the match. 'Where were you gunna take the taxi?'

'Straight to your place, man. I've got the letter on me.'

'I've pushed off from there.'

'But what happened, son, I thought it was so near for work and everything?'

Willie took a deep draw at his cigarette, put his head back as if swallowing an injury and then blew smoke at it, with narrowed eyes; there was a line between them already, his father noticed. 'Didn't work out at Twyford's Electric. So I had to find a cheaper room until I get fixed up.'

'But I thought they told you there was prospects, son?'

'I'm going to see someone at the cement works Monday. Friend of mine says he'll fix me up. And there's a job going at a motor spares firm, too. I don't want to jump at anything.'

'For Pete's sake, no. You must think of your future. Fancy about Twyford's, eh, they started up in the thirties, one of the first. But I suppose the old boy's dead now. Watch out for the motor spares outfit – I don't trust that game.'

They were still standing on the platform; Willie was leaning against one of the struts that held up the roof, smoking and feeling a place near his left sideburn where he had nicked himself. That poor kid would never be able to get a clean shave – his skin had never come right. He seemed to have forgotten about the luggage.

'So where you staying now, Willie?' Everyone from the train had left.

'I'm at another chap's place. There's a bed on the stoep. There's five people in the house, only three rooms. They can't put you up.'

'What's wrong with a hotel?' Manie Swemmer consoled, chivvying, cheerful. 'Come let's take this lot and get into town. I'll get a room at the Lusaka Hotel, good Lord, do I remember that place. I know all about the posh new one out on Ridgeway, too. But I don't have to splash it. The Lusaka'll do me fine.'

Willie was shaking his head, hang-dog.

'You'll never get *in*, man, Dad. You don't know – you won't get a room in this place. It's the independence anniversary next week –'

'When? The anniversary, eh –' He was pleased to have arrived for a festival.

'I dunno. Monday, I think. You haven't a hope.'

'Wait a minute, wait a minute.' They were gathering the luggage. Manie Swemmer had put on his hat to emerge into the town, although he had suddenly realized that the night was very hot. He looked at his son.

'I thought maybe it's the best thing if you go straight on to the Copper Belt,' said Willie. 'To Thys.'

'To Thys?' He lifted the hat to let the air in upon his head.

'I dunno about a train, but it's easy to thumb a lift on the road.'

'The Regent!' Manie Swemmer said. 'Is there still a Regent Hotel? Did you try there?'

'What you mean try, Dad, I told you, it's no use to *try*, you'll never get *in* –'

'Well, never mind, son, let's go and have a beer there, anyway. Okay?' Manie Swemmer felt confused, as if the station itself were throwing back and forth all sorts of echoes. He wanted to get out of it, never mind where. There was only one clear thought; silly. He must put new buttons on the kid's shirt. A man who has brought up two youngsters and lived alone a long time secretly knows how to do these things.

Lusaka was a row of Indian stores and the railway station, facing each other. In the old days.

Manie Swemmer was a heavy man but he sat delicately balanced, forward, in the taxi, looking out under the roof at the new public buildings and shopping centres lit up round paved courts in Cairo Road, the lights of cars travelling over supermarkets and milk bars. 'The post office? Ne-ver!' And he could not stop marvelling at it, all steel and glass, and a wide parking-lot paved beside it. Here and there was a dim landmark – one of the Indian stores whose cracked veranda had been a quay above the dust of the road – with a new shopfront but the old tin roof. No more sewing machines going under the hands of old natives on the verandas; even just in passing, you could see the stuff in the smart window displays was factory-made. Fishing tackle and golf clubs: shiny sets of drums and electric guitars; a grubby-looking little bar with kaffir music coming out. 'Looks as if it should be down in the location, eh?' He laughed, pointing it out to Willie. There were quite a few nicely-dressed natives about, behaving themselves, with white shirts and ties. The women in bright cotton dresses, the latest styles and high-heeled shoes. And everywhere, Europeans in cars. 'Ah, but the old trees are still going strong!' he said to Willie. Along the middle of the Cairo Road there was the same broad island with red-flowering trees, he recognized the shape of the blooms although he couldn't see their colour. Willie was sitting back, smoking. He said, 'They don't leave you alone, with their potatoes and I don't know what.' He wasn't looking, but was speaking of the natives who hung around even after dark under the trees – venders, young out-of-works.

The way to the Regent was too short for Manie Swemmer's liking. He could have done with driving around a bit; this kind of confusion was different – exciting, like being blindfolded, whirled around, and then left to feel your way about a room you knew well. But in no time they were at the hotel, and that had changed and hadn't changed, too. The old rows of rooms in the garden had been connected with a new main building, but the 'garden' was still swept earth with a few hibiscus and snake plants.

They found themselves in what had been the veranda and was now closed in with glass louvres and called the terrace lounge. Willie made no suggestions, and his father, chatting and commenting in the husky undertone he used among other people, was misled by the layout of the hotel as he remembered it. 'Never mind, never mind! What's the odds. We'll have a drink before we start any talking, man, why not? This'll do all right.' With his big behind in its neat grey flannels rising apologetically towards the room, he supervised the stowing of his two suitcases and newspaper parcel beside the small table where he urged Willie to sit. He ordered a couple of beers, and looked around. The place was filling up with the sort of crowd you get on hot evenings; one or two families with kids climbing about the chairs, young men buying their girls a drink, married couples who hadn't gone home after the office – men alone would be in the pub itself. There was only one coloured couple – not blacks, more like Cape Coloureds. You'd hardly notice them. Willie didn't know anyone. They went, once again, over the questions and answers they had exchanged over Willie's prospects of a new job. But it had always been hard to know what Willie was thinking, even when he was quite a little kid; and Manie Swemmer's attention kept getting out of range, around the room, to the bursts of noise that kept coming, perhaps when some inner door connected with the bar was opened – to the strange familiar town outside, and the million-and-one bugs going full blast for the night with the sound of sizzling, of clocks being wound and ratchets jerking. 'What a machine shop, eh?' he said; but of course, living there five years, Willie wouldn't even be hearing it any more.

'Who's running the place these days?' he suggested to Willie confidentially, when the beer was drunk. 'You know the chap at all?'

'Well, I mean I know who he is. Mr Davidson. We come here sometimes. There's a dance, first Saturday of the month.'

'Do you think he'd know you?'

'Don't know if he knows me,' said Willie.

'Well, come on, let's see what we can do.' Manie Swemmer asked the Indian waiter to keep an eye on the luggage for a moment, and was directed to the reception desk. Willie came along behind him. A redhead with a skin that would dent blue if you touched it said, 'Full up, sir, I'm sorry, sir –' almost before Manie Swemmer began speaking. He put his big, half-open fist on the counter, and smiled at her with his head cocked: 'Now listen here, young miss, I come all the way from a place you never heard of, Bontebokspruit, and I'm sure you can find me just a bed. Anywhere. I've travelled a lot and I'm not fussy.' She smiled sympathetically, but there it was – nothing to offer. She even ran her ballpoint down the list of bookings once again, eyebrows lifted and the pretty beginnings of a double chin showing.

'Look, I lived in this town while you were still a twinkle in your father's eye – I'd like to say hello to Mr Davidson, anyway. D'you mind, eh?'

She called somewhere behind a stand of artificial roses and tulips, 'Friend of Mr Davidson's here. Can he come a minute?'

He was a little fellow with a recognizable way of hitching his arms forward at the elbow to ease his shirt cuffs up his wrists as he approached: ex-barman. He had a neat, patient face, used to dealing with trouble.

'Youngster like you wouldn't remember, but I lived in this hotel thirty years ago – I helped build this town, put up the first reservoir. Now they tell me I'll have to sleep in the street tonight.'

'That's about it,' the manager said.

'I can hear you're a Jock, like me, too!' Manie Swemmer seized delightedly upon the hint of a Scots accent. 'Yes, you may not believe it but my grandmother was a Miss Swan. From the Clyde. Agnes Swan. I used to wear the kilt when I was a kiddie. Yes, I did! An old Boer like me.'

The little man and the receptionist conferred over the list of bookings; she knew she was right, there was nothing. But the man said, 'Tell you what I'll do. There's this fellow from Delhi. He h's a biggish single I could m'be put another bed in. I promised him he'd have it to himself, but still an' all. He can't object to someone like yourself, I mean.'

'There you are! The good old Regent! Didn't I say to you, Willie?' Willie was leaning on the reception desk smoking and looking dazedly at the high heel of his Chelsea boot; he smiled down the side of his mouth again.

'I'll apologize for barging in on this chap, don't you worry, I'll make it all right. You say from Delhi – India?' Manie Swemmer added suddenly. 'You mean an Indian chappie?'

'But he's not one of your locals,' said the manager. 'Not one of these fellows down here. A businessman, flown in this morning on the V.C.10.'

'Oh, he's well-dressed, a real gentleman,' the receptionist reassured in the wide-eyed recommendation of something she wouldn't care to try for herself.

'That's the way it is,' the manager said, in confidence.

'Okay, okay, I'll buy. I'm not saying a word!' said Manie Swemmer. 'Ay, Willie? Somewhere to lay my head, that's all I ask.'

The redhead took a key out of the nesting boxes numbered on the wall: 'Fifty-four, Mr Davidson? The boy'll bring your luggage, sir.'

'Good Lord, you've got to have a bit of a nerve or you don't get anywhere, eh?' Manie walked gaily close beside his son along the corridors with their path of flowered runner and buckets of sand filled with cigarette-stubs, stepping round beer bottles and tea-trays that people had put outside their doors. In the room the servant opened for him, he at once assumed snug possession. 'I hope the Oriental gentleman's only going to stay one night. This'll do me fine.' A divan, ready made-up with bedding and folded in the middle like a wallet, was wheeled in. He squeaked cupboards open, forced up the screeching steel fly-screens and pushed the windows wide – 'Air, air, that's what we need.' Willie sat on the other bed, whose cover already had been neatly turned back to allow a head to rest on the pillow; the dent was still there. The chap's things were on the dressing-table. Willie fingered a pair of cuff-links with red stones in them. There was a tissue-paper airmail edition of some London newspaper, an open tin of cough lozenges and a gold-tooled leather notebook. Rows of exquisitely neat figures, and then writing like something off a fancy carpet: 'Hell, look at this, eh?' said Willie.

'Willie, I always taught you to respect other people's belongings no matter who they are.'

Willie dropped the notebook finickily. 'Okay, okay.'

Manie Swemmer washed, combed his moustache and the back of his head where there was still some hair, put back on again the tropical-weight jacket he had bought specially for the trip. 'I never used to look sloppy, not even when the heat was at its height,' he remarked to Willie. Willie nodded whether he had been listening to what you said or not.

When they had returned the key to the reception desk Willie said, 'We gunna eat now, Dad,' but there wasn't a soul in the dining room but a young woman finishing supper with her kiddies, and if there was one thing that depressed Manie Swemmer it was an empty hotel dining room.

In fact, he was attracted to the bar with a mixture of curiosity and shyness, as if Manie Swemmer, twenty-three years old, in bush jacket and well-pressed shorts, might be found drinking there. He strolled through the garden, Willie behind him, listening to the tree-frogs chinking away at the night. In spite of the town, you could still smell woodsmoke from the natives' fires. But youngsters don't notice these things. The street entrance to the bar was through a beer garden now, screened by lattice. Coloured bulbs poked red and blue light through the pattern of slats and dark blotches of creeper. There were loud voices in the local native lingo and the coughs of small children. 'It's for them, let's go this way,' Willie said, and he and his father went back into the hotel and entered the bar from the inside door.

It was full, all right. Manie Swemmer had never been what you would call a drinker, but for a man who lives alone there is no place where he feels at home the way he does among men in a bar. And yet there were blacks. Oh yes, that was something. Blacks sitting at the tables, and some of them not too clean or well-dressed, either. Looked like boys from the roads, labourers. Up at the bar were the white men, the wide backs and red necks almost solidly together; a black face or two above white shirts at the far end. The backs parted for father and son: they might have been expected. 'Well, what's the latest from Thys, man?' Manie Swemmer was at ease at last, wedged between the shoulder of a man telling a story with large gestures, and the bar counter ringed shinily, like the dark water at Gysbert's dam.

'Nothing. Oh this girl. He's got himself engaged to this doll Lynda Thompson.'

'Good grief, so he must have written! The letter's missed me. Getting engaged! Well, I've picked the right time, eh, independence anniversary and my son's engagement! We've got something to drink to, all right. When's the engagement going to be?'

'Oh it was about ten days ago. A party at her people's place in Kitwe. I couldn't get a lift up to the Copper Belt that weekend.'

'But if I'd known! Why'n't Thys send me a telegram, man! I'd have taken my leave sooner!'

Willie said nothing, only looked sideways at the men beside him.

Manie Swemmer took a deep drink of his beer. 'If he'd sent a telegram, man! Why'n't he let me know? I told him I was coming up the middle of the month. Why not just send a telegram at least?'

Willie had no answer. Manie Swemmer drank off his beer and ordered another round. Now he said softly, in Afrikaans, 'Just go to the post office and write out a telegram eh?'

Willie shrugged. They drank. The swell of other people's spirits, the talk and laughter around them lifted Manie Swemmer from the private place where he was beached. 'Well, I'll go up and look at Miss Lynda Thompson for myself in a few days. Kitwe's a beautiful town, eh? What's the matter with the girl, is he ashamed of her or what? Is she bowlegged and squint?' He laughed. 'Trust old Thys for that!'

At some point the shoulder pressing against his had gone without his noticing. A native's voice said in good English, 'Excuse me, did you lose this?' The black hand with one of those expensive calendar watches at the wrist held out a South African two-rand note.

Manie Swemmer began struggling to get at his pockets. 'Hang on a tick, just let me . . . yes, must be mine, I pulled it out by mistake to pay with . . . thanks very much.'

'A pleasure.'

One of the educated kind, some of them have studied at universities in America, even. And England was just pouring money into the hands of these people, they could go over and get the best education going, better than whites could afford. Manie Swemmer said to Willie, but in a voice to be overheard, because after all, you didn't expect such honesty of a native, it was really something to be encouraged: 'I thought I'd put away all my money from home when I took out my Zambian currency in the train. Two rand! Well, that would have been the price of a few beers down the drain!'

The black said, 'The price of a good bottle of brandy down there.' He wore a spotless bush jacket and longs; spotless.

'You've been to South Africa?' said Manie Swemmer.

'You ever heard of Fort Hare College? I was there four years. And I used to spend my holidays with some people in Germiston. I know Johannesburg well.'

'Well, let me buy you a South African brandy. Come on, man, why not?' The black man smiled and indicated casually that his bottle of beer already had been put before him. 'No, no, man, that'll do for a chaser; you're going to have a brandy with me, eh?' Manie Swemmer's big body curved over the bar as he agitated for the attention of the barman. He jolted the black man's arm and almost threw Willie's glass over. 'Sorry – come on, there – two brandies – wait a minute, have you got Senator? D'you want another beer, Willie?' The kid might drink brandy on his own but he wasn't going to get it from his father.

'You'll get a shock when you have to pay.' The black chap was amused. He had taken a newspaper out of his briefcase and was glancing over the headlines.

'Brandy's expensive here, eh? The duty and that. When I was up on the Copper Belt as a youngster we had to drink it to keep going. Brandy and quinine. It was a few bob a bottle. That's how I learnt to drink brandy.'

'Is that so?' The black man spoke kindly. 'So you know this country quite a long time.'

Manie Swemmer moved his elbow within half-an-inch of a nudge – 'I'll bet I knew it before you did – before you were born!'

'I'm sure, I'm sure.' They laughed. Manie Swemmer looked excitedly from the man to his son, but Willie was mooning over his beer, as usual. The black man – he told his name but who could catch their names – was something in the Ministry of Local Government, and he was very interested in what Manie Swemmer could tell him of the old days; he listened with those continual nods of the chin that showed he was following carefully; a proper respect – if not for a white man, then for a man as old as his father might be. He could still speak Afrikaans, Manie Swemmer discovered. He said a few sentences in a low voice but Manie Swemmer was pretty sure he could have carried on a whole conversation if he'd wanted to. 'You'll excuse me if I don't join you, but you'll have another brandy?' the black man offered. 'I have a meeting in' – he looked at the watch – 'less than half-an-hour, and I must keep a clear head.'

'Of course! You've got responsibility, now. I always say, any fool can learn to do what he's told, but when it comes to making the decisions, when you got to shift for yourself, that's the time you've either got it up here, or ... It doesn't matter who or what you are ...'

The man had slipped off the bar stool, briefcase between chest and arm. 'Enjoy your holiday ...'

'Everything of the best!' Manie Swemmer called after him. 'I'll tell you something, Willie, he may be black as the ace of spades, but that's a gentleman. Eh? You got to be open-minded, otherwise you can't move about in these countries. But that's a gentleman!'

'Some of them put on an act,' said Willie. 'You get them wanting to show how educated they are. The best thing is don't take any notice.'

'What's the name of that feller was talking to me?' Manie Swemmer asked the white barman. He wanted to write it down so he'd be able to remember when he told the story back home.

'You know who that is? That's Thompson Gwebo, that's one of the Under Minister's brothers,' the barman said. 'When he married last November they had their roast oxen and all that at his village, but the wedding reception for the government people and white people and so on was here. Five tiers to the cake. Over three hundred people. Mrs Davidson did the snacks herself.'

They began to chat, between interruptions when the barman was called away to dispense drinks. Two or three beers had their effect on Willie, too; he was beginning to talk, in reluctant spates that started with one of his mumbled remarks, half-understood by his father, and then developed, through his father's eager questions, into the bits and pieces of a life that Manie Swemmer pieced together. 'This feller said...' 'Which one was that, the manager or your mate?' 'No, the one I told you ... the one who was supposed to turn up at the track...' 'What track?' 'Stock car racing ... there was this feller asked me to change the plugs...'

In a way, it was just like the old days up there. Nobody thought about going home. Not like Buks Jacobs's place, the pub empty over dinner-time. This one was packed. The white men were solid at the bar again, but the blacks at the tables – the labourers – were getting rowdy. They were joined by a crowd of black ducktails in jeans who behaved just like the white ones you saw in the streets of Johannesburg and Pretoria. They surged up and down between the tables and were angrily hit off, like flies, by the labourers heavily drunk over their beer: one lifted his bottle and brought it down on the back of one of the hooligans' hands; there was a roar. A black lout in a shirt with 007 printed across it kept jolting against Manie Swemmer's shoulder in the brand-new tropical jacket. Manie Swemmer went on talking and ignored him, but the hooligan taunted in English – 'Sorry!' He did it again: 'Sorry!' The drunken black face with a fleck of white matter at the corner of each eye breathed over him. If it'd been a white man Manie Swemmer wouldn't have stood for it, he'd have punched him in the nose. And at home if a native – but at home it couldn't happen; here he was, come up to have a look, and he'd been in some tough spots before – Good Lord, those gyppos in Egypt, they didn't all smell of roses, either. He knew how to hold himself in if he had to.

Then another native – one in a decent shirt and tie – came over and said something angrily, in their own language, to the hooligans. He said to the barman in English. 'Can't you see these men are making a nuisance of themselves? Why don't you have them thrown out?'

The barman was quick to take the support. 'These people should be outside in the beer garden!' he said to the company at large. 'Go on. I don't want trouble in here.' The hooligans drifted away from the bar counter but would not go out. Manie Swemmer had not noticed the decently-dressed native leave, but suddenly he appeared, quiet and business-like, with two black policemen in white gloves. 'What's the complaint?' one shouldered past Willie to ask the barman. 'Making a nuisance of themselves, those over there.' There was a brief uproar; of course natives are great ones for shouting. But the black hooligans were carted away by their own policemen like a bunch of scruffy dogs; no nonsense.

'No nonsense!' said Manie Swemmer, laughing and putting his hand over Willie's forearm. 'D'you see that? Good Lord, they've got marvellous physiques, that pair. Talk about smart! That's something worth seeing!' Willie giggled; his dad was talking very loud; he was talking to everyone in the place, joking with everyone. At last they found themselves at dinner, after half-past nine it must have been. There were shouts of laughter from other late diners, telling stories. Manie Swemmer began to think very clearly and seriously, and to talk very seriously to Willie, about the possibility of moving up here, himself. 'I've still a lot of my life ahead of me. Must I see out my time making money for Abel Barends? In Bonteboksspruit? Why shouldn't I start out on my own again? The place is going ahead!'

The jolly party left the dining room and all at once he was terribly tired: the journey, the arrival, the first look around – it left him winded like too hearty a slap on the back. 'Let's call it a day, son,' he said, and Willie saw him to the room.

But the key would not open the door. Willie investigated by the flare of a match. 'S'bolted on the inside.' They rapped softly, then hammered. 'Well I'm damned,' said Manie Swemmer. 'The Indian.' And he had been going to tell him about how many years Y. S. Mia had had a store near the farm.

They went down to the reception desk. The redhead thrust her tongue in a bulge between lower lip and teeth, in consternation. 'Have you knocked?' 'The blooming door down!' said Manie Swemmer. 'Mind you, I thought as much,' the girl said. 'He was on his high horse when he came back and saw your bed and things. I mean I don't know what the fuss was about – as I said to him, it isn't as if we've put an African in with you, it's a white man. And him Indian himself.'

'Well, what're you going to do about my dad?' Willie said suddenly.

'What can I do?' She made a peaked face. 'Mr Davidson's gone off to Kapiri Mposhi, his mother's broken her hip at eighty-one. I can't depend on anyone else here to throw that chap out. And if he won't even answer the door.'

Manie Swemmer said nothing. Willie waited, but all he could hear was his father's slow breathing, with little gasps on the intake. 'But what about my dad?'

She had her booking list out again. They waited. 'Tell you what. No. – There's a room with four beds out in the old wing, we keep it, you know – sometimes now, these people come in and you daren't say no. They don't want to pay for more than one room for the lot. It was booked, I mean, but it's after eleven now and no one's showed up, so I should think you could count on it being all right...'

Manie Swemmer put his big forearm and curled hand on the reception desk like a dead thing. 'Look,' he said. 'The coolie, all right, I didn't say anything. But don't put me in with an African, now, man! I mean, I've only just got here, give me a bit of time. You can't expect to put me in with a native, right away, first thing.'

'Oh I should think it would be all right,' she said in her soothing, effusive way, something to do with some English accent she had. 'I wouldn't worry if I was you. It's late now. Very unlikely anyone'd turn up. Don't you think?'

She directed him to the room. Willie went with him again. Across the garden; the old block, the way it was in the old days. There was no carpet in the passage; their footsteps tottered over the unevennesses of cracked granolithic. When Willie had left him, he pulled down the bedding of the best-looking bed to have a good look at the sheets, opened the window, and then, working away at it with a grunt that was almost a giggle, managed to drive the rusty bolt home across the door.

Livingstone's Companions

In the house that afternoon the Minister of Foreign Affairs was giving his report on the President's visit to Ethiopia, Kenya and Tanzania. 'I would like to take a few minutes to convey to you the scene when we arrived at the airport,' he was saying, in English, and as he put the top sheet of his sheaf of notes under the last, settling down to it, Carl Church in the press gallery tensed and relaxed his thigh muscles – a gesture of resignation. 'It's hard to describe the enthusiasm that greeted the President everywhere he went. Everywhere crowds, enormous crowds. If those people who criticize the President's policies and cry neo-colonialism when he puts the peace and prosperity of our country first –'

There were no Opposition benches since the country was a one-party state, but the dissident faction within the party slumped, blank-faced, while a deep hum of encouragement came from two solid rows of the President's supporters seated just behind Carl Church.

'... those who are so quick to say that our President's policies are out of line with the OAU could see how enthusiastically the President is received in fellow member-states of the OAU, they would think before they shout. They would see it is they who are out of line, who fail to understand the problems of Pan-Africa, they who would like to see our crops rot in the fields, our people out of work, our development plans come to a full stop' – assent swarmed, the hum rose – 'and all for an empty gesture of fist-shaking' – the two close-packed rows were leaning forward delightedly; polished shoes drummed the floor – 'they know as well as you and I will not free the African peoples of the white-supremacy states south of our borders.'

The Foreign Minister turned to the limelight of approval. The President himself was not in the House; some members watched the clock (gift of the United States Senate) whose graceful copper hand moved with a hiccup as each minute passed. The Speaker in his long curly wig was propped askew against the tall back of his elaborate chair. His clerk, immobile, with the white pompadour, velvet bow and lacy jabot that were part of the investiture of sovereignty handed down from the British, was a perfect *papier-mâché* blackamoor from an eighteenth-century slave trader's drawing-room.

The House was panelled in local wood whose scent the sterile blast of the air-conditioning had not yet had time to evaporate entirely. Carl Church stayed on because of the coolness, the restful incense of new wood – the Foreign Minister's travelogue wasn't worth two lines of copy. Between the Minister and the President's claque the dialogue of banal statement and deep-chested response went on beamingly, obliviously. '... can assure you ... full confidence lies in ...'

Suddenly the Speaker made an apologetic but firm gesture to attract the Minister's attention: 'Mr Minister, would it be convenient to adjourn at this point...?'

The claque filed jovially out of the House. The Chamberlain came into the foyer carrying his belly before turned-out thighs, his fine African calves looking well in courtier's stockings, silver buckles flashing on his shoes. Waylaid on the stairs by another journalist, the Minister was refusing an interview with the greatest amiability, in the volume of voice he had used in the House, as if someone had forgotten to turn off the public address system.

With the feeling that he had dozed through a cinema matinee, Carl Church met the glare of the afternoon as a dull flash of pain above his right eye. His hired car was parked in the shade of the building – these were the little ways in which he made some attempt to look after himself: calculating the movement of the sun when in hot countries, making sure that the hotel bed wasn't damp, in cold ones. He drove downhill to the offices of the broadcasting station, where his paper had arranged Telex facilities. In the prematurely senile building, unfinished and decaying after five years, the unevenness of the concrete floors underfoot increased his sensation of slowed reactions. He simply looked in to see if there was anything for him; the day before he had sent a long piece on the secessionist movement in the Southern Province and there just might be a word of commendation from the Africa desk. There *was* something: '100 YEARS ANNIVERSARY ROYAL GEOGRAPHICAL SOCIETY PARTY SENT SEARCH FOR LIVINGSTONE STOP YOU WELL PLACED RETRACE STEPS LIVINGSTONES LAST JOURNEY SUGGEST LAKES OR INTERIOR STOP THREE THOUSAND WORDS SPECIAL FEATURE 16TH STOP THANKS BARTRAM.'

He wanted to fling open bloody Bartram's bloody door and give him his Livingstone – words were in his mouth, overtaking each other.

Oh yes. *Church is out there, he'll come up with the right sort of thing. Remember His 'Peacock Throne' piece?*

Oh yes. He had been sent to Iran for the coronation of the Shahanshah, he was marked down to have to do these beautiful, wryly-understated sidelights. Just as a means of self-expression, between running about after Under Ministers and party bosses and driving through the bush at a hundred in the shade to look at rice fields planned by the Chinese and self-help pig farms run by the Peace Corps and officially non-existent guerrilla training camps for political refugees from neighbouring countries.

He could put a call through to London. How squeakily impotent the voice wavering across the radio telephone! Or he could Telex a blast; watch all the anticipated weariness, boredom and exasperation punching a domino pattern on clean white tape.

Slowly pressure subsided from his temples. He was left sulkily nursing the grievance: don't even realize the 'lakes and interior' are over the border! In the next country. Don't even know that. The car whined up the hill again (faulty differential this one had) to the office full of dead flies and posters of ski slopes where the airline agency girl sat. There was a Viscount next day, a local Dakota the day after. 'I'll wait-list you. You're sure to get on. Just be at the airport half-an-hour early.'

He was there before anybody. Such a pretty black girl at the weigh-bay; she said with her soft, accented English, 'It looks good. You're top of the list, don't worry, sir.' 'I'm not worried, I assure you.' But it became a point of honour, like the obligation to try to win in some silly game – once you'd taken the trouble to get to the airport, you must succeed in getting away. He watched the passengers trailing or hurrying up with their luggage and – smug devils – presenting their tickets. He tried to catch the girl's eye now and then to see how it was going. She gave no sign, except, once, a beautiful airline smile, something she must have learnt in her six weeks' efficiency and deportment course. Girls were not beautiful, generally, in this part of Africa; the women of Vietnam had spoilt him for all other women, anyway. In the steps of Livingstone, or women of the world, by our special correspondent. But even in his mind, smart phrases like that were made up, a picture of himself saying them, Carl A. Church, the foreign correspondent in the air-conditioned bar (when asked what the American-style initial stood for, the story went that he had said to a bishop, 'Anti, Your Grace'). Under his absurdly tense attention for each arrival at the weigh-bay there was the dark slow movement of the balance of past and present that regulates the self-estimate by which one really manages to live. He was seeing again – perhaps for the first time since it happened, five? six? years ago – a road in Africa where the women were extremely beautiful. She was standing on the edge of the forest with a companion, breasts of brown silk, a water-mark of sunlight lying along them. A maroon and blue *pagne* hid the rest of her. On a sudden splendid impulse he had stopped the car (that one had a worn clutch) and offered her money, but she refused. Why? The women of that country had been on sale to white men for a number of generations. She refused. Why not? Well, he accepted that when it came to women, whom he loved so well, his other passion – the desire to defend the rights of the individual of any colour or race – did not bear scrutiny.

Now a blonde was up at the weigh-bay for the second or third time; the black girl behind it was joined by an airline official in shirt-sleeves. They consulted a list while the blonde went on talking. At last she turned away and, looking round the echoing hall with the important expression of someone with a complaint to confide, this time came and sat on the bench where he waited. Among her burdens was a picture in brown paper that had torn over the curlicues of the gilt frame. Her thin hands had rings thrust upon them like those velvet Cleopatra's needles in the jewellers'. She puts on everything she's got, when she travels; it's the safest way to carry it. And probably there's a pouch round her middle containing the settlement from her last ex-husband. Carl Church had noticed the woman before, from some small sidetrack of his mind, even while she existed simply as one of the lucky ones with a seat on the plane. She was his vintage, that's why; the blond page-boy broken into curling locks by the movement of her shoulders, the big red mouth, the high heels, the girlish floral beach-dress – on leaves during the war, girls his own age looked like that. But this one had been out in the sun for twenty years. Smiled at him; teeth still good. Ugly bright blue eyes, cheap china. She knew she still had beautiful legs, nervous ankles all hollows and tendons. Her dead hair tossed frowsily. He thought, tender to his own past: she's horrible.

'This's the second morning I've sat here cooling my heels.' Her bracelets shook, dramatizing exasperation. 'The second day running. I only hope to God I'm on this time.'

He said, 'Where're you trying to get to?' But of course he knew before she answered. He waited a moment or two, and then strolled up to the weigh-bay. 'Still top of the list, I hope?' – in an undertone. The airline man, standing beside the black beauty, answered brusquely, 'There's just the one lady before you, sir.' He began to argue. 'We can't help it, sir. It's a compassionate, came through from the town office.' He went back and sat down.

She said, 'You're going on the same plane?'

'Yes.' Not looking her way, the bitch, he watched with hope as boarding time approached and there were no new arrivals at the weigh-bay. She arranged and rearranged her complicated hand luggage; rivalry made them aware of one another. Two minutes to boarding-time, the airline girl didn't want him to catch her eye, but he went over to her just the same. She said, cheerfully relieved of responsibility, 'Doesn't look as if any-one's going to get a seat. Everybody's turned up. We're just checking.'

He and the blonde lady were left behind. Hostility vanished as the others filed off down the Red Route. They burst into talk at once, grumbling about the airline organization.

'Imagine, they've been expecting me for days.' She was defiantly gay.

'Dragging out here for nothing – I was assured I'd get a seat, no no trouble at all.'

'Well, that's how people are these days – my God, if I ran my hotel like that. Simply re-lax, what else can you do? Thank heaven I've got a firm booking for tomorrow.'

A seat on tomorrow's plane, eh; he slid out of the con-versation and went to look for the reservations counter. There was no need for strategy, after all; he got a firm booking, too. In the bus back to town, she patted the seat beside her. There were two kinds of fellow travellers, those who asked questions and those who talked about themselves. She took the bit of a long cigarette-holder between her teeth and quoted her late hus-band, told how her daughter, a 'a real little madam', at board-ing school, got on like a house on fire with her new husband, said how life was what you put into it, as she always reminded her son; people asked how could one stand it, up there, miles away from everything, on the lake, but she painted, she was interested in interior decorating, she'd run the place ten years by herself, took some doing for a woman.

'On the lake?'

'Gough's Bay Hotel.' He saw from the stare of the blue eyes that it was famous – he should have known.

'Tell me, whereabout are the graves, the graves of Living-stone's companions?'

The eyes continued to stare at him, a corner of the red mouth drew in proprietorially, carelessly unimpressed. 'My graves. On my property. Two minutes from the hotel.'

He murmured surprise. 'I'd somehow imagined they were much farther north.'

'And there's no risk of bilharzia *whatever,*' she added, apparently dispelling a rumour. 'You can water-ski, goggle-fish – people have a marvellous time.'

'Well, I may turn up someday.'

'My dear, I've never let people down in my life. We'd find a bed somewhere.'

He saw her at once, in another backless flowered dress, when he entered the departure lounge next morning. 'Here we go again' – distending her nostrils in mock resignation, turning down the red lips. He gave her his small-change smile and took care to lag behind when the passengers went across the runway. He sat in the tail of the plane and opened the copy of Livingstone's last Journals, bought that morning. *Our sympathies are drawn out towards our humble hardy companions by a community of interests, and, it may be, of perils, which make us all friends.* The book rested on his thighs and he slept through the hour-and-a-half journey. Livingstone had walked it, taking ten months and recording his position by the stars. This could be the lead for his story, he thought: waking up to the recogniton of the habits of his mind like the same old face in the shaving mirror.

The capital of this country was hardly distinguishable from the one he had left. The new national bank with air-conditioning and rubber plants changed the perspective of the row of Indian stores. Behind the main street a native market stank of dried fish. He hired a car, borrowed a map from the hotel barman and set out for 'the interior' next day, distrusting – from long experience – both car and map. He had meant merely to look up a few places and easy references in the journals, but had begun to read and gone on half the night. *A wife ran away, I asked how many he had; he told me twenty in all: I then thought he had nineteen too many. He answered with the usual reason. 'But who would cook for strangers if I had but one?' ... It is with sorrow that I have to convey the sad intelligence that your brother died yesterday morning about ten o'clock ... no remedy seemed to have much effect. On the*

20th he was seriously ill but took soup several times and drank claret and water with relish ... A lion roars mightily. The fish-hawk utters his weird voice in the morning, as if he lifted up to a friend at a great distance, in a sort of falsetto key ... The men engaged refuse to go to Matipa's, they have no honour ... Public punishment to Chirango for stealing beads, fifteen cuts; diminished his load to 40 lbs ... In four hours we came within sight of the lake, and saw plenty of elephants and other game.

How enjoyable it would have been to read the Journals six thousand miles away, in autumn, at home, in London. As usual, once off the circuit that linked the capital with the two or three other small towns that existed, there were crossroads without signposts, and place-names that turned out to be one general store, an African bar and a hand-operated petrol pump, unattended. He was not fool enough to forget to carry petrol and he was good at knocking up the bar owners (asleep during the day). As if the opening of the beer refrigerator and the record player were inseparably linked – as a concept of hospitality if not mechanically – African jazz jog-trotted, clacked and drummed forth while he drank on a dirty veranda. Children dusty as chickens gathered. As he drove off the music stopped in mid-record.

By early afternoon he was lost. The map, sure enough, failed to indicate that the fly-speck named as Moambe was New Moambe, a completely different place in an entirely different direction from that of Old Moambe, where Livingstone had had a camp, and had talked with chiefs whose descendants were active in the present-day politics of their country (another lead). Before setting out, Carl Church had decided that all he was prepared to do was take a car, go to Moambe, take no more than two days over it and write a piece using the journey as a peg for what he did know something about – this country's attempt to achieve a form of African socialism. That's what the paper would get, all they would get, except the expense account for the flight, car and beers. (The beers were jotted down as 'Lunch, Sundries, Gratuities, £3. 10.' No reason, from Bartram's perspective, why there shouldn't be a Livingstone Hilton in His Steps.) But when he found he had missed Moambe and past three in the afternoon was headed in the wrong direction, he turned the car savagely in the road and made for what he hoped would turn out to be the capital. All they would get would be the expense account. He stopped and asked the way of anyone he met, and no one spoke English. People smiled and instructed the foreigner volubly, with many gestures. He had the humiliation of finding himself twice back at the same crossroads where the same old man sat calmly with women who carried dried fish stiff as Chinese preserved ducks. He took another road, any road, and after a mile or two of hesitancy and obstinacy – turn back or go on? – thought he saw a signpost ahead. This time it was not a dead tree. A sagging wooden finger drooped down a turn-off: GOUGH'S BAY LAZITI PASS.

The lake.

He was more than a hundred miles from the capital. With a sense of astonishment at finding himself, he focused his existence, here and now, on the empty road, at a point on the map. He turned down to petrol, a bath, a drink – that much, at least, so assured that he did not have to think of it. But the lake was farther away than the casualness of the sign would indicate. The pass led the car whining and grinding in low gear round silent hillsides of white rock and wild fig trees leaning out into ravines. This way would be impassable in the rains; great stones scraped the oilsump as he disappeared into steep streambeds, dry, the sand wrung into hanks where torrents had passed. He met no one, saw no hut. When he coughed, alone in the car he fancied this noise of his thrown back from the stony face of hill to hill like the bark of a solitary baboon. The sun went down. He thought, there was only one good moment the whole day: when I drank that beer on the veranda, and the children came up the steps to watch me and hear the music.

An old European image was lodged in his tiredness: the mirage, if the road ever ended, of some sort of Mediterranean resort, coloured umbrellas, a street of white hotels beside water and boats. As the road unravelled from the pass into open bush, there came that moment when, if he had had a companion, they would have stopped talking. Two, three miles; the car rolled in past the ruins of an arcaded building to the barking of dogs, the horizontal streak of water behind the bush, outhouses and water tanks, a raw new house. A young man in bathing trunks with his back to the car stood on the portico steps, pushing a flipper off one foot with the toes of the other. As he hopped for balance he looked round. Blond wet curls licked the small head on the tall body, vividly empty blue eyes were the eyes of some nocturnal animal dragged out in daylight.

'Can you tell me where there's a hotel?'

Staring, on one leg: 'Yes, this's the hotel.'

Carl Church said, foolishly pleasant, 'There's no sign, you see.'

'Well, place's being redone.' He came, propping the flippers against the wall, walking on the outside edges of his feet over the remains of builders' rubble. 'Want any help with that?' But Carl Church had only his typewriter and the one suitcase. They struggled indoors together, the young man carrying flippers, two spearguns and goggles. 'Get anything?' 'Never came near the big ones.' His curls sprang and drops flowed from them. He dropped the goggles, then a wet gritty flipper knocked against Carl Church. 'Hell, I'm sorry.' He dumped his tackle on a desk in the passage, looked at Carl Church's case and portable, put gangling hands upon little hips and took a great breath: 'Where those boys are when you want one of them – that's the problem.' 'Look, I haven't booked,' said Church. 'I suppose you've got a room?'

'What's today? Full up, weekends.' Even his eyelashes were wet. The skin on the narrow cheekbones was whitened as if over knuckles.

'Thursday. I think I met someone on the plane –'

'Go on –' The face cocked in attention.

'She runs a hotel here ...?'

'Madam in person. D'jou see who met her? My stepfather?' But Carl Church had not seen the airport blonde once they were through customs. 'That's Lady Jane all right. Of course she hasn't turned up here yet. So she's arrived, eh? Well thanks for the warning. Just a sec, you've got to sign,' and he pulled over a leather register, yelling, 'Zelide, where've you disappeared to –' as a girl with a bikini cutting into heavy red thighs appeared and said in the cosy, long-suffering voice of an English provincial, 'You're making it all wet, Dick – oh give here.'

They murmured in telegraphic intimacy. 'What about number 16?' 'I thought a chalet.' 'Well, I dunno, it's your job, my girl –' She gave a parenthetic yell and a barefoot African came from the back somewhere to shoulder the luggage. The young man was dismantling his speargun, damp backside hitched up on the reception desk. The girl moved his paraphernalia patiently aside. 'W'd you like some tea in your room, sir?'

'Guess who w's on the plane with him. Lady Godiva. So we'd better brace ourselves.'

'Dickie! Is she really?'

'In person.'

The girl led Carl Church out over a terrace into a garden where rondavels and cottages were dispersed. It was rapidly getting dark, only the lake shone. She had a shirt knotted under her breasts over the bikini, and when she shook her shaggy brown hair – turning on the light in an ugly little outhouse that smelled of cement – a round, boiled face smiled at him. 'These chalets are brand new. We might have to move you Saturday, but jist as well enjoy yourself in the meantime.' 'I'll be leaving in the morning.' Her cheeks were so sunburned they looked as if they would bleed when she smiled. 'Oh, what a shame. Aren't you even going to have a go at spear-fishing?' 'Well, no; I haven't brought any equipment or anything.' He might have been a child who had no bucket and spade; 'Oh not to worry, Dick's got all the gear. You come out with us in the morning, after breakfast – okay?' 'Fine,' he said, knowing he would be gone.

The sheets of one bed witnessed the love-making of previous occupants; they had not used the other. Carl Church stumbled around in the dark looking for the ablution block – across a yard, but the lightswitch did not work in the bathroom. He was about to trudge over to the main house to ask for a lamp when he was arrested by the lake, as by the white of an eye in a face hidden by darkness. At least there was a towel. He took it and went down in his pants, feeling his way through shrubs, rough grass, over turned-up earth, touched by warm breaths of scent, startled by squawks from lumps that resolved into fowls, to the lake. It held still a skin of light from the day that had flown upward. He entered it slowly; it seemed to drink him in, ankles, knees, thighs, sex, waist, breast. It was cool as the inside of a mouth. Suddenly hundreds of tiny fish leapt out all round him, bright new tin in the warm, dark, heavy air.

... I enclose a lock of his hair; I had his papers sealed up soon after his decease and will endeavour to transmit them all to you exactly as he left them.

Carl Church endured the mosquitoes and the night heat only by clinging to the knowledge, through his tattered sleep, that soon it would be morning and he would be gone. But in the morning there was the lake. He got up at five to pee. He saw now how the lake stretched to the horizon from the open arms of the bay. Two bush-woolly islands glided on its surface; it was the colour of pearls. He opened his stale mouth wide and drew in a full breath, half-sigh, half-gasp. Again he went down to the water and, without bothering whether there was anybody about, took off his pyjama shorts and swam. Cool. Impersonally cool, at this time. The laved mosquito bites stung pleasurably. When he looked down upon the water while in it, it was no longer nacre, but pellucid, a pale and tender green. His feet were gleaming tendrils. A squat spotted fish hung near his legs, mouthing. He didn't move, either. Then he did what he had done when he was seven or eight years old, he made a cage of his hands and pounced – but the element reduced him to slow motion, everything, fish, legs, glassy solidity, wriggled and flowed away and slowly undulated into place again. The fish returned. On a dead tree behind bird-spattered rocks ellipsed by the water at this end of the beach, a fish-eagle lifted its head between hunched white shoulders and cried out; a long whistling answer came across the lake as another flew in. He swam around the rocks through schools of fingerlings as close as gnats, and hauled himself up within ten feet of the eagles. They carried the remoteness of the upper air with them in the long-sighted gaze of their hooded eyes; nothing could approach its vantage; he did not exist for them, while the gaze took in the expanse of the lake and the smallest indication of life rising to its surface. He came back to the beach and walked with a towel round his middle as far as a baobab tree where a black man with an ivory bangle on either wrist was mending nets, but then he noticed a blue bubble on the verge – it was an infant afloat on some plastic beast, its mother in attendance – and turned away, up to the hotel.

He left his packed suitcase on the bed and had breakfast. The dining room was a veranda under sagging grass matting; now, in the morning, he could see the lake, of course, while he ate. He was feeling for change to leave for the waiter when the girl padded in, dressed in her bikini, and shook corn flakes into a plate. 'Oh hullo, sir. Early bird you are.' He imagined her lying down at night just as she was, ready to begin again at once the ritual of alternately dipping and burning her seared flesh. They chatted. She had been in Africa only three months, out from Liverpool in answer to an advertisement – receptionist/secretary, hotel in beautiful surroundings. 'More of a holiday than a job,' he said. 'Don't make me laugh' – but she did. 'We were on the go until half-past one, night before last, making the changeover in the bar. You see the bar used to be here –' she lifted her spoon at the wall, where he now saw mildew-traced shapes beneath a mural in which a girl in a bosom-laced peasant outfit appeared to have given birth, through one ear, Rabelaisian fashion, to a bunch of grapes. He had noticed the old Chianti bottles, by lamplight, at dinner the night before, but not the mural. 'Dickie's got his ideas, and then she's artistic, you see.' The young man was coming up the steps of the veranda that moment, stamping his sandy feet at the cat, yelling towards the kitchen, blue eyes open as the fish's had been staring at Carl Church through the water. He wore his catch like a kilt, hooked all round the belt of his trunks.

'I been thinking about those damn trees,' he said.

'Oh my heavens. How many's still there?'

'*There* all right, but nothing but blasted firewood. Wait till she sees the holes, just where she had them dug.'

The girl was delighted by the fish: 'Oh pretty!'

But he slapped her hands and her distraction away. 'Some people ought to have their heads read,' he said to Carl Church. 'If you can tell me why I had to come back here, well, I'd be grateful. I had my own combo, down in Rhodesia.' He removed the fish from his narrow middle and sat down on a chair turned away from her table.

'Why don't we get the boys to stick 'em in, today? They could've died after being planted out, after all, ay?'

He seemed too gloomy to hear her. Drops from his wet curls fell on his shoulders. She bent towards him kindly, wheedlingly, meat of her thighs and breasts pressing together. 'If we put two boys on it, they'd have them in by lunch-time? Dickie? And if it'll make her happy? Dickie?'

'I've got ideas of my own. But when Madam's here you can forget it, just forget it. No sooner start something – just get started, that's all – she chucks it up and wants something different again.' His gaze wavered once or twice to the wall where the bar had been. Carl Church asked what the fish were. He didn't answer, and the girl encouraged, 'Perch. Aren't they, Dickie? Yes, perch. You'll have them for your lunch. Lovely eating.'

'Oh what the hell. Let's go. You ready?' he said to Church. The girl jumped up and he hooked an arm round her neck, feeling in her rough hair.

'Course he's ready. The black flippers'll fit him – the stuff's in the bar,' she said humouringly.

'But I haven't even got a pair of trunks.'

'Who cares? I can tell you I'm just-not-going-to-worry-a-damn. Here Zelide, I nearly lost it this morning.' He removed a dark stone set in a Christmas-cracker baroque ring from his rock-scratched hand, nervous-boned as his mother's ankles, and tossed it for the girl to catch. 'Come, I've got the trunks,' she said, and led Carl Church to the bar by way of the reception desk, stopping to wrap the ring in a pink tissue and pop it in the cash box.

The thought of going to the lake once more was irresistible. His bag was packed; an hour or two wouldn't make any difference. He had been skin-diving before, in Sardinia, and did not expect the bed of the lake to compare with the Mediterranean, but if the architecture of undersea was missing, the fish one could get at were much bigger than he had ever caught in the Mediterranean. The young man disappeared for minutes and rose again between Carl Church and the girl, his Gothic Christ's body sucked in below the nave of ribs, his goggles leaving weals like duelling scars on his white cheekbones. Water ran from the tarnished curls over the bright eyeballs without seeming to make him blink. He brought up fish deftly and methodically and the girl swam back to shore with them, happy as a retrieving dog.

Neither she nor Carl Church caught much themselves. And then Church went off on his own, swimming slowly with the borrowed trunks inflating above the surface like a striped Portuguese man-of-war, and far out, when he was not paying attention but looking back at the skimpy white buildings, the flowering shrubs and even the giant baobab razed by distance and the optical illusion of the heavy waterline, at eye-level, about to black them out, he heard a fish-eagle scream just overhead; looked up, looked down, and there below him saw three fish at different levels, a mobile swaying in the water. This time he managed the gun without thinking; he had speared the biggest.

The girl was as impartially overjoyed as when the young man had a good catch. They went up the beach, laughing, explaining, a water-intoxicated progress. The accidental bump of her thick sandy thigh against his was exactly the tactile sensation of contact with the sandy body of the fish, colliding with him as he carried it. The young man was squatting on the beach now, his long back arched over his knees. He was haranguing, in an African language, the old fisherman with the ivory bracelets who was still at work on the nets. There were dramatic pauses, accusatory rises of tone, hard jerks of laughter, in the monologue. The old man said nothing. He was an Arabized African from far up the lake somewhere in East Africa, and wore an old towel turban as well as the ivory; every now and then he wrinkled back his lips on tooth-stumps. Three or four long black dugouts had come in during the morning and were beached; black men sat motionless in what small shade they could find. The baby on his blue swan still floated under his mother's surveillance – she turned a visor of sunglasses and hat. It was twelve o'clock; Carl Church merely felt amused at himself – how different the measure of time when you were absorbed in something you didn't earn a living by. 'Those must weigh a pound a piece,' he said idly, of the ivory manacles shifting on the net-mender's wrists.

'D'jou want one?' the young man offered. (*My graves*, the woman had said, *on my property*.) 'I'll get him to sell it to you. Take it for your wife.'

But Carl Church had no wife at present, and no desire for loot; he preferred everything to stay as it was, in its place, at noon by the lake. Twenty thousand slaves a year had passed this way, up the water. Slavers, missionaries, colonial servants – all had brought something and taken something away. He would have a beer and go, changing nothing, claiming nothing. He plodded to the hotel a little ahead of the couple, who were mumbling over hotel matters and pausing now and then to fondle each other. As his bare soles encountered the smoothness of the terrace steps he heard the sweet, loud, reasonable feminine voice, saw one of the houseboy-waiters racing across in his dirty jacket – and quickly turned away to get to his room unnoticed. But with a perfect instinct for preventing escape, she was at once out upon the dining room veranda, all crude blues and yellows – hair, eyes, flowered dress, a beringed hand holding the cigarette away exploratively. Immediately, her son passed Church in a swift, damp tremor. 'Well, God, look at my best girl – mm-MHH ... madam in per-son.' He lifted her off her feet and she landed swirling giddily on the high heels in the best tradition of the Fred Astaire films she and Carl Church had been brought up on. Her laugh seemed to go over her whole body. 'Well?' 'And so, my girl?' They rocked together. 'You been behaving yourself in the big city?' 'Dickie – for Pete's sake – he's like a spaniel –' calling Carl Church to witness.

A warm baby-smell beside him (damp crevices and cold cream) was the presence of the girl. 'Oh, Mrs Palmer, we were so worried you'd got lost or something.'

'My dear. My you're looking well –' The two vacant, inescapable blue stares took in the bikini, the luxuriously inflamed skin, as if the son's gaze were directed by the mother's. Mrs Palmer and the girl kissed but Mrs Palmer's eyes moved like a lighthouse beam over the wall where the bar was gone, catching Carl Church in his borrowed swimming trunks. 'Wh'd'you think of my place?' she asked. 'How, d'you like it here, eh? Not that I know it myself, after two months ...' Hands on hips, she looked at the peasant girl and the mildewed outlines as if she were at an exhibition. She faced sharply round and her son kissed her on the mouth: 'We're dying for a beer, that's what. We've been out since breakfast. Zelide, the boy –'

'Yes, he *knows* he's on duty on the veranda today – just a minute, I'll get it –'

Mrs Palmer was smiling at the girl wisely. 'My dear, once you start doing their jobs for them ...'

'Shadrach!' The son made a megaphone of his hands, shaking his silver identification bracelet out of the way. The girl stood, eagerly bewildered.

'Oh it's nothing. Only a minute –' and bolted.

'Where is the bar, now, Dickie?' said his mother as a matter of deep, polite interest.

'I must get some clothes on and return your trunks,' Carl Church was saying.

'Oh, it makes a world of difference. You'll see. You can move in that bar. Don't you think so?' The young man gave the impression that he was confirming a remark of Church's rather than merely expressing his own opinion. Carl Church, to withdraw, said, 'Well, I don't know what it was like before.'

She claimed him now. 'It was here, in the open, of course, people loved it. A taverna atmosphere. Dickie's never been overseas.'

'Really *move*. And you've got those big doors.'

She drew Church into the complicity of a smile for grown-ups, then remarked, as if for her part the whole matter were calmly accepted, settled, 'I presume it's the games room?'

Her son said to Church, sharing the craziness of women,

'There never was a games room, it was the lounge, can you see a lot of old birds sitting around in armchairs in a place like this?'

'The lounge that was going to be redecorated as a games room,' she said. She smiled at her son.

The girl came back, walking flat-footed under a tray's weight up steps that led by way of a half-built terrace to the new bar. As Carl Church went to help her she breathed, 'What a performance.'

Mrs Palmer drew on her cigarette and contemplated the steps: 'Imagine the breakages.'

The four of them were together round beer bottles. Church sat helplessly in his borrowed trunks that crawled against his body as they dried, drinking pint after pint and aware of his warmth, the heat of the air, and all their voices rising steadily. He said, 'I must get going,' but the waiter had called them to lunch three times; the best way to break up the party was to allow oneself to be forced to table. The three of them ate in their bathing costumes while madam took the head, bracelets colliding on her arms. He made an effort to get precise instructions about the best and quickest route back to the capital, and was told expertly by her, 'There's no plane out until Monday, nine-fifteen, I suppose you know that.' 'I have no reason whatever to doubt your knowledge of plane schedules,' he said, and realized from the turn of phrase that he must be slightly drunk, on heat and the water as much as beer.

She knew the game so well that you had only to finger a counter unintentionally for her to take you on. 'I told you I never let anyone down.' She blew a smokescreen; appeared through it. 'Where've they put you?'

'Oh, he's in one of the chalets, Mrs Palmer,' the girl said. 'Till tomorrow, anyway.'

'Well, there you are, re-lax,' she said. 'If the worst comes to the worst, there's a room in my cottage.' Her gaze was out over the lake, a tilting, blind brightness with black dugouts appearing like sunspots, but she said, 'How're my jacarandas coming along? Someone was telling me there's no reason why they shouldn't do, Dickie. The boys must make a decent trench round each one and let it *fill up* with water once a week, *right* up, d'you see?'

The effect of travel on a man whose heart is in the right place is that the mind is made more self-reliant; it becomes more confident of its own resources – there is greater presence of mind. The body is soon well-knit; the muscles of the limbs grow hard as a board ... the countenance is bronzed and there is no dyspepsia.

Carl Church slept through the afternoon. He woke to the feeling of helplessness he had at lunch. But no chagrin. This sort of hiatus had opened up in the middle of a tour many times – lost days in a blizzard on Gander airport, a week in quarantine at Aden. This time he had the Journals instead of a Gideon Bible. *Nothing fell from his lips as last words to survivors. We buried him today by a large baobab tree.* There was no point in going back to the capital if he couldn't get out of the place till Monday. His mind was closed to the possibility of trying for Moambe, again; that was another small rule for self-preservation: if something goes wrong, write it off. He thought, it's all right here; the dirty, ugly room had as much relevance to 'spoiling' the eagles and the lake as he had had to the eagles when he climbed close. On his way down to the lake again he saw a little group – mother, son, receptionist – standing round the graveside of one of the holes for trees. Dickie was still in his bathing trunks.

Church had the goggles and the flippers and the speargun, and he swam out towards the woolly islands – they were unattainably far – and fish were dim dead leaves in the water below him. The angle of the late-afternoon sun left the underwater deserted, filled with motes of vegetable matter and sand caught by oblique rays of light. Milky brilliance surrounded him, his hands went out as if to feel for walls; there was the apprehension, down there, despite the opacity and tepidity, of night and cold. He shot up to the surface and felt the day on his eyelids. Lying on the sand, he heard the eagles cry now behind him on the headland, where trees held boulders in their claws, now over the lake. A pair of piebald kingfishers squabbled, a whirling disk, in mid-air, and plummeted again and again. Butterflies with the same black and white markings went slowly out over the water. The Arabized fisherman was still working at his nets.

Some weekend visitors arrived from the hotel, shading their eyes against the sheen of the lake; soon they stood in it like statues broken off at the waist. Voices flew out across the water after the butterflies. As the sun drowned, a dhow climbed out of its dazzle and dipped steadily towards the beach. It picked up the fisherman and his nets, sending a tiny boat ashore. The dhow lay beating slowly, like an exhausted bird. The visitors ran together to watch as they would have for a rescue, a monster – any sign from the lake.

Carl Church had been lying with his hand slack on the sand as on a warm body; he got up and walked past the people, past the baobab, as far along the beach as it went before turning into an outwork of oozy reeds. He pushed his feet into his shoes and went up inland, through the thorn bushes. As soon as he turned his back on it, the lake did not exist; unlike the sea that spread and sucked in your ears even when your eyes were closed. A total silence. Livingstone could have come upon the lake quite suddenly, and just as easily have missed it. The mosquitoes and gnats rose with the going down of the sun. Swatted on Church's face, they stuck in sweat. The air over the lake was free, but the heat of day cobwebbed the bush. *We then hoped that his youth and unimpaired constitution would carry him through ... but about six o'clock in the evening his mind began to wander and continued to. His bodily powers continued gradually to sink till the period mentioned when he quietly expired ... there he rests in sure and certain hope of a glorious Resurrection.* He thought he might have a look at the graves, the graves of Livingstone's companions, but the description of how to find them given him that morning by the young man and the girl was that of people who know a place so well they cannot imagine anyone being unable to walk straight to it. A small path, they said, just off the road. He found himself instead among ruined arcades whose whiteness intensified as the landscape darkened. It was an odd ruin: a solid complex of buildings, apparently not in bad repair, had been pulled down. It was the sort of demolition one saw in a fast-growing city, where a larger structure would be begun at once where the not-old one had been. The bush was all around; as far as the Congo, as far as the latitude where the forests began. A conical anthill had risen to the height of the arcades, where a room behind them must have been. A huge moon sheeny as the lake came up and a powdery blue heat held in absolute stillness. Carl Church thought of the graves. It was difficult to breathe; it must have been hell to die here, in this unbearable weight of beauty not shared with the known world, licked in the face by the furred tongue of this heat.

Round the terrace and hotel the ground was pitted by the stakes of high heels; they sounded over the floors where everyone else went barefoot. The shriek and scatter of chickens opened before a constant coming and going of houseboys and the ragged work-gang whose activities sent up the regular grunt of axes thudding into stumps, and the crunch of spades gritting into earth. The tree-holes had been filled in. Dickie was seen in his bathing trunks but did not appear on the beach. Zelide wore a towelling chemise over her bikini, and when the guests were at lunch went from table to table bending to talk softly with her rough hair hiding her face. Carl Church saw that the broken skin on her nose and cheeks was repaired with white cream. She said confidentially, 'I just wanted to tell you there'll be a sort of beach party tonight, being Saturday. Mrs Palmer likes to have a fire on the beach, and some snacks – you know. Of course, we'll all eat here first. You're welcome.'

He said, 'How about my room?'

Her voice sank to a chatty whisper, 'Oh it'll be all right, one crowd's cancelled.'

Going to the bar for cigarettes, he heard mother and son in there. 'Wait, wait, all that's worked out. I'mn'a cover the whole thing with big blow-ups of the top groups, the Stones and the Shadows and suchlike.'

'Oh grow up, Dickie my darling, you want it to look like a teenager's bedroom?'

Church went quietly away, remembering there might be a packet of cigarettes in the car, but bumped into Dickie a few minutes later, in the yard. Dickie had his skin-diving stuff and was obviously on his way to the lake. 'I get into shit for moving the bar without telling the licensing people over in town, and then she says let's have the bar counter down on the beach tonight – all in the same breath, that's *nothing* to her. At least when my stepfather's here he knows just how to put the brake on.'

'Where is he?'

'I don't know, something about some property of hers, in town. He's got to see about it. But he's always got business all over, for her. I had my own band, you know, we've even toured Rhodesia. I'm a solo artist, really. Guitar, I compose my own stuff. I mean, what I play's original, you see. Night club engagements and such-like.'

'That's a tough life compared with this,' Church said, glancing at the speargun.

'Oh, this's all right. If you learn how to do it well, y'know? I've trained myself. You've got to concentrate. Like with my guitar. I have to go away and be *undisturbed*, you understand – right away. Sometimes the mood comes, sometimes it doesn't. Sometimes I compose all night. I got to be left *in peace*.' He was fingering a new thick silver chain on his wrist. 'Lady Jane, of course. God knows what it cost. She spends a fortune on presents. You sh'd see what my sister gets when she's home. And what she gave my stepfather – I mean before, when they weren't married yet. He must have ten pairs of cuff-links, gold, I don't know what.' He sat down under the weight of his mother's generosity. Zelide appeared among the empty gas-containers and beer crates outside the kitchen. 'Oh, Dickie, you've had no lunch. I don't think he ever tastes a thing he catches.' Dickie squeezed her thigh and said coldly. 'S'best time, now. People don't know it. Between now and about half-past three.'

'Oh Dickie, I wish you'd eat something. And he's got to play tonight.' They watched him lope off lightly down the garden. Her hair and the sun obscured her. 'They're both artistic, you see, that's the trouble. What a performance.'

'Are you sorry you came?'

'Oh no. The weather's so lovely, I mean, isn't it?'

It was becoming a habit to open Livingstone's Journals at random before falling stunned-asleep. *Now that I am on the point of starting another trip into Africa I feel quite exhilarated: when one travels with the specific object in view of ameliorating the condition of the natives every act becomes ennobled.* The afternoon heat made him think of women, this time, and he gave up his siesta because he believed that day-dreams of this kind were not so much adolescent as – worse – a sign of approaching age. He was getting – too far along, for pauses like this; for time out. If he were not preoccupied with doing the next thing, he did not know what to do. His mind turned to death, the graves that his body would not take the trouble to visit. His body turned to women; his body was unchanged. It took him down to the lake, heavy and vigorous, reddened by the sun under the black hairs shining on his belly.

The sun was high in a splendid afternoon. In half an hour he missed three fish and began to feel challenged. Whenever he dived deeper than fifteen or eighteen feet his ears ached much more than they ever had in the sea. Out of training, of course. And the flippers and goggles lent by the hotel really did not fit properly. The goggles leaked at every dive, and he had to surface quickly, water in his nostrils. He began to let himself float aimlessly, not diving any longer, circling around the enormous boulders with their steep polished flanks like petrified tree-trunks. He was aware, as he had been often when skin-diving, of how active his brain became in this world of silence; ideas and images interlocking in his mind while his body was leisurely moving, enjoying at once the burning sun on his exposed shoulders and the cooling water on his shrunken penis – good after too many solitary nights filled with erotic dreams.

Then he saw the fish, deep down, twenty feet maybe, a yellowish nonchalant shape which seemed to pasture in a small forest of short dead reeds. He took a noble breath, dived with all the power and swiftness he could summon from his body, and shot. The miracle happened again. The nonchalant shape became a frenzied spot of light, reflecting the rays of the sun in a series of flashes through the pale blue water as it swivelled in agony round the spear. It was – this moment – the only miracle Church knew; no wonder Africans used to believe that the hunter's magic worked when the arrow found the prey.

He swam up quickly, his eyes on the fish hooked at the end of the spear, feeling the tension of its weight while he was hauling it and the line between spear and gun straightened. Eight pounds, ten, perhaps. Even Dickie with his silver amulets and bracelets couldn't do better. He reached the surface, hurriedly lifted the goggles to rid them of water, and dived again: the fish was still continuing its spiralling fight. He saw now that he had not transfixed it, only the point of the spear had penetrated the body. He began carefully to pull the line towards him; the spear was in his hand when, with a slow motion, the fish unhooked itself before his eyes.

In its desperate, thwarted leaps it had unscrewed the point and twirled it loose. This had happened once before, in the Mediterranean, and since then Church had taken care to tighten the spearhead from time to time while fishing. Today he had forgotten. Disappointment swelled in him. Breathlessness threatened to burst him like a bubble. He had to surface, abandoning the gun in order to free both arms. The fish disappeared round a boulder with the point of the harpoon protruding from its open belly amid flimsy pinkish ribbons of entrails; the gun was floating at mid distance between the surface and the bed of the lake, anchored to the spear sunk in dead reeds.

Yet the splendour of the afternoon remained. He lay and smoked and drank beer brought by a waiter who roamed the sand, flicking a napkin. Church had forgotten what had gone wrong, to bring him to this destination. He was *here*; as he was not often fully present in the places and situations in which he found himself. It was some sort of answer to the emptiness he had felt on the bed. Was this how the first travellers had borne it, each day detached from the last and the next, taking each night that night's bearing by the stars?

Madam – Lady Jane in person – had sent down a boy to pick up bottle tops and cigarette stubs from the water's edge. She had high standards. (She had said so in the bar last night.

'The trouble is, *they'll* never be any different, they just don't know how to look after anything.') This was the enlightenment the explorers had brought the black man in the baggage he portered for them on his head. This one was singing to himself as he worked. If the plans that were being made in the capital got the backing of the World Bank and the U.N. Development Fund and all the rest of it, his life would change. Whatever happened to him, he would no longer be measured by the standard that had been set by people who maintained it by using him to pick up their dirt. Church thought of the ruin (he'd forgotten to ask what it was) – Lady Jane's prefabricated concrete blocks and terrazzo would fall down more easily than that.

He had had a shirt washed and although he was sweating under the light-bulb when he put it on for dinner, he seemed to have accustomed himself to the heat, now. He was also very sunburned. The lady with the small child sat with a jolly party of Germans in brown sandals – apparently from a Lutheran Mission nearby – and there was a group of men down from the capital on a bachelor binge of skin-diving and drinking who were aware of being the life of the place. They caught out at Zelide, her thick feet pressed into smart shoes, her hair lifted on top of her head, her eyes made up to twice their size. She bore her transformation bravely, smiling. 'You are coming down to the beach, arnch you?' She went, concerned, from table to table. Mrs Palmer's heels announced her with the authority of a Spanish dancer. She had on a strapless blue dress and silver sandals, and carried a little gilt bag like an outsize cigarette box. She joined the missionary party: '*Wie geht's*, Father, have you been missing me?' Dickie didn't appear. Through the frangipani, the fire on the beach was already sending up scrolls of flame.

Church knew he would be asked to join one group or another and out of a kind of shame of anticipated boredom (last night there had been one of those beer-serious conversations about the possibility of the end of the world: 'They say the one thing'll survive an atomic explosion is the ant. The ant's got something special in its body, y'see') he went into the empty bar after dinner. The little black barman was almost inaudible, in order to disguise his lack of English. There was an array of fancy bottles set up on the shelves but most seemed to belong to Mrs Palmer's store of *objets d'art*: 'Is finish'.' Church had to content himself with a brandy from South Africa. He asked whether a dusty packet of cigarillos was for sale, and the barman's hand went from object to object on display before the correct one was identified. Church was smoking and throwing darts as if they were stones, when Dickie came in. Dickie wore a dinner jacket; his lapels were blue satin, his trousers braided, his shirt tucked and frilled; his hands emerged from ruffles and the little finger of the left one rubbed and turned the baroque ring on the finger beside it. He hung in the doorway a moment like a tall, fancy doll; his mother might have put him on a piano.

Church said, 'My God, you're grand,' and Dickie looked down at himself for a second, without interest, as one acknowledges one's familiar working garb. The little barman seemed flattered by Dickie's gaze.

'Join me?'

Dickie gave a boastful, hard-wrung smile. 'No thanks. I think I've had enough already.' He had the look his mother had had, when Church asked her where her hotel was. 'I've been drinking all afternoon. Ever since a phone call.'

'Well you don't look it,' said Church. But it was the wrong tone to take up.

Dickie played a tattoo on the bar with the ringed hand, staring at it. 'There was a phone call from Bulawayo, and a certain story was repeated to me. Somebody's made it their business to spread a story.'

'That's upsetting.'

'It may mean the loss of a future wife, that's what. My fiancée in Bulawayo. Somebody *took the trouble* to tell her there's a certain young lady in the hotel here with me. Somebody had nothing better to do than make trouble. But that young lady is my mother's secretary-receptionist, see? She works here, she's *employed*, just like me. Just like I'm the manager.'

From country to country, bar to bar, Church was used to accepting people's own versions of their situations, quite independently of the facts. He and Dickie contemplated the vision of Dickie fondling Zelide in the garden as evidence of the correctness of his relations with the secretary-receptionist. 'Couldn't you explain?'

'Usually if I'm, you know, depressed and that, I play my guitar. But I've just been strumming. No, I don't think I'll have any more tonight, I'm full enough already. The whole afternoon.'

'Why don't you go to Bulawayo?'

Dickie picked up the darts and began to throw them, at an angle, from where he sat at the bar; while he spoke he scored three bull's eyes. 'Huh, I think I'll clear out altogether. Here I earn fifty quid a month, eh? I can earn twenty pounds a night – *a night* – with a personal appearance. I've got a whole bundle of my own compositions and one day, boy – there's got to be one that hits the top. One day it's got to happen. All my stuff is copyright, you see. Nobody's gonna cut a disc of my stuff without my permission. I see to that. Oh I could play you a dozen numbers I'm working on, they're mostly sad, you know – the folk type of thing, that's where the money is now. What's a lousy fifty quid a month?'

'I meant a quick visit, to put things straight.'

'Ah, somebody's mucked up my life, all right' – he caught Church's eye as if to say, you want to see it again – and once again planted three darts dead-centre. 'I'll play you some of my compositions if you like. Don't expect too much of my voice, though, because as I say I've been drinking all afternoon. I've got no intention whatever of playing for them down there. An artist thrown in, fifty quid a month, they can think again.' He ducked under the doorway and was gone. He returned at once with a guitar and bent over it professionally, making adjustments. Then he braced his long leg against the bar rail, tossed back his skull of blond curls, began a mournful lay – broke off: 'I'm full of pots, you know, my voice' – and started again, high and thin, at the back of his nose.

It was a song about a bride, and riding away, and tears you

cannot hide away. Carl Church held his palm round the brandy glass to conceal that it was empty and looked down into it. The barman had not moved from his stance with both hands before him on the bar and the bright light above him beating sweat out of his forehead and nose like an answer exacted under interrogation. When the stanza about death and last breath was reached, Dickie said, 'It's a funny thing, me nearly losing my engagement ring this morning, eh? I might have known something' – paused – and thrummed once, twice. Then he began the song over again. Carl Church signalled for the brandy bottle. But suddenly Mrs Palmer was there, a queen to whom no door may be closed. 'Oh show a bit of spunk! Everyone's asking for you. I tell him, everyone has to take a few cracks in life, am I right?'

'Well, of course.'

'Come on then, don't encourage him to feel sorry for himself. My God, if I'd sat down and cried every time.'

Dickie went on playing and whispering the words to himself.

'Can't you do something with him?'

'Let's go and join the others, Dickie,' Church said; he drank off the second brandy.

'One thing I've never done is let people down,' Mrs Palmer was saying. 'But these kids've got no sense of responsibility. What'd happen without me I don't know.'

Dickie spoke. 'Well you can have it. You can have the fifty pounds a month and the car. The lot.'

'Oh yes, they'd look fine without me, I can tell you. I would have given everything I've built up over to him, that was the idea, once he was married. But they know everything at once, you know, you can't teach them anything.'

'Come on Dickie, what the hell – just for an hour.'

They jostled him down to the fire-licked faces on the beach. A gramophone was playing and people were dancing barefoot. There were not enough women, and men in shorts were drinking and clowning. Dickie was given beer; he made cryptic remarks that nobody listened to. Somebody stopped the gramophone with a screech and Dickie was tugged this way and that in a clamour to have him play the guitar. But the dancers put the record back again. The older men among the bachelors opposed the rhythm of the dancers with a war dance of their own: Hi-zoom-a-zoom-ba, zoom-zoom-zoom. Zelide kept breaking away from her partners to offer a plate of tiny burnt sausages like bird-droppings. HI-ZOOM-A-ZOOM-BA – ZOOM-ZOOM-ZOOM. Light fanned from the fire showed the dancers as figures behind gauze, but where Church was marooned, near the streaming flames, faces were gleaming, gouged with grotesque shadow. Lady Jane had a bottle of gin for the two of them. The heat of the fire seemed to consume the other heat, of the night, so that the spirit going down his gullet snuffed out on the way in a burning evaporation. HI-ZOOM-A-ZOOM-BA. At some point he was dancing with her, and she put a frangipani flower in his ear. Now Dickie, sitting drunk on a box with his long legs at an angle like a beetle's, wanted to play the guitar but nobody would listen. Church could make out from the shapes Dickie's mouth made that he was singing the song about the bride and riding away, but the roar of the bachelors drowned it: Hold him down, you Zulu warrior, hold him down, you Zulu Chief-chief-ief. Every now and then a slight movement through the lake sent a soft, black glittering glance in reflection of the fire. The lake was not ten feet away but as time went by Church had the impression that it would not be possible for him to walk down, through the barrier of jigging firelight and figures, and let it cover his ankles, his hands. He said to her, topping up the two glasses where they had made a place in the sand, 'Was there another hotel?'

'There's been talk, but no one else's ever had the initiative, when it comes to the push.'

'But whose was that rather nice building, in the bush?'

'Not *my* idea of a hotel. My husband built it in forty-nine. Started it in forty-nine, finished it fifty-two or -three. Dickie was still a kiddie.'

'But what happened? It looks as if it's been deliberately pulled down.'

CHIEF-UH-IEF-UH-IEF-IEF-IEF. The chorus was a chanting grunt.

'It was what?'

She was saying, '... died, I couldn't even give it away. I always told him, it's no good putting up a bloody palace of a place, you haven't got the class of person who appreciates it. Too big, far too big. No atmosphere, whatever you tried to do with it. People like to feel cosy and free and easy.'

He said, 'I liked that colonnaded veranda, it must have been rather beautiful,' but she was yanked away to dance with one of the bachelors. Zelide wandered about anxiously: 'You quite happy?' He took her to dance; she was putting a good face on it. He said, 'Don't worry about them, they're tough. Look at those eyes.'

'If there was somewhere to go,' she said. 'It's not like a town, not like at home, you know – you can just disappear. Oh there she is, for God's sake –'

He said to Mrs Palmer, 'That veranda, before you bulldozed it –' but she took no notice and attacked him at once: 'Where's Dickie? I don't see Dickie.'

'I don't know where the hell Dickie is.'

Clinging to his arm she dragged him through the drinkers, the dancers, the bachelors, round the shadowy human lumps beyond the light that started away from each other, making him give a snuffling laugh because they were like the chickens that first day. She raced him stumbling up the dark terraces to Dickie's cottage, but it was overpoweringly empty with the young man's smell of musky leather and wet wool. 'I tell you, he'll do something to himself.' Ten yards from the bungalows and the main house, the bush was the black end of the world; they walked out into it and stood helplessly. A torch was a pale, blunt, broken stump of light. 'He'll do away with himself,' she panted. Church was afraid her breathing would turn to hysterics. 'Come on, now, come on,' he coaxed her back to the lights burning in the empty hotel. She went, but steered towards quarters he had not noticed or visited. There were lamps in pink shades. Photographs of her in the kind of dress she was wearing that night, smiling over the head of an infant Dickie. A flowered sofa they sat down on, and a little table with filigree boxes and a lighter shaped like Aladdin's lamp and gilt-covered matchbooks with *Dorothy* stamped across the corner.

'Take some,' she said, and began putting them in his pockets, both outer pockets of his jacket and the inner breast pocket. 'Take some, I've got hundreds.' She dropped her head against him and let the blonde curls muffle her face. 'Like his father did,' she said. 'I know it. I tell you I know it.'

'He's passed out somewhere, that's all.' She smelled of Chanel No 5, the only perfume he could identify, because he had bought it on the black market for various girls in Cairo during the war. Where she leant on him her breasts were warmer than the rest of her.

'I tell you I know he'll do something to himself sooner or later. It runs in families, I know it.'

'Don't worry. It's all right.' He thought: an act of charity. It was terribly dark outside; the whole night was cupped round the small flickering of flames and figures, figures like flames, reaching upwards in flame, snatched by the dark, on the beach. He knew the lake was there; neither heard nor seen, quite black. The lake. The lake. He felt, inevitably, something resembling desire, but it was more like a desire for the cool mouth of waters that would close over ankles, knees, thighs, sex. He was drunk and not very capable, and felt he would never get there, to the lake. The lake became an unslakeable thirst, the night-thirst, the early-morning thirst that cannot stir a hand for the surcease of water.

When he awoke sometime in his chalet, it was because consciousness moved towards a sound that he could identify even before he was awake. Dickie was playing the guitar behind closed doors somewhere, playing again and again the song of the bride and the riding away.

Zelide wore her bikini, drawing up the bill for him in the morning. The demarcation lines at shoulder-straps and thighs had become scarlet weals; the sun was eating into her, poor cheerful adventuring immigrant. She had been taken up by the bachelors and was about to go out with them in their boat. 'Maybe we'll bump into each other again,' she said.

And of course they might; handed around the world from country to country, minor characters who crop up. There was an air of convalescence about the hotel. On the terrace, empty bottles were coated with ants; down at the beach, boys were burying the ashes of the bonfire and their feet scuffed over the shapes – like resting-places flattened in grass by cattle – where couples had been secreted by the night. He saw Mrs Palmer in a large sun hat, waving her tough brown arms about in command over a gang who, resting on their implements, accepted her as they did sun, flies, and rain. Two big black pairs of sunglasses – his own and hers – flashed back and forth blindly as they stood, with Zelide, amid the building rubble in the garden.

'Don't forget to look us up if ever you're out this way.'

'One never knows.'

'With journalists, my God, no, you could find yourself at the North Pole! We'll always find a bed for you. Has Dickie said good-bye?'

'Say good-bye to him for me, will you?'

She put out her jingling, gold-flashing hand and he saw (as if it had been a new line on his own face) the fine, shiny tan of her forearm wrinkle with the movement. 'Happy landings,' she said.

Zelide watched him drive off. 'You've not forgotten anything? You'd be surprised at people. I don't know what to do with the stuff, half the time.' She smiled and her stomach bulged over the bikini; she had the sort of pioneering spirit, the instincts of self-preservation appropriate to her time and kind.

Past the fowls, water tanks and outhouses, the hot silent arcades of the demolished hotel, the car rocked and swayed over the track. Suddenly he saw the path, the path he had missed the other day, to the graves of Livingstone's companions. It was just where Dickie and Zelide had said. He was beyond it by the time he understood this, but all at once it seemed absurd not even to have gone to have a look, after three days. He stopped the car and walked back. He took the narrow path that was snagged with thorn bushes and led up the hill between trees too low and meagre of foliage to give shade. The earth was picked clean by the dry season. Flies settled at once upon his shoulders. He was annoyed by the sound of his own lack of breath; and then there, where the slope of the hill came up short against a steep rise, the gravestones stood with their backs to rock. The five neat headstones of the monuments commission were surmounted each by an iron cross on a circle. The names, and the dates of birth and death – the deaths all in the last quarter of the nineteenth century – were engraved on the granite. A yard or two away, but in line with the rest, was another gravestone. Carl Church moved over to read the inscription: *In Memory of Richard Alastair Macnab, Beloved Husband of Dorothy and Father of Richard and Heather, died 1957.* They all looked back, these dead companions, to the lake, the lake that Carl Church (turning to face as they did, now) had had silent behind him all the way up; the lake that, from here, was seen to stretch much farther than one could tell, down there on the shore or at the hotel: stretching still – even from up here – as far as one could see, flat and shining, a long way up Africa.

An Intruder

Someone had brought her along; she sat looking out of the rest of the noisy party in the nightclub like a bush-baby between trees. He was one of them, there was no party without him, but under the cross-fire of private jokes, the anecdotes and the drinking he cornered her, from the beginning, with the hush of an even more private gentleness and tenderness: 'The smoke will brown those ears like gardenia petals.' She drank anything so long as it was soft. He touched her warm hand on the glass of lemonade; 'Pass the water,' he called, and dipping his folded handkerchief in among the ice cubes, wrung it out and drew the damp cloth like cool lips across the inside of her wrists. She was not a giggler despite her extreme youth, and she smiled the small slow smile that men brought to her face without her knowing why. When one of the others took her to dance, he said seriously, 'For God's sake don't breathe your damned brandy on her, Carl, she'll wilt.' He himself led her to the dark crowded circle in shelter, his arms folded round her and his handsome face pressed back at the chin, so that his eyes looked down on her in reassurance even while the din of bouzouki and drum stomped out speech, stomped through bones and flesh in one beat pumped by a single bursting heart.

He was between marriages, then (the second or third had just broken up – nobody really knew which), and this was always a high time, for him. They said, Seago's back in circulation; it meant that he was discovering his same old world anew, as good as new. But while he was setting off the parties, the weekend dashes here and there, the pub-crawls, he was already saying to her mother as he sat in the garden drinking coffee, 'Look at the mother and see what you're getting in the daughter. Lucky man that I am.'

Marie and her mother couldn't help laughing and at the same time being made to feel a little excited and worldly. His frail little marmoset – as he called her – was an only child, they were mother-and-daughter, the sort of pair with whom a father couldn't be imagined, even if he hadn't happened to have been dispensed with before he could cast the reminder of a male embrace between them in the form of a likeness or gesture they didn't share. Mrs Clegg had earned a living for them both, doing very pale pastels of the children of the horsey set, and very dark pastels of African women for the tourist shops. She was an artist and therefore must not be too conventional: she knew James Seago had been married before, but he was so attractive – so charming, so considerate of Marie and her and such a contrast to the boys of Marie's own age who didn't even bother to open a car door for a woman – there was something touching about this man, whose place was in a dinner-jacket among the smart set, appreciating the delicacy of the girl. 'You don't mind if I take her out with my ruffian friends? You'll let me look after her?' – In the face of this almost wistful candour and understanding, who could find any reality in his 'reputation' with women? He came for Marie night after night in his old black Lancia. His ruddy, clear-skinned face and lively eyes blotted out the man her mother heard talked about, the creation of gossip. He was – no, not like a son to her, but an equal. When he said something nice, he was not just being kind to an older woman. And his photograph was often on the social page.

In the nightclubs and restaurants he liked to go to he drank bottle after bottle of wine with friends and told his mimicking stories, all the time caressing Marie like a kitten. Sometimes he insisted that she literally sit on his knees. She spoke little, and when she did it was to utter, slow, sensible things that commanded a few seconds' polite attention before the voices broke out at one another again. But on his knees she did not speak at all, for while he was gesturing, talking, in response to the whole cave of voices and music and movement, she felt his voice through his chest rather than heard him and was filled, like a child bottling up tears, with appalling sexual desire. He never knew this and when he made love to her – in his bed, in the afternoons, because he kept the evenings for his friends – she was as timid and rigid as if she had never been warmed by lust. He had to coax her: 'My little marmoset, my rabbit-nose, little teenage-doll, you will learn to like this, really you will . . .' And in time, always using the simple words with which some shy pet is persuaded to drink a saucer of milk, he taught her to do all the strange things she would not have guessed were love-making at all, and that he seemed to enjoy so much. Afterwards, they would go home and have tea with her mother in the garden.

With his usual upper-class candour, he constantly remarked that he hadn't a bean; but this, like his reputation with women, didn't match the facts of his life as Marie and her mother knew them. He had enough money for the luxuries of bachelor life, if not for necessities. There was the old but elegant Lancia and there were always notes in the expensive crocodile-skin wallet (an inscription on a silver plate, from a former wife, inside) to pay the hotel managers and *restaurateurs* he was so friendly with, though he lived in a shabby room in an abandoned-looking old house rented by a couple who were his close friends. His English public school accent got him a number of vague jobs on the periphery of influential business groups, where the crude-speaking experts felt themselves hampered in public relations by their South African inarticulateness; these jobs never lasted long. Wifeless and jobless after many wives and jobs, he still appeared to be one of those desirable men who can take anything they want of life if they think it worth the bother.

Marie, gravely fluffing out her dark hair in the ladies' rooms of nightclubs where old attendants watched from their saucers of small change, wondered what she would say when her mother found out about the afternoons in James's room. But before this could happen, one day in the garden when she was out of earshot, he said to her mother, 'You know, I've been making love to her, I know one shouldn't . . .? But we'll be able to get married very soon. Perhaps next year.'

He was looking after Marie, as she walked into the house,

with the rueful, affectionate gaze with which one marks a child growing up. Mrs Clegg was irresistibly tempted to fit the assumption that she took sexual freedom for granted: after all, she was an artist, not a bourgeois housewife. She decided, again, his frankness was endearingly admirable; he was human, Marie was beautiful, what else could you expect?

The marriage was put off several times – there was some business of his trying to get back his furniture from his divorced wife, and then there was a job connected with an Angolan diamond-mining company that didn't come off. At last he simply walked in one morning with the licence and they were married without Marie or her mother going to the hairdresser or any friends being told. That night there was a surprise for his bride: apparently two of his best friends were arriving on a visit from England, and all their old friends were to meet them at the airport and go straight to their favourite nightclub, the place where, incidentally, he and Marie had met. The bouzouki player was persuaded to carry on until nearly five in the morning, and then they went to someone's house where the champagne was produced as the sky pinkened and the houseboy came in with his dust-pan and brush. Marie did not drink and she repaired her perfect makeup every hour; though pale, she was as fresh and circumspect among their puffy faces and burning eyes at the end of the night as she was at the beginning. He slept all next day and she lay contentedly beside him in the room in the old house, watching the sun behind the curtains try first this window and then the next. But no one could get in; he and she were alone together.

They found a flat, not a very pleasant one, but it was only temporary. It was also cheap. He was so amusing about its disadvantages, and it was such fun to bob in and out of each other's way in the high dark cell of a bathroom every morning, that after the dismay of her first look at the place, she really ceased to see the things she disliked about it so much – the fake marble fireplace and the thick mesh burglar-proofing over all the windows. 'What are these people afraid of?' Her tiny nostrils stiffened in disdain.

'Angel ... your world is so pink and white and sweet-smelling ... there are stale women with mildew between their breasts who daren't open doors.'

She put up white gauzy curtains everywhere, and she went about in short cotton dressing-gowns that smelt of the warm iron. She got a part-time job and saved to buy a scrubbed white wood dining table and chairs, and a rose silk sari to make up as a divan cover. 'Damned lawyers twiddling their thumbs. When'll I see my furniture from that freckled bitch,' he said. The wife-before-the-last, a Catholic, was referred to as 'Bloody-minded Mary, Our Lady of the Plastic Peonies' because, looking back on it, what he really couldn't stand about her was the habit she had of putting artificial flowers on the table among real leaves. He seemed to have parted from these women on the worst of terms and to dismiss his association with them – a large part of his life – as a series of grotesque jokes.

'What do you think you'd call me if we were divorced?'

'You...' He took Marie's head between his hands and smoothed back the hair from her temples, kissing her as if trying with his lips the feel of a piece of velvet. 'What could anyone say about you.' When he released her she said, going deep pink from the ledges of her small collar-bones to her black eyes, all pupil: 'That sugar-tit tart.' The vocabulary was his all right, coming out in her soft, slow voice. He was enchanted, picked her up, carried her round the room. 'Teenage-doll! Marmoset-angel! I'll have to wash your mouth out with soap and water!'

They continued to spend a lot of time at nightclubs and drinking places. Sometimes at eleven o'clock on a weekday night, when lights were going out in bedrooms all over the suburb, he would take the old Lancia scrunching over the dark drive of someone's house, and while Marie waited in the car, stand throwing gravel at a window until his friends appeared and could be persuaded to get dressed and come out. He and his friends were well known in the places they went to and they stayed until they were swept out. Manolis or Giovanni, the Greek or Italian owner, would sit deep in the shadows, his gaze far back in fatigue that ringed his eyes like a natural marking, and watch these people who were good business and would not go to bed: these South Africans who did not know any better. Sometimes she and the proprietor in whose blood the memory of Dionysiac pleasures ran were the only spectators left. James, her husband, did not appear drunk during these sessions, but next day he would remember nothing of what he had said or done the night before. She realized that she, too, sitting on his lap while he murmured loving things into her ear under the talk, was blacked out along with the rest. But she had seen envy behind the expressions of other women that suggested they wouldn't care for such an exhibition of affection.

There were people who seemed to know him whom he didn't remember at all, either; a man who came up to them as they were getting out of the car in town one day and laid a hand on his shoulder – 'James...'

He had looked round at the man, casual, edgy, with the patient smile of someone accosted by a stranger.

'James ... What's the matter? Colin –'

'Look, old man, I'm sorry, but I'm afraid –'

'Colin. Colin. The Golden Horn Inn, Basutoland.'

He continued to look into the man's face as if at an amiable lunatic, while the man's expression slowly changed to a strange, coquettish smile. 'Oh I see. Well, that's all right, James.'

She supposed they must have been drinking together once.

Sometimes she wondered if perhaps he had been as crazy about those other women, his wives, as he was about her, and did not remember: had forgotten other wild nights in the wine that washed them all out. But that was not possible; she enjoyed the slight twinge of jealousy she induced in herself with the thought. She was going to have a baby, and he had never had a child with anyone else. She said, 'You haven't a child somewhere?'

'Breed from those gorgons? Are you mad?'

But coarse words were not for her; he said to her mother, 'Do you think I should have given her a child? She's a little girl herself.' He kissed and petted her more than ever, the signs of her womanhood saddened and delighted him, like precocity.

She did not talk to him about after the baby was born, about a bigger flat – a little house, perhaps, with a garden? – and where to dry napkins and not being able to leave a baby at night. In the meantime, they had a good time, just as before.

And then one night – or rather one early morning – something awful happened that made it suddenly possible for her to speak up for a move, napkins, the baby as a creature with needs rather than as a miraculous function of her body. They had been at Giovanni's until the small hours, as usual, there had been some occasion for celebration. She drove home and they had gone to bed and into a sleep like a death – his from drink, hers from exhaustion. Pregnancy made her hungry and she woke at eight o'clock to the church bells of Sunday morning and slid out of bed to go to the kitchen. She bumped into a chair askew in the passage, but in her sleepy state it was nothing more significant than an obstacle, and when she reached the kitchen she stood there deeply puzzled as if she had arrived somewhere in sleep and would wake in the presence of familiar order in a moment.

For the kitchen was wrecked; flour had been strewn, syrup had been thrown at the walls, soap powder, milk, cocoa, salad oil were upset over everything. The white muslin curtains were ripped to shreds. She began to shake; and suddenly ran stumbling back to the bedroom.

He lay fast asleep, as she had lain, as they both had lain while this – Thing – happened. While Someone. Something. In the flat with them.

'James,' she screamed hoarsely whispering, and flung herself on him. His head came up from under his arm, the beard strong-textured in the pink firm skin; he frowned at her a moment, and then he was holding her in a kind of terror of tenderness. 'Marmoset. Rabbit.' She buried her head in the sleep-heat between his shoulder and neck and gestured fiercely back at the door.

'Christ almighty! What's wrong?'

'The kitchen! The kitchen!'

He struggled to get up.

'Don't go there.'

'Sweetling, tell me, what happened?'

She wouldn't let him leave her. He put his two hands round her stone-hard belly while she controlled shuddering breaths. Then they went together into the other rooms of the flat, the kitchen, the living room, and the dark hole of a bathroom, her bare feet twitching distastefully like a cat's at each step. 'Just look at it.' They stood at the kitchen door. But in the living room she said, '*What is it?*' Neither of them spoke. On each of the three divisions of the sofa cushions there was a little pile, an offering. One was a slime of contraceptive jelly with hair-combings – hers – that must have been taken from the waste-paper basket in the bedroom; the other was toothpaste and razor blades; the third was a mucous of half-rotted vegetable matter – peelings, tea leaves, dregs – the intestines of the dust-bin.

In the bathroom there were more horrors; cosmetics were spilt, and the underwear she had left there was arranged in an obscene collage with intimate objects of toilet. Two of her pretty cotton gowns lay in the bath with a bottle of liqueur emptied on them. They went again from room to room in silence. But the mess spoke secretly, in the chaos there was a jeering pattern, a logic outside sense that was at the same time *recognizable*, as a familiar object turned inside-out draws a blank and yet signals. There was something related only to them in this arrangement without values of disrelated objects and substances; it was, after all, the components of their daily existence and its symbols. It was all horrible; horribly familar, even while they were puzzled and aghast.

'This flat. The light has to be on in the bathroom all day. There's no balcony where the baby could sleep. The washing will never dry. I've never been able to get rid of the black beetles in the kitchen, whatever I put down.'

'All right, angel, poor angel.'

'We can't live here. It's not a place for a baby.'

He wanted to phone for the police but it did not seem to occur to her that there could be a rational explanation for what had happened, a malicious and wicked intruder who had scrawled contempt on the passionate rites of their intimacy, smeared filth on the cosy contemporary home-making of the living room, and made rags of the rose silk cover and the white muslin curtains. To her, evil had come out of the walls, as the black beetles did in the kitchen.

It was not until some days had passed and she had calmed down – they found another flat – that the extraordinariness of the whole business began to mean something to her: she and James had gone round the flat together, that morning, and there wasn't a door or window by which anyone could have got in. Not a pane was broken and there was that ugly burglar-proofing, anyway. There was only one outer door to the flat, and she had locked it when they came home and put the key, as usual, on the bedside table; if someone had somehow managed to steal the key, how could they have put it back on the table after leaving the flat, and how could the door have been left bolted on the inside? But more amazing than how the intruder got in, why had he done so? Not a penny or a piece of clothing had been stolen.

They discussed it over and over again, as he kept saying, 'There must be an explanation, something so simple we've missed it. Poltergeists won't do. Are you sure there couldn't have been someone hiding in the flat when we came home, marmoset-baby? Did either of us go into the living room before we went to bed?' – For of course he didn't remember a thing until he woke and found she had flung herself on him terrified.

'No. I told you. I went into the living room to get a bottle of lime juice, I went into all the rooms,' she repeated in her soft, slow, reasonable voice; and this time, while she was speaking, she began to know what else he would never remember, something so simple that she had missed it.

She stood there wan, almost ugly, really like some wretched pet monkey shivering in a cold climate. But she was going to have a child, and – yes, looking at him, she was grown-up, now, suddenly, as some people are said to turn white-haired overnight.

Open House

Frances Taver was on the secret circuit for people who wanted to find out the truth about South Africa. These visiting journalists, politicians and churchmen all had an itinerary arranged for them by their consular representatives and overseas information services, or were steered around by a 'foundation' of South African business interests eager to improve the country's image, or even carted about to the model black townships, universities and beerhalls by the South African State Information service itself. But all had, carefully hidden among the most private of private papers (the nervous ones went so far as to keep it in code), the short list that would really take the lid off the place: the people one must see. A few were names that had got into the newspapers of the world as particularly vigorous opponents or victims of apartheid; a missionary priest, a lawyer or two, a writer, a newspaper editor or an outspoken bishop. Others were known only within the country itself, and were known about by foreign visitors only through people like themselves who had carried the short list before. Most of the names on it were white names – which was rather frustrating, when one was after the real thing; but it was said in London and New York that there *were* still ways of getting to meet Africans, provided you could get hold of the right white people.

Frances Taver was one of them. Had been for years. From the forties when she had been a trade union organizer and run a mixed union of garment workers while this was legally possible; in the fifties, after her marriage, when she was manager of a black-and-white theatre group before that was disbanded by new legislation; to the early sixties, when she hid friends on the run from the police – Africans who were members of the newly-banned political organizations – before the claims of that sort of friendship had to be weighed against the risk (for white as well as black) of the long spells of detention without trial introduced to betray it.

Frances Taver had few friends left now, and she was always slightly embarrassed when she heard an eager American or English voice over the telephone announcing an arrival, a too-brief stay (of course), and the inevitable fond message of greetings to be conveyed from so-and-so – whoever it was who happened to have supplied the short list. A few years ago it had been fun and easy to make these visitors an excuse for a gathering that quite likely would turn into a party. The visitor would have a high old time learning to dance the *kwela* with black girls; he would sit fascinated, trying to keep sober enough to take it all in, listening to the fluent and fervent harangue of African, white, and Indian politicals, drinking and arguing together in a paradox of personal freedom that, curiously, he couldn't remember finding where there were *no* laws against the mixing of races. And no one enjoyed his fascination more than the objects of it themselves; Frances Taver and her friends were amused, in those days, in a friendly way, to knock the 'right' ideas slightly askew.

In those days: that was how she thought of it; it seemed very long ago. She saw the faces, sometimes, a flash in an absence filled with newspaper accounts of trials, hearsay about activities in exile, chance remarks from someone who knew someone else who had talked over the fence with one who was under house arrest. Another, an African friend banned for his activities with the African National Congress, who had gone 'underground', came to see her at long intervals, in the afternoons when he could be sure the house would be empty. Although she was still youngish, she had come to think of 'those days' as her youth; and he was a vision strayed from it.

The voice on the telephone, this time, was American – soft, cautious – no doubt the man thought the line was tapped. Robert Greenman Ceretti, from Washington; while they were talking, she remembered that this was the political columnist who had somehow been connected with the Kennedy administration. Hadn't he written a book about the Bay of Pigs? Anyway, she had certainly seen him quoted.

'And how are the Brauns – I haven't heard for ages –' She made the usual inquiries about the well-being of the mutual acquaintance whose greetings he brought, and he made the usual speech about how much he was hoping he'd be able to meet her? She was about to say, as always, come to dinner, but an absurd recoil within her, a moment of dull panic, almost, made her settle for an invitation to drop in for a drink two days later. 'If I can be of any help to you, in the meantime?' she had to add; he sounded modest and intelligent.

'Well, I do appreciate it. I'll look forward to Wednesday.'

At the last minute she invited a few white friends to meet him, a doctor and his wife who ran a tuberculosis hospital in an African reserve, and a young journalist who had been to America on a leadership exchange programme. But she knew what the foreign visitor wanted of her and she had an absurd – again, that was the word – compulsion to put him in the position where, alas, he could ask it. He was a small, cosy, red-headed man with a chipmunk smile, and she liked him. She drove him back to his hotel after the other guests had left, and they chatted about the articles he was going to write and the people he was seeing – had he been able to interview any important Nationalists, for example? Well, not yet, but he hoped to have something lined up for the following week, in Pretoria. Another thing he was worried about (here it came), he'd hardly been able to exchange a word with any black man except the one who cleaned his room at the hotel. She heard her voice saying casually, 'Well, perhaps I might be able to help you, there,' and he took it up at once, gravely, gratefully, sincerely, smiling at her – 'I hoped you just might. If I could only get to talk with a few ordinary, articulate people. I mean, I think I've been put pretty much in the picture by the courageous white people I've been lucky enough to meet – people like you and your husband – but I'd like to know a little at first hand about what Africans themselves are thinking. If you could fix it, it'd be wonderful.'

Now it was done, at once she withdrew, from herself rather

than him. 'I don't know. People don't want to talk any more. If they're doing anything, it's not something that can be talked about. Those that are left. Black and white. The ones you ought to see are shut away.'

They were sitting in the car, outside the hotel. She could see in his encouraging, admiring, intent face how he had been told that she, if anyone, could introduce him to black people, hers, if anyone's, was the house to meet them.

There was a twinge of vanity: 'I'll let you know. I'll ring you, then, Bob.' Of course they were already on first-name terms; lonely affinity overleapt acquaintance in South Africa when likeminded whites met.

'You don't have to say more than when and where. I didn't like to talk, that first day, over the phone,' he said.

They always had fantasies of danger. 'What can happen to you?' she said. Her smile was not altogether pleasant. They always protested, too, that their fear was not for themselves, it was on your behalf, etc. 'You've got your passport. You don't live here.'

She did not see Jason Madela from one month's end to the next but when she telephoned him at the building where she remembered him once having had an office on the fringe of the white town, he accepted the invitation to lunch just as if he had been one of the intimates who used to drop in any time. And then there was Edgar, Edgar Xixo the attorney, successor to her old friend Samson Dumile's practice; one could always get him. And after that? She could have asked Jason to bring someone along, perhaps one of the boxing promoters or gamblers it amused him to produce where the drinks were free – but that would have been too obvious, even for the blind eye that she and Jason Madela were able to turn to the nature of the invitation. In the end she invited little Spuds Butelezi, the reporter. What did it matter? He was black, anyway. There was no getting out of the whole business, now.

She set herself to cook a good lunch, just as good as she had ever cooked, and she put out the drinks and the ice in the shelter of the glassed-in end of the big veranda, so that the small company should not feel lost. Her fading hair had been dyed to something approximating its original blonde and then streaked with grey, the day before, and she felt the appearance to be pleasingly artificial; she wore a bright, thick linen dress that showed off sunburned shoulders like the knobs of well-polished furniture, and she was aware that her blue eyes were striking in contrast with her tough brown face. She felt Robert Greenman Ceretti's eyes on her, a moment, as he stood in the sunny doorway; yes, she was also a woman, queening it alone among men at lunch. 'You mix the Martinis, there's a dear,' she said. 'It's such a treat to have a real American one.' And while he bent about over bottles with the neatness of a small man, she was in and out of the veranda, shepherding the arrival of the other guests. 'This is Bob – Bob Ceretti, here on a visit from the States – Edgar Xixo.'

'Jason, this is Bob Ceretti, the man who has the ear of presidents –'

Laughter and protests mingled with the handing round of the drinks. Jason Madela, going to fat around the nape but still handsome in a frowning, Clark Gable way, stood about glass in hand as if in the habit acquired at cocktail parties. With his air of being distracted from more important things by irresistibly amusing asides, he was correcting a matter of terminology for Robert Ceretti – 'No, no, but you must understand that in the townships, a "situation" is a different thing entirely – well, *I'm* a situation, f'rinstance –' He cocked his smile, for confirmation, to Xixo, whose eyes turned from one face to another in obedient glee – 'Oh, you're the *muti* man!' 'No, wait, but I'm trying to give Bob an obvious example' – more laughter, all round – '– a man who wears a suit every day, like a white man. Who goes to the office and prefers to talk English.'

'You think it derives from the use of the word as a genteelism for "job"? Would you say? You know – the Situations Vacant column in the newspapers?' The visitor sat forward on the edge of his chair, smiling up closely. 'But what's this "*muti*" you mentioned, now – maybe I ought to have been taking notes instead of shaking Frances's Martini pitcher.'

'He's a medicine man,' Xixo was explaining, while Jason laughed – 'Oh for God's sake!' and tossed off the rest of his gin, and Frances went forward to bring the late arrival, Spuds

Butelezi, in his lattice-knit gold shirt and pale blue jeans, into the circle. When the American had exchanged names and had Spuds by the hand, he said, 'And what's Spuds, then?'

The young man had a dough-shaped, light-coloured face with tiny features stuck in it in a perpetual expression of suspicious surprise. The Martinis had turned up the volume of voices that met him. 'I'll have a beer,' he said to Frances; and they laughed again.

Jason Madela rescued him, a giant flicking a fly from a glass of water. 'He's one of the egg-heads,' he said. 'That's another category altogether.'

'Didn't you used to be one yourself, Jason?' Frances pretended a reproof: Jason Madela would want a way of letting Ceretti know that although he was a successful businessman in the township, he was also a man with a university degree.

'Don't let's talk about my youthful misdemeanours, my dear Frances,' he said, with the accepted light touch of a man hiding a wound. 'I thought the men were supposed to be doing the work around here – I can cope with that,' and he helped her chip apart the ice-cubes that had welded together as they melted. 'Get your servant to bring us a little hot water, that'll do it easily –'

'Oh, I'm really falling down on the job!' Ceretti was listening carefully, putting in a low 'Go on' or 'You mean?' to keep the flow of Xixo's long explanation of problems over a travel document, and he looked up at Frances and Jason Madela offering a fresh round of drinks.

'You go ahead and talk, that's the idea,' Frances said.

He gave her the trusting grin of some intelligent small pet. 'Well, you two are a great combination behind the bar. Real team-work of long association, I guess.'

'How long is it?' Frances asked, drily but gaily, meaning how many years had she and Jason Madela been acquaintances, and, playfully making as if to anticipate a blow, he said, 'Must be ten years and you were a grown-up girl even then' – although both knew that they had seen each other only across various rooms perhaps a dozen times in five years, and got into conversation perhaps half as often.

At lunch Edgar Xixo was still fully launched on the story of his difficulties in travelling back and forth to one of the former British Protectorates, now small, newly-independent states surrounded by South African territory. It wasn't, he explained, as if he were asking for a passport: it was just a travel document he wanted, that's all, just a piece of paper from the Bantu Affairs Department that would allow him to go to Lesotho on business and come back.

'Now have I got this straight – you'd been there sometime?' Ceretti hung over the wisp of steam rising from his soup like a seer over a crystal ball.

'Yes, yes, you see, I had a travel document –'

'But these things are good for one exit and re-entry only.' Jason dispatched it with the good-humoured impatience of the quickwitted. 'We blacks aren't supposed to want to go wandering about the place. Tell them you want to take a holiday in Lourenço Marques – they'll laugh in your face. If they don't kick you downstairs. Oppenheimer and Charlie Engelhard can go off in their yachts to the South of France, but Jason Madela?'

He got the laugh he wanted, and, on the side, the style of his reference to rich and important white industrialists as decent enough fellows, if one happened to know them, suggested that *he* might. Perhaps he did, for all Frances Taver knew; Jason would be just the kind of man the white establishment would find if they should happen to decide they ought to make a token gesture of being in touch with the African masses. He was curiously reassuring to white people; his dark suits, white shirts, urbane conversation and sense of humour, all indistinguishable from their own and apparently snatched out of thin air, made it possible for them to forget the unpleasant facts of the life imposed on him and his kind. How tactful, how clever he was, too. She, just as well as any millionaire, would have done to illustrate his point; she was culpable: white, and free to go where she pleased. The flattery of being spared passed invisibly from her to him, like a promissory note beneath the table.

Edgar Xixo had even been summoned to The Greys, Special Branch headquarters, for questioning, he said – 'And I've never belonged to any political organization, they know there've never been any charges against me. I don't know any political refugees in Lesotho, I don't want to *see* anybody – I have to go up and down simply because of business, I've got this agency selling equipment to the people at the diamond diggings, it could be a good thing if . . .'

'A little palm-grease, maybe,' said Jason Madela, taking some salad.

Xixo appealed to them all, dismayed. 'But if you offer it to the wrong one, that's the . . .? In my position, an attorney!'

'Instinct,' said Madela. 'One can't learn it.'

'Tell me,' Ceretti signalled an appreciative refusal of a second helping of duck, while turning from his hostess to Madela. 'Would you say that bribery plays a big part in daily relations between Africans and officials? I don't mean the political police, of course – the white administration? Is that your experience?'

Madela sipped his wine and then turned the bottle so that he could read the label, saying meanwhile, 'Oh not what you'd call graft, not by your standards. Small stuff. When I ran a transport business I used to make use of it. Licences for the drivers and so on. You get some of these young Afrikaner clerks, they don't earn much and they don't mind who they pick up a few bob from. They can be quite reasonable. I was thinking there might be someone up at the Bantu Affairs offices. But you have to have a feeling for the right man' – he put down the bottle and smiled at Frances Taver – 'Thank heaven I'm out of it, now. Unless I should decide to submit some of my concoctions to the Bureau of Standards, eh?' and she laughed.

'Jason has broken the white monopoly of the hair-straightener and blood-purifier business,' Frances said gracefully, 'and the nice thing about him is that he has no illusions about his products.'

'But plenty of confidence,' he said. 'I'm looking into the possibilities of exporting my pills for men, to the States. I think the time's just ripe for American blacks to feel they can buy back a bit of old Africa in a bottle, eh?'

Xixo picked about his leg of duck as if his problem itself

were laid cold before them on the table. 'I mean, I've said again and again, show me anything on my record –'

The young journalist, Spuds Butelezi, said in his heavy way, 'It might be because you took over Samson Dumile's show.'

Every time a new name was mentioned the corners of Ceretti's eyes flickered narrow in attention.

'Well, that's the whole thing!' Xixo complained to Ceretti. 'The fellow I was working for, Dumile, was mixed up in a political trial and he got six years – I took over the *bona fide* clients, that's all, my office isn't in the same building, nothing to do with it – but that's the whole thing!'

Frances suddenly thought of Sam Dumile, in this room of hers, three – two? – years ago, describing a police raid on his house the night before and roaring with laughter as he told how his little daughter said to the policeman, 'My father gets very cross if you play with his papers.'

Jason picked up the wine bottle, making to pass it round – 'Yes, please do, please do – what happened to the children?' she said. Jason knew whose she meant; made a polite attempt. 'Where are Sam's kids?'

But Edgar Xixo was nodding in satisfied confirmation as Ceretti said, 'It's a pretty awful story. My God. Seems you can never hope to be in the clear, no matter how careful you are. My God.'

Jason remarked, aside, 'They must be around somewhere with relatives. He's got a sister in Bloemfontein.'

The dessert was a compound of fresh mangoes and cream, an invention of the house: '*Mangoes Frances*' said the American. 'This is one of the African experiences I'd recommend.' But Jason Madela told them he was allergic to mangoes and began on the cheese which was standing by. Another bottle of wine was opened to go with the cheese and there was laughter – which Robert Ceretti immediately turned on himself – when it emerged out of the cross-talk that Spuds Butelezi thought Ceretti had something to do with an American foundation. In the sympathetic atmosphere of food, drink, and sunshine marbled with cigarette smoke, the others listened as if they had not heard it all before while Butelezi, reluctant to waste the speech he had primed himself with, pressed Ceretti with his claim to a study grant that would enable him to finish his play. They heard him again outlining the plot and inspiration of the play – 'right out of township life' as he always said, blinking with finality, convinced that this was the only necessary qualification for successful authorship. He had patiently put together and taken apart, many times, in his play, ingredients faithfully lifted from the work of African writers who got published, and he was himself African: what else could be needed but someone to take it up?

Foundation or no foundation, Robert Ceretti showed great interest. 'Do you know the play at all, Frances? I mean' (he turned back to the round, wine-open face of the young man) 'is it far enough along to show to anybody?' And she said, finding herself smiling encouragingly, 'Oh yes – an early draft, he's worked on it a lot since then haven't you – and there's been a reading...?'

'I'll certainly get it to you,' Butelezi said, writing down the name of Ceretti's hotel.

They moved back to the veranda for the coffee and brandy. It was well after three o'clock by the time they stood about, making their good-byes. Ceretti's face was gleaming. 'Jason Madela's offered to drop me back in town, so don't you worry, Frances. I was just saying, people in America'll find it difficult to believe it was possible for me to have a lunch like this, here. It's been so very pleasant – pleasant indeed. We all had a good time. He was telling me that a few years ago a gathering like this would be quite common, but now there aren't many white people who would want to risk asking Africans and there aren't many Africans who would risk coming. I certainly enjoyed myself ... I hope we haven't put you out, lingering so long ... it's been a wonderful opportunity ...' Frances saw them to the garden gate, talking and laughing; last remarks and thanks were called from under the trees of the suburban street.

When she came back alone the quiet veranda rang tense with vanished voices, like a bell tower after the hour has struck. She gave the cat the milk left over from coffee. Someone had left a half-empty packet of cigarettes; who was it who broke matches into little tents? As she carried the tray into the deserted kitchen, she saw a note written on the back of a bill taken from the spike. HOPE YOUR PARTY WENT WELL.

It was not signed, and was written with the kitchen ballpoint which hung on a string. But she knew who had written it; the vision from the past had come and gone again.

The servants Amos and Bettie had rooms behind a granadilla vine at the bottom of the yard. She called, and asked Bettie whether anyone had asked for her? No, no one at all.

Her African National Congress friend from underground must have heard the voices in the quiet of the afternoon, or perhaps simply seen the cars outside, and gone away. She wondered if he knew who was there. Had he gone away out of consideration for her safety? They never spoke of it, of course, but he must know that the risks she took were carefully calculated, very carefully calculated. There was no way of disguising that from someone like *him*. Then she saw him smiling to himself at the sight of the collection of guests: Jason Madela, Edgar Xixo, and Spuds Butelezi – Spuds Butelezi, as well. But probably she was wrong, and he would have come out among them without those feelings of reproach or contempt that she read into the idea of his gait, his face. HOPE YOUR PARTY WENT WELL. He may have meant just that.

Frances Taver knew Robert Ceretti was leaving soon, but she wasn't quite sure when. Every day she thought; I'll phone and say good-bye. Yet she had already taken leave of him, that afternoon of the lunch. Just telephone and say good-bye. On the Friday morning, when she was sure he would be gone, she rang up the hotel, and there it was, the soft, cautious American voice. The first few moments were awkward; he protested his pleasure at hearing from her, she kept repeating, 'I thought you'd be gone...' Then she said, 'I just wanted to say – about that lunch. You mustn't be taken in –' He was saying, 'I've been so indebted to you, Frances, really you've been great.'

'– not phonies, no, that's not what I mean, on the contrary, they're very real, you understand?'

'Oh, your big good-looking friend, he's been marvellous.

Saturday night we were out on the town, you know.' He was proud of the adventure but didn't want to use the word '*shebeen*' over the telephone.

She said, 'You must understand. Because the corruption's real. Even they've become what they are because things are the way they are. Being phoney is being corrupted by the situation ... and that's real enough. We're made out of *that*.'

He thought maybe he was finding it difficult to follow her over the telephone, and seized upon the word: 'Yes, the "situation" – he was able to slip me into what I gather is one of the livelier places.'

Frances Taver said, 'I don't want you to be taken in –'

The urgency of her voice stopped his mouth, was communicated to him even if what she said was not.

'– by anyone,' the woman was saying.

He understood, indeed, that something complicated was wrong, but he knew, too, that he wouldn't be there long enough to find out, that perhaps you needed to live and die there, to find out. All she heard over the telephone was the voice assuring her, 'Everyone's been marvellous ... really marvellous. I just hope I can get back here some day – that is, if they ever let me in again ...'

Rain-Queen

We were living in the Congo at the time; I was nineteen. It must have been my twentieth birthday we had at the *Au Relais,* with the Gattis, M. Niewenhuys, and my father's site manager. My father was building a road from Elisabethville to Tshombe's residence, a road for processions and motorcades. It's Lubumbashi now, and Tshombe's dead in exile. But at that time there was plenty of money around and my father was brought from South Africa with a free hand to recruit engineers from anywhere he liked; the Gattis were Italian, and then there was a young Swede. I didn't want to leave Johannesburg because of my boy-friend, Alan, but my mother didn't like the idea of leaving me behind, because of him. She said to me, 'Quite honestly, I think it's putting too much temptation in a young girl's way. I'd have no one to blame but myself.' I was very young for my age, then, and I gave in. There wasn't much for me to do in E'ville. I was taken up by some young Belgian married women who were only a few years older than I was. I had coffee with them in town in the mornings, and played with their babies. My mother begged them to speak French to me; she didn't want the six months there to be a complete waste. One of them taught me how to make a chocolate mousse, and I made myself a dress under the supervision of another; we giggled together as I had done a few years before with the girls at school.

Everyone turned up at the *Au Relais* in the evenings, and in the afternoons when it had cooled off a bit we played squash – the younger ones in our crowd, I mean. I used to play every day with the Swede, and Marco Gatti. They came straight from the site. Eleanora Gatti was one of those Mediterranean women who not only belong to a different sex, but seem to be a species entirely different from the male. You could never imagine her running or even bending to pick something up; her white bosom in square-necked dresses, her soft hands with rings and jewel-lidded watch, her pile of dark hair tinted a strange tarnished marmalade-colour that showed up the pallor of her skin – all was arranged like a still-life. The Swede wasn't married.

After the game Marco Gatti used to put a towel round his neck tennis-star fashion and his dark face was gilded with sweat. The Swede went red and blotchy. When Marco panted it was a grin, showing white teeth and one that was repaired with gold. It seemed to me that all adults were flawed in some way; it set them apart. Marco used to give me a lift home and often came in to have a drink with my father and discuss problems about the road. When he was outlining a difficulty he had a habit of smiling and putting a hand inside his shirt to scratch his breast. In the open neck of his shirt some sort of amulet on a chain rested on the dark hair between his strong pectoral muscles. My father said proudly, 'He may look like a tenor at the opera, but he knows how to get things done.'

I had never been to the opera; it wasn't my generation. But when Marco began to kiss me every afternoon on the way home, and then to come in to talk to my father over beer as usual, I put it down to the foreignness in him. I said, 'It seems so funny to walk into the room where Daddy is.' Marco said, 'My poor little girl, you can't help it if you are pretty, can you?'

It rains every afternoon there, at that time of year. A sudden wind would buffet the heat aside, flattening paper against fences in the dust. Fifteen minutes later – you could have timed it by the clock – the rain came down so hard and noisy we could scarcely see out of the windscreen and had to talk as loudly as if we were in an echoing hall. The rain usually lasted only about an hour. One afternoon we went to the site instead of to my parent's house – to the caravan that was meant to be occupied by one of the engineers but never had been, because everyone lived in town. Marco shouted against the downpour, 'You know what the Congolese say? "When the rain comes, quickly find a girl to take home with you until it's over." ' The caravan was just like a little flat, with everything you needed. Marco showed me – there was even a bath. Marco wasn't tall (at home the girls all agreed we couldn't look at any boy under six foot) but he had the fine, strong legs of a sportsman, covered with straight black hairs, and he stroked my leg with his hard yet furry one. That was a caress we wouldn't have thought of, either. I had an inkling we really didn't know anything, at home.

The next afternoon Marco seemed to be taking the way directly to our house, and I said in agony, 'Aren't we going to the caravan?' It was out, before I could think. 'Oh my poor darling, were you disappointed?' He laughed and stopped the car there and then and kissed me deep in both ears as well as the mouth. 'All right, the caravan.' We went there every weekday afternoon – he didn't work on Saturdays, and the wives came along to the squash club. Soon the old Congolese watchman used to trot over from the labourers' camp to greet us when he saw the car draw up at the caravan; he knew I was my father's daughter. Marco chatted with him for a few minutes, and every few days gave him a tip. At the beginning, I used to stand by as if waiting to be told what to do next, but Marco had what I came to realize must be adult confidence. 'Don't look so worried. He's a nice old man. He's my friend.'

Marco taught me how to make love, in the caravan, and everything that I had thought of as 'life' was put away, as I had at other times folded the doll's clothes, packed the Monopoly set and the sample collection, and given them to the servant. I stopped writing to my girlfriends; it took me weeks to get down to replying to Alan's regular letters, and yet when I did so it was with a kind of professional pride that I turned out a letter of the most skilful ambiguity – should it be taken as a love-letter, or should it not? I felt it would be beyond his powers – powers of experience – to decide. I alternately pitied him and underwent an intense tingling of betrayal – actually cringing away from myself in the flesh. Before my parents and in the company of friends, Marco's absolutely unchanged behaviour mesmerized me: I acted as if nothing had happened because for him it was really as if nothing had happened. He was not pretending to be natural with my father and mother – he *was* natural. And the same applied to our behaviour in the presence of his wife. After the first time he made love to me I had looked forward with terror and panic to the moment when I should have to see Eleanora again; when she might squeeze my hand or even kiss me on the cheek as she sometimes did in her affectionate, feminine way. But when I walked into our house that Sunday and met her perfume and then all at once saw her beside my mother talking about her family in Genoa, with Marco, my father, and another couple sitting there – I moved through the whirling impression without falter. Someone said, 'Ah here she is at last, our Jillie!' And my mother was saying (I had been riding with the Swede), 'I don't know how she keeps up with Per, they were out dancing until three o'clock this morning –' and Marco, who was twenty-nine (1st December, Sagittarius, domicile of Jupiter), was saying, 'What it is to be young, eh?', and my father said, 'What time did you finally get to bed, after last night, anyway, Marco –' and Eleanora, sitting back with her plump smooth knees crossed, tugged my hand gently so that we should exchange a woman's kiss on the cheek.

I took in the smell of Eleanora's skin, felt the brush of her hair on my nose; and it was done, forever. We sat talking about some shoes her sister-in-law had sent from Milan. It was something I could never have imagined: Marco and I, as we really were, didn't exist here; there was no embarrassment. The Gattis, as always on Sunday mornings, were straight from eleven o'clock Mass at the Catholic cathedral, and smartly dressed.

As in most of these African places, there was a shortage of white women in Katanga and my mother felt much happier to see me spending my time with the young married people than she would have been to see me taken up by the mercenaries who came in and out of E'ville that summer. 'They're experienced men,' she said – as opposed to boys and married men, 'and of course they're out for what they can get. They've got nothing to lose; next week they're in another province, or they've left the country. I don't blame them. I believe a girl has to know what the world's like, and if she is fool enough to get involved with that crowd, she must take the consequences.' She seemed to have forgotten that she had not wanted to leave me in Johannesburg in the company of Alan. 'She's got a nice boy at home, a decent boy who respects her. I'd far rather see her just enjoying herself generally, with you young couples, while we're here.' And there was always Per, the Swede, to even out the numbers; she knew he wasn't 'exactly Jillie's dream of love'. I suppose that made him safe, too. If I was no one's partner in our circle, I was a love-object, handed round them all, to whom it was taken for granted that the homage of a flirtatious attitude was paid. Perhaps this was supposed to represent my compensation: if not the desired of any individual, then recognized as desirable by them all. 'Oh of course, you prefair to dance with Jeelie,' Mireille, one of the young Belgians, would say to her husband, pretending offence. He and I were quite an act, at the *Au Relais*, with our cha-cha. Then he would whisper to her in their own language, and she would giggle and punch his arm.

Marco and I were as famous a combination on the squash court as Mireille's husband and I were on the dance floor. This was the only place, if anyone had had the eyes for it, where our love-making showed. As the weeks went by and the love-making got better and better, our game got better and better. The response Marco taught me to the sound of spilling grain the rain made on the caravan roof held good between us on the squash court. Sometimes the wives and spectators broke into spontaneous applause; I was following Marco's sweat-oiled excited face, anticipating his muscular reactions in play as in bed. And when he had beaten me (narrowly) or we had beaten the other pair, he would hunch my shoulders together within his arm, laughing, praising me in Italian to the others, staggering about with me, and he would say to me in English, 'Aren't you a clever girl, eh?'; only he and I knew that that was what he said to me at other times. I loved that glinting flaw in his smile, now. It was Marco, like all the other things I knew about him: the girl cousin he had been in love with when he used to spend holidays with her family in the Abruzzi mountains; the way he would have planned Tshombe's road if he'd been in charge – 'But I like your father, you understand? – it's good to work with your father, you know?'; the baby cream from Italy he used for the prickly heat round his waist.

The innocence of the grownups fascinated me. They engaged in play-play, while I had given it up; I began to feel arrogant among them. It was pleasant. I felt arrogant – or rather tolerantly patronizing – towards the faraway Alan, too. I said to Marco, 'I wonder what he'd do if he knew' – about me; the caravan with the dotted curtains, the happy watchman, the tips, the breath of the earth rising from the wetted dust. Marco said wisely that Alan would be terribly upset.

'And if Eleanora knew?'

Marco gave me his open, knowing, assured smile, at the same time putting the palm of his hand to my cheek in tender parenthesis. 'She wouldn't be pleased. But in the case of a man –' For a moment he was Eleanora, quite unconsciously he mimicked the sighing resignation of Eleanora, receiving the news (seated, as usual), aware all the time that men were like that. Other people who were rumoured or known to have had lovers occupied my mind with a special interest. I chattered on the subject, '... when this girl's husband found out, he just walked out of the house without any money or anything and no one could find him for weeks,' and Marco took it up as one does what goes without saying: '– Well of course. If I think of Eleanora with someone – I mean – I would become mad.'

I went on with my second-hand story, enjoying the telling of all its twists and complications, and he laughed, following it with the affectionate attention with which he lit everything I said and did, and getting up to find the bottle of Chianti, wipe out a glass and fill it for himself. He always had wine in the caravan. I didn't drink any but I used to have the metallic taste of it in my mouth from his.

In the car that afternoon he had said maybe there'd be a nice surprise for me, and I remembered this and we lay and wrangled teasingly about it. The usual sort of thing: 'You're learning to be a real little nag, my darling, a little nag, eh?' 'I'm not going to let go until you tell me.' 'I think I'll have to give you a little smack on the bottom, eh, just-like-this, eh?' The surprise was a plan. He and my father might be going to the Kasai to advise on some difficulties that had cropped up for a construction firm there. It should be quite easy for me to persuade my father that I'd like to accompany him, and then if Marco could manage to leave Eleanora behind, it would be almost as good as if he and I were to take a trip alone together. 'You will have your own room?' Marco asked. I laughed. 'D'you think I'd be put in with Daddy?' Perhaps in Italy a girl wouldn't be allowed to have her own hotel room. Now Marco was turning his attention to the next point: 'Eleanora gets sick from the car, anyway – she won't want to come on bad roads, and you can get stuck, God knows what. No, it's quite all right, I will tell her it's no pleasure for her.' At the prospect of being in each other's company for whole days and perhaps nights we couldn't stop smiling, chattering and kissing, not with passion but delight. My tongue was loosened as if I *had* been drinking wine.

Marco spoke good English.

The foreign turns of phrase he did have were familar to me. He did not use the word 'mad' in the sense of angry. 'I would become mad': he meant exactly that, although the phrase was not one that we English-speaking people would use. I thought about it that night, alone, at home; and other nights. Out of his mind, he meant. If Eleanora slept with another man, Marco would be insane with jealousy. He said so to me because he was a really honest person, not like the other grownups – just as he said, 'I like your father, eh? I don't like some of the things he does with the road, but he is a good man, you know?' Marco was in love with me; I was his treasure, his joy, some beautiful words in Italian. It was true; he was very, very happy with me. I could see that. I did not know that people could be so happy; Alan did not know. I was sure that if I hadn't met Marco I should never have known. When we were in the caravan together I would watch him all the time, even when we were dozing I watched out of slit eyes the movement of his slim nostril with its tuft of black hair, as he breathed, and the curve of his sunburned ear through which capillary-patterned light showed. Oh Marco, Eleanora's husband, was beautiful as he slept. But he wasn't asleep. I liked to press my feet on his as if his were pedals and when I did this the corner of his mouth smiled and he said something with the flex of a muscle somewhere in his body. He even spoke aloud at times: my name. But I didn't know if he knew he had spoken it. Then he would lie with his eyes open a long time, but not looking at me, because he didn't need to: I was there. Then he would get up, light a cigarette, and say to me, 'I was in a dream ... oh, I don't know ... it's another world.'

It was a moment of awkwardness for me because I was entering the world from my childhood and could not conceive that, as adults did – as he did – I should ever need to find surcease and joy elsewhere, in another world. He escaped, with me. I entered, with him. The understanding of this I knew would come about for me as a transfiguration of the gold tooth from a flaw into a characteristic had come. I still did not know everything.

I saw Eleanora nearly every day. She was very fond of me; she was the sort of woman who, at home, would have kept attendant younger sisters round her to compensate for the children she did not have. I never felt guilty towards her. Yet, before, I should have thought how awful one would feel, taking the closeness and caresses that belonged, by law, to another woman. I was irritated at the stupidity of what Eleanora said; the stupidity of her not knowing. How idiotic that she should tell me that Marco had worked late on the site again last night, he was so conscientious, etc. – wasn't I with him, while she made her famous veal scaloppini and they got overcooked? And she was a nuisance to us. 'I'll have to go – I must take poor Eleanora to a film tonight. She hasn't been anywhere for weeks.' 'It's the last day for parcels to Italy, tomorrow – she likes me to pack them with her, the Christmas parcels, you know how Eleanora is about these things.' Then her aunt came out from Italy and there were lunches and dinners to which only Italian-speaking people were invited because the signora couldn't speak English. I remember going there one Sunday – sent by my mother with a contribution of her special ice-cream. They were all sitting round in the heat on the veranda, the women in one group with the children crawling over them, and Marco with the men in another, his tie loose at the neck of his shirt (Eleanora had made him put on a suit), gesturing with a toothpick, talking and throwing cigar butts into Eleanora's flower-trough of snake cactus.

And yet that evening in the caravan he said again, 'Oh good God, I don't want to wake up ... I was in a dream.' He had appeared out of the dark at our meeting-place, barefoot in espadrilles and tight thin jeans, like a beautiful fisherman.

I had never been to Europe. Marco said, 'I want to drive with you through Piemonte, and take you to the village where my father came from. We'll climb up to the walls from the church and when you get to the top – only then – I'll turn you round and you'll see Monte Bianco far away. You've heard nightingales, eh – never heard them? We'll listen to them in the pear orchard, it's my uncle's place, there.'

I was getting older every day. I said, 'What about Eleanora?' It was the nearest I could get to what I always wanted to ask him: 'Would you still become mad?'

Would you still become mad?

And now?

And now – two months, a week, six weeks later?

Now would you still become mad?

'Eleanora will spend some time in Pisa after we go back to Italy, with her mother and the aunts,' he was saying.

Yes, I knew why, too; knew from my mother that Eleanora was going to Pisa because there was an old family doctor there who was sure, despite everything the doctors in Milan and Rome had said, that poor Eleanora might still one day have a child.

I said, 'How would you feel if Alan came here?'

But Marco looked at me with such sensual confidence of understanding that we laughed.

I began to plan a love affair for Eleanora. I chose Per as

victim not only because he was the only presentable unattached man in our circle, but also because I had the feeling that it might just be possible to attract her to a man younger than herself, whom she could mother. And Per, with no woman at all (except the pretty Congolese prostitutes good for an hour in the rain, I suppose) could consider himself lucky if he succeeded with Eleanora. I studied her afresh. Soft white goose-flesh above her stocking-tops, breasts that rose when she sighed – that sort of woman. But Eleanora did not even seem to understand that Per was being put in her way (at our house, at the *Au Relais*) and Per seemed equally unaware of or uninterested in his opportunities.

And so there was never any way to ask my question. Marco and I continued to lie making love in the caravan while the roof made buckling noises as it contracted after the heat of the day, and the rain. Tshombe fled and returned; there were soldiers in the square before the post office and all sorts of difficulties arose over the building of the road. Marco was determined, excitable, harassed and energetic – he sprawled on the bed in the caravan at the end of the day like a runner who has just breasted the tape. My father was nervous and didn't know whether to finish the road. Eleanora was nervous and wanted to go back to Italy. We made love and when Marco opened his eyes to consciousness of the road, my father, Eleanora, he said, 'Oh for God's sake, *why* . . . it's like a dream . . .'

I became nervous too. I goaded my mother: 'The Gattis are a bore. That female Buddha.' I developed a dread that Eleanora would come to me with her sighs and her soft-squeezing hand and say, 'It always happens with Marco, little Jillie, you mustn't worry. I know all about it.'

And Marco and I continued to lie together in that state of pleasure in which nothing exists but the two who make it. Neither roads, nor mercenary wars, nor marriage, nor the claims and suffering of other people entered that tender, sensual dream from which Marco, although so regretfully, always returned.

What I dreaded Eleanora might say to me was never said,

either. Instead my mother told me one day in the tone of portentous emotion with which older women relive such things, that Eleanora, darling Eleanora, was expecting a child. After six years. Without having to go to Pisa to see the family doctor there. Yes, Eleanora had conceived during the rainy season in E'ville, while Marco and I made love every afternoon in the caravan, and the Congolese found themselves a girl for the duration of a shower.

It's years ago, now.

Poor Marco, sitting in Milan or Genoa at Sunday lunch, toothpick in his fingers, Eleanora's children crawling about, Eleanora's brothers and sisters and uncles and aunts around him. But I have never woken up from that dream. In the seven years I've been married I've had – how many lovers? Only I know. A lot – if you count the very brief holiday episodes as well.

It *is* another world, that dream, where no wind blows colder than the warm breath of two who are mouth to mouth.

No Place Like

The relief of being down, out, and on the ground after hours in the plane was brought up short for them by the airport building: dirty, full of up-ended chairs like a closed restaurant. *Transit? Transit?* Some of them started off on a stairway but were shooed back exasperatedly in a language they didn't understand. The African heat in the place had been cooped up for days and nights; somebody tried to open one of the windows but again there were remonstrations from the uniformed man and the girl in her white gloves and leopard-skin pillbox hat. The windows were sealed, anyway, for the air-conditioning that wasn't working; the offender shrugged. The spokesman that every group of travellers produces made himself responsible for a complaint; at the same time some of those sheep who can't resist a hole in a fence had found a glass door unlocked on the far side of the transit lounge – they were leaking to an open passage-way: grass, bougainvillaea trained like standard roses, a road glimpsed there! But the uniformed man raced to round them up and a cleaner trailing his broom was summoned to bolt the door.

The woman in beige trousers had come very slowly across the tarmac, putting her feet down on this particular earth once more, and she was walking even more slowly round the dirty hall. Her coat dragged from the crook of her elbow, her shoulder was weighed by the strap of a bag that wouldn't zip over a package of duty-free European liquor, her bright silk shirt opened dark mouths of wet when she lifted her arms. Fellow-glances of indignance or the seasoned superiority of a sense of humour found no answer in her. As her pace brought her into the path of the black cleaner, the two faces matched perfect indifference: his, for whom the distance from which these people came had no existence because he had been nowhere outside the two miles he walked from his village to the airport; hers, for whom the distance had no existence because she had been everywhere and arrived back.

Another black man, struggling into a white jacket as he unlocked wooden shutters, opened the bar, and the businessmen with their hard-top briefcases moved over to the row of stools. Men who had got talking to unattached women – not much promise in that now; the last leg of the journey was ahead – carried them glasses of gaudy synthetic fruit juice. The Consul who had wanted to buy her a drink with dinner on the plane had found himself a girl in red boots with a small daughter in identical red boots. The child waddled away and flirtation took the form of the two of them hurrying after to scoop it up, laughing. There was a patient queue of ladies in cardigans waiting to get into the lavatories. She passed – once, twice, three times in her slow rounds – a woman who was stitching petit-point. The third time she made out that the subject was a spaniel dog with orange-and-black-streaked ears. Beside the needlewoman was a husband of a species as easily identifiable as the breed of dog – an American, because of the length of bootlace, slotted through some emblem or badge, worn in place of a tie. He sighed and his wife looked up over her glasses as if he had made a threatening move.

The woman in the beige trousers got rid of her chit for Light Refreshment in an ashtray but she had still the plastic card that was her authority to board the plane again. She tried to put it in the pocket of the coat but she couldn't reach, so she had to hold the card in her teeth while she unharnessed herself from the shoulder-bag and the coat. She wedged the card into the bag beside the liquor packages, leaving it to protrude a little so that it would be easy to produce when the time came. But it slipped down inside the bag and she had to unpack the whole thing – the hairbrush full of her own hair, dead, shed; yesterday's newspaper from a foreign town; the book whose jacket tore on the bag's zip as it came out; wads of pink paper handkerchiefs, gloves for a cold climate, the quota of duty-free cigarettes, the Swiss pocket knife that you couldn't buy back home, the wallet of travel documents. There at the bottom was the shiny card. Without it, you couldn't board the plane again. With it, you were committed to go on to the end of the journey, just as the passport bearing your name committed you to a certain identity and place. It was one of the nervous tics of travel to feel for the reassurance of that shiny card. She had wandered to the revolving stand of paperbacks and came back to make sure where she had put the card: yes, it was there. It was not a bit of paper; shiny plastic, you couldn't tear it up – indestructible, it looked, of course they use them over and over again. *Tropic of Capricorn. Kamasutra. Something of Value.* The stand revolved and brought round the same books, yet one turned it again in case there should be a book that had escaped notice, a book you'd been wanting to read all your life. If one were to find such a thing, here and now, on this last stage, this last stop . . . She felt strong hope, the excitation of weariness and tedium perhaps. They came round – *Something of Value, Kamasutra, Tropic of Capricorn.*

She went to the seat where she had left her things and loaded up again, the coat, the shoulder-bag bearing down. Somebody had fallen asleep, mouth open, bottom fly-button undone, an Austrian hat with plaited cord and feather cutting into his damp brow. How long had they been in this place? What time was it where she had left? (Some airports had a whole series of clock-faces showing what time it was everywhere.) Was it still yesterday, there? – Or tomorrow? And where she was going? She thought, I shall find out when I get there.

A pair of curio venders had unpacked their wares in a corner. People stood about in a final agony of indecision: What would he do with a thing like that? Will she appreciate it, I mean? A woman repeated as she must have done in bazaars and shops and market-places all over the world: I've seen them for half the price . . . But this was the last stop of all, the last chance *to take back something*. How else stake a claim? The last place of all the other places of the world.

Bone bracelets lay in a collapsed spiral of overlapping circles. Elephant-hair ones fell into the pattern of the Olympic symbol. There were the ivory paper-knives and the little pictures of palm trees, huts and dancers on black paper. The vender, squatting in the posture that derives from the necessity of the legless beggar to sit that way and has become as much a mark of the street professional – in such towns as the one that must be somewhere behind the airport – as the hard-top brief-case was of the international businessman drinking beer at the bar, importuned her with the obligation to buy. To refuse was to upset the ordination of roles. He was there to sell 'ivory' bracelets and 'African' art; they – these people shut up for him in the building – had been brought there to buy. He had a right to be angry. But she shook her head, she shook her head, while he tried out his few words of German and French (*billig, bon marché*) as if it could only be a matter of finding the right cue to get her to play the part assigned to her. He seemed to threaten, in his own tongue, finally, his head in its white skull-cap hunched between jutting knees. But she was looking again at the glass case full of tropical butterflies under the President's picture. The picture was vivid, and new; a general successful in a coup only months ago, in full dress uniform, splendid as the dark one among the Magi. The butterflies, relic of some colonial conservationist society, were beginning to fall away from their pins in grey crumbs and gauzy fragments. But there was one big as a bat and brilliantly emblazoned as the general: something in the soil and air, in whatever existed out there – whatever 'out there' there was – that caused nature and culture to imitate each other . . .?

If it were possible to take a great butterfly. Not take back; just take. But she had the Swiss knife and the bottles, of course. The plastic card. It would see her onto the plane once more. Once the plastic card was handed over, nowhere to go but across the tarmac and up the stairway into the belly of the plane, no turning back past the air-hostess in her leopard-skin pillbox, past the barrier. It wasn't allowed; against regulations. The plastic card would send her to the plane, the plane would arrive at the end of the journey, the Swiss knife would be handed over for a kiss, the bottles would be exchanged for an embrace – she was shaking her head at the curio vender (he had actually got up from his knees and come after her, waving his pictures), *no thanks, no thanks.* But he wouldn't give up and she had to move away, to walk up and down once more in the hot, enclosed course dictated by people's feet, the up-ended chairs and tables, the little shored-up piles of hand-luggage. The Consul was swinging the child in red boots by its hands. It was half-whimpering, half-laughing, yelling to be let down, but the larger version of the same model, the mother, was laughing in a way to make her small breasts shake for the Consul, and to convey to everyone how marvellous such a distinguished man was with children.

There was a gritty crackle and then the announcement in careful, African-accented English, of the departure of the flight. A kind of concerted shuffle went up like a sigh: at last! The red-booted mother was telling her child it was silly to cry, the Consul was gathering their things together, the woman was winding the orange thread for her needlework rapidly round a spool, the sleepers woke and the beer-drinkers threw the last of their foreign small change on the bar counter. No queue outside the Ladies' now and the woman in the beige trousers knew there was plenty of time before the second call. She went in and, once more, unharnessed herself among the crumpled paper towels and spilt powder. She tipped all the liquid-soap containers in turn until she found one that wasn't empty; she washed her hands thoroughly in hot and then cold water and put her wet palms on the back of her neck, under her hair. She went to one of the row of mirrors and looked at what she saw there a moment, and then took out from under the liquor bottles, the Swiss knife and the documents, the hairbrush. It was full of hair; a web of dead hairs that bound the bristles together so that they could not go through a head of live hair. She raked her fingers slowly through the bristles and was aware of a young Indian woman at the next mirror, moving quickly and efficiently about an elaborate toilet. The Indian back-combed the black, smooth hair cut in Western style to hang on her shoulders, painted her eyes, shook her ringed hands dry rather than use the paper towels, sprayed French perfume while she extended her neck, re-pleated the green and silver sari that left bare a small roll of lavender-grey flesh between waist and *choli.*

This is the final call for all passengers.

The hair from the brush was no-colour, matted and coated with fluff. Twisted round the forefinger (like the orange thread for the spaniel's ears) it became a fibrous funnel, dusty and obscene. She didn't want the Indian girl to be confronted with it and hid it in her palm while she went over to the dustbin. But the Indian girl saw only herself, watching her reflection appraisingly as she turned and swept out.

The brush went easily through the living hair, now. Again and again, until it was quite smooth and fell, as if it had a memory, as if it were cloth that had been folded and ironed a certain way, along the lines in which it had been arranged by professional hands in another hemisphere. A latecomer rushed into one of the lavatories, sounded the flush and hurried out, plastic card in hand.

The woman in the beige trousers had put on lipstick and run a nailfile under her nails. Her bag was neatly packed. She dropped a coin in the saucer set out, like an offering for some humble household god, for the absent attendant. The African voice was urging all passengers to proceed immediately through Gate B. The voice had some difficulty with *l*'s, pronouncing them more like *r*'s; a pleasant, reasoning voice, asking only for everyone to present the boarding pass, avoid delay, come quietly.

She went into one of the lavatories marked 'Western-type toilet' that bolted automatically as the door shut, a patent device ensuring privacy; there was no penny to pay. She had the coat and bag with her and arranged them, the coat folded and balanced on the bag, on the cleanest part of the floor. She thought what she remembered thinking so many times before: not much time, I'll have to hurry. That was what the plastic card was for – surety for not being left behind, never. She had it stuck in the neck of the shirt now, in the absence of a convenient pocket; it felt cool and wafer-stiff as she put it there but had quickly taken on the warmth of her body. Some tidy soul determined to keep up Western-type standards had closed the lid and she sat down as if on a bench – the heat and the weight of the paraphernalia she had been carrying about were suddenly exhausting. She thought she would smoke a cigarette; there was no time for that. But the need for a cigarette hollowed out a deep sigh within her and she got the pack carefully out of the pocket of her coat without disturbing the arrangement on the floor. All passengers delaying the departure of the flight were urged to proceed immediately through Gate B. Some of the words were lost over the echoing intercommunication system and at times the only thing that could be made out was the repetition, Gate B, a vital fact from which all grammatical contexts could fall away without rendering the message unintelligible. Gate B. If you remembered, if you knew Gate B, the key to mastery of the whole procedure remained intact with you. Gate B was the converse of the open sesame; it would keep you, passing safely through it, in the known, familiar, and inescapable, safe from caves of treasure and shadow. *Immediately. Gate B. Gate B.*

She could sense from the different quality of the atmosphere outside the door, and the doors beyond it, that the hall was emptying now. They were trailing, humping along under their burdens – the petit-point, the child in red boots – to the gate where the girl in the leopard-skin pillbox collected their shiny cards.

She took hers out. She looked around the cell as one looks around for a place to set down a vase of flowers or a note that mustn't blow away. It would not flush down the outlet; plastic doesn't disintegrate in water. As she had idly noticed before, it wouldn't easily tear up. She was not at all agitated; she was simply looking for somewhere to dispose of it, now. She heard the voice (was there a shade of hurt embarrassment in the rolling *r*-shaped *l*'s) appealing to the passenger who was holding up flight so-and-so to please ... She noticed for the first time that there was actually a tiny window, with the sort of pane that tilts outwards from the bottom, just above the cistern. She stood on the seat-lid and tried to see out, just managing to post the shiny card like a letter through the slot.

Gate B, the voice offered, *Gate B*. But to pass through Gate

B you had to have a card, without a card Gate B had no place in the procedure. She could not manage to see anything at all, straining precariously from up there, through the tiny window; there was no knowing at all where the card had fallen. But as she half-jumped, half-clambered down again, for a second the changed angle of her vision brought into sight something like a head – the top of a huge untidy palm tree, up in the sky, rearing perhaps between buildings or above shacks and muddy or dusty streets where there were donkeys, bicycles and bare-foot people. She saw it only for that second but it was so very clear, she saw even that it was an old palm tree, the fronds rasping and sharpening against each other. And there was a crow – she was sure she had seen the black flap of a resident crow.

She sat down again. The cigarette had made a brown aureole round itself on the cistern. In the corner what she had thought was a date-pit was a dead cockroach. She flicked the dead cigarette butt at it. Heel-taps cluttered into the outer room, an African voice said, Who is there? Please, are you there? She did not hold her breath or try to keep particularly still. There was no one there. All the lavatory doors were rattled in turn. There was a high-strung pause, as if the owner of the heels didn't know what to do next. Then the heels rang away again and the door of the Ladies' swung to with the heavy sound of fanned air.

There were bursts of commotion without, reaching her muffledly where she sat. The calm grew longer. Soon the intermittent commotion would cease; the jets must be breathing fire by now, the belts fastened and the cigarettes extinguished, although the air-conditioning wouldn't be working properly yet, on the ground, and they would be patiently sweating. They couldn't wait for ever, when they were so nearly there. The plane would be beginning to trundle like a huge perambulator, it would be turning, winking, shuddering in summoned power.

Take off. It was perfectly still and quiet in the cell. She thought of the great butterfly; of the general with his beautiful markings of braid and medals. Take off.

So that was the sort of place it was: crows in old dusty palm trees, crows picking the carrion in open gutters, legless beggars threatening in an unknown tongue. Not Gate B, but some other gate. Suppose she were to climb out that window, would they ask her for her papers and put her in some other cell, at the general's pleasure? The general had no reason to trust anybody who did not take Gate B. No sound at all, now. The lavatories were given over to their own internal rumblings; the cistern gulped now and then. She was quite sure, at last, that flight so-and-so had followed its course; was gone. She lit another cigarette. She did not think at all about what to do next, not at all; if she had been inclined to think that, she would not have been sitting wherever it was she was. The butterfly, no doubt, was extinct and the general would dislike strangers, the explanations (everything has an explanation) would formulate themselves, in her absence, when the plane reached its destination. The duty-free liquor could be poured down the lavatory, but there remained the problem of the Swiss pocket knife. And yet – through the forbidden doorway: grass, bougainvillaea trained like standard roses, a road glimpsed there!

The Life of the Imagination

As a child she did not inhabit their world, a place where whether the so-and-sos would fit in at dinner, and whose business it was to see that the plumber was called, and whether the car should be traded in or overhauled were the daily entries in a ledger of living. The sum of it was the comfortable, orderly house, beds with turned-down sheets from which nightmares and dreams never overstepped the threshold of morning, good night kisses as routine as the cleaning of teeth, a woman stating her truth, 'Charles would never eat a warmed-over meal,' a man defining his creed, 'One thing I was taught young, the value of money.'

From the beginning, for her, it was the mystery and not the carefully knotted net with which they covered it, as the high-wire performer is protected from the fall. Instead of dust under the beds there was (for her) that hand that Malte Laurids Brigge saw reaching out towards him in the dark beneath his mother's table. Only she was not afraid; as she read, later, he was; she recognized, and grasped it.

And she never let go.

She did not make the mistake of thinking that because of this she must inevitably be able to write or paint; that was just another of the axioms that did for them (Barbara has such a vivid imagination, she is so artistic). She knew it was one thing to have entry to the other world, and another entirely to bring something of it back with you. She studied biology at the university for a while (the subject, incising soft fur and skin to get at the complexities beneath, lured her, and they heard there were good positions going for girls with a B.Sc. degree) but then left and took a job in a municipal art gallery. She began by sorting sepia postcards and went on to dust Chinese ceramic roof-tiles and to learn how to clean paintings. The smell of turpentine, size and coffee in the room where she and the director worked was her first intimacy. They wondered how she could be so happy there, cut off from the company of young people, and once her father remarked half-meaningfully that he hoped the director wouldn't get any ideas.

The director had many ideas, including the only one her father thought of. He was an oldish man – to her, at the time, anyway – with the proboscis-face that often goes with an inquiring mind, and a sudden nakedness of tortoiseshell-coloured eyes when he took off his huge glasses. His wife said, 'It's wonderful for Dan to have you working for him. He's always been one of those men who are at their best mentally only when they are more or less in love.' He told his assistant the story of Wu Ch'eng-ên's characters, the monkey, the pilgrim Tripitaka, Sandy, Pigsy and the two horses she had dusted, as well as giving her a masterly analysis of the breakdown of feudalism in relation to the success of the Long March. He had a collection of photographs he had taken of intricate machinery and microphotography of the cells of plants, and together, using her skill in dissecting rats and frogs and grasshoppers, they added blow-ups of animal tissue. He kissed her occasionally, but rather as if that were simply part of the order of the cosmos; his lips were thin, now, and he knew it. It was through him that she met and fell in love with the young architect whom she married, and with whom she went to Japan, where he had won a scholarship to the University of Tokyo. They wandered about the East and Europe together for a year or two (it was just as her parents expected; she had no proper home) and then came back to South Africa where he became a very successful architect indeed and made an excellent living.

It was as simple and confounding as that. Government administration as well as the great mining and industrial companies employed him to design one public building after another. He and Barbara had a serene, self-effacing house on a *kopje* outside Pretoria – the garden demonstrated how well the spare, indigenous thorn trees of the Middle Veld followed the

Japanese architectural idiom. They had children. Barbara remained, in her late thirties, a thin, tall creature with a bony face darkened by freckles, good-looking and much given to her own company. Money changed her dress little, and her tastes not at all; she was able to indulge them rather more. She had a *pondokkie* down in the Low Veld, on the Crocodile River, where she went sometimes in the winter to stay for a week or two on her own. Marriage was not possible, of course. Certainly not of true minds, because if one is ever going to find release from the mesmerism of appearances one is condemned to make the effort by oneself. And daily intimacy was an inevitable attempt to avoid this that left one sharing bed, bathroom and table, solitary as in any crowd. She and Arthur, her husband, knew it; they got on almost wordlessly well, now and then turned instinctively to each other, and were alone, he with his work and she with her books and her *pondokkie*. They made their children happy. The school headmaster said they were the most 'creative' children that had ever passed through his hands (Barbara's children are so artistic, Barbara's children are so imaginative).

They got measles and ran sudden fevers at awkward times, just like other children, however, and one evening when Barbara and Arthur were about to go out to dinner, Pete was discovered to have a high temperature. The dinner was for a visiting Danish architect who had particularly requested to meet Arthur, so he went on ahead while Barbara stayed to see what the doctor would say. She had not been particularly pleased to hear that the family doctor was away on holiday in Europe and his locum tenens would be coming instead. He was perhaps a little surprised to be met at the door by a woman in evening dress – the house itself was something that made unexpected demands on the attention of people who had not seen anything like it before. She felt the necessity to explain her appearance, partly to disguise the slight hostility she felt towards him for being a substitute for a reassuring face – 'We were just going out when I noticed my son looked like a beetroot.'

He smiled. 'It's a change from curlers and dressing-gowns.'

And they stood there, she in her long dress, he with a coat and brown bag, as if for a split second the situation of their confrontation was not clear; had they bumped into one another, stupidly both dodging in the same direction to avoid colliding in the street? Then the lapse closed and they proceeded to the bedroom where Pete and Bruce sat up in their beds expectantly. Pete said, 'That's not our doctor.'

'No, I know, this is Doctor Asher, he's looking after everybody while Doctor Dickson's away.'

'You won't give me an injection?' said Pete.

'I don't think you've got the sort of sickness that's going to need an injection,' the man said. 'Anyway, I give injections so fast you don't even know they've happened. Really.'

The little one, Bruce, giggled, flopped back in bed and pulled the sheet over his mouth.

The doctor said, 'You mustn't laugh at me. You can ask my children. One, two – before you can count three – it's done.'

Bruce said to him, 'It's not nice to swank.'

The doctor looked up over his open bag and appeared to flinch at this grown-up dictum. 'I'm sorry. I won't do it any more.'

When he had examined Pete he prescribed a mixture that Dr Dickson had often given the children; Barbara went to look in the medicine chest, and there was an almost full bottle there. Pete had swollen glands at the base of his skull and under the jawline. 'We'll watch it,' the doctor said, as Barbara preceded him down the passage. 'I've seen several cases of glandular fever since I've been here. Ring me in the morning if you're worried.' Again they stood in the entrance, she with her hands hanging at the sides of her long skirt, he getting into his coat. He was no taller than she, and probably about the same age, but tired, with the travel-worn look of general practitioners, perpetually lugging a bag around with them. His hair was a modified version of the sort of Julius Caesar cut affected by architects, journalists and advertising men; doctors usually stuck to short back and sides. She thanked him, using his name, and he remarked, pausing at the door, 'By the way, it's Usher – with a U.'

'Oh, I'm sorry – I misheard, over the phone. Usher.'

He was looking up and around the house. 'Japanese style, isn't it? They grow those miniature trees – amazing. There was an article about them the other day, I can't remember where I ... What d'you call it?'

She had kept from childhood an awkward gesture of jerking her chin when embarrassed. One look at the house and people racked their brains for something apposite to say and up came those horrible little stunted trees. 'Oh yes. Bonsai. Thank you very much. Good night.'

When he had gone she went at once to give Pete his medicine and the nanny the telephone number of the hotel where the dinner was being held. Afterwards, she remembered with a detached clarity those few minutes before she left the house, when she was in and out of her son's room: the light that seemed reddish, with the stuffy warmth of childhood colouring it, the stained rugs, the nursery-school daubs stuck on the walls, Dora's cheerfully scornful African voice and the hoist of her big rump as she bent about tidying up, the smell of fever on Pete's lips as she kissed him and the encounter, under the hand she leaned on, with the comforting midden of a child's bed – bits of raw potato he had been using as ammunition in a pea-shooter, the hard shape of a piece of jigsaw puzzle, the wooden spatula the doctor had used to flatten his tongue. And it seemed to her that even at the time, she had had a rare momentary vision of herself (she was not a woman given to awareness of creating effects). She had thought – moving between the small beds slowly because of the long dress, perfumed and painted – this is the image of the mother that men have often chosen to perpetuate, the autobiographers, the Prousts. This is what I may be for one of these little boys when I have become an old woman with bristles on her chin, dead.

Pete was better next day. The doctor came at about half past one, when the child was asleep and she was eating her lunch off a tray in the sun. The servant led the doctor out onto the terrace. He didn't want to disturb her; but she was simply having a snack, as he could see. He sat down while she told him about the child. She had a glass of white wine beside her plate of left-over fish salad – the wine was a left-over, too, but still, what interest could that be to him, whether or not she habitually bibbed wine alone at lunch? The man looked with real pleasure round the calm and sunny terrace and she felt sorry for him because he thought bonsai trees were wonderful. 'Have a glass of wine – it's lovely and cold.' Her bony feet were bare in the winter sun. He refused; of course, a doctor can't do as he likes. But he took out a pipe, and smoked that. 'The sun's so pleasant, I must say Pretoria has its points.' They were both looking at her toes, on each foot the second one was crooked; it was because the child was asleep, of course, that he sat there. He told her that he came from Cape Town, where it rained all winter. They went upstairs to look at the child; he was breathing evenly and soundlessly. 'Leave him,' the doctor said. Downstairs he added, 'Another day or two in bed, I'd say. I'd like to check those glands again.'

He came just before two the following day. This time he accepted a cup of coffee. It was just as it had been yesterday; it might have been yesterday. It was almost the same time of day. The sun had exactly the same strength. They sat on the broad brick seat with its thick cushion. His pipe smoke hung a little haze before their eyes. She was telling him the child was so much better that it really was impossible to keep him in bed, when he looked at her amusedly, as if he had found them both out – himself and her – and his arm, with the hand curved to bring her to him, drew her in. They kissed and without thinking at all whether she wanted to kiss him or not, she found herself anxious to be skilful. She seemed to manage very well because the kissing went on for minutes, their heads turning this way and that as their mouths slowly detached and met.

And so it began. When they drew back from each other the words flew to her: why this man, for heaven's sake – why you? And because she was ashamed of the thought, she said aloud instead, 'Why me?'

He found this apparent unawareness of her own attractions so moving that he kissed her fiercely, answering, for her, both questions, the spoken and unspoken.

While they were kissing she became aware of the slightest, quickest sideways movement of the one slate-coloured eye she could see, a second before she herself heard the squeak of the servant's sandshoes approaching from within the house. They drew apart, she in jerky haste, he with composed swiftness so that the intimacy between them held good even while he put his pipe in his pocket, took out a prescription pad and was remarking, when the servant picked up the coffee tray, 'It mightn't be a bad idea to keep some sort of mild antipyretic in the house, not as strong as that mixture he's been having, I mean, but...'

So it began. The love-making, the absurdities of concealment; even the acceptance of the knowledge that this hard-working doctor with the sickle-line of a smile cut down either side of his mouth, and the brown, coarse-grained forehead, had gone through it all before, perhaps many times. So it began, exactly as it was to be.

They made love the first time in the flat he was living in temporarily. It was a ravishing experience for both of them and when it was over – for the moment – they knew that they must turn their attention urgently and at once to the intensely practical business of how, when and where they were to continue to be together. After a month his wife came up from Cape Town and things were more difficult. He had taken a house for his family; the sublet flat with other people's books and sheets and bric-à-brac, in which he and Barbara were the only objects familiar to each other, became a paradise lost. They drove then, separately, all the way to Johannesburg to spend an afternoon together in an hotel (Pretoria was too small a place for one to expect to go unrecognized). He was tied to his endless working hours; they had nowhere to go. Their problem was passion but they could hope for only the most down-to-earth, realistic solutions. One could not flinch from them. After the last patient left the consulting rooms in the evening the building was deserted – an office block. He made little popping noises on his pipe as he decided they would be quite safe there. Deaf and blind with anticipation of the meeting, she would come from the side street where her car was parked, through the dark foyer, past the mops and bucket of the African cleaner, up in the lift with its glowing eye showing as it rose through successive levels, then along the corridors of closed doors and commercial nameplates until she was there: Dr J. McDow Dickson, M.B.B.Ch. Edin. Consulting Hours, Mornings 11–1, Afternoons 4–6. On the old day-bed in Dr Dickson's anteroom they made love, among the medical insurance calendars and the desk accessories advertising antibiotics. Once the cleaner was heard turning his pass-key in the waiting-room door; once someone (a patient, no doubt) hammered at it for a while, and then went away. She had always been sure, without censure, that shabby love-affairs would be useless, for her. She learnt that shabbiness is the judgement of the outsider, the one left in the cold; there are no shabby love-affairs for those who are the lovers.

They met wherever and however and for whatever length of time they could, but still by far the greater part of their time was spent apart. Communications, movements, meeting-places – all this had to be settled as between two secret agents whom the world must not suspect to be in contact. In order to plan strategy, each had to brief the other about the normal pattern of his life: this was how they got to know, bit by bit, that yawning area of each other's lives that existed outside one another's arms. 'On Thursday nights I'm always alone because Arthur takes a seminar at the university.' 'You can safely ring me any Sunday morning between eight and nine because Yvonne goes to Mass.'

So his wife was a Catholic. Well, yes, but he was not. Of course that meant that his children were being brought up as Catholics. One evening when he and Barbara were putting on their clothes again in the consulting rooms she had seen the picture of the three little girls, under the transparent plastic slot in his wallet. White-blond hair, short and straight as a nylon toothbrush, ribbon sashes, net petticoats, white socks held by elastic – the children of one of those nice, neat pretty women who look after them just as carefully as they used to take care of their dolls. Barbara never met her. He said that the local doctors' wives were being very kind – she was playing tennis regularly at the house of one, and another had little girls the same age who had become inseparable from his girls. If he and Barbara met at the consulting rooms on Friday evenings, he had to keep an eye on his watch – 'Bridge night,' he said, doggedly, resignedly. Sometimes he said, 'Blast bridge night.'

Between embraces, confessions, questions came easily, up to a point. 'You lead a very different life,' he said.

He meant 'from mine'. Or from hers, perhaps – his wife's.

Lying there, Barbara pulled a dismissing face.

'Oh yes.' He did not want to be excepted, indulged, out of love; he had his own regard for the truth. 'What was wrong about the Japanese trees, that time – that first night I came to your house – what did I say? There was such a look on your face.'

'Oh that. The bonsai business.' The reproach was for herself; he didn't understand the shrinking in repugnance from 'good taste' – well, wasn't the shrinking as daintily fastidious, in its way, as the 'good taste' itself? You went whoring after one concept or the other of your own sensibility. 'Not different at all,' – she returned to his original remark; she had this quality, he noticed, of keeping a series of remarks you had passed laid out before her, and then unhesitatingly turning to pick up this one or that – 'It's like putting a net into the sea. You bring up small fish or big fish, weeds, muck, little bright bits of things. But the water, the element that's living – that's drained away.'

'– So tonight it's bridge,' she added, putting out her hand to caress his chest.

He took the pipe out of his mouth. 'When you're down at the Crocodile,' he said – they called her *pondokkie* that because it was on the Crocodile River – 'What are you doing there, when you're alone?'

She lay under his gaze; she felt the quality she had for him, awkwardly, as if he had stuck a jewel on her forehead. She didn't answer.

'Reading, eh? Reading and thinking your own thoughts.' For years he had barely had time to get through the medical journals.

She was seeing the still, dry stretch to the horizon, each

thorn bush like every other thorn bush, the narrow cattle paths leading back on themselves through the clean, dry grass, the silence into which one seemed to fall, at midday, as if into an airpocket; the silence there would be one day when one's heart stopped, while everything went on as it did in that veld silence, the hard trees waiting for sap to rise, the dead grass waiting to be sloughed off the new under rain, the boulders cracking into new forms under frost and sun.

But alive under her hand was the hair of his breast, still damp and soft from contact with her body, and she said, keeping her teeth together, 'I wish we could go there. I wish we were in bed there now.'

That winter she did not go once to the shack. It had become nothing but a shelter where they could have made love, whole nights and days. There were so many hours when they could not see each other. Could not even telephone; he was at home with his family, she with hers. Such slow stretches of mornings, thawing in the sun; such long afternoons when the interruption of her children was a monstrous breaking-in upon – what? She was doing nothing. She saw him as she had once watched him without his being aware of her, crossing the street and walking the length of a block to their meeting-place: a slight man with a pipe held between his teeth in a rather brutal way, a smiling curve of the mouth denied by the downward, inward lines of brow and eyelids as his head bobbed. In his hand the elegant pigskin bag she had given him because it was easy to explain away as the gift of some grateful patient. He sees nobody, only where he is going. Sitting at dinner-parties or reading at night, she saw him like this in broad daylight, crossing the street, bag in hand. It seemed she could follow him through all the hill-cupped small city, make out his back among all others, crossing the square past Dr Dolittle in his top hat (that was what her little boys thought the statue of President Kruger was), doing the rounds in the suburbs, the car full of pipe-smoke and empty phials with their necks snapped off, the smile a grim habit, greeting no one.

Sometimes he materialized at her own door – he'd had a call

in the neighbourhood, or told the nurse so, anyway. It would be in the morning, when the boys were at school and Arthur was at the town studio. He always went straight to the telephone and rang up the consulting rooms, so that he'd be covered if his car happened to be seen: 'Oh Birdie, I'm around Muckleneuk – if there's anyone I ought to drop in on out this way? My next call will be the Wilson child, Waterkloof Road, so –' Then they would sit on the terrace again and have coffee. And he would give his expert glance round doors and windows before kissing her; he smelt of the hospital theatre he had been in, or the soap he had washed his hands with in other people's houses. He wore a pullover his mother had sent him, he had pigskin gloves. Yvonne had bought him – he smiled, telling it – because she thought the smart new bag made his old ones look so shabby. For Barbara there was the bloom on him of the times when he was not with her.

She had never been in his house, of course, and she did not know the disposition of the rooms, or the sound of voices calling through it in the early morning rush to get to school and hospital rounds (she knew he got up very early, before she would even be awake), or the kind of conversation that came to life over drinks when friends were there, or the atmosphere, so strongly personal in every house, of the hour late at night when outsiders have gone and doors are being locked and lights switched off, one by one.

She had never been with him in the company of other people (unless one counted Pete and Bruce) and she did not know how he would appear in their eyes, or what his manner would be. She listened with careful detachment when he telephoned the nurse; he had a tired, humorous way with her – but that was just professional camaraderie, with a touch of the flirtatiousness that pleases old ladies. Once or twice he had had to phone his wife in Barbara's presence: it was the anonymous telecommunication of long marriage – 'Yvonne? I'm on my way. Oh, twenty minutes or so. Well, if he does, say I'll be in any time after nine. Yes. No, I won't. See you.'

When they were together after love-making they talked about their past lives and discussed his future. He intended, within the next year, to go to America to do what he had always wanted – biological research. They discussed in great detail the planning of his finances: he had sold his practice in Cape Town in order to be able to keep his family while studying on a grant he'd been promised. The six months' locum-tenancy was a stop-gap between selling the practice and taking up the grant in Boston. He had moments of deep uncertainty: he should have gone ten years ago, young and single-minded – but, helplessly, even then there was a girl, marriage, babies. From the depths of his uncertainty, he and Barbara looked at each other like two prisoners who wake up and find themselves on the floor of the same cell. He said, as if for what it was worth, 'I love you.' They became absorbed again in the questions of how he should best use his opportunities in America, and under whom he should try to get the chance to work. And then it was time to get dressed, time up, time to go, time to be home to change for his bridge evening, time to be home to receive Arthur's friends. Standing in the lift together they were silent, weary, at one. They left the consulting-room building separately; as she walked away he became again that figure crossing streets, going in and out of houses and car, pigskin doctor's bag in hand, seeing nobody, only where he was going.

Her mind constructed snatches of dialogue, like remembered fragments of a play. She was following him home to the bridge table (she had never played card games) or the dinner-table – there was a roast, that would be the sort of thing, a brown leg of pork with apple sauce, and he was carving, knowing what cut each member of the little family liked best. The white-haired, white-socked little girls had washed their hands. The bridge players talked with the ease of colleagues, the wives were saying, 'John wouldn't touch it,' 'I must say the only thing he always does remember is when to pay the insurance,' 'I can't get anyone to do shirt collars properly.' She had the feeling his wife bought his clothes for him; but the haircut – that he chose for himself. As he chose her, Barbara, and other women. On Sundays she lay with an unread book on the terrace or laughed and talked without listening among Arthur's friends (they all seemed to be Arthur's friends, now) and he was running about some clean, hard tennis court, red in the face, agile, happy perhaps, in the mindless happiness of physical exercise. She was not jealous, only slightly excited by the thought of him with her completely out of mind. Or perhaps this Sunday they had taken the children on some outing. Once when she had visualized him all afternoon on that tennis court, he had happened to mention that Sunday afternoon had been swallowed up in a family outing – the children had heard about a game park in Krugersdorp. The plain, white-haired little girl clambered over him to see better; was he irritated? Or was he smoothing the hair behind the child's ears with that lover's gesture of his, also, perhaps, a father's gesture? She read over again a paragraph in the book lying between her elbows on the grass: '... the word *lolo* means both "soul" and "butterfly" ... the dual meaning is due to the fact that the chrysalis resembles a shrouded corpse and that the butterfly emerges from it like the soul from the body of a sleeping man.' But the idea had no meaning for her. The words floated on her mind; no, a moth, quite an ordinary-looking, protectively-coloured moth, not noticed going about the streets, quickly crossing the square in the early evening, coming softly along the corridor, touching softly. Fierily, making quick the sleeping body.

One night when she had the good luck to be alone for a few days (Arthur was in the Cape), he was able to slip away and come to her at home. This rare opportunity required careful planning, like every other arrangement between them. He said he was going to a meeting of the medical association; she had an early dinner, to be sure the servants would be out of the way. She saw to it that all the windows of the house except those of her bedroom should be in darkness, so that any unexpected caller would presume she had gone to bed and not disturb her. In fact, she did lie on her bed, fully dressed, waiting for him. She had given him the key of the side door, off the terrace, that afternoon. He came with a quiet, determined hesitancy, through another man's house. He had never been into the bedroom before but he knew where the children's rooms were. When she heard him reach the passage where a turn divided the parents' quarters from the children's, she got up and went softly to meet him. But the little boys were asleep, long ago. She took his two clean hands, dryly cold from the winter night, in hers, and then they crept along together. In the bedroom, when she had shut the door behind them, she was cold and trembling, as if she too had just found shelter.

He had to leave not long after the time the meeting would end; now, because this was her own bed, in her own home, she lay there naked, flung back under the disarray of bedclothes, and watched him dress alone. He took her brush and put it through his hair before the mirror, with a quick, knowing look at himself. He sat on the bed, like a doctor, to embrace her a last time. She watched him softly release the handle of the door, almost without a click, as he closed it on her, heard him going evenly, quietly down the corridor, listened to the faint creak and stir of him making his way through the big living room, and then, after a pause, heard the clip of his footsteps dying away across the terrace. The engine of the car started up: shadows from its lights flew across the bedroom windows.

She put up her hand to switch off the bed lamp but did not move her head or body. She lay in the dark for a long time just as he had left her; perhaps she slept. There seemed to be a dark wind blowing through her hollow mind; she was awake, and there was a night wind come up, the cold gale of the winter veld, pressing against the walls and windows like pressure in one's ears. A thorn branch scrabbled on the terrace wall. She heard dry leaves swirl and trail across the flagstones. And irregularly, at long intervals, a door banged without engaging its latch. She tried to sleep or to return to sleep, but some part of her mind waited for the impact of the door in the wind. And it came, again and again. Slowly, reasoned thought cohered round the sound: she identified the direction from which it came, her mind travelled through the house the way he had gone, and arrived at the terrace door. The door banged, with a swinging shudder, again.

He's left the door open. She saw it; saw the gaping door, and the wind bellying the long curtains and sending papers skimming about the room, the leaves sailing in and slithering across the floors. The whole house was filling up with the wind. There had been burglaries in the suburb lately. This was one of the few houses without an alarm system – she and Arthur had refused to imprison themselves in the white man's fear of attack on himself and his possessions. Yet now the door was open like the door of a deserted house and she found herself believing, like any other suburban matron, that someone must enter. They would come in unheard, with that wind, and approach through the house, black men with their knives in their hands. She, who had never submitted to this sort of fear ever in her life, could hear them coming, hear them breathe under their dirty rag masks and their *tsotsi* caps. They had killed an old man on a farm outside Pretoria last week; someone described in the papers as a mother of two had held them off, at her bedside, with a golf club. Multiple wounds, the old man had received, multiple wounds.

She was empty, unable to summon anything but this stale fantasy, shared with the whole town, the whole white population. She lay there possessed by it, and she thought, she violently longed – they will come straight into the room and stick a knife in me. No time to cry out. Quick. Deep. Over.

The light came instead. Her sons began to play the noisy whispering games of children, about the house in the very early morning.

Africa Emergent

He's in prison now, so I'm not going to mention his name. It mightn't be a good thing, you understand. – Perhaps you think you understand too well; but don't be quick to jump to conclusions from five or six thousand miles away: if you lived here, you'd understand something else – friends know that shows of loyalty are all right for children holding hands in the school playground; for us they're luxuries, not important and maybe dangerous. If I said, I was a friend of so-and-so, black man awaiting trial for treason, what good would it do him? And, who knows, it might draw just that decisive bit more attention to me. *He*'d be the first to agree.

Not that one feels that if they haven't got enough in my dossier already, this would make any difference; and not that he really was such a friend. But that's something else you won't understand; everything is ambiguous, here. We hardly know, by now, what we can do and what we can't do; it's difficult to say, goaded in on oneself by laws and doubts and rebellion and caution and – not least – self-disgust, what is or is not a friendship. I'm talking about black and white, of course. If you stay with it, boy, on the white side in the country clubs and garden suburbs if you're white, and on the black side in the locations and beerhalls if you're black, none of this applies, and you can go all the way to your segregated cemetery in peace. But neither he nor I did.

I began mixing with blacks out of what is known as an outraged sense of justice, plus strong curiosity, when I was a student. There were two ways – one was through the white students' voluntary service organization, a kibbutz-type junket where white boys and girls went into rural areas and camped while they built school classrooms for African children. A few coloured and African students from their segregated universities used to come along too, and there was the novelty, not without value, of dossing down alongside them at night, although we knew we were likely to be harbouring Special Branch spies among our willing workers, and we dared not make a pass at the coloured or black girls. The other way – less hard on the hands – was to go drinking with the jazz musicians and journalists, painters and would-be poets and actors who gravitated towards whites partly because such people naturally feel they can make free of the world, and partly because they found an encouragement and appreciation there that was sweet to them. I tried the V.S.O. briefly, but the other way suited me better; anyway, I didn't see why I should help this Government by doing the work it ought to be doing for the welfare of black children.

I'm an architect and the way I was usefully drawn into the black scene was literally that: I designed sets for a mixed-colour drama group got together by a white director. Perhaps there's no urban human group as intimate, in the end, as a company of this kind, and the colour problem made us even closer. I don't mean what *you* mean, the how-do-I-feel-about-that-black-skin stuff; I mean the daily exasperation of getting round, or over, or on top of the colour-bar laws that plagued our productions and our lives. We had to remember to write out 'passes' at night, so that our actors could get home without being arrested for being out after the curfew for blacks, we had to spend hours at the Bantu Affairs Department trying to arrange local residence permits for actors who were being 'endorsed out' of town back to the villages to which, 'ethnically', apparently, they belonged although they'd never set eyes on them, and we had to decide which of us could play the sycophant well enough to persuade the Bantu Commissioner to allow the show to go on the road from one Group Area, designated by colour, to another, or to talk some town clerk into getting his council to agree to the use of a 'white' public hall by the mixed cast. The black actors' lives were in our hands, because they were black and we were white, and could, must, intercede for them. Don't think this made everything love and light between us; in fact it caused endless huffs and rows. A white woman who'd worked like a slave acting as P.R.O.-cum-wardrobe-mistress hasn't spoken to me for years because I made her lend her little car to one of the chaps who'd worked until after the last train went back to the location, and then he kept it the whole weekend and she couldn't get hold of him because, of course, location houses rarely have telephones and once a black man has disappeared among those warrens you won't find him till he chooses to surface in the white town again. And when this one did surface, he was biting, to me, about white bitches' 'patronage' of people they secretly still thought of as 'boys'. Yet our arguments, resentments and misunderstandings were not only as much part of the intimacy of this group as the good times, the parties and the love-making we had, but were more – the defining part, because we'd got close enough to admit argument, resentment and misunderstanding between us.

He was one of this little crowd, for a time. He was a dispatch clerk and then a 'manager' and chucker-out at a black dance club. In his spare time he took a small part in our productions now and then, and made himself generally handy; in the end it was discovered that what he really was good at was front-of-house arrangements. His tubby charm (he was a large young man and a cheerful dresser) was just the right thing to deal with the unexpected moods of our location audiences when we went on tour – sometimes they came stiffly encased in their church-going best and seemed to feel it was vulgar to laugh or respond to what was going on, on stage; in other places they rushed the doors, tried to get in without paying, and were dominated by a *tsotsi*, street urchin, element who didn't want to hear anything but themselves. He was the particular friend – the other, passive half – of a particular friend of mine, Elias Nkomo.

And here I stop short. How shall I talk about Elias? I've never even learnt, in five years, how to think about him.

Elias was a sculptor. He had one of those jobs – messenger 'boy' or some such – that literate young black men can aspire to in a small gold-mining and industrial town outside Johannesburg. Somebody said he was talented, somebody sent him to me – at the beginning, the way for every black man to find himself seems inescapably to lead through a white man. Again, how can I say what his work was like? He came by train to the black people's section of Johannesburg central station, carrying a bulky object wrapped in that morning's newspaper. He was slight, round-headed, tiny-eared, dunly dressed, and with a frown of effort between his eyes, but his face unfolded to a wide, apologetic yet confident smile when he realized that the white man in a waiting car must be me – the meeting had been arranged. I took him back to my 'place' (he always called people's homes that) and he unwrapped the newspaper. What was there was nothing like the clumps of diorite or sandstone you have seen in galleries in New York, London or Johannesburg, marked 'Africa Emergent', 'Spirit of the Ancestors'.

What was there was a goat, or goat-like creature, in the way that a centaur is a horse-like, man-like creature, carved out of streaky knotted wood. It was delightful (I wanted to put out my hand to touch it), it was moving in its somehow concrete diachrony, beast-men, coarse wood–fine workmanship, and there was also something exposed about it (one would withdraw the hand, after all).

I asked him whether he knew Picasso's goats? He had heard of Picasso but never seen any of his work. I showed him a photograph of the famous bronze goat in Picasso's own house; thereafter all his beasts had sex organs as joyful as Picasso's goat's udder, but that was the only 'influence' that ever took, with him. As I say, a white man always intercedes in some way, with a man like Elias; mine was to keep him from those art-loving ladies with galleries who wanted to promote him, and those white painters and sculptors who were willing to have him work under their tutelage. I gave him an old garage (well, that means I took my car out of it) and left him alone, with plenty of chunks of wood.

But Elias didn't like the loneliness of work. That garage never became his 'place'. Perhaps when you've lived in an overcrowded yard all your life the counter-stimulus of distraction becomes necessary to create a tension of concentration. No – well all I really mean is that he liked company. At first he came only at weekends, and then, as he began to sell some of his work, he gave up the messenger job and moved in more or less permanently – we fixed up the 'place' together, putting in a ceiling and connecting water and so on. It was illegal for him to live there in a white suburb, of course, but such laws breed complementary evasions in people like Elias and me and the white building inspector didn't turn a hair of suspicion when I said that I was converting the garage as a flat for my wife's mother. It was better for Elias once he'd moved in; there was always some friend of his sharing his bed, not to mention the girls who did; sometimes the girls were shy little things almost of the kitchenmaid variety, who called my wife 'madam' when they happened to bump into her, crossing the garden, sometimes they were the bewigged and painted actresses from the group who sat smoking and gossiping with my wife while she fed the baby.

And *he* was there more often than anyone – the plump and cheerful front-of-house manager; he was married, but as happens with our sex, an old friendship was a more important factor in his life than a wife and kids – if that's a characteristic of black men, then I must be black under the skin, myself. Elias had become very involved in the theatre group, anyway, like *him*; Elias made some beautiful *papier mâché* gods for a play by a Nigerian that we did – 'spirits of the ancestors' at once amusing and frightening – and once when we needed a singer he surprisingly turned out to have a voice that could phrase a madrigal as easily as whatever the forerunner of Soul was called – I forget now, but it blared hour after hour from the garage when he was working. Elias seemed to like best to work when the other one was around; *he* would sit with his fat boy's legs rolled out before him, flexing his toes in his fashionable shoes, dusting down the lapels of the latest thing in jackets, as he changed the records and kept up a monologue contentedly punctuated by those soft growls and sighs of agreement, those sudden squeezes of almost silent laughter – responses possible only in an African language – that came from Elias as he chiselled and chipped. For they spoke in their own tongue, and I have never known what it was they talked about.

In spite of my efforts to let him alone, inevitably Elias was 'taken up' (hadn't I started the process myself, with that garage?) and a gallery announced itself his agent. He walked about at the opening of his one-man show in a purple turtle-necked sweater I think his best friend must have made him buy, laughing a little, softly, at himself, more embarrassed than pleased. An art critic wrote about his transcendental values and plastic modality, and he said, 'Christ, man, does he dig it or doesn't he?' while we toasted his success in brandy chased with beer – brandy isn't a rich man's sip in South Africa, it's made here and it's what people use to get drunk on.

He earned quite a bit of money that year. Then the gallery-owner and the art critic forgot him in the discovery of yet another interpreter of the African soul, and he was poor again, but he had acquired a patroness who, although she lived far away, did not forget him. She was, as you might have thought, an American lady, very old and wealthy according to South African legend but probably simply a middle-aged widow with comfortable stock holdings and a desire to get in on the cultural ground floor of some form of art collecting not yet overcrowded. She had bought some of his work while a tourist in Johannesburg. Perhaps she did have academic connections with the art world; in any case, it was she who got a foundation to offer Elias Nkomo a scholarship to study in America.

I could understand that he wanted to go simply in order to go: to see the world outside. But I couldn't believe that at this stage he wanted or could make use of formal art-school disciplines. As I said to him at the time, I'm only an architect, but I've had experience of the academic and even, God help us, the frenziedly non-academic approach in the best schools, and it's not for people who have, to fall back on the jargon, found themselves.

I remember he said, smiling, 'You think I've found myself?'

And I said, 'But you've never been lost, man. That very first goat wrapped in newspaper was your goat.'

But later, when he was refused a passport and the issue of his going abroad was much on our minds, we talked again. He wanted to go because he felt he needed some kind of general education, general cultural background that he'd missed, in his six years at the location school. 'Since I've been at your place I've been reading a lot of your books. And man, I know nothing. I'm as ignorant as that kid of yours there in the pram. Right, I've picked up a bit of politics, a few art terms here and there – I can wag my head and say "plastic values" all right, eh? But man, what do I know about life? What do I know about how it all works? How do I know *how* I do the work I do? Why we live and die? – If I carry on here I might as well be carving walking sticks,' he added. I knew what he meant: there are old men, all over Africa, who make a living squatting at a decent distance from tourist hotels, carving fancy walking sticks from local wood, only one step in sophistication below the 'African Emergent' school of sculptors so rapturously acclaimed by gallery owners. We both laughed at this, and following the line of thought suggested to me by this question to himself: 'How do I know how I do the work I do?', I asked him whether in fact there was any sort of traditional skill in his family? As I imagined, there was not –he was an urban slum kid, brought up opposite a municipal beerhall among paraffin-tin utensils and abandoned motor-car bodies which, perhaps curiously, had failed to bring out a Duchamp in him but from which, on the contrary, he had sprung, full-blown, as a classical expressionist. Although there were no rural walking-stick carvers in his ancestry, he did tell me something I had no idea would have been part of the experience of a location childhood – he had been sent, in his teens, to a tribal initiation school in the bush and been circumcised according to rite. He described the experience vividly.

Once all attempts to get him a passport had failed, Elias's desire to go to America became something else, of course: an obsessive resentment against confinement itself. Inevitably, he was given no reason for the refusal. The official answer was the usual one – that it was 'not in the public interest' to reveal the reason for such things. Was it because 'they' had got to know he was 'living like a white man'? (Theory put to me by one of the black actors in the group.) Was it because a critic had dutifully described his work as expressive of the 'agony of the emergent African soul'? Nobody knew. Nobody ever knows. It is enough to be black; blacks are meant to stay put, in their own ethnically-apportioned streets in their own segregated areas, in those parts of South Africa where the government says they belong. Yet – the whole way our lives are manoeuvred, as I say, is an unanswered question – Elias's best friend suddenly got a passport. I hadn't even realized that *he* had been offered a scholarship or a study grant or something, too; *he* was invited to go to New York to study production and the latest acting teachniques (it was the time of the Method rather than Grotowski). And *he* got a passport, 'first try' as Elias said with ungrudging pleasure and admiration; when someone black got a passport, then, there was a collective sense of pleasure in having outwitted we didn't quite know what. So they went together, *he* on his passport, and Elias Nkomo on an exit permit.

An exit permit is a one-way ticket, anyway. When you are granted one at your request but at the government's pleasure, you sign an undertaking that you will never return to South Africa or its mandatory territory, South West Africa. You pledge this with signature and thumb-print. Elias Nkomo never came back. At first he wrote (and he wrote quite often) enthusiastically about the world outside that he had gained, and he seemed to be enjoying some kind of small vogue, not so much as a sculptor as a genuine, real live African Negro who was sophisticated enough to be asked to comment on this and that: the beauty of American women, life in Harlem or Watts, Black Power as seen through the eyes, etc. He sent cuttings from *Ebony* and even from *The New York Times Magazine*. He said that a girl at *Life* was trying to get them to run a piece on his work; his work? – well, he hadn't settled down to anything new, yet, but the art centre was a really swinging place, Christ, the things people were doing, there! There were silences, naturally; we forgot about him and he forgot about us for weeks on end. Then the local papers picked up the sort of news they are alert to from all over the world. Elias Nkomo had spoken at an anti-apartheid rally. Elias Nkomo, in West African robes, was on the platform with Stokely Carmichael.

'Well, why not? He hasn't got to worry about keeping his hands clean for the time when he comes back home, has he?' – My wife was bitter in his defence. Yes, but I was wondering about his work – 'Will they leave him alone to work?' I didn't write to him, but it was as if my silence were read by him: a few months later I received a cutting from some university art magazine devoting a number to Africa, and there was a photograph of one of Elias's wood sculptures, with his handwriting along the margin of the page – *I know you don't think much of people who don't turn out new stuff but some people here seem to think this old thing of mine is good.* It was the sort of wry remark that, spoken aloud to me in the room, would have made us both laugh. I smiled, and meant to write. But within two weeks Elias was dead. He drowned himself early one morning in the river of the New England town where the art school was.

It was like the refusal of the passport; none of us knew why. In the usual arrogance one has in the face of such happenings, I even felt guilty about the letter. Perhaps, if one were thousands of miles from one's own 'place', in some sort of a bad way, just a small thing like a letter, a word of encouragement from someone who had hurt by being rather niggardly with encouragement in the past . . .? And what pathetic arrogance, at that! As if the wisp of a letter, written by someone between other preoccupations, and in substance an encouraging lie (how splendid that your old work is receiving recognition in some piddling little magazine) could be anything round which the hand of a man going down for the second time might close.

Because before Elias went under in that river he must have been deep in forlorn horrors about which I knew nothing, nothing. When people commit suicide they do so apparently out of some sudden self-knowledge that those of us, the living, do not have the will to acquire. That's what's meant by despair, isn't it – what they have come to know? And that's what one means when one says in extenuation of oneself, *I knew so little about him, really*. I knew Elias only in the self that he had presented at my 'place'; why, how out of place it had been, once, when he happened to mention that as a boy he had spent weeks in the bush with his circumcision group! Of course we – his friends – decided out of the facts we knew and our political and personal attitudes, why he had died: and perhaps it is true that he was sick to death, in the real sense of the phrase that has been forgotten, sick unto death with homesickness for the native land that had shut him out for ever and that he was forced to conjure up for himself in the parody of 'native' dress that had nothing to do with his part of the continent, and the shame that a new kind of black platform-solidarity forced him to feel for his old dependence, in South Africa, on the friendship of white people. It was the South African government who killed him, it was culture shock – but perhaps neither our political bitterness nor our glibness with fashionable phrases can come near what combination of forces, within and without, led him to the fatal baptism of that early morning. *It is not in the private interest that this should be revealed.* Elias never came home. That's all.

But his best friend did, towards the end of that year.

He came to see me after he had been in the country some weeks – I'd heard he was back. The theatre group had broken up; it seemed to be that, chiefly, he'd come to talk to me about: he wanted to know if there was any money left in the kitty for him to start up a small theatrical venture of his own, he was eager to use the know-how (his phrase) he'd learned in the States. He was really plump now and he wore the most extraordinary clothes. A Liberace jacket. Plastic boots. An Afro wig that looked as if it had been made out of a bit of karakul from South West Africa. I teased him about it – we were at least good enough friends for that – asking him if he'd really been with the guerrillas instead of Off-Broadway? (There was a trial on at home, at the time, of South African political refugees who had tried to infiltrate through South West Africa.) And felt slightly ashamed of my patronage of his taste when he said with such good humour, 'It's just a fun thing, man, isn't it great?' I was too cowardly to bring the talk round to the point: Elias. And when it couldn't be avoided, I said the usual platitudes and he shook his head at them – 'Hell, man,' and we fell silent. Then he told me that that was how he had got back – because Elias was dead, on the unused portion of Elias's air ticket. *His* study grant hadn't included travel expenses and he'd had to pay his own way over. So he'd had only a one-way ticket, but Elias's scholarship had included a return fare to the student's place of origin. It had been difficult to get the airline to agree to the transfer; he'd had to go to the scholarship foundation people, but they'd been very decent about fixing it for him.

He had told me all this so guilelessly that I was one of the people who became angrily indignant when the rumour began to go around that he was a police agent: who else would have the cold nerve to come back on a dead man's ticket, a dead man who couldn't ever have used that portion of the ticket himself, because he had taken an exit permit? And who could believe the story, anyway? Obviously, *he* had to find some way of explaining why he, a black man like any other, could travel freely back and forth between South Africa and other countries. He had a passport, hadn't he? Well, there you were. Why should *he* get a passport? What black man these days had a passport?

Yes, I was angry, and defended him, by proof of the innocence of the very naïveté with which – a black man, yes, and therefore used to the necessity of salvaging from disaster all his life, unable to afford the nice squeamishness of white men's delicacy – he took over Elias's air ticket because he was alive and needed it, as he might have taken up Elias's coat against the cold. I refused to avoid him, the way some members of the remnant of our group made it clear they did now, and I remained stony-faced outside the complicity of those knowing half-smiles that accompanied the mention of his name. We had never been close friends, of course, but he would turn up from time to time. He could not find theatrical work and had a job as a travelling salesman in the locations. He took to bringing three or four small boys along when he visited us; they were very subdued and whisperingly well-behaved and well-dressed in miniature suits – our barefoot children stared at them in awe. They were his children plus the children of the family he was living with, we gathered. He and I talked mostly about his difficulties – his old car was unreliable, his wife had left him, his commissions were low, and he could have taken up an offer to join a Chicago repertory company if he could have raised the fare to go back to America – while my wife fed ice-cream and cake to the silent children, or my children dutifully placed them one by one on the garden swing. We had begun to be able to talk about Elias's death. He had told me how, in the weeks before he died, Elias would get the wrong way on the moving stairway going down in the subway in New York and keep walking, walking up. 'I thought he was foolin' around, man, you know? Jus' climbin' those stairs and goin' noplace?'

He clung nostalgically to the American idiom; no African talks about 'noplace' when he means 'nowhere'. But he had abandoned the Afro wig and when we got talking about Elias he would hold his big, well-shaped head with its fine, shaven covering of his own wool propped between his hands as if in an effort to think more clearly about something that would never come clear; I felt suddenly at one with him in that gesture, and would say, 'Go on.' He would remember another example of how Elias had been 'acting funny' before he died. It was on one of those afternoon visits that he said, 'And I don't think I ever told you about the business with the students at the college? How that last weekend – before he did it, I mean – he went around and invited everybody to a party, I dunno, a kind of feast he said it was. Some of them said he said a barbecue – you know what that is, same as a *braaivleis*, eh? But one of the others told me afterwards that he'd told them he was going to give them a real African feast, he was going to show them how the country people do it here at home when somebody gets married or there's a funeral or so. He wanted to know where he could buy a goat.'

'A goat?'

'That's right. A live goat. He wanted to kill and roast a goat for them, on the campus.'

It was round about this time that *he* asked me for a loan. I think that was behind the idea of bringing those pretty, dressed-up children along with him when he visited; he wanted firmly to set the background of his obligations and responsibilities before touching me for money. It was rather a substantial sum, for someone of my resources. But he couldn't carry on his job without a new car, and he'd just got the opportunity to acquire a really good second-hand buy. I gave him the money in spite of – because of, perhaps – new rumours that were going around then that, in a police raid on the house of the family with whom he had been living, every adult except himself who was present on that night had been arrested on the charge of attending a meeting of a banned political organization. His friends were acquitted on the charge simply through the defence lawyer's skill at showing the *agent provocateur*, on whose evidence the charge was based, to be an unreliable witness – that is to say, a liar. But the friends were promptly served with personal banning orders, anyway, which meant among other things that their movements were restricted and they were not allowed to attend gatherings.

He was the only one who remained, significantly, it seemed impossible to ignore, free. And yet his friends let him stay on in the house; it was a mystery to us whites – and some blacks, too. But then so much becomes a mystery where trust becomes a commodity on sale to the police. Whatever my little show of defiance over the loan, during the last year or two we have reached the stage where if a man is black, literate, has 'political' friends and white friends, *and* a passport, he must be considered a police spy. I was sick with myself – that was why I gave him the money – but I believed it, too. There's only one way for a man like that to prove himself, so far as we're concerned: he must be in prison.

Well, *he* was at large. A little subdued over the fate of his friends, about which he talked guilelessly as he had about the appropriation of Elias's air ticket, harassed as usual about money, poor devil, but generally cheerful. Yet our friendship, that really had begun to become one since Elias's death, waned rapidly. It was the money that did it. Of course, he was afraid I'd ask him to begin paying back and so he stopped coming to my 'place', he stopped the visits with the beautifully dressed and well-behaved black infants. I received a typed letter from him, once, solemnly thanking me for my kind co-operation etc., as if I were some business firm, and assuring me that in a few months he hoped to be in a position, etc. I scrawled a note in reply, saying of course I darned well hoped he was going to pay the money he owed, sometime, but why, for God's sake, in the meantime, did this mean we had to carry on as if we'd quarrelled? Damn it all, he didn't have to treat me as if I had some nasty disease, just because of a few rands?

But I didn't see him again. I've become too busy with my own work – the building boom of the last few years, you know; I've had the contract for several shopping malls and a big cultural centre – to do any work for the old theatre group in its sporadic comings-to-life. I don't think he had much to do with it any more, either; I heard he was doing quite well as a salesman and was thinking of marrying again. There was even a – yet another – rumour, that he was actually building a house in Dube, which is the nearest to a solid bourgeois suburb a black can get in these black dormitories outside the white man's city, if you can be considered to be a bourgeois without having freehold. I didn't need the money, by then, but you know how it is with money – I felt faintly resentful about the debt anyway, because it looked as if now *he* could have paid it back just as well as *I* could say I didn't need it. As for the friendship, he'd shown me the worth of that. It's become something the white man must buy just as he must buy the co-operation of police stool-pigeons. Elias has been dead five years; we live in our situation as of now, as the legal phrase goes; one falls back on legal phrases as other forms of expression become too risky.

And then, two hundred and seventy-seven days ago, there was a new rumour, and this time it was confirmed, this time it was no rumour. *He* was fetched from his room one night and imprisoned. That's perfectly legal, here; it's the hundred-and-eighty-day Detention Act. At least, because he was something of a personality, with many friends and contacts in particular among both black and white journalists, the fact has become public. If people are humble, or of no particular interest to the small world of white liberals, they are sometimes in detention for many months before this is known outside the eye-witness of whoever happened to be standing by, in house or street, when they were taken away by the police. But at least we all know where *he* is: in prison. They say that charges of treason are being prepared against him and various others who were detained at the same time, and still others who have been detained for even longer – three hundred and seventy-one days, three hundred and ten days – the figures, once finally released, are always as precise as this – and that soon, soon they will be brought to trial for whatever it is that we do not know they have done, for when people are imprisoned under the Detention Act no one is told why and there are no charges. There are suppositions among us, of course. Was he a double agent, as it were, using his *laissez-passer* as a police spy in order to further his real work as an underground African nationalist? Was he just unlucky in his choice of friends? Did he suffer from a dangerous sense of loyalty in place of any strong convictions of his own? Was it all due to some personal, unguessed-at bond it's none of our business to speculate about? Heaven knows – those police-spy rumours aside – nobody could have looked more unlikely to be a political activist than that cheerful young man, second-string, always ready to jump up and turn over the record, fond of Liberace jackets and aspiring to play Le Roi Jones Off-Broadway.

But as I say, we know where he is now; inside. In solitary most of the time – they say, those who've also been inside. Two hundred and seventy-seven days he's been there.

And so we white friends can purge ourselves of the shame of rumours. We can be pure again. We are satisfied at last. He's in prison. He's proved himself, hasn't he?